MW01380366

Rate

Donna Gene Stankey

ISBN 978-1-0980-4737-5 (paperback)
ISBN 978-1-0980-4738-2 (digital)

Christian Faith Publishing, Inc.
832 Park Avenue
Meadville, PA 16335
www.christianfaithpublishing.com

Printed in the United States of America

CONTENTS

CHAPTER 1

One small kerosene lamp on the dresser softly illuminated the room, revealing the figure of a woman lying under a slightly askew counterpane. She obviously had recently given birth, and now she lay back in a state of complete exhaustion. A thick braid of dark hair lay over her right shoulder, a few tendrils of hair curled around her moist face, the face itself looked wan and drawn, the smudges under the eyes proclaimed it had not been an easy delivery, and the hours of labor had taken their toll. The intense blue eyes showed none of this tiredness of the body as they sought her husband seated near the bed. They were bright blue, but the expression in them, as they rested on the man, held none of the warmth and love that one would expect. They were cold—as cold and frosty as chunks of ice in a glass.

The man held the sleeping babe tenderly in his arms and watched the small red face with love radiating from the tender brown eyes.

From the depths of the double bed came the petulant voice.

"Well, Millie, I hope you're satisfied now that you have a son. We don't need any more children, do we?" She waited for his answer, and since none was forthcoming, she said sharply, "Millie!"

"What was that, Miney?"

"I said we don't need more children. You'll not be putting me through months of discomfort and this final agony again. Will you, Milford?" she demanded. "You have your son, and I have my daughter."

"You're right, Miney. Two's enough, but a man needs a son." He touched a huge forefinger tentatively to the baby's wealth of dark hair. "Yep, a man needs a son. Someone to carry on the family name. I'm sorry for what you had to go through. I wish I could've borne the pain for you."

"Humph. What's a man know about the pain of childbearing? They have a few moments' pleasure, but the woman's the one who pays the price. All those weeks of getting larger and larger, not being able to move like they ought, the backaches, and the always being tired. Then, the pain. Why God ever made it so a woman has to suffer so is beyond me. But no more, Millie. You don't need more children."

"I've said all right. You're tired. Now, get some rest whilst this little fellow is sleeping. I'll send Lena in to see if she can do anything for you, and then you get some rest. You hear?"

It was the eighteenth of December, and the year was 1893. Already winter lay heavy on the land. In spite of the roaring stove only a short distance away in the next room, the room was chilly. Frost had been creeping slowly up the windowpanes as the evening progressed. From the northwest, the wind was gusting furiously; and the puny, man-made structure trembled at its fury. In the corner of one window, a sparkling drift of sugar-fine snow was appearing on the windowsill from an unseen crack.

The man rose to place the sleeping child in a cradle that had been lovingly hand-carved by Miney's grandfather Barnes, when he lived in the state of New York, for babes that had long since grown to manhood and womanhood. As he turned to leave, the voice came peevishly from the bed again.

"What are we to call him? I hadn't even considered a boy's name. I was just that certain I'd have another girl. I prayed and prayed and felt that God would not force me to have a boy. Oh, Millie, I just didn't want a boy, and I don't want him now. I never even wanted another child, but had it been a girl, I could have loved her."

She started to sob great racking sobs that shook her sparse frame.

"Now, now, Miney. Don't take on so." He patted the hand lying on the coverlet. "He's a fine, healthy baby, and you should be thankful for that. God no doubt has His reasons. We'll call him Ralph Horatio. We needed a son to pass Pa's name to another generation. *Horatio* is a good name—one you don't hear every day, and I rather take a notion to *Ralph*. Do try to rest. You're overwrought. Tomorrow things will look brighter, you'll see. ' Sides, I'll fetch Blanche right after dinner. I know you've missed her these last few days."

He stooped quickly and planted a kiss on her brow and left.

He was a huge man, six foot three, broad-shouldered, and his 235 pounds sat easily on his large frame. The years of hard work had produced muscle and left no room for fat. His features were coarse, his hair straight and dark, and a large mustache all but hid his upper lip; his eyes were dark brown and warm and crinkled in the corners when he laughed. There was a hidden look of strength in them as though they could be unrelenting and stubborn if the provocation came. He moved gracefully for such a large man as he quietly left his wife's room.

He would sleep on the couch the same as he had been doing for the past several nights; that way, he could hear her if she called, and he could keep the fire going without disturbing her. She needed her rest after her ordeal, and maybe, when she felt better, she would be in a better frame of mind. Besides, he didn't want either she or the babe to take a chill. He knew this sometimes happened after childbirth, and he intended to guard against any such event. He had his son, and God willing, he intended to keep him.

Mina quit her sobbing shortly after he left. What was she to do? She felt no love for that boy child who lay in the cradle, but then, she had felt no sudden surge of maternal love when her daughter had been born four and a half years ago. However, Blanche had been a beautiful baby, but this one—he was red, and with all that hair, he looked like a monkey. She remembered the shock when Lena had held him up for her to see, proudly announcing it was a healthy boy. Maybe it was just the bitter disappointment, the feeling of being cheated after all those months of hating the child growing within her. Well, he was here now, and although she had half hoped he would die at birth, he was healthy and strong. She would have to make the best of it and carry the burden God had seen fit to give her. Thinking thus, she slept.

The thermometer slowly crept toward the zero mark, and past midnight, when Millie looked out after poking up the fire, he observed the wind had died and the full moon hung in a star-studded sky. He noted with satisfaction the storm had abated, for he had promised Miney to fetch Blanche, and he didn't relish the thought of

7

the three and a half miles under blizzard conditions. He looked in on the babe and his wife. The lamp had been turned down low, but he could see that she was sleeping peacefully.

Mayhap she'll feel better about the boy come morning, he mused. At any rate, he hoped so.

He knew she had never wanted children, but he hadn't known until after they were married. It wasn't something a proper young woman discussed with a man, even if he was her intended. Mina had been brought up proper. Why, he'd never even been allowed to kiss her until after she'd promised to marry him. They'd been married eight years last month, and it had been a good life. She'd been a good mother to Blanche, but then, Miney was a lot more likely to take to a girl than a boy. Even in her Sunday school class, it was the girls she enjoyed. She was glad when the class got so large Richard had taken the boys and left her only the girls.

"She'll help raise him right," he said half aloud, "but even a boy needs love afore he's growed to manhood."

The babe stirred and started to fret.

"Millie! The boy's wakening."

"I'm here, Miney. No use to rouse Lena. I'll bring him to you."

"Are you to change him? No doubt he'll be sopping wet."

"Reckon I can. My fingers ben't always all thumbs, you know. Lena was tired, and I was restless anyways."

She nursed the baby dutifully. He suckled noisily, taking to the breast much better than some. As soon as his comforts were attended to, he slept again. Millie hoped he would always be this way. Perhaps if he wasn't much trouble, Miney would learn to love him the sooner.

He wasn't certain Miney fell asleep as fast as she seemed. He thought she was playing possum and would like to have said something more to her. He wanted to tell her he cared for her, but he was afraid of disturbing her. She looked pretty in the soft lamp glow. He liked to see her with her hair down, loose instead of in a braid. She had such beautifully soft hair, so thick and dark. Why, her braid was almost as large as his wrist, and her hair was so long she had to move it aside so's not to sit on it. Her skin was delicately fair. She was so persnickety about herself, always wore her sunbonnet and gloves so's she never got tanned like most farm women.

He remembered how he'd been taken with her when they were in school together. He and some of the older boys came to school in the wintertime when things were slack on the farms and Pa hadn't needed him to help with the store and livery stable except before and after school; sometimes, some of the girls who went to school from fall till spring would help them with their ciphering or spelling. Almina Smith had been the best speller in the whole darned school. Why, he remembered the spelling bees they'd had, and Miney had always spelled the rest of them down even though some of them had had more schooling than she.

Then he remembered lunchtime when she and some of the others had sat around singing, and he'd been too bashful to go and sit beside her. There came a day when she'd smiled at him sweetly and asked if he wanted to sit with her to eat lunch. From that time on, he'd known she preferred him to the other boys, and he'd been mightily pleased. He'd known right then that when he was old enough, he'd ask her to marry him. Yep, he was mighty lucky to have her for his wife, and he'd liked to have told her so, but then, he reckoned she knew anyways.

He returned to the leather couch where he had made his bed. He hadn't bothered to undress, for somehow it didn't seem fitten to put on a nightshirt when a body didn't intend to get into a bed. He knew the night would pass quickly, and then, it would be time for chores. Lena, a neighbor from up on the Ridge Road, would have to go home after breakfast, but he'd stop by and bring Lorin, Miney's half sister, home when he fetched Blanche from Mother Smith's.

Lorin had expected to stay for Miney's lying-in. She probably would have been here, only the lad had jumped the gun a mite, and there'd been no time to fetch her. He'd barely had time to fetch the doctor. Lucky it was that Blanche had already been spending a few days with her grandmother. It had also been fortunate Lena was handy and could come. Of course, she couldn't be expected to stay since she had to care for her own family.

Maybe having Lorin around would be good for Miney. Lorin was the older by almost twenty years and had been married twenty-two or twenty-three years already, he forgot which. She had had only one child, Georgie, who was almost seventeen. Guess she'd never wanted any more of her own, but she had always liked her nieces and nephews. He knew she would love the baby even though it was a boy. Mayhap some of her excitement over the boy would rub off on Miney. At least it couldn't hinder any.

Millie was right in surmising that Miney had only pretended to drop off to sleep. She had sensed that he had something more on his mind, but had been in no mood to listen to him. Her stomach felt a little queasy, and her abdomen was sore as though her insides too had rebelled at having that foreign body growing there. She sensed she was bleeding more than was good, so she gently kneaded her belly and felt the uterus harden once more. Now, where had she learned that? Anyway, it seemed to help. She felt beat—simply dragged out. Didn't seem like this birth had been any easier than the first, yet folks were always saying the second child gave less trouble. Lot they knew.

Blanche had been a breech birth and very difficult. Miney still remembered her mother hovering over the bed telling the doctor to turn that baby so it would come right, but the doctor had said it couldn't be done. Ma had told him she'd seen her husband do it numerous times, only the old doctor had just shaken his head.

This one had lain crossways for a spell and then had come feet-first. Just proved she was never meant to have children. She still felt bitter because it was a boy. She felt resentment toward Millie because it was all his fault. If men didn't have to be like animals, but they were. From some of the hints the older women dropped, perhaps she was luckier than some. At least she had only two children, and some of her girlhood chums already had three or four. It was still Millie's fault. How was she ever to enjoy taking care of the child? It was her duty, she knew, and she'd not neglect the tyke, but love him? Well... now, that was something else.

Ma had scoffed at her ideas when she had tried to talk to her. 'Course Ma had been married twice; her first husband, Elisher Fuller, had dropped dead even though he was only twenty-seven and left her with two small girls. That had been Lorin and Mary. Then, she'd married Pa and had Ettie and her. Of course, Pa had had four boys by his first wife who'd died, but they were a lot older than Miney, and she scarcely knew them. Jim had been around the most, in between trips to Oregon—he'd made the round trip by wagon train twice— and she was right fond of him, she guessed. He'd always been kind to his little half sister, letting her ride his horse even though they hadn't had a proper sidesaddle. She'd learned to crook her leg around the saddle horn and had managed right enough. Leastways, Jim hadn't made fun of her when she'd taken a tumble the first time she'd tried sidesaddle. She had ridden straddle at first, only Ma had said it was unbecoming of a lady to straddle a horse and show off her legs even if she was only a little girl. Jim was a right good brother, she'd have to admit, so just maybe boys weren't all bad. Ma had been lucky to have girls if she had to have four children. Why couldn't she have been just as lucky, wondered Miney as she finally drifted back to sleep.

CHAPTER 2

"Ma, Ma, I'm home." A dark-haired little girl of four rushed through the dining room to the bedroom and flung herself into her mother's waiting arms. "Oh, Ma, I missed you so."

"Did you, precious, did you? Ma missed you too. My, my, but your face is cold."

"Blanche," said a matronly woman from the doorway, "come get your cold wraps off before you give your mother a chill."

"Oh, let her be, Lorin. She's all right." Mina hugged the child to her again, and her face shone with love.

True, Blanche was a beautiful child. Her rich, dark-brown hair hung in long pigtails tied with large bows, her brown eyes were dark and flashing, her cheeks were rosy from the cold, her round face still held its childish look, but there was something about the mouth, as though she was only happy and gay as long as no one crossed her, and she possessed a stubborn streak that was difficult to surmount. She tossed off her hat and threw her muff on the bed.

"Ma, are you sick? Pa told me you was in bed. Are you sick?" Her face showed concern.

"Ma's only tired, love. Auntie Lorin will take care of you for a few days whilst I rest. Now, let Auntie Lorin help you out of your wraps. Then you can tell Ma what you did while at Grandma's."

Just then the baby started a coaxing, crying sound. Blanche noticed the cradle for the first time. She went hesitantly over to the crib and peered in. Her eyes widened in surprise.

"A baby!" she exclaimed. "Oh, Ma, a baby? Is it ours? To keep? Where did it come from?" she wondered.

"God sent him to us, love. That is your little brother."

"A boy, Ma?" she asked in disbelief. "I don't want a brother. Tell God to take him back. I don't want a brother. I want a sister. Tell God to take him back and give me a sister. Give him to someone else."

"Hush, child," said Lorin sharply.

"I don't care. I don't want him. Ma, do we have to keep him?" she asked beseechingly.

"Yes, Blanche, we have to keep him."

"But I don't want a brother," she wailed.

Just then, Millie came to the door.

"Blanche, that will do," he said sternly. "This is your little brother, Ralph. Now, you are a lot bigger than him, so's you'll have to help your ma care for him. He needs a lot of care whilst he's so small. Surely you can be a big girl and give Ma some help, can't you?"

"No, I won't," she screamed. "I hate him, I hate him. I don't want him," she said, stamping her foot to emphasize her feelings. "You can just take him and feed him to the pigs."

"Blanche, that is enough."

Millie would have taken hold of her, but Miney gave him a withering look and said, "Come here, love. Of course you don't have to help Ma. You're my baby yet. Auntie Lorin will take care of him for a few days and you too, but I'll be here to love you. Now, get out of your wraps, and then we'll talk. Do it for Ma."

Blanche moved away. As she passed the cradle, she wrinkled up her nose and muttered, "I still don't want him, and you can't make me want him."

Lorin took her by the hand and led her from the room, thinking, *Poor little Ralph. His will be a hard row to hoe. He's strong and healthy, which is the most important thing. Some folks just don't count their blessings.*

"Miney, you have got to quit siding in with Blanche. She's strong-willed enough, and you make matters worse. She has to accept Ralph, and you have got to help."

"How can I when I feel just as the child does? I didn't ask to have him, you know."

"Let's not start that again. He's here, and he's ours just as much as Blanche is. It's up to you to teach her to love her brother. I'll not tolerate any more of these outbursts and hollering that she hates him, so either you help her to change or *I* will."

"All right, Millie. I'll try."

"You do just that."

His chin had that peculiar set to it she knew so well. Obstinate, she called it, but she knew that once he had spoken, God in heaven couldn't make him change his mind. If she wanted to handle Blanche in her own way, she had better get instantaneous results, for Millie was done fooling around. She heaved a sigh and wondered just what the best approach would be. Blanche was a Setterington to the core with maybe even an overdose of pride and stubbornness.

For a little mite, Ralph had certainly caused plenty of trouble—and him not even two days old. Maybe it wasn't right, poor child, since he was hardly to blame for being here. Of course, in her eyes, neither was she. Ralph was here solely because of the carnal appetite of the man who had begot him. Well, she had to do something—that much was certain. Millie meant what he said, and she knew he wasn't above using a heavy hand on Blanche's backsides if she had another outburst.

Miney pondered the situation for some moments.

Presently, Blanche returned to sit on the bed and show Ma a new book Grandmother Setterington had given her. Miney noticed with satisfaction that the child seemed completely at ease, as if she had completely forgotten the babe sleeping contentedly in the nearby cradle. Perhaps things would right themselves without her scolding Blanche. She knew from past experience that Blanche was much easier to get along with if she wasn't crossed in any way. Of course, she hadn't exactly let the child run wild, but one got much further with her if she was led instead of pushed. Like Ma always said, a body got more flies with sugar than with vinegar.

She helped Blanche read from a book that contained nursery rhymes. The drawings seemed to fascinate the little girl, and she made up her own stories to go along with them. She was cheerful and serene.

The afternoon passed, and when Ralph awoke and cried, Blanche marched stoically from the room, unequivocally ignoring the presence of another being. At least she wasn't raising verbal objections, so Millie should be satisfied.

After all, it was quite a change for Blanche to have a baby in the house. She had never been around other small children except at church and had never played with boys at all. What else was one to expect from the child? If Millie wasn't so cantankerous at times, he'd be able to understand the child's way of thinking better. Of course, men never did try to cotton to a woman's way of thinking. If only God had seen fit to give her a girl. She knew she shouldn't question the wisdom of God and hastily asked His forgiveness.

That night, she prayed long and fervently, asking Him to help her accept this burden He had thrust upon her. She tried to understand, knowing full well that mere mortals were not intended to understand the role God intended for them to play in their itinerant life on earth. Whatever His reason, she must not question, but must do her best to live up to His expectations. Somehow, after prayer, she felt better, and her burden seemed lighter. It was always thus when one asked God for help.

Christmas was only four days away, and Miney felt rather helpless confined to bed. Of course, Lorin seemed to be enjoying the preparations, and Blanche was excited about helping her aunt in the kitchen.

Lorin was good with children, no doubt about that. Lorin—with her short, stout figure and somewhat odd ways with oldsters—just seemed to appeal to the little ones no matter whose they were. 'Course when Lorin was younger, she hadn't liked children either. Why, Pa and Ma had practically raised Georgie. Lorin had acted as though she was scared of him when he was a baby. Guess Mary was the only one of the girls who took after Ma since Mary loved babies—hers and anyone else's. Still, Lorin had always been good with Blanche.

At least no one expected to have Lorin home to be preparing for the holidays. Norm and Georgie would come out here for dinner. They would enjoy being here just as much as if they'd had dinner at home. Probably more since she was sure she and Millie set a more bountiful table. Norm's job at the cheese factory to the west didn't pay much, and Norm did spend a lot at the saloon although Lorin was never one to complain. Norm Duncan was easygoing although Miney thought a little shiftless too—so whatever suited Lorin, suited him too.

The kitchen was a flurry of activity. Lorin had already made several kinds of cookies, popcorn balls, and candy. Now, Blanche sat at the table busily stringing popcorn on a string to put on the Christmas tree Pa had promised to get today. She was a serious child and kept at the work diligently. Lorin watched her from where she was stirring up batter for a suet pudding. Most four-year-olds would have grown tired of this tedious task long before now, but Blanche, her brow slightly puckered, worked tirelessly.

"Why don't you let that be a while, Blanche?"

"I've got to be finished afore the tree gets here. Pa said he'd bring one today, an' it's getting dark. He's sure to be home soon. I've got to hurry 'cause I've this much to do."

She held up the bowl showing the remaining kernels.

"He said he'd bring the tree today, but he didn't say a thing 'bout gettin' it set up," Lorin reminded.

"He will too, he will too. He promised, Auntie Lorin, he promised."

"No, child. Now, your pa will have chores to see to soon's he gets here, and there won't be no time for settin' up Christmas trees. Not this night at least," she explained patiently.

"I'll ask Ma. She'll want it up too."

With that, Blanche slid off her chair and ran to her mother's bedroom. Lorin could hear the demanding tone of her voice as she accosted her mother. However, judging from the outburst of crying, Miney must have given her the same response. Poor tyke, she was dead set on having her tree up tonight. It was a shame to disappoint her; however, chores came first, and with the weather still hovering at the zero mark, it only made things worse. Animals had to be looked after good if they was to do all right in weather like this. They were God's creatures too, and man had an obligation to take care of them just as the shepherds of old had tended their flocks. Blanche would simply have to learn that the world didn't turn for her sake alone.

A few minutes later, Blanche came bursting from her mother's room.

"Auntie Lorin, Auntie Lorin, I hear sleigh bells. Pa's home. Can you see my tree? Can you?"

"It's too dark to see that far. You'll have to wait till he's put up the team, and then he'll likely bring it onto the porch."

"I want to see it now."

She pressed her nose against the pane of glass, making it steam with her breath, which she promptly wiped away with her hand.

"Child, come away from that window. Now, I'll have to wash the glass where you've made marks. Your ma would never rest easy if she knew the window was streaked on Christmas. It is too dark to see, so come here. You get the table ready so we can eat when your pa gets in."

"Do I have to? I'd rather watch here."

"Blanche," came the stern reply.

"All right."

The round table was made of oak with drop leaves, which could be lowered to make a small rectangular top; it was covered with a bright-red checkered tablecloth. There was no cheesecloth to be folded this winter weather, only the steel forks and knives to get from the drawer, spoons from the spoonholder at the center of the table, plates to be turned over to be right side up, and cups to be set in place. These were the everyday dishes, and she could handle them. Ma didn't quite trust her to set table on Sundays, when they used their best china, which had come from England, because Ma was so afraid she would break or chip them. She guessed Auntie Lorin was right; Pa would be starved after being out in the cold for so long. Perhaps if she was real good and pleased him, he would at least bring the tree inside the house. It was worth the effort anyway.

"Put a napkin on your ma's tray. Maybe if you'd be right careful, you could carry it to her. I'll fix hers before your pa gets here to set down."

Lorin dished up a plate of victuals, poured a cup of milk and set it on the tray. She knew Miney would have preferred tea, but milk was better for her whilst she was nursing the little fellow.

"Can I take it, Auntie Lorin? Can I?"

The Christmas tree was momentarily forgotten. Lorin had lured Blanche with the chance to be thought of as a big girl. Miney would be pleased, Blanche knew, and for the most part at least, she liked to please her mother. Mostly, it was because she thrived on praise. It gave her a sense of being loved, and in this respect, Blanche was a normal child—she needed to know she was loved and wanted.

"Careful, love. Don't try to walk too fast. P'raps I'd better carry the milk," said Lorin as the tray tilted dangerously. "Miney, here's your supper."

"My, my, and who's your little helper?"

"It's me, Ma. And I never spillded it neither."

"Of course you didn't. You're a big girl now and such a help to Auntie Lorin. Ma is so proud of her little sweetheart."

Blanche beamed.

"I hear your pa on the steps, Blanche," put in Lorin. "We'd best get his vittles on the table so's he can set and eat. It's right frosty out there, and he'll need hot food to help thaw his innards out."

"My tree, my tree. Has he got my tree?" Blanche rushed from the room. Millie had just come in the door and was taking off his heavy mackinaw. "Pa, Pa, where's my tree?"

"What tree?"

"My Christmas tree, Pa. You didn't forget, did you?" Her bottom lip started to quiver. "Did you, Pa?"

Millie swung his daughter high in the air before cradling her in his arms.

"A Christmas tree, is it? Don't you have a kiss for your father first?"

"Your face is freezing," she observed, placing her hands on his cheeks, "but where's my tree, Pa? Where's my tree?"

"Well, now, just supposing I plumb forgot?"

"Oh, Pa, you…you didn't."

Tears filled the large brown eyes. The man gave a hearty laugh and said, "Look out the window." He held her down to see, and there, in the soft lamp glow as she shaded her eyes, she saw a magnificent tree leaning against the side of the house.

She threw her arms around his neck and cried, "It's beautiful. Can we bring it in?"

"We'll see. Right now, that food smells awful good, and I'm near famished."

The meal was a hearty one designed for a man who did hours of hard, manual labor and needed an ample meal to satisfy his appetite. There was corned beef, boiled potatoes with plenty of butter, thick slices of bread with apple butter, squash, cabbage fixed with vinegar, and mince pie for dessert. A meal like that stuck to a man's ribs.

The meal finished, Millie looked at the wistful face of his small daughter. Blanche had learned at an early age that wheedling her father did no good. Her mother was a different story. She could usually get her own way with Miney, but Millie was not likely to cater to the whims of a child, or anyone for that matter.

He was a man of many moods. Sometimes, he was so good-natured that he would laugh till he cried over some incident. At these times, his brown eyes danced in merriment. Then, on occasion, he was at the opposite extreme. His eyes could shelter cold fury, and his curt, abrupt words would cut like a sharply honed razor.

Even though Blanche realized he was in a particularly affable mood this night, she bided her time, watching him out of the corner of her eye. She knew better than to bring up the subject of the Christmas tree again. When Pa made up his mind, he would let her know, but until then, she must wait, albeit none too patiently. Already her stubbornness and her unwillingness to show her feelings were as a seed being carefully nurtured by the most patient horticulturist. She had glanced his way only once, then asked to be excused and had started to help Lorin clear off the table as a dutiful young girl should. Millie looked at her with pride in his heart. In his eyes, she was beautiful, and he loved her dearly. Now, he had a son, and it filled him with contentment. He was a very lucky man, and as such, he felt generous.

"That was a mighty fine meal, Lorin. Always did say you made a right good mince pie."

"Why, thank you kindly, Millie. You know full well Miney is a far better cook than I ever been, but it sounds good anyways." She laughed as she started to do dishes, humming softly to herself.

"Blanche, come here."

She came to stand in front of her father and regard him solemnly, her eyes unblinking.

"Well, girl, do you think we should bring that scrawny, old tree into the house?"

"Oh, Pa, it's not scrawny. It's beautiful. Can we?"

"Yes, child, we'll bring it in and set it up, but mind you, the trimming will have to wait until tomorrow. Understand?"

"Yes, Pa," she answered meekly. Well, at least she had won half the battle. "Pa, can we put candles on the tree this year?"

She eyed her father wistfully, hardly daring to breathe as she awaited his reply.

"Now, Blanche, I've explained to you before how dangerous they be. More'n one family has had a fire because of candles on their tree. However, we'll see. Mayhap we can light them for just a few minutes on Christmas Eve. I know your ma would like that too."

Blanche smiled inwardly. She maybe hadn't won the whole battle, but she had gained a slight advantage. It was always to be counted in her favor when Pa didn't come out with an out-and-out no from the very first. After all, she knew from listening to the parents of the children in her Sunday school class that it wasn't everyone who had a Christmas tree. Some folks just didn't hold with such frivolous things. Like as not they just didn't want to take the time and effort to go out and chop the tree and haul it in from the woods. She was certainly glad her father didn't mind doing a little work when it gave his daughter so much pleasure.

My, how she did want candles on her tree. She had seen a picture of one in a magazine at Grandmother's, and it did look scrumptious. If'n Pa would just let them be lighted for even a little while. She sighed audibly as she sat quietly watching her father fasten the tree in its stand. She remembered last year they had put colored candles on the tree, but they had not been lighted. Well, even an unlit candle was better than no candle at all. She was glad she had finished stringing the popcorn—the white always looked so pretty nestled against the dark-green needles of the pine.

Last year, Ma had bought a few shiny ornaments, and even though she had regretted her extravagance later, Blanche had been thrilled. There was an angel, a deer, and some birds—not many, but they looked nice hanging on the tree. Of course, this year Ma hadn't been to the store to buy any more.

Seemed awful odd Ma had got so tired just at the time when God had sent them that new baby. Now, why had she started thinking about him? He sure didn't look like much, and she wisht God had given her a sister instead, but Ma said we was not to question what the good Lord did—at least not if we ever expected to get to heaven. So she guessed she'd not ask why anymore, but she didn't have to like him, and they couldn't make her like him if she didn't want to. *Ralph.* She didn't even like the name. She liked the name Rob, but no one had considered asking her what she liked. She knew Ma didn't like that new baby either; she could just tell by Ma's actions, but Pa sure seemed taken with him and looked awful funny holding that mite of a thing in his big hands, talking to him just like that baby really could understand what he was saying.

Guess Pa did still love her since he had got such a lovely tree. In the past week, she had wondered many times if her father still loved her. She could be sitting on his lap, yet if that boy cried, Pa was quick to go see why. Auntie Lorin catered to him too. She had held him and rocked him all one afternoon when she said he had a touch of the colic. Seemed like for such a small thing, he had disrupted the whole household.

Blanche was suffering from an acute case of jealousy that was not soon to abate.

On Christmas Eve, Miney got out of bed for the first time since Ralph's birth. It was a mite soon, but she had wanted to sit up for a spell. Millie helped her from the bedroom to the rocking chair covered with quilts so she could be snugly wrapped while she sat there. He placed a warmed soapstone at her feet. He had already checked that the fire was burning well, giving off plenty of heat.

The tree had been trimmed, and Millie had finally relented and promised Blanche that for a while, the few candles could be lighted. Miney read the story of that birth of long ago, and Blanche sat in awe as she listened to her mother's voice. Miney read well, and she never tired reading of the birth of the Savior. Blanche, listening to the steady intonation of her mother's voice, found herself wondering what present she would receive from Santa in the morn. She knew this was naughty and that good little girls were not supposed to think of presents whilst Ma was reading, so she tried to concentrate on the words even though she didn't understand them all.

It was difficult to listen for long. She watched the crackling flames showing behind the isinglass in the door of the square, nickel-trimmed stove, which sat along the north wall of the parlor. They didn't always use this room in the evenings, but this was where there had been room for the small tree, and it was where the organ stood across the room from the stove. Mina's rocker was pulled up near the stove to keep her from drafts, and Millie had piled the firebox of the stove full before getting her from bed. The floor had no large rug, but scattered here and there were crocheted rugs that Miney had made herself, and one was a braided wool rug made from old coats Mother Setterington had been going to throw away. It was Miney's pride and joy because it not only had the usual navy and gray, but had a tan and wine braid in the heavy wool fabric. It would last for years.

Just as Blanche's mind started to wander again, Miney closed the book, and Blanche heaved a sigh of relief. Lorin moved to the organ and started to play some Christmas carols. Blanche and Miney joined in the singing while Millie lighted the candles. He knew he was doing this against his better judgment, but then, he was trying to humor both Blanche and Miney. Mayhap if he was a little nicer and gave in on something like this, they'd be inclined to take a little more kindly to the boy. At least he had had the foresight to fetch two buckets of water should the need arise.

The tree did look pretty, no doubt about that, and as the soft candlelight was reflected in happiness in his wife's eyes, he knew it was worth the risk. Miney looked happy for the first time since Ralph's arrival. However, he didn't delude himself for one moment.

He knew this would pass, but at least she was happy tonight, which seemed like a good omen. Mayhap from now on, things would get better and Miney would learn to love the boy.

Blanche would undoubtedly learn to love him too when she got over this period of jealousy. Miney needed to be a little more strict with the girl. She was strong-willed for her age and needed to be curbed. Guess maybe she took after his side of the family a little too much since Pa was one of the most obstinate men he'd ever known. Why, when he and John had been boys at home, they had learned that once their father made up his mind to something, nothing in heaven or on earth could make him change his mind or admit he was wrong. Still, Pa had a good many fine qualities. His word was his bond. Everyone knew that Rate Setterington was as good as his word.

Rate. Now, that's what Pa had always been called far and wide instead of *Horatio*. Guess that would be good to call the boy too. Pa would never be one to admit it, but Millie was sure it would be pleasing to him to have his first grandson called after him. Miney didn't hold too much for nicknames, so's he didn't suppose she would ever call him anything but Ralph. Be that as it may, he'd call him Rate.

Miney's voice brought him back to his surroundings.

"Millie, perhaps you should put the candles out now. Some of them are burning low. My, but they do look pretty."

"Ma, does he have to?"

"Yes, precious. Did you really like them?"

"They were just wonderful. Ma, this is the bestest Christmas ever."

Just then, the babe started to fret, and Lorin moved quickly to bring him from the cradle. It was as though a curtain had ended the final act of a play. The light went out of Miney's eyes, and Blanche's mouth was set in the petulant fashion so peculiar to her.

"See. He knew he was being left out, and he didn't like it one little bit," crooned Lorin as she nestled the babe in her arms. He quieted when he found a fist to suck. "He's hungry, poor tyke. Do you want to nurse him now, Miney? He acts starved."

"Hand him here," she replied, dutifully holding out her arms to receive the child.

The glow had gone from her face, and once more her eyes had that expression in them that denoted duty as opposed to pleasure. The mother holding a nursing babe should have been reminiscent of the Madonna and child of eons ago, but this scene failed miserable at any similarity.

Millie felt a constriction on his heart as he watched his wife and son. Would there ever come a time when Miney would look at the boy with love in her eyes? He felt doubt creep over him and possess his body like some unknown demon. Generally not a religious man, he closed his eyes for a moment and thought, *Please, dear God in heaven, make her love that child she holds. Help her to be the mother he needs. Please, God, remove this obsession she has about not wanting the boy.* For a man such as he, who perhaps sometimes doubted whether God existed, this was an act born of desperation.

He noted that Blanche, in spite of herself, had sidled over to her mother and was watching with great curiosity as the boy suckled. Before, she had always ignored the fact that he had to eat and had needs that must be tended. Mayhap it was the spirit of the evening— the utter peace that had emulated the scene before the intrusion of the babe. Time would at least make her tolerate her brother, if not love him, of that he was certain.

The days passed, and in late January came the expected warm weather and thaw. It was a welcome relief from the bitter cold that had relentlessly throttled the land. At least during the day, the sun shone brightly and rivulets of water found their way to the snow and ice-clogged ditches. The huge piles of snow lessened visibly each day. However, these warm days were only a hint of what would eventually come, and once more the snow came with a howling fury from out of the northwest.

The stock huddled together in bunches, their backs to the driving snow, and refused to drink more than a few sips of the icy water where Millie broke the ice on the tank so they might reach it. They only wanted back in the comparatively warm shelter of the barn. For two days it was not fit for man nor beast, and then, the snow ceased while the frosty cold persisted.

The stoves ate firewood with an insatiable appetite. The wood-box seemed to be always near empty, and several times a day, Millie brought wood inside from the pile he had already corded on the porch. Normally, Mina could have saved him some of this effort, but being in her present state of mind, she was not so inclined.

She felt that it served him right to have the added chore. After all, didn't she have a lot more to do now? Maybe he thought that taking care of a baby wasn't much work. Well, she knew better. Washing the mounds of diapers every other day and hanging them behind the stove to dry was a never-ending task. That boy, no matter how often he was checked, seemed like he was always wet. Just think what it would have been if a body hadn't dried the wet diapers and used them twice before washing, a body would have spent all their time just doing diapers. It never occurred to Miney not to care for Ralph as she should. No, God had added him as an unwelcome burden to her life, but she would care for him as any good mother should.

Millie had been up town, so he had driven down to ask Miney's mother if she wanted to come out to the farm to see Miney and the baby. Mary had welcomed the chance since she did love tiny babies and had fretted because she had not seen her grandson as yet. She knew Vine and Rate had driven out to see him, Rate being especially proud because he now had a grandson named after him.

The day had gone well, and Mary had cuddled and held the baby to her heart's content. She thought he was simply adorable. Of course, she had been extremely careful not to neglect Blanche since Mary didn't want her darling granddaughter to think she was unloved now that there was a new baby in the house. Mary's heart held enough love for half the children of the world; she was ready to befriend any little waif, no matter who the parents were.

It was near time for Millie to take Mary home. She had opened the drawers of the buffet looking for something and now was opening Miney's bureau drawers.

"Ma, whatever are you looking for?"

"That heavy white wool shawl you have."

"Goodness, whatever for?"

"Well, since you don't want the baby, said you just knew you couldn't tolerate him, I thought I'd take him along home with me, so I need that shawl to bundle him in."

"Oh, Ma! You know I'm not about to give him up."

"Aren't you?"

"Of course not," snapped Miney somewhat peevishly. "You knew I'd want him after he was here. He's not all that much trouble," she added lamely.

"But you were so determined you didn't want another child, and if memory serves me right, Millie had to put up with a shrew for several months."

"I know, Ma, and I truly am sorry. I guess I still wish the baby had been a girl, but it does no good to wish. I'm not sure I'll make a very good mother for a boy," she explained sadly.

"Of course you will. All he needs is love, the same as Blanche does. Well, if you're certain you want to keep him, I guess I don't need the shawl after all."

Mary smiled a knowing smile. Miney had not yet come to love the lad, and Mary felt a little sad because in her heart, she knew Blanche undoubtedly would always come first in Miney's affections; yet, Mary also felt certain that Miney would come to care for the boy more than she'd like to admit. At least Mary knew her daughter well enough to know that Mina would never neglect her duty. It was certainly evident that Millie was proud of his son. How nice they had a boy to carry on the family name because *Setterington* was certainly a fine Old English name.

Miney stood over a tub of hot water, scrubbing one of Millie's dirty shirts. Her back ached, and she was right glad this was the last of the washing. She'd like for a chance to set and rest a spell, but it was time to start peeling potatoes for dinner.

She had been on her feet all morning except for the half hour it took to nurse the child. He had gone back to sleep as usual, and she had returned to the washing. She supposed she should be thankful he was such a good baby. To be fed, changed, and kept warm seemed to be all he needed. To be sure, he spent less time sleeping than what he had at first, but he didn't cry for attention as some babies did.

Of course, he seemed to sense when Millie was in the house, and if he was to fret, it was likely to be then. Millie was quick to pick him up and cuddle him. Sometimes, that bothered her, Millie making a fool of himself over a son. Men wouldn't be so anxious to have sons if they had to spend nine months carrying them, and she could just hear how they would beller over labor pains.

Woman's lot was a sorry one most of the time. Man's work was from sun to sun all right, but a woman's work just never was done since there was always sewing and patching to be done by lamplight. Work, work all day, and then work at night too while the menfolk sat and read or played checkers.

Sewing had never been her best talent anyway. Somehow, things just never seemed to fit as good as they ought. Now, Lorin and Mary and Ma, they could turn a mighty fine seam. Of course, their embroidery couldn't hold a candle to hers and Mary's crocheting—well, the less said about that, the better. Miney loved to make fancy lace, and even the pillowcases she used on her bed had lovely wide edges of lace. Most women saved such things for the guest room, but Miney used hers every day.

Long before she knew she would get married, she had made things for her hope chest. Somehow, thinking of all the pretty things she had crocheted, she felt less tired, and her backache had lessened too. She put the shirt through the wringer and then hung it behind the stove to dry. Some of the other clothes needed turning to finish drying them.

She would have Millie empty the wash water. That was one more chore he could help her with whilst she had to wash in the kitchen. She wished they had more room. Millie had promised to build another room, but it hadn't been done as yet. This summer she would not be put off with promises. It would be much easier to get it done before the boy got to where he would be getting around and needed watching every minute so's he wouldn't get himself hurt. She was still thinking of a new kitchen when Millie came in for his midday meal.

Lambing time came, and the nights and days became as one. Millie ate at odd hours, and Miney knew she was expected to have a hot meal whenever he chose to want one. It was just one more thing with which a farm woman had to contend. Millie became irritable, but she understood that it was from lack of sleep since it seemed as though he scarcely came to bed. Thus far, thirty ewes had lambed, and they had fifty-five lambs to prove it, only five ewes giving single birth. She reckoned that might be near a record. Millie had taken such good care of them that not one ewe had refused to own one of her lambs as was so often the case. They had fifty more to go, and then they could return to normal living again.

Of course, she was right proud that Millie wasn't shiftless and lazy like some. He was a good farmer and a husband of whom a woman could be proud. It was only fitting that she do her share, and right now that seemed to be having something hot on the stove at all hours and not complaining if Millie did seem a little short with her.

Sometimes, she wished they didn't keep such a huge flock of sheep since sheep were always so much trouble at lambing time. She had ventured to suggest to Millie that hogs or cows were less trouble, so why not increase the amount of hogs and sell off some of the sheep. Millie had been quick to point out that wool brought a fair price, lambs sold good, and the sheep were invaluable to help clear the brushland back of the ditch, which crossed the property a little more than a third of the way back to the west. He knew that sooner or later, he'd clear that land and put it under the plow, and the sheep helped get rid of the pesky brush. Mina had resigned herself that the sheep were here to stay, and she would just have to put up with them.

Of course, she remembered how a few years ago sheep had been worth next to nothing. Millie had leased out a flock of twenty-five ewes to Rod Dekker, north of Elsie. In three years, Millie was to get back double. Well, when the three years were up, sheep were such a drug on the market Millie hadn't even felt them to be worth going after. At least times had improved since then.

CHAPTER 3

R alph grew and changed with each passing week. While he never
seemed jubilant over seeing his mother, even though she was the
one who tended to most of his needs, it was for his father he saved
his smiles and gurgles of delight. Millie would hold him, talk to him,
and play with him by the hour in the evening after the day's work was
finished. Ralph looked forward to these moments. He often regarded
his mother with that solemn expression of his, his face betraying no
emotion, but the large brown eyes watching her every move. Perhaps
even at this tender age he sensed that caring for him was not done
with love, merely fostered by a sense of duty.

Spring came, and Millie's work increased as the planting season
was at hand. He and the hired man spent long hours in the field, and
evenings found him tired from his day's toil. He found the time with
his son relaxing, and he seldom failed to play with the baby each night.

By the time Ralph was seven months old, he had learned to
hitch himself along when placed on the floor, and Miney could no
longer leave him unattended and expect him to be where she had put
him. It seemed to Miney he was always dirty. Try as she would, she
could not keep him clean. She had scrubbed the wide board floor
with strong lye soap until the boards were fairly bleached white, but
still the lad managed to look as if she never changed his clothes. Of
course, he could have gone faster, but the long dress and petticoat
hampered his movements; however, he was still a good baby and
seldom cried. Sometimes, Blanche would play with him, and on rare
occasions, she made him laugh aloud. He still saved his boisterous
laughs for his father, who tossed him into the air for the simple pleasure of hearing his son laugh. Heights never frightened Rate even at
this early age.

Miney sometimes grudgingly admitted to herself that he was not a very demanding baby. At the same age, Blanche had been much more trouble. Somehow, Blanche had always expected everyone to cater to her. Mother Setterington hadn't helped either because she and Father had spoiled Blanche from the very first.

Lavina was forever saying, "Rate, she does look like Baby, doesn't she? See how she smiles, just like my little girl."

"Yes, Vine, she truly does."

"Sometimes when she laughs, it sounds so much like Baby."

"I know, Vine. You still miss Emma, and so do I. Perhaps that is why Milt had such an adorable daughter. It was God's way of easing our hurt."

Baby was little Emma, who had died in January the same year Blanche had been born although she had only been four years old. It was true, she had been a charming child, and by being some six years younger than Ruby, she had been the pet of the family. Of course, Mother Setterington had been past forty at Emma's birth, so perhaps that was why the baby had been so special.

Miney would most assuredly have liked to assert herself. After all, Blanche was Miney's child even if she did happen to be the first grandchild. Miney was the one who had borne all the discomforts, so it rankled her to have her domineering mother-in-law tell her how to raise the girl. Trouble was, Miney was afraid of Lavina Setterington. She sensed that underneath, Millie was still in awe of his parents, so she had no misconceived notion of his ever taking her part in any disagreement. Like as not, he would side with his mother, no matter what. It wasn't that Millie didn't have a mind of his own either—he had plenty of backbone. It was just that Mother was that sort of a woman; even Father knuckled under to her at times. Millie had been brought up well and taught to respect his elder's judgment, and this sort of upbringing dies hard.

Now, Ma was different—a lot different. 'Course life had been a lot harder for Ma than Mother Setterington. Ma's first husband had dropped dead whilst they were moving from New York State to Michigan in a covered wagon. They had been almost to Vernon when he died. Mary had been just thirteen months old, and even Lorin, who had been seven, scarcely remembered her own father.

Ma and Grandfather Barnes had been pretty hard put to make do until she met Pa and married him. Soon, they'd moved to the log cabin south of the main four corners in Elsie, and this was where she and Ettie had spent their early years. Ma was easygoing and didn't think she had to run everyone's life. Pa had been a doctor and had been gone all hours of the day or night, so Ma had learned to get by.

Mother Setterington would never have tolerated such a haphazard life—hers had to be a regular routine, her house the nicest in town, her clothes the finest. Ma and Pa hadn't had as much, but they had always eaten well because a lot of people paid Pa in food, when they paid him at all. Guess Mother Setterington felt just because her husband was such a good provider, she had to be allowed extra privileges. Well, Miney didn't like it, but there was nothing much she could do about it. Although Blanche was spoiled, she was such a winsome child when she wanted to be, it was hard not to let her have her way. Millie wasn't quite as taken with her wiles as the rest of the family, but that was because he was so besotted with his son.

Ralph was turning out to be a fetching little fellow in looks. She supposed it did make her feel proud when friends and neighbors said what a good-looking baby he was. Guess maybe he did have Millie's eyes, and she had always thought Millie had nice eyes. She liked them best when they danced with merriment and the crinkles showed in the corners. 'Course Millie was a handsome man. She was proud of him and proud to be his wife. Guess maybe she shouldn't feel badly because she had a boy who quite likely would grow up to be something like his father. She guessed Millie was right; a man should have a son to keep up the family name. *Setterington* was a distinguished name, and it would be a shame to have it die out. Besides, Ralph was growing nicely and was a good-natured baby. Things could be a heap worse.

"Ma! Ma! Wake up."

Blanche stood by her mother's bed gently tapping Miney's arm. The room was shrouded in darkness, but Blanche's white muslin nightgown stood out in relief, giving her a spectral appearance. Her voice was hushed, yet urgent.

"Ma!" she said a little louder.

Miney had been sleeping with the soundness of first sleep, which comes after a tiring day.

"Blanche. Land's sakes, child, what is it?"

"I'm afeared, Ma. I hearded noises."

"What kind of noises?"

"I don't know, and that's why I'm afeared," the child explained patiently in a whisper.

After a moment, Miney said, "I don't hear a thing except the crickets and an old tree toad."

"Come on, Ma. Just you come into the parlor, and you can hear."

"Well, all right."

Miney threw back the sheet, took Blanche's hand, and went through the dining room into the parlor. Just then, there was a sharp, loud report, unmistakably the sound of a rifle.

"There, Ma. You heard it. Was it a gun?"

Her eyes became wide and frightened at the unknown, and she pressed closer to her mother.

"I think so. There it went again. There's more than that though. Sounds like Ralph does when he bangs on my pots and pans with a spoon."

Just then, Millie came to stand beside them.

"What in thunderation is going on? Can't a man be left alone to get a decent night's sleep?"

"Blanche was frightened because some strange noises woke her up. Honestly, Millie, it did sound like a gunshot from up on the Ridge. But there's a lot more commotion. Listen, doesn't it sound like hollering?"

"Quite likely. Heard some of the fellows talking when I was up town the other day, and I think tonight was when they planned to chivaree Wally Hiers and Sarah."

"That's right. They've been married over two weeks, so that is likely what's going on."

"Ma, what's a chivaree? Does it hurt?"

"Not at all, sweetheart, unless you perhaps count a person's dignity." Miney laughed. "It is just a bunch of folks getting together to tease newlyweds. They always wait until the young couple have gone to bed. Then, they sneak around the house, some into the house, and if they're lucky, even right up to the bedroom door, and then they start ringing cowbells, banging on old kettles or circle saws or anything that makes a lot of noise. 'Course, at the first sound, it makes the couple jump right out of their hide. Sometimes, they make them come out in their nightgown and nightshirt, and they might even take them for a ride on a wagon. It is all meant in fun, and usually everyone just accepts it as inevitable."

"I don't think I'd like it much."

"Well, dear, by the time you are old enough to get married, perhaps they will no longer do these things."

"Are you women going to stand here jawing all night? I'm going back to bed."

Miney took Blanche upstairs and kissed her goodnight once again. Now that Blanche knew the origin of the strange sounds, Miney was certain the child would soon drop off to sleep. If it hadn't been that the sounds carried so well on the summer night air, what with all the windows and doors being open, Blanche probably would never have heard a thing. No wonder the child was afraid since she had recognized a gunshot. During the day, it was not a sound to draw any undue attention, but after sundown, it was cause for speculation. 'Course Ralph had slept through the whole thing, which was just as well.

Miney returned to bed, but now she was wide-awake. She heard the clock on the shelf strike eleven and knew she had had over an hour of good slumber, which was enough to make her feel restless now. She thought about her daughter. Ma had certainly been right— Blanche was the most important person in Miney's small world. Ralph was a cunning little fellow, she thought begrudgingly, yet he was forever trying her patience to the utmost.

Sometimes, she wondered how Mother Setterington had ever coped with both Millie and John because she just felt it was from the Setterington side of the family that Ralph inherited these characteristics. Everyone knew that Father had been wild when he was young; well, at least he had done a lot of things that he frowned on now. Like Millie could remember that his father used to frequent the saloon. In fact, Millie remembered that he often was with his father when Horatio stepped into the saloon; he could recall being sat up on the bar while his father ordered him a sarsaparilla and a whiskey for himself. Now, Father never drank spirits—not even hard cider.

No, Horatio Setterington had not always been the God-fearing man he was now. He had always been as good as his word, but one had had to pay close attention to what Father said, or they sometimes got the wrong impression. Why, she remembered when she was a young girl, Pa had traded horses thinking he was getting an extremely good bargain. As it turned out, the one he got was a heaver. When Pa had first noticed the young mare wasn't breathing right, he could hardly believe his eyes. Miney had heard him tell his wife about the transaction. He had ended by saying, "Rate Setterington just beat me out of a good horse. He's just too clever. I guess he only told me that this one was young, and I was too trusting to look her over carefully. You just can't trust a horse trader."

Father was still an astute businessman, and if you dealt with him, you had better read carefully what you were signing. However, he never lied. All was there for anyone to read, it was just that he was very clever about wording any contract he drew up. The man was made for the business world.

That summer, Miney got her wish as Millie did build on to the house. Now, she finally had the kitchen with plenty of cupboards instead of a kitchen-dining room combination like she had been putting up with for years. It did seem nice. That was something a woman needed—a kitchen, if she was to cook for hungry men at threshing time. True, she had wanted it a little larger, but Millie had said that making the wall even with the narrow porch off the dining room to the north was good enough; then too, he hadn't seen fit to put in a pantry like she had wanted. Shermans up on the corner had a mighty fine pantry. One door led into the kitchen, and the other door went into the dining room, so's it was real handy, but Millie said what with the cellar, she didn't really need one.

Perhaps he was right. There was a cellarway connecting the house from the west kitchen door to the door of the huge stone cellar. Not everyone had such a fine place as that to keep their canned goods and vegetables. It was a large building, about fifteen feet by twenty with stone walls almost two feet thick. Even potatoes would keep there without freezing except in the very coldest part of the winter. The floor was dirt, and they had bins for potatoes, carrots, cabbage, onions, and squash. It was cold, but nearly always stayed just above freezing. There were plenty of shelves for the jars of canned fruits and vegetables so painstakingly put up by Mina along with the jars of pickles; also, a place for the crocks that held the fried-down pork, sauerkraut, and dills. Come butchering time, there was room for smoked hams and bacon to hang from a rafter. In the cellarway, which did get as cold as outdoors, there were hooks for an occasional carcass of a freshly butchered sheep or the hind of a beef to provide fresh beefsteak for a time. Yes, it was all pretty handy, and Miney had much for which to be thankful.

Millie was better than some husbands as he did try to get her labor-saving devices. Just before Ralph was born, he had bought her a wringer, which proved to be ever so much better than having to twist the clothes by hand. Besides, it got more water out than she could get out by twisting, so's the clothes dried a lot sooner. Not any of the neighbor women were as fortunate as yet. Ma would have been glad to have had such a convenience. Of course, Mother Setterington had had one for years, but Miney's was newer, and she just bet it was a lot better, she thought as she grinned smugly.

With a mother like his, it was no wonder Millie gave a thought to the woman's welfare. Mother had always had a hired woman to do cleaning in the house ever since Miney knew her.

Mother had grown soft with the years because she hadn't always had such luxury. When they were first married, she had had to do for herself. Mother was just plumb lucky she had married a man like Horatio Setterington. Everything he tried made money for him.

Her life had had its share of sorrow. She had borne seven children, but four of those seven were buried in the village cemetery. Shortly after they had moved to Elsie, Lavina had been blessed with a tiny baby girl, only to have the Lord take her at the age of four months. A bitter blow indeed. Then, had come John, a fine, healthy boy. Pearl, Edward, and Ruby had been born next, but now both Pearl and Edward rested in the graveyard with Annie B. Then, almost seven years after Ruby, when Lavina had been forty-three years old, little Emma had been born. It was the same year that Millie and Mina had been married. My, how both Rate and Lavina had adored that child. Then, when only four, she had joined her brother and sisters in the grassy plot in the cemetery. Lavina had found it difficult indeed to reconcile herself to the death of yet another daughter.

Both John and Millie had been healthy, strapping lads, seldom sick, but Ruby had been small and rather frail looking. After little Emma, lovingly called Baby, had died, Mother Setterington had lavished all of her affection on Ruby, and now Blanche came in for a major portion. Ruby was spoiled, and Father Setterington had indulged his wife in this. Mother had seen to it that Ruby had done very few chores around the house. However, those boys had always had to toe the line. At least Mother had brought Millie up to give some consideration to a woman's work, so she supposed she should be thankful for that.

If only Mother wasn't such an interfering soul. Miney recalled when she and Millie had first moved into the farmhouse right after their wedding trip to Manistique. They had invited Mother and Father over for Saturday evening supper. Miney had been more than a little anxious about cooking for her in-laws, but Ma had taught her well, and she knew she could cook as well as most. Her baking was better than a lot of women she knew. Well, anyway, the supper had gone pretty well, but then, Mother had inspected the house. She hadn't liked where Miney had the couch, nor the library table, nor one of the rockers, nor the organ. Well, she'd made it plain that the next time she came out, she expected the furniture to be arranged as she suggested. Miney had looked to Millie for support, but he had given her that noncommittal look of his, and she knew for certain there would be no help forthcoming from him.

She had answered meekly, "Of course, Mother, I'm sure it would look better where you suggest. I'll try to get it moved first thing next week."

She had felt anything but meek, only Mother had such a formidable look, she hadn't dared argue. Millie certainly came by his set ways honestly. From the looks of things, he got it from both sides of the family, the Reynolds as well as the Setteringtons. Well, she'd known when she married him that his folks were much respected and looked up to as leaders in the community. Mother had always bossed the women of the church, but Miney had never really figured on Mother bossing her. Well, while she might have to put up with it, she didn't have to like it.

Blanche had donned her nightgown while Miney folded her petticoat and neatly draped her dress on the chair. Miney folded back the coverlet and held the sheet up for Blanche to crawl into bed.

"Not yet, Ma. I have to say my prayers first. Aunt Ruby said I must never go to bed without saying my prayers."

"When did Aunt Ruby tell you all this?" asked Miney, a slight edge to her voice.

"The last time I stayed at Grandmother's. When we went to bed, Aunt Ruby knelt with me and teached me to fold my hands and teached me what to say."

"*Taught*, sweetheart, *taught*."

"Well, she taught me what to say."

"All right, Blanche, is it all right if Ma listens?"

"Oh, yes, Ma. I'd like that. Then, you can tuck me in just like afore."

Blanche knelt by her bed, folded her hands, closed her eyes, and in her sweet, childish voice, began, "Now I lay me down to sleep, I pray the Lord my soul to keep. If I should die before I wake, I pray the Lord my soul to take. God bless Pa and Ma and Ralph and bless Grandma and Grandmother and Grandfather and Aunt Ruby. Amen. There, Ma, now you can tuck me in."

"That was very nice, Blanche. It was nice of Aunt Ruby to teach you. I guess Ma just hadn't realized what a big girl you are getting to be. I'm glad Ruby is so nice to you."

"Aunt Ruby is awful nice, Ma. She doesn't ever yell at me like Grandmother does, and she does nice things. Why, one day she took me down town special and bought me some candy. She always tucks me in bed when I'm at Grandmother's." Noting the look on her mother's face, she added, "Of course, I like it lots better when you put me to bed and kiss me goodnight."

Back downstairs, Mina gave thought to the episode just finished. So Ruby had taught Blanche her prayers. Miney felt just a small twinge of jealousy, knew it was wrong, and quickly asked forgiveness. It was just that she hadn't thought of Blanche as being that old, and yet, the child was five. Of course, it was nice that Ruby cared so much for her small niece. Still, Miney did feel just a little cheated that someone else had shared these precious moments with her daughter. Where her daughter was concerned, Mina did like to be the most important personage, and she rather disliked sharing the child with others.

By the time Ralph had reached his first birthday, he was an ordinary toddler. He had cut his teeth on time and with a minimum of discomfort; in fact, he had seldom been ailing. When he was ten months old, he had started pulling himself up to anything he could grasp firmly, and by that first birthday, he was taking several steps on his own.

A few months later, he went on the run most of the time. Mina couldn't keep track of him and soon discovered she had no sooner taught him to leave one thing alone, when he cheerfully moved on to something else. My, my, boys were certainly a lot different than girls. Blanche had never wanted to get her hands dirty even as a little tyke, but the lad, now, was something else to reckon with. When he discovered that eggs broke when dropped, much to her chagrin, he had rather enjoyed feeling the slimy mess. She walloped, scolded, slapped hands, and used the word *no* so much, she was afraid he would never learn any other word. Ralph took it all in stride. He was seldom punished twice for the same thing—he simply discovered something new to do.

What angered Miney almost more than Ralph's infraction of rules was to catch Millie surreptitiously smiling or trying very hard to suppress an out-and-out chuckle at some of the boy's antics. It was bad enough to have a constant battle raging between mother and son without having the feeling that one's husband found the whole situation quite hilarious. On more than one occasion, Miney voiced her thoughts to Millie, only to meet with his infuriating calm over the entire situation.

Sometimes, she wished she could look at life with Millie's easy-going nature. He often said, "What will be, will be." And Millie truly believed his words. Worrying never did a person a mite of good, but Miney hadn't arrived at any method to keep from worrying. Take Ralph for instance. Did it do her one bit of good to worry about what he'd get into next? Not at all. So far, it had never kept him out of anything. Another thing, from the way Millie played with the boy now, she could just visualize what it was going to be like when Ralph was older. It would be like having a free-forall in the house.

'Course the other day it had been her turn to laugh although very quietly and to herself. It seemed that Cash Waldron and Millie had sat hunched over the checkerboard, which lay on their knees, neither saying a word, each intent on his game when Ralph had come running by, freshly invigorated by his afternoon nap. Well, Ralph had stumbled, hit the checkerboard, and scattered checkers every way for Sunday. Millie had looked slightly perturbed as he said, "I guess that ends that game, Cash. Good thing for you since I was going to lick you anyhow." They had argued good-naturedly as they found the checkers and set the board up for a new game.

The thought crossed Miney's mind that it would have been even more comical if there had at least been one lost checker.

CHAPTER 4

The day promised to be hot. There was not even a hint of a breeze, and even though it was not yet noon, the sun beat down relentlessly from a cloudless sky. Mina wiped perspiration from her brow before reaching for another shirt to hang on the line. Lawsy, but she was glad this was the last batch of clothes to hang up, that is, all except Millie's overalls. She always hoped for a nice wind on washday since it not only dried the clothes in a hurry, it made them soft to touch. Today, they'd be like boards unless she ironed everything. If it was this hot tomorrow, she certainly wasn't going to keep a fire going just so's she could heat irons. Of course, she would have to iron Millie's good shirt, and she supposed she would end up doing the everyday ones too; however, she would just fold the dish towels and flat things even if it did go against her grain.

"Wonder where that boy got to?" she said aloud.

Ralph at nineteen months was a handful. Why, that boy could move quicker'n scat and was always into some mischief. He had the biggest bump of curiosity she had ever heard tell of, which often resulted in some sort of mess for her to clean up. Still, she had to admit he was becoming a fetching child, and everyone commented on how well-behaved he was in church. 'Course they didn't get to see him at home, or they would think differently, no doubt about that.

The clothes on the line, she came through the house to the kitchen, dropped her basket, glanced into the bedroom searching for Ralph. She returned to the dining room, looked out the north door, and there he was, by the huge cottonwood tree, the rear wheel of his little wagon caught on a large stone. With a child's usual frustration, he had never considered backing the wagon and detouring around the rock; his method of attack was to jerk the wagon over the stone, and with every tug, he was very angrily and clearly shouting, "Damn! Damn! Damn!"

Miney rushed out of the house to chastise her son. Now, where had he picked up such language? Millie, no doubt. Even though Millie never used such language in her presence, she had long surmised that he used that kind of verbiage. Well, she would just have a talk with him about that. She was not going to have her son using swear words. Why, if she let this go on, the next thing she knew, he would be taking the Lord's name in vain. She would speak to Millie about this, and in the future, he could just watch his language. After all, this was one thing that wasn't exactly the boy's fault. Now, this was no small concession on her part because it wasn't often Miney was this generous with the child.

She brought Rate into the house where she could keep an eye on him. She hooked the screen doors so he couldn't be off while her back was turned. It was time to start getting dinner, and she had no time to be chasing down her small son. Millie expected a large midday meal, regardless the weather, and he expected it promptly at noon.

Miney often wondered just how Millie knew when to quit for noon since he never carried a watch to the field like most menfolk did. But watch or no watch, he would walk through the door all washed up and ready to sit down to the table just as the clock was striking twelve. Sometimes, when the firewood was a trifle green, or maybe just a little damp, so's she hadn't been able to get the fire going like it ought, and things refused to boil even with the stove lids removed, so the pots sit right over the fire, she felt more than a mite irritated because he was always so punctual. Not that Millie ever said anything if he was to wait a few minutes; he simply sat down with that certain look on his face and waited. Still, he sometimes bragged to others how Miney always had his meals on time, so she guessed that made up for all the effort it cost.

Millie often was a man of few words, neither complaining about things nor expressing satisfaction. Sometimes, she wisht he would tell her when things pleased him. She could tell by his looks that he was pleased, but it still wasn't quite the same as if he had actually said something. Oh, well, best to count her blessings, she supposed. Maybe how he felt was a heap more important than his saying his thoughts. 'Course she had heard other women tell how their man always told them what good cooks they were, such good housekeepers, the best seamstress, and like as not when they were talking with other menfolk, they'd do nothing but complain. Sometimes, Millie would tell her what had been said. Men gossiped just as much as women did, she had figured out, and they weren't always complimentary about their womenfolk. At least she never had cause to think Millie ever spoke ill of her to anyone else. In fact, Millie was a first-rate husband, and she could put up with his lack of compliments or flowery language; she guessed actions did speak louder than words.

That night, when she mentioned the incident to Millie, he had simply chuckled and said, "Why, Miney, you're accusing me of swearing. Now, have you ever heard me swear?"

"Well, no. I don't rightly think I ever have."

"Well then, do you honestly think I'd use such language?"

"You just might. If you don't, where'd the child hear it?" she asked accusingly.

"Blesst if I know. Maybe he heard it in church."

"Millie!" came the horrified cry.

"Now, Miney, don't the preacher talk about hell and being damned? Who's to say Rate didn't pick up the word there? You'll have to admit it just might be possible."

Millie gave another chuckle, and his eyes danced with pleasure as Miney considered this remote possibility. He knew that he had planted a seed of doubt in her mind as to where to place the blame. Reckon he would have to be a mite more careful with his choice of words when the boy was around. Still, when things didn't go quite according to Hoyle, it was awful easy to let a *damn* slip into one's remarks. Now, who would've thought the boy would be so quick to pick up a stray word like that and use it in the proper way too. My, what if Rate had used the word in front of Ma; there'd have been some fireworks then. Still, Millie gave another chuckle and spoke to his perplexed wife.

"Like as not the boy learned his lesson. He's sharp as a tack, and he'll know better than to use the word again. Now, don't you fret."

With that he dismissed the episode from his mind and went contentedly to sleep.

Blanche came hobbling into the kitchen, her face plainly showing pain, her cheeks tear-streaked although she was now in complete control of her emotions.

"Ma, I'm just never going outdoors again."

"And why not?"

"I just stepped on a nail. That's why. Seems like I'm always stepping on nails. I try to be so careful, but every old board must have a whole bunch of nails sticking out of it."

"It only seems that way. Here. Let Ma take a look."

Blanche sat down in a kitchen chair and stuck her foot out for Mina to examine. Sure enough, on the ball of the foot was the telltale sign: a small hole with blood oozing from it.

"Never mind now. It'll be fine."

Miney took a knife from the cabinet drawer and disappeared down the steps into the stone cellar. There, she sliced off a piece of fat, salt pork. Upon returning to the kitchen, she grabbed the pepper shaker and made the white meat completely black with the pepper, sneezing once as a little got up her nose.

"Now, young lady, you hold that in place while I get a rag to tie around it."

Miney went to the ragbag and extracted a bit of an old sheet; she tore off a strip about two inches wide and three feet long.

"There. That should do it. Hold your foot up so's I can reach it better."

"Yes, Ma."

Miney wrapped the sheeting around the foot, anchored it by passing it around the ankle, and then tore the strip in half far enough back so she could use the ends as ties around the foot. It was easy to tell that she had performed this same task numerous times before.

"There you are, Blanche. And please try to be more careful."

"Ma, I told you, I do try to be careful. I don't like getting hurt, and I don't like having a hunk of salt pork tied on me. I don't do it on purpose," she explained.

"I know you don't, sweetheart. I guess it just seems like you don't watch where you are stepping. Run along now."

Blanche limped off. She'd not be going outside to play again today, that's for sure. Blamed old nails anyway. Why did Pa always have to leave old boards lying around? She found her Mother Goose book and settled down, repeating to herself as many of the rhymes as she could remember.

"Blanche. Blanche Setterington, you come here this instant."

"I'm coming, Ma," came the reply from the upstairs.

Blanche had been playing with her dolls, intentionally keeping out of sight because she had heard Ma mention to Pa that she intended to make soap today. Blanche knew that this job was hard work and that her part of the task was to mind her little brother and keep him out of Ma's way. Now, if there was one task Blanche intensely disliked, it was minding Ralph. She had to keep her eye on him every minute, or he'd wander off like as not. Ma was always afeared he'd get hurt on something. Especially she didn't like having him underfoot whilst she made soap. Ma knew Elzie Brewbaker, Wilson and Alice's boy, who, when he was only a little tyke, had taken a swallow of lye from a tub thinking the liquid was cider, and it near killed him. Some said his throat was never right after that and that he could hardly eat sometimes. Well, Ma didn't want anything like that happening to Ralph; therefore, she expected Blanche to keep Ralph otherwise occupied.

"What did you want, Ma?" Blanche asked innocently.

"You know very well what I want, missy. I have to hurry if I'm going to get that batch of soap done before dinnertime, and you know full well you're to mind Ralph."

"He's all right, Ma. See, he's just playing there on the floor with those old spools."

"Like as not that won't last long. Now, you take care you don't let him run off."

Mina, finished with her orders, returned to the kitchen, gathered up the container of fatty meat rinds and scraps of fat meat, and dumped them into the iron kettle. Next, she brought in the lye to add to the mixture. This was no commercial lye, but a lye obtained from making a pile of the wood ashes they cleared out of the stove daily, allowing water to seep through, and collecting the ensuing mixture in a wooden tub. She stirred up the fire a mite and added another stick of wood as the mixture had to boil. There. That much was done, but she had to keep the fire going good to keep it bubbling, and she had to stir it so the fat would not stick on the sides and burn; after all this trouble, she hardly wanted to spoil it. As she stirred the mixture thoughtfully, she heard Ralph start to cry.

With a note of exasperation in her voice, she called, "Blanche, what's wrong?"

"Nothing, Ma," came the innocent reply.

"Why is Ralph crying?"

"Honest, Ma, I don't know. He just started bawling for no reason at all."

Mina left the stove long enough to take a peek into the dining room where the children were playing. Here they sat, facing each other with all of Ralph's spools behind Blanche, and when he reached for one, she hit his hand; of course, he howled momentarily. Just as Mina stepped into the room, Rate walloped his sister right in the face.

"Ma! Ma! Ralph hit me," shouted Blanche.

"You deserved it, Blanche Lenore. What ails you anyhow? Now, you just straighten up, missy, or I'll give you something to cry about. For shame teasing your little brother that way. Ralph, you mustn't hit sister even if she is naughty. You're a great big boy, and she's only a girl. Now, there'll be no more fighting this morning from the both of you."

With that ultimatum, Miney returned to her project of soapmaking. Not long before it was time to start making dinner, the rinds had been skimmed off, the mess had congealed and been put in containers ready for use. Miney was glad to have that chore out of the way for a while. She didn't like this job even a little bit, but it was just something that was necessary, no matter whether one liked the job or not.

July 5, 1895, and Blanche's sixth birthday. She had wanted a party this year, but Ma had said maybe next year. Well, if Ma wouldn't have one for her next year, she'd just ask Grandmother and Grandfather. Bet they'd see that she got a party if she was careful to ask them real nice. Bet the reason Ma wouldn't let her have one this year was because of Ralph. That baby was always into something. It wasn't because Ma didn't punish him either; my, but he sure got his backsides swatted plenty. Served him right though—and to think one day in Sunday school Fern had said she thought he was real sweet and she wisht she had a little brother just like him. Of course, she could say that since she didn't have either a little brother or a little sister. There was just Bert and Archie, who were lots older than she. Some people sure were lucky.

Blanche wouldn't have minded having a sister quite so much, but a brother—ugh! The less said, the better. She had to watch him like a hawk, or she just knew he'd break her doll. He hadn't learned to be careful with anything. At least Ma had made her a cake, and she had a new dress for everyday; Aunt Lorin had given her a book, Grandma Smith had made her a new petticoat, and she didn't know what she'd get from Grandmother and Grandfather. Like as not they'd be over in the evening and bring her something. Whatever it was, it would be far nicer than anything the others had given her.

It was always thus. She doubted if Grandfather had much to do with what she got, but Grandmother seemed to know what little girls liked. Last year, it had been Alice, her very nicest doll. Then, at that Christmas in the old house, the one Blanche scarcely remembered, they had given her that tiny washbowl and pitcher so daintily trimmed with flowers. She had never seen a toy like them before, and none of her girlfriends had anything quite as nice. Fern had really been extremely envious. However, she had no idea what they would give her this time, but whatever it was, she was sure she would like it.

Blanche was right; shortly after supper, Grandmother and Grandfather drove into the yard. Miney had scarcely had time to get her supper dishes done, and she still wore her apron. Well, much she cared. If Mother Setterington had as much work to do as she did, she was certain Mother wouldn't look as if she had just stepped out of a bandbox.

Lavina and Horatio settled themselves after giving Blanche a rather large box from Christian's in Owosso. The little girl had scarcely been able to untie the strings, she was so excited. When she did get it open, she let out a squeal of delight for there lay the prettiest blue voile dress, white gloves, and a dainty matching parasol. My, Grandmother certainly did know what would strike a small girl's fancy.

After Blanche had modeled her dress, much to everyone's satisfaction, Lavina brought up the subject on her mind.

"Mina, are you going to send Blanche to school come fall?"

"Why, I hadn't given it much thought, Mother. I do suppose since she is six, she should start. Some don't go until seven, but if I waited another year, that would make her seven and a half, so I think it best she go this fall. Besides, she already knows most of her letters," she added proudly.

"Have you given any thought as to where she will attend school?"

"Why, Stafford, where else," stated a puzzled Miney. "It's only a mile and a half from here. That's right handy for living in the country," she explained.

"Well, now, Mina, Rate and I've been talking it over, and we feel that we don't want our granddaughter going to a shoddy country school. We shall take her into town to live with us, and she can have the advantages of a town school."

"You want me to let her stay with you?" Mina asked incredulously.

"I know you're thinking that you'll miss the lass," put in Horatio, "but you must consider Blanche and what's best for her."

"I am considering Blanche, and her place is in her own home with her own father and mother. Millie wouldn't want her to be away from us either, I can tell you," asserted Miney with a bravado she scarcely felt.

"Now, Mina, you give it some thought, and I'm certain you'll see we are right. Besides, it isn't as though she had no friends in town, and really, just who does she have here except perhaps one of the Moores or Clarks. You do want Blanche to grow into a lady, don't you?"

"Of course I do, Mother Setterington, but—"

"Well, then, say no more. She can come home for the weekends or on vacations. Milford can just bring her in each Monday morning and pick her up on Friday night. You know how quickly the days pass, and you'll still have Ralph for company."

Mother acted as if it were all settled. Miney was sure that just this once Millie would oppose his mother. Not have Blanche around to enjoy? Mother had better realize Blanche's parents would decide where she went to school. Millie simply wouldn't hear of Blanche being gone all week either. He loved Blanche just as much as she did, and they certainly weren't going to give up their daughter just to please the whim of Mother Setterington. Somehow, Miney had the feeling that Father Setterington didn't give a hoot one way or the other, but was merely finding it expedient to humor Mother's wishes. Well, they'd just see.

Suppose the school in Elsie was better, and Miney wasn't sure it was, but suppose it did have more to offer, was that still sufficient reason to uproot Blanche from her own home? Goodness knows, she spent enough time with them as it was. Of course, at Stafford, Blanche's only classmates would be the children of farmers, but Miney could see no harm in that; after all, Blanche's parents were farmers, and Miney felt Millie was just as good as any man—better than some since he neither smoked nor drank and wasn't one mite lazy.

If the rest of the evening seemed a little strained, neither Lavina nor Horatio gave any indication that they sensed it. If anything, they seemed a little more relaxed and talkative and waited for almost an hour after Millie came in from chores before leaving to go home. They even played with Ralph, and Grandfather would swing the child up to sit on his broad shoulders because the boy laughed so. Oh, yes, they were most agreeable, and Millie had no reason to suspect what a turmoil his wife's mind was in, nor did he find out until after the children were in bed.

"Millie, just you guess what your mother wants now."

"Miney, I have no idee what Ma would be wanting. I've never been able to outguess her yet."

"Well, she wants Blanche to stay with them and go to school in Elsie. Now, what do you think of that?"

"Hmmmm. Ma suggested that, did she. Did Pa have anything to say, or did Ma do all the talking?"

"You know how your mother is, she did most of the talking, and when Father did say something, he agreed with Mother as usual."

"Perhaps we should give it some consideration."

"Milford Horatio Setterington, do you mean to tell me you will just sit there and calmly say we should consider giving our daughter away? Just what kind of a father are you? Don't you love Blanche, or is it only your son you care about?" accused a distraught Miney.

"Of course that isn't true, and you know full well I love Blanche, but you know that once Ma and Pa make up their mind to something, they are powerful hard to dissuade."

"Milford, when are you going to be man enough to stand up to your parents? Aren't you a grown man yet?"

"Miney, that's not fair. Ma and Pa have always been good to us. They gave us a good price on the farm here. They think they have Blanche's best interest at heart, and perhaps they do."

"How can you be so shortsighted? Mother and Father still consider you a boy, and they must make your decisions—just like the time Father sold your yoke of oxen just because he considered $300 a good price for the beasts, even if you hadn't wanted to sell them. He didn't even give you the money, just put it against what we still owed for the farm."

"I know, but Pa felt he was doing me a favor because that was really more than they were worth," Millie offered lamely.

"And how about your inheritance from your grandfather? One thousand dollars, wasn't it? You said that Father kept what belonged to you and John until you were twenty-one."

"I know, Miney. But he paid us interest, so it was all fair and square. I hadn't had need of the money until we were married. Pa just kept it safe for me."

"You were only twenty when we married," she reminded.

"Well, Pa just did what he thought was best. Still, that has nothing to do with this. You know Blanche would have to walk to school as I'd not have time to take her each day, and being's she's a girl, I'd not trust her with a horse just yet, and besides, there's no shed to put a horse in at school as you know. Anyway, I don't suppose these farm children are taught manners like the ones in town. You know yourself that is true. Ma wants her to be a young lady."

"She wants her spoiled, that's what she wants. She likes her dressed better than we can afford, and she wants her to be older than her years. Mother doesn't help Blanche to get on with other girls her own age at all. Besides, I would miss her so," she said beseechingly. "Please, Millie, just this once stand up to your mother."

"All right, Miney." He sighed. "I'll try, but Ma can be awful stubborn when she's made up her mind to something. There are times when even Pa has to give in to her, you know that as well as I do."

When Millie went into the bedroom to go to bed, Miney quickly changed into her nightgown. It never occurred to her that it was unusual that she had never once undressed in the same room with her husband in all these years of marriage, nor would she ever. For Millie always undressed and dressed in the bedroom, while she did so by the woodstove in the dining room. While she may have borne him two children, her body was still her own, and she was always glad when he was sufficiently tired to no more than give her arm a loving pat and grumble goodnight when she stealthily slipped in beside him. Tonight was no exception, and in a few moments, his deep, regular breathing announced that he was sleeping soundly.

She felt more than a little irritated with him because he could so easily dismiss the problem that would confront them come September. She was not going to have her daughter taken away from her, mother-in-law or no mother-in-law. No sir, Mother Setterington was just going to have to learn that Blanche belonged with her parents, and that was that.

Miney was hurrying to get the dinner dishes done. She wanted to get to the depot in time to meet Lorin's train, which was due at two thirty. A week ago today, Lorin and Blanche had left to go visit Ettie in Traverse City. Mina had been more than a little surprised that Blanche had wanted to accompany Lorin because Miney knew Blanche wasn't very fond of either aunt; then, she remembered how much the child liked Ettie's husband, George. She supposed he had been the attraction since Uncle Doc, as Blanche called him, was by far her favorite uncle.

Miney had found the time without her daughter lonesome indeed. Of course, Blanche was often gone for a day or two, staying with Mary, Ma, or Mother and Father Setterington, but this had been a whole week.

Apparently, Ralph had missed his sister too because sometimes if Blanche was in a particularly congenial mood, she would play with the lad. She often pulled him in his little wagon to his shouts of "Go, horsey, go!" and sometimes she sat with him on the floor and rolled a solid glass ball—the one with the figure of a white cat in it, which had belonged to Aunt Ruby—to him so he could catch it between his outspread legs. All this week he had been more mischievous than ever; she supposed it was just out of boredom.

After having spent a lonesome week, Miney was all the more certain she did not want Blanche going to town to school come fall. Why, one week had been bad enough. Perhaps if Ralph were just a little older where he could carry on some sort of conversation, but he wasn't. The good Lord knew Millie was a far cry from a good conversationalist. Much of the time he sat without making any effort to converse with her, and if she persisted, he was likely to tell her to keep still, which was just a polite way of telling her to shut up. Oh, well, she supposed she shouldn't complain since he was such a hard worker and a good provider.

She finished in the kitchen, changed her dress, washed Ralph's face and hands and changed his dress. Next, she went to the barn and threw the lightweight, driving harness on black Old Mikey; then, she led him out to the buggy and hitched him up. Ralph had followed instructions and had waited patiently at the doorway of the dining room while his mother performed these tasks.

"Come on, Ralph. Ma's ready now."

Ralph came out the door, across the narrow porch, and over to where Miney stood by the buggy. She lifted him into the buggy, then, holding the lines, climbed into the buggy to sit beside her son. She slapped Mikey's back with the lines, and the old horse moved off at a slow trot.

"'Dap, Mikey. Mikey, go fast."

"Well, Ralph, that's about as fast as Old Mikey goes anymore. He's a pretty old horse, you know. He once belonged to Grandfather Setterington, but we've had him since we first got married."

"I likes Mikey," he confided.

They took the Ridge Road, and when they came to the corner to turn toward the cemetery, Mikey quickly took a swing into the corner of the field instead of staying on the road.

Miney laughed. "Poor Old Mikey. If I don't watch you, you always take us through here. Guess it hardly matters."

The horse had a split front foot, which was drawn together by the shoe he wore, and Millie had surmised the soft dirt of the field felt better to his foot than the gravel of the roadbed because Mikey took this route whenever the driver wasn't paying enough attention and he could catch them unawares. It was because of his hoof that the horse could never be allowed to go unshod.

Miney checked the watch on the chain around her neck; they were going to be at the station before two thirty, so unless the train was early—and this was almost unheard-of—they would be there in plenty of time.

They passed the main four corners, passed the business block, and turned north at the second corner. There was only one road leading to the depot. They went past the gristmill, across a track that was just a siding leading to the long low coal shed, and continued on to the depot.

The depot was a squat, low, wooden building, the siding being wide boards placed vertically, which had weathered to a dull gray. The roof had an overhang, so on the platform side, near the tracks, the roof gave protection to the passengers on the platform. A blackboard hung on the wall where the stationmaster posted the expected time of arrival of the trains from different directions, east or west.

Inside the depot, from the cramped stationmaster's office and ticket window, the telegraph key clicked monotonously. The benches looked hard and uncomfortable, and Miney noted they were not any too clean since they, like everything else, were covered with a fine, sooty dust. The windows were grimy, and the sills were heavily laden with cindery dust. Miney took her handkerchief and dusted a place for she and Ralph to sit. Seemed as though they could keep the place cleaner than this. Several other people waited; a few had satchels and were no doubt traveling someplace, while others were apparently meeting someone.

Ed Hawes came into the station. He drove the surrey from the large hotel on the main four corners, and it was his job to meet every train to provide transportation from the depot to the hotel. There probably was a carriage waiting from Wolf's Hotel, which was the smaller hotel on the east end of town, because they too usually had a guest or two come in on each train.

Must be near time, thought Miney. Just then came the sound of a whistle from the west. Miney and Ralph moved out to the platform. By now, a number of people were there waiting as the huffing engine, black smoke billowing from the smokestack, drew nearer the station. Ralph's eyes grew round and large as he watched the huge engine, shrouded in a cloud of steam, drift slowly past, then the coal car, the mail car, the baggage car, and finally the passenger cars. The brakes screeched, the cars jolted to a standstill, each one taking its turn at jostling the car in front. The conductors swung down and placed a small footstool by the steps of the cars, and the passengers began to disembark. The baggage car door slid open, and suitcases and valises were handed to the station agent to be placed on a waiting hand-propelled cart that stood on extremely high wheels.

Miney clutched Ralph's pudgy, little hand while she scanned the crowd for a glimpse of her daughter. Then, she saw Lorin place her hand in the conductor's outstretched hand as he helped her down the steps; he then turned to Blanche, placed his hands around her childish waist, and swung the child down to stand her on the boardwalk.

"Lorin. Blanche. Over here."

Blanche saw Miney, pushed past an elderly couple, and ran most unladylike to her mother.

"Ma, Ma. Oh, Ma, I'm so glad to be home."

Miney enveloped her daughter in her arms, gave her a resounding kiss, then turned to greet her sister. How Mina's spirits soared now that she had her daughter back again. She even noticed that

Blanche had given her little brother a bonebreaking hug, and for once, he had not shoved her away. She guessed Ralph was as pleased as she was to have Blanche home.

"Ma, Grandma let me go over to Aunt Mary's to play with Lelah all by myself yesterday."

"I guess you're plenty big enough to go that little distance by yourself. It's hardly like Mary lived clear across town."

In truth, Mary lived only a block to the west on the north side of the street.

"Well, she never has before. Maybe it's because I'm six now."

"Presume that must be it. And how is your aunt Mary and uncle Jap and the rest?"

"They's all right. They was just eating supper. They eat kinda late if you ask me. Guess Uncle Jap don't get home from work very early. Anyway, they were eating when I got there, so Aunt Mary invited me to eat with them."

"That was nice."

"I suppose so, but they had sweet potatoes."

"What was wrong with that?"

"Do you like them?"

"They aren't my favorite food, but I like them."

"Whyn't we ever have them then?" asked Blanche suspiciously.

"Your pa doesn't care for them, so I just never bothered. Didn't you like them?"

"Not at all. Honest, Ma, I could hardly get them down, and I was almost afraid they'd make me throw up. But I managed," she added triumphantly.

"Good for you. I'm glad you remembered to be polite."

"Aunt Mary offered me seconds, but I said I was full. Lelah and Frank, they took seconds, but, Ma, they tasted just awful, and I'll never, never eat them again as long as I live," she declared vehemently.

The day after Labor Day, Blanche enrolled for her first year of school—at Elsie.

Whether having Blanche with them all week was more tiring than Lavina had anticipated or whether it was to help soothe Mina's ruffled feathers, Blanche stayed one week with her grandmother and grandfather Setterington and the next week with Grandma Smith.

The difference in the two households was from one end of the scale to the other. Horatio and Lavina had one of the most beautiful homes in Elsie, inside as well as out. It was a new dwelling, only finished last spring. The nine-foot ceilings left room above each doorway for an intricate grilled work; the open stairway was beautiful; the rooms were spacious and furnished with the most attractive furniture of the period; carpets covered the floors, which was not a common practice except for the very well-to-do; and they had a bathroom, an almost unheard-of luxury.

Still, in all this luxury, Blanche was always to feel just a little alien. Her bedroom was on the second floor, down a long hall and around the corner. Grandmother had bought her a tiny lamp for her very own to light her way to bed. It had a dainty red bowl to hold the oil, a small clear chimney, but the shaft of light it emitted was not much more than from a candle.

Blanche hated bedtime. The passage was long and dark, and she had to get her nightgown from the hall closet just outside her bedroom door. Now, in this closet, Grandfather kept a plug (high silk) hat, which he no longer wore, and that hat cast the largest, scariest shadow you could imagine. She knew exactly what was causing the shadow, but somehow, it looked so different in the nighttime. She usually grabbed her nightgown from the hook as quickly as possible, slammed the door, and rushed into the sanctity of her room. She never felt quite at ease until she was safely in bed.

Never once had she voiced her fears to anyone. Grandmother would have scoffed at the idea of a six-year-old girl being afraid of shadows. Instead, Blanche just set her lips in a firm line, stiffened her spine, and did what had to be done, thinking that each night it would be easier. It never was.

The week with Grandma Smith was completely different. Her house was rather shabbily furnished; no carpets, only crocheted or woven rag rugs; there was no inside bathroom or running water; but here was love, warmth, and a coziness so lacking in the Setterington house.

The thinness of Mary Smith's care-worn face was accentuated by her hair being parted in the middle and pulled severely to the back to be worn in a bun; her nose seemed oversize in the smallness of her face, and her hair couldn't quite camouflage the prominent ears, but the eyes radiated a kindness for everyone. She was a small woman who always wore knitted slipper-sox with a soft leather sole which enabled her to move rather noiselessly around the house. Her explanation for this was that shoes hurt her feet, so she wore them only when she went outside or away from home.

Her first evening there, Blanche had followed her grandmother into the pantry to wipe the supper dishes. She had learned not to be tardy when Grandmother Setterington did dishes if she didn't want some caustic remark about how easy it was for someone her age to do the work. Well, she'd expected to perform the same service for Grandma Smith, but Grandma had said, "What are you intending to do?"

"Wipe the dishes for you, Grandma."

"You go play. I've nothing else that needs doing, and you've a long time ahead of you to do dishes."

"Thank you, Grandma. You're nice."

"Well, get along with you and enjoy yourself. You're only young once, my dear."

It was little wonder that Blanche felt more love for this small, kind, warmhearted Scotswoman than she felt for the cold, domineering Lavina Setterington. Money could never buy a child's love, and Blanche was no exception, so while Lavina gave her money and material things, it was Mary who gave her love and understanding.

CHAPTER 5

Fridays were always good days, since Mina looked forward to having her daughter home. Usually, Blanche was bubbling over with events that had happened at school. At times like these, mother and daughter were particularly close. Blanche could always make Miney laugh as she related the week's events. By the same token, Miney did dread Mondays as it made her face another lonesome week. Millie wasn't much of a talker, and Ralph was too young yet, besides having the disadvantage of being a boy and not being interested in woman things.

Blanche was drying the dishes as Mina washed. She had been lost in thought, and her actions had been mostly mechanical. Finally, she broke out of her reverie, watched her mother a moment, then ventured a question.

"Ma, do you understand Grandmother?"

"Land's sakes, child, what kind of a question is that?"

"Well, do you understand her?" she persisted.

"What don't you understand?" countered Miney.

"For one thing, she's always hollering at me for something. 'Blanche, don't slouch. Blanche, sit more like a lady. Blanche, it's time to do dishes the minute we get up from the table. Blanche, couldn't you see that thread on the carpet? It is much easier for you to bend over than it is for me.' It seems as if I never do anything to suit her and yet—" She paused as if pondering what to say next.

"And yet," prompted her mother, pausing in the act of washing a plate.

"Well, you know how you and Pa always give me money each week to buy what I need for school? Well, that second week with her, Grandmother showed me where she keeps her milk money.

You know she sells what milk they don't use from their cow. She keeps that money separate in a dish in the cupboard, and she says to me, 'Blanche, this is as much yours as it is mine, so when you want money, you are to help yourself to whatever you need.' But, Ma, I just couldn't take her money, not for anything. 'Sides, you and Pa give me what I really need. Anyway, I hadn't taken any. Then, last week I went to the drawer to get my purse, and instead of the nickel I knew I had, I had seventy-five cents more. Grandmother hadn't said a word, but I just know she put the money there."

"That was very nice of her, Blanche, and I hope you appreciate it. Did you thank her?"

"Well, no, because…well, I guess it was because I don't know for certain she was the one who put it there. I suppose I should thank her. But, Ma, I just don't understand how she can holler at me for every little thing and then be so nice in other ways."

"I expect she feels she is doing it for your own good. She wants you to be a nice young lady. Of course, Ma already knows you're a fine young lady and a mighty pretty one too."

Miney hugged the child close and gave her a kiss, and neither one seemed to mind the wet, soapy hands.

"Blanche, you certainly are getting taller. I notice it more when I don't see much of you."

"Ma, Mrs. Wooley told me I look like you."

"Did she now? Well, maybe when I was younger, but you are far prettier."

Miney had finally started on the pots and pans, and the potato kettle was blackened on the bottom where Miney had removed the stove lid and set the kettle directly over the fire so it would boil more quickly.

"Blanche, just look at this kettle. Will you get Ma the scouring rag, please?"

"Yes, Ma."

The scouring rag was a cloth that hung behind the stove to be used for just this one purpose. It became blackened so that no amount of scrubbing ever got it clean again. At least this saved the dishrag from getting in this condition. Blanche wetted the cloth in the reservoir, then pulled open the ashpit door, and dipped the cloth in the ashes from the stove.

"That enough, Ma?"

"Yes, that's fine for now." She began to scrub away at the soot-blackened pan.

Mina had intentionally changed the subject. She was as much at a loss to understand her mother-in-law as was her daughter. Lavina Setterington was like no one else she knew. She knew for a fact that Blanche often ran to Ma's, half in tears over something Mother Setterington had done or said. Yet, the child still liked to go there. Of course, part of the attraction was the beautiful house, the furnishings that found their equal nowhere in Elsie. Yet, Mina felt all those worldly, material possessions did not make up for the warmth and love that seemed to be lacking. She knew, of course, that both Mother and Father Setterington must care deeply for those who belonged to them, but they certainly had odd ways of showing it. Father had been dreadfully strict with John and Millie when they were boys, never giving them a thing they hadn't earned. When he punished them, he had used a buggy whip.

In fact, Mother herself told of the time she had thought John was going to die from one such whipping. She had his clothes all laid out and intended to dress the boy because she would have been ashamed to have had anyone see the marks on his body and know his father had beaten him so badly. At times like this, Father was a hard, cruel man, and yet, Millie always defended his father by saying, "Pa was always just. We asked for what we got."

Somehow, Miney always felt that Father had been proud of his boys even if he couldn't unbend enough to show it. Millie had never held all those lickings against his father, and Millie had been upset because now that John was older, he not only had no respect for their father, but there were times when John actually hated Horatio.

Blanche certainly liked school. Bertha and Alden Brown, who lived on what later would be known as the Tabor Farm, taught the first and second grade. Blanche liked both of them and thought them quite the nicest teachers anyone could possibly have. Although she often confided to Miney that she liked spending the week with Grandma Smith much better than being with Grandmother and Grandfather, she never complained about school.

Strange, thought Miney, how money could not buy a child's love. A child remained completely candid. Goodness, Ma's house had been built on to so many times it was just a haphazard affair. None of the upstairs bedrooms had floors at the same level, so a person went either up or down, depending on which room one was entering. 'Course Ma's rooms weren't carpeted either—she only had rag rugs scattered here and there. She pumped her water from a well in the backyard and didn't even have a sink in the kitchen. She did her dishes by setting a dishpan on a wide board in the pantry, washed and scrubbed for so many years, it had ridges where the grain was hard and hadn't worn down with the rest of the board.

At Lavina's house, the water was pumped into a tank in the attic, so by the force of gravity, they at least had running cold water in the kitchen. They also had a bathroom: a sink, a stool with a chain pull tank to flush it, and a bathtub, which sat in a frame about fifteen inches off the floor; the front of the boxed-in frame opened up, and under the tub sat a kerosene burner, which could be lighted to heat the water in the tub for a bath; the ledge protruding out from the bathtub served as a place to step on to get into the tub. Quite a luxury for 1895.

Naturally, Lavina had carpets in the parlor, the sitting room, and the bedrooms. The furniture was beautiful. Blanche was especially intrigued with the cupola on the northwest comer, which was a playroom. Access to this small "doll house," as Blanche called it, was by way of a ladder—the steps of which were carpeted—through a small doorway. Ruby had a small, toy piano, about two feet wide, in this little room that Blanche sometimes played. Of course, once in a while several wasps crawled in from a crack under the eaves, and Blanche would be afraid to go up there. Usually, Aunt Ruby or Grandfather saw to killing the intruders.

Even though times had been hard for the past few years, it had very little effect on the Setterington household. Horatio perhaps grumbled a little over what he considered Vine's little extravagances, but he still good-naturedly paid the bills. Lavina might have worn her dresses longer than usual, but the material was still the best that money could buy, and Horatio's suits and coats were still of an expensive cut.

Ma was a different story. Her meager income covered her bare necessities, and only by being the frugal little Scotswoman she was did she manage to have enough left over to now and then buy gifts for her family. Miney often thought that even if money had been more easily come by for Ma, her mother would have been just as close with a penny. Mary Smith was not born to be a spendthrift.

At Thanksgiving time, Blanche had come home all excited because Mr. and Mrs. Brown had put a transfer of a turkey on the large blackboard in the front of the room. They had used transfers at Halloween time too, only with this big, old turkey, they had used red chalk to color his wattles so he looked ever so much more life-like. Blanche had been intrigued as had the other students. No one had foreseen how much more difficult the red chalk was going to be to wash off the board. The white came off easily, but the red took soap and plenty of elbow grease to remove it completely. Still, the Browns felt it was worth all the effort because the children enjoyed it so much.

Mina had been doing some crocheting, Millie was busy doing some bookwork for the farm, while Ralph had been looking at the pictures in one of Blanche's old books. She looked up at the clock on the shelf and noticed it was high time she was getting Ralph to bed. She sighed, putting aside her needlework. My, she hated to quit just now, but it would always keep, she knew; and if Ralph didn't get his rest, he would be ornery tomorrow.

"Ralph, come along now and get your nightshirt on for bed. Take care of the book first."

"I wants to read. I not sleepy," he objected.

"You just come along to bed, and we'll see how sleepy you are." She laughed.

Knowing that further arguing would avail him nothing, he put the book under the library table and went with his mother into the bedroom where she lighted the lamp on the dresser. She sat in the chair and started to unbutton his dress.

"I do it. I do it."

"All right. You do it, but don't dawdle."

His chubby fingers very carefully worked to get the buttons undone. He managed one, then two, but Miney was tired of waiting.

"Here, Ralph, let Ma help. It will go better when you're a little bigger." She removed his dress and petticoat, then exclaimed, "Goodness, Ralph, where's your fetty bag?"

His face took on an impish look as he said, "Don't know."

"Land's sakes, you must have taken it off. Now, where is it?"

The "fetty" bag normally hung on a string around his neck and was a small bag that was filled with asafetida, a dark-colored resinous material that literally stunk to high heaven. Its purpose? Why, everyone knew it kept colds and almost everything else away. For anyone to have to put up with such a stench, it had to be good for something.

"What did you do with it? Tell Ma."

"It stinks," he observed.

"I know you don't like the smell, and I guess I don't either, but do you want to get sick?"

Rate shook his head.

"Well, then, what did you do with it?"

Ralph clamped his mouth firmly shut.

"Millie, Ralph has taken his fetty bag off, and he won't tell me where it is. See if he'll tell you."

"Those blamed things stink enough seems like your nose should be able to ferret it out." Millie gave a little chuckle.

"Millie, don't tease."

"I'm sorry, Miney." He came to the doorway. "Rate, tell Ma where you put your fetty bag. By golly, boy, you should be glad you only have to wear a stinken old bag around your neck. When I was a lad, if I got a cold, my mother fed me chicken manure."

"Millie! She didn't."

"So help me, Miney, she used to find the droppings with white on them, and she collected the white part. It had the most gosh-awful taste of anything I ever tried. It always made me gag, but Ma just told me to hush and swallow it anyhow. See how lucky you are," he said to Ralph.

Ralph eyed his father solemnly as if to digest what his father had just said.

Finally, he said, "I gits."

He dashed over to his cradle, dropped down on all fours, and crawled under it. Almost immediately, he backed out, the fatty bag clutched in one hand.

"Here I find."

Miney took it from his outstretched hand.

"It smells," he said as he wrinkled up his nose with displeasure.

"I know, but Ma only does it to keep you from getting sick."

She put it back around his neck, dropped his nightshirt over his head, then gave him a quick hug.

Millie felt a surge of satisfaction at her display of affection for the boy. True, Blanche would always come first, but Miney did have a love of sorts for Rate, of that he was certain. Sometimes, he felt she just hated to admit how much the lad had squirmed his way into her heart.

Of course, Millie realized that Miney did miss Blanche a great deal, and there had been times lately when the weather had been so bad Blanche hadn't been home for two weeks at a stretch. He also knew that Ralph's constant disregard for rules angered her as much as it amused him. In truth, Millie was proud of his young son and was secretly glad he seemed to be all boy.

"Why," he'd been heard to say, "I'd not give a nickel for a boy who couldn't think of some harmless mischief to get into now and again."

By his own standards, Ralph was near priceless.

Blanche could hardly wait to get home. Usually she and Millie had very little to say to each other on the way home. Somehow, Pa was never one to carry on long conversations. He often went on the theory that children should be seen and not heard. He generally asked her how the week had gone and seemed to want only a short, perfunctory answer. Normally, the ride seemed short, but today it seemed as though the horse was plodding along at its slowest gait. Still, she hesitated to ask her father if they could go a little faster.

At long last, they arrived home. Curbing her excitement, Blanche sauntered into the house, set her valise by the stairway door, then went into the kitchen where Miney was preparing supper.

After giving her mother a hug and a kiss, she exclaimed, "Ma, guess what Grandmother is doing for me."

"Blanche, I have no idea. With Mother Setterington, it is hard to tell."

"She's giving me a party, that's what."

"How nice. When?"

"The next week I'm at her place. Guess it was Wednesday night when just out of the blue she says, 'Blanche, would you like to give a party for some of your little friends?' Ma, it just took me so by surprise. Of course, I said I'd really like to have one. Sometimes Grandmother can be awful nice. Well, anyway, she asked me who I'd like to invite because she would have to send out invitations. Well, I started naming those friends I knew she approved of. You know, Fern Wooley, Bertha Meyers, and Hazel Hamilton. Then, she asked me why I didn't ask Berthie Love. Ma, always before she has never had anything good to say about Berthie and her parents. She always finds fault because they have five children and are too poor to dress and feed them like Grandmother considers proper."

"I know, Blanche, I've heard her numerous times."

"When I said I guessed I'd not invite her, Grandmother told me I was being inconsiderate. She told me she thought I should pay more attention to what the good Lord taught—that we should be kind to those less fortunate than ourselves and on and on. Honest, Ma, I like Berthie, only I never dared have her over to Grandmother's because of the way Grandmother has always talked before. Ma, I just never know how to please her, and I'll just never, never understand her."

"Blanche, your grandmother means well, I'm sure, but I am inclined to agree with you. I don't understand her either."

At that Blanche gave a laugh, then said, "I'm sure glad you're my mother and that you aren't one bit like Grandmother."

"Thank you, dear. I'm certainly glad you are my daughter. Ma is very proud of you."

The next week that Blanche stayed at the Setteringtons, she had her party. Lavina always did things with a flourish, and this party was no exception. She made candies in different colors, and the candies were arranged on a platter in the form of a flower. My, it did look pretty, and the girls oohed and aahed over it much to Blanche's delight. There were games and prizes, which delighted everyone. If Berthie Love seemed to feel out of place, it was not because Blanche didn't do her best to make the girl feel at ease.

Then, just before the girls left, Lavina made a rather cutting remark regarding the condition of the parlor saying that she thought a group of well-brought-up young ladies would certainly have learned to be neater. Blanche was furious! The other girls were embarrassed. Why, oh why, did Grandmother always ruin things? This was a question Blanche was to ask herself often about her grandmother. It just seemed that Lavina had a knack for spoiling her good intentions with some ill-timed remark.

Once again it was Blanche's week to stay with her grandmother and grandfather Setterington. Tuesday night, things really livened up since Horatio's two brothers, Albert and George, arrived from Canada to spend a few days. There had been seven children in Horatio's family, four boys and three girls. Blanche heard the brothers discussing Vest (for *Sylvester*), Victoria, Caroline, and the eldest, Mary Alice.

At first, Blanche was rather shy around these two hulking creatures who were her great-uncles. They were as large as Pa, and Great-Uncle Albert had a beard, and both of them had snapping, black eyes just like Grandfather. However, it wasn't long before she discovered a major difference—Grandfather's brothers were not nearly as stern; they laughed easily and heartily. In fact, they both played with her, large as she was, by tossing her up in the air, which set her squealing and laughing, much to Lavina's dislike. Little they cared if Lavina didn't like this unladylike conduct. They were not to be intimidated by their sister-in-law.

Blanche was getting a ride on Great-Uncle Albert's back as he crawled around the parlor and sitting room on all fours. All of a sudden, she heard a roar, and glancing around, she beheld a huge bear, teeth bared, coming slowly toward her and her horse. Blanche slipped to one side, off the broad back, her mouth made movements, yet no sound came forth; she stood petrified watching the slow and clumsy advance of the animal. Finally, she screamed as the bear made a lunge. She screamed again and again and started to run.

"Blanche, Blanche, look, it's only me, your uncle George. Here, girl, I'm no bear," cried George as he threw off the bearskin rug from Lavina's sitting room.

Blanche stopped, turned around, and skeptically surveyed the scene. Albert picked her up and said harshly, "Now, George, see what you've done. You've scared the livin' daylights out of her."

"I didn't mean to. Here, Blanche, see, it's just me. I thought sure you'd recognize your grandma's bearskin rug. All right, sweetie?"

At that moment, Lavina charged in from the kitchen like a wildcat ready to protect her kittens.

"See what you've done with your little boy pranks? Scared this child half to death. Seems like the two of you will never know enough to act like grown men," she berated, the tone of her voice heavy with unveiled sarcasm.

"Now, Vine, we didn't mean no harm," put in Albert.

"'Course we didn't. She's all right now, aren't you, Blanche?" asked George with somewhat more assurance than he felt. "Tell your grandma you're not afeared anymore."

By now Blanche had regained her aplomb. Very haughtily she replied, "I knowed it was you all the time, Uncle George. I was just funnin' with you."

Both men laughed uproariously. They realized the child had been monstrously frightened, only she was too proud and too much a Setterington to admit it. Rate certainly had himself a granddaughter, not the usual sort, one with the breeding of a good Englishman. She'd go far in this world, and it would be all of her own doing they were sure.

That weekend when Blanche went home, she brought up the subject as she and Mina did the supper dishes.

"Ma, did Great-Uncle George and Great-Uncle Albert come out here?"

"Yes, child, they were out here for dinner on Thursday. Didn't they say?"

"No...um, at least I didn't hear them." She paused, then asked, "Ma, did they tell you about me getting scared of Great-Uncle George?"

"Oh, you mean when he had the bearskin rug on? Yes, he mentioned it. He felt very badly because he frightened you."

"I told him I wasn't afeared, but it wasn't rightly so. Ma, when I first saw that old bear a comin' at me, I was so scared I couldn't even holler. Then, the whole thing just made me mad at myself 'cause I knowed Grandmother had that old bearskin rug, and I should have known that there's no real live bears around here and that none could get in the house anyways. Well, they was sorry, an' I knew that, but I just couldn't admit that I was scared stiff, so I told a little fib and said I knew who it was all the time. Was that being sinful? Was it, Ma?'

"Of course, Blanche, I don't usually condone your telling a falsehood, but I think in this case, it might be permissible. Uncle George and Uncle Albert had no business treating you so. Supposing you'd have died of fright?"

"Oh, Ma, they didn't intend to scare me. They really are lots of fun. My, but we laughed and played. They are so different from Grandfather that I can hardly make it seem possible they are his brothers. 'Course Pa and Uncle John aren't much alike either," she added as an afterthought.

Miney silently agreed. Millie was still held down by his father's thumb while John flaunted his independence. John and Grace made quite a pair. Grace talked back to Mother, and John did anything of which he was sure his parents would disapprove. Mother Setterington just knew it was the bad influence of his wife that led John astray, but Miney knew differently. It took a deal of courage on their part, and she and Millie had never had that much courage.

"Ma, how's Grandma Smith ever get her groceries?"

"Buys them. Same as anyone else."

"I mean who goes uptown for her? She just never seems to go anyplace, but she always has what food she needs."

"I expect Mary or Lorin do her shopping for her."

"Grandma never complains, but she said yesterday that since Christmas was almost here, she supposed she'd have to go uptown to get her shopping done. Then she added that she dreaded it more each year since her old bones grumbled more each year. What did she mean?"

"I expect Ma was referring to her lumbago. It is hard for her to walk very far because her joints are stiff. I can't remember the time when her feet didn't give her trouble. As long as I can remember, she's always worn those slipper-sox with the leather soles because she said shoes hurt her feet. We always attended church as a family when I was little—it's only been lately that Ma hasn't gone to church—and Ma could hardly wait until we got home to get out of her shoes. Never saw anyone who could undo buttons any faster. Sometimes, I think Ma has such a wide foot her shoes don't fit like they ought."

Blanche digested this piece of information.

"Does she only go uptown at Christmastime?"

"Mostly, I guess. She always has yarn for knitting, but I suppose Lorin gets that for her. Ma wouldn't know what to do with herself if she didn't have something to knit."

"Does she buy presents for everyone?"

"Well, she gets some little things for all her grandchildren, and if she can stretch her money far enough, she gets for the rest of us. The little ones come first. Ma doesn't have much of an income, you know."

"I'm glad she gets me something. I don't mind if it isn't much."

"I know, dear, you would like anything you got just because you love your grandma."

"She is so good to me, Ma. She just never hollers or finds fault."

Miney knew that Blanche was thinking that even though her grandmother Setterington was very good about buying her presents, she sometimes spoiled it all by finding fault with something Blanche had or hadn't done.

While some folks never put up a Christmas tree in their own home because they felt these festivities made what should be a solemn occasion worldly, the Baptist Church usually had two trees, tall enough to touch the ceiling, one on either side of the stage. Christmas was a time of celebration, and the church felt that the spirit of giving coincided with the wonderful event of Christ's birth; thus, they encouraged not only their own members, but anyone from the community to attend their Christmas program and exchange gifts after the program was finished.

Parents sneaked presents to the church all during the day of the program to be hung on one of the trees. While this was the only Christmas many families had, Lavina always had her family with her on Christmas Day; therefore, Blanche only received some small gift—a bar of scented soap, a lacy handkerchief, a stick of peppermint—nothing of any consequence.

The child would always remember what it was like to get her first peek at the huge trees, covered with presents as she and her family came through the double doors at the back of the church. How longingly she looked at the dolls of all sizes, some exquisitely beautiful in their silk dresses with real hair curling around their faces; how badly she wanted one of those dolls to be hers. Each year she was disappointed.

Blanche spoke her piece and then went to sit with Grandmother and Grandfather since Ma was helping with the program. Blanche eyed each tree in turn. They looked beautiful with all those presents that had been hung on them and piled underneath the heavy, green boughs. She counted fourteen dollies. There was one that took her fancy more than any of the others; it was not as large as some, but it had blond hair and a beautiful blue silk dress. More than anything in the world, Blanche wanted that doll. Maybe this year would be different. Maybe Ma and Pa had got her a doll this year. She had made it very plain that she would like another dolly. Grandmother and Grandfather had given her one over a year ago, but Blanche wanted a new one. Besides, a girl needed more than one doll with which to play.

The program finished, and it was time for the tree. The minister called off the names of children who hurried to the front to claim their presents. Blanche watched the first few dolls go to some other little girls. She had a sinking feeling; she knew it was going to be the same as last year and the year before. The minister took down the doll in the blue dress. Blanche held her breath. When the minister called some other little girl's name, Blanche released her breath in one great sigh. It didn't really matter what she got, or if she got anything at all; nothing mattered now that she realized that once again none of the dolls were to be hers.

If anyone noticed how unusually quiet Blanche became, no one said anything. Perhaps it was merely thought that the child was tired since it had been a long day. However, never again was Blanche to foster false hopes for more than a trinket from church. Her family never realized how important the church party was to her; she had her presents at home from Santa, and then they had a tree at Grandmother Setterington's, where she had gifts from the rest of the family. What else could a child wish to have?

Miney was sewing a dress for herself. She sat at the dining room table taking dainty stitches to gather the sleeve to fit the wristband. Frankie Keenan was on her hands and knees in the kitchen scrubbing the wood floor, which was worn smooth by constant use. Near her left hand was the pail of warm, sudsy water into which she dipped the stiff brush she used with her vigorous right hand to scrub the wide boards.

Frankie backed up a little, but didn't pull the pail along with her. Since she had partly turned her body to reach farther to her right, she did not see Ralph backing up in direct line with her pail. Splat! Frankie turned to find Ralph wedged into her pail of water. His feet just missed touching the floor, and his struggles were accomplishing nothing. His yells brought Miney hurrying into the kitchen.

"Land's sakes, Ralph, however did you do that?"

"Frankie pushed me," was the indignant reply.

At that, both women broke out laughing. Miney extricated her dripping son from the bucket of water.

"Now, stand still so I can get you out of these wet clothes. You'll catch your death of pneumonia if we don't hurry. Frankie, did you ever see anyone who can get into more trouble?"

"Somehow, Miney, I think things have only just begun. I have an idee that the older he gits, the more trouble he will git into. Still, he did look comical stuck in that bucket. Imagine him sayin' I pushed him, the little dickens."

Miney hastened to get Ralph's dress, petticoats, and undergarments changed. Even his undershirt was wet. Goodness, that boy managed to find trouble somehow. Blanche had never been half the bother. She supposed Millie would think it hilarious since he usually viewed such things from a much different point of view. Of course,

Ralph had looked funny with his behind stuck in the pail. She chuckled again as she hung his clothes behind the stove to dry. She guessed the look on his face was the best part. Perhaps Frankie was right, and this was only the beginning; she surmised that if this was so, he had inherited an extra-large dose from the Setterington side of the family.

There were times when Millie still played a prank on someone although Miney viewed it as being childish. John was much the same, and neither of them showed anger if someone teased them; they simply bided their time and then returned the favor, so to speak. Both men had a terrific sense of humor, which often surprised people because both of them were also noted for being the most obstinate of men in any sort of argument.

*****

Spring came early this year, and the month of April ushered in mild nights and still milder days. The grass greened, the buds swelled on the trees; on some they had reached the bursting point, and the green of dainty leaves peeked out. Millie had already broadcast a field of oats where the corn had stood last year and had done some plowing for this year's field of corn. The moist earth had rolled over nicely and had been just wet enough to make the job of holding the plow in the ground and guiding it easier than usual. The pastures had greened, and the hayfields were far advanced from what they usually were this early in the season. Miney was glad to have the rainy days past so Ralph could be let outdoors to play. Sure made him easier to handle if he wore off some of that energy outside. The fresh air seemed to make him sleepier than usual, so he took a longer afternoon nap. This was always a welcome respite.

*****

Blanche had been over to Fern Wooley's house since school. She realized it was getting close to suppertime and knew she shouldn't have stayed this long, but she and Fern were having such a good time. Now, she hurried her steps even though it was one of those warm spring afternoons that made a person want to dawdle, watching the fleecy white clouds drift slowly along the azure sky; notice the tiny leaves showing on the box elders and maples, the fat buds of the hickories and walnuts; listen for the call of birds so recently returned from the South and watch them searching for nesting materials: a piece of grass, a scrap of yam, a torn thread. All the wonders of the rebirth of a season unfolded before her eyes, and she would like to have remained out-of-doors longer, only she daren't. She opened the front door quietly, half hoping that if Grandmother was busy in the kitchen, she wouldn't notice her stealthy entrance.

"Blanche? It's high time you came home. Come and get table set this very minute."

Blanche put her knapsack on a chair, took off her light coat, and hurried to the kitchen.

"Goodness, child, look at you. Your hair is pulled out of one of your braids, there's a black smudge on your cheek, your hands are positively filthy. Why can't you learn to be ladylike? After all, you are not a boy, although you do seem to do your best to be one. Thank the good Lord Ruby was never such a trial. Now, scrub those hands before you touch a single plate. Blanche, is that a tear in your dress? No, I guess it is just a streak of dirt. Why can't you be more careful of your clothes?"

Lavina turned her attention back to her cooking. Rate would be here to supper promptly at six. Perhaps this was where Millie had learned his promptness for meals because Lavina's household ran like clockwork.

Blanche hastened to the bathroom, washed her hands and the smudge from her cheek. She hesitated a moment, took a deep breath, squared her shoulders, which were broad for a girl—the Setterington build had shown up here too since Blanche was tall for her age as well—compressed her lips in a thin determined line, and reentered the kitchen. She went busily to her work in the hopes she would incur no further remonstrance from her grandmother. However, this just didn't seem to be her day for keeping out of trouble. She dropped a glass. Grandmother scolded and berated. At supper, she was told to sit straight at the table, not to fill her mouth so full, and it seemed to Blanche the list was endless.

She had hardly put the last dish in its place and hung the dish-towel neatly on the rack before she tore out of the front door, not caring one whit how hard she slammed it, across the dusk darkening street, between two houses, down a path to Grandma Smith's back door. She was crying big sobs as she burst unceremoniously into the kitchen.

Mary Smith raised her eyes from her knitting to peer at her granddaughter through steel-rimmed glasses. Shaking her head sadly, she asked, "What has that woman done now?"

"Oh, Grandma," sobbed the little girl; all her stubborn Setterington pride that had kept her spine as straight as a poker and the tears at bay while in Lavina's presence deserted her now. She threw herself into her grandmother's waiting arms and sobbed out the entire story.

"There, there, child. Now, dry those tears. Crying just spoils the looks of those pretty brown eyes. Come now, things aren't as bad as they seem. I baked a fresh batch of cookies today. Do you think one would make you feel better? There now, that's better. I do love to see you smile."

"Grandma, you are the best grandma a girl ever had. I love you."

"Go on with you now. I'm a useless old woman—"

"You are not. Why, if you weren't here, I'd have to stay with Grandmother Setterington all the time," came the horrified thought.

"Blanche, I'm sure Vine loves you as much as I do. She just shows it in a different way. You must try to be understanding and tolerant. Remember she and your grandfather are very good to you."

Blanche sighed. "I suppose you're right, but it just seems as though I never please her no matter how hard I try. Grandfather doesn't have much to say to me, so he doesn't complain. Still, she does buy me things," she added somewhat grudgingly.

Blanche ate not one, but two of her grandmother's big, filled cookies. My, sitting here munching cookies, listening to Grandma talk as her knitting needles clicked while her fingers flew to manip-ulate the yarn in a seemingly effortless motion, was satisfying.

Grandma's house wasn't nearly as beautiful, only it sure was a lot more homey. No one hollered if she slouched or even if she dropped a crumb or two. Here was complete serenity, and Blanche hated to leave this sanctuary to return to the lioness's den, but then, all good things must come to an end. It was only the darkness of night that kept Blanche from dallying on her return trip to the huge white Setterington home.

Blanche never knew how her grandmother Setterington felt about these absences. Lavina knew exactly where Blanche went and, without a doubt, knew the reason. She thought of Mary as being too soft-hearted, and she was sure Mary spoiled Blanche because she was not nearly as demanding when it came to obedience. Not once did it occur to Lavina that the love Mary so readily gave was much more important to a very young girl. However, she accepted these outbursts and chose to ignore them, never even chiding the child when she returned.

Lavina had never been demonstrative with her own children once they were past the baby stage except perhaps with Emma. Of course, she had been older then, and Emma had been a beautiful, charming child. She seldom showed Ruby affection although it had always been evident that Ruby came in for a much larger portion of her mother's love than either John or Millie.

People around town often felt that Ruby was spoiled. Lavina would have been the last to admit this even though she realized that she had never expected the exemplary conduct from Ruby that she did of Blanche.

Of course, Blanche was such a strong, active child, and Ruby had always been much more frail. Perhaps Lavina lived in constant fear that this one remaining daughter would be snatched from her as had the other three. That Blanche was robust and healthy was a constant reminder of her own child's suspected infirmities. Besides, Lavina knew Mina was not nearly capable of raising a girl as she should be raised—at least when that girl was Lavina's very first granddaughter.

CHAPTER 6

The summer of 1896, election year, the rural community of Elsie kept a close eye on politics. The farmer's lot had not been a good one. Cleveland's second term and the panic of 1893 had seen a continued agricultural depression. Millie was not nearly as concerned with the next Democratic candidate as he was with the man the Republicans would put up to oppose him. Millie was firmly convinced that it was time for a party change in the White House. On June 16, the Republican Convention at St. Louis nominated William McKinley, former Ohio congressman, for the presidency. In July, the Democrats nominated William Jennings Bryan.

"Yessiree, Miney, this McKinley fellow talks a heap o' sense."

"How do you know? Seems like the politicians always talk in circles. I tried reading some of those pamphlets you brought home, and I'm afraid I wasn't much impressed."

"Just like a woman. McKinley knows more about the farm problem than does Bryan. Dave Watson and I were talking just the other day that if McKinley gets elected, farm prices are bound to go up. Lord knows they can't go much lower."

"I know, dear. It seems a shame for you to put so many hours of hard work in the fields, and we get so little for what we sell."

"Wouldn't be quite so bad if the price of tools, harness, and everything we use didn't keep going up. Are you and Rate ready?"

"I guess so. Just let me get my bonnet."

It was Saturday, and their day to drive into town for groceries. Millie left to hitch up the team; and Miney, bonnet tied carefully in place, took Ralph by the hand and waited for Millie to drive up. They were to bring Blanche home too. She'd been visiting at Mary's this week, so they'd have to stop there for a spell. Just before she helped Rate into the surrey, Millie said, "Rate, show your ma what Mr. Watson and I taught you in town the other afternoon."

Ralph quickly doffed his hat, swung it around his head, and shouted, "Hurrah for McKinley."

"Lawsy, Millie, whatever gave you such an idea?" Miney laughed.

"Don't rightly know, but the men all got a chuckle out of him. Every time they'd ask him what he thought of Bryan and McKinley, he'd shout, 'Hurrah for McKinley.' I tell you, Miney, the boy's keen as a newly honed razor."

At this moment, Millie's pride in his son was evident. However, time brought about a change. Perhaps pride would appear when Millie talked to someone else, but never did any words of praise come from him in Ralph's presence. It was quite likely a trait inherited from Horatio, who, it was generally known, was very much like his father, John. Perhaps it could be termed a Setterington characteristic—at least among the males of the line.

Mina made her way slowly to the house. She had been doing some hoeing in the garden; then, when she had bent to pull a weed from the row of carrots, her hip had caught, and for a moment, she could not move. The pain made her momentarily dizzy. Dear, what an inconvenient time for that hip to start bothering. She limped toward the garden path, biting her lower lip to keep back the tears.

No one had ever known why Miney's hip behaved thus. For months it would function as any normal hip, and then, sometimes for no apparent reason, it would hurt terribly. On more than one occasion, when she had been lifting something heavy, a shooting pain would make her cry out in agony. Sometimes, the hip even swelled and remained swollen for several days, giving her a look of deformity.

She had made it to the house and now cautiously lowered herself into a rocking chair. She squirmed a little to get herself into a position that was the least uncomfortable since no position completely relieved the pain. Wouldn't you know this would happen when there were two extra hands to feed for supper.

Just then, Blanche came into the room.

"Ma, what's wrong? You look awful white."

"It's my hip. I was working in the garden, and it just caught for no reason at all."

"Oh, Ma, I'm sorry. We've got Jake and Jim here for supper, haven't we?"

"That's right."

"Well, maybe I can help. If I brought you the potatoes, you could peel them sitting there, then I could wash them off and put them on to cook."

"Thank you, Blanche, but Ma doesn't like to have you take care of the fire. I'm so afraid you'll get burned."

"But, Ma, I'm getting big now."

"I know you are, sweetheart, only Ma doesn't want you to get hurt. If you bring things to me, I can stand pretty well in one place, it is the walking that bothers most. Ma appreciates that you want to help."

Mina looked at her daughter's worried face. She did not like to have Blanche concerned because Mina felt a child's world was a special one—time enough to have worries when they were older. She would just grit her teeth and bear the pain and do what had to be done. She knew Millie would help with putting Ralph to bed since she'd not be able to lift the lad; but in a kitchen, he was like a bull in a china shop. She knew she would have to get the meal for hungry men and do the dishes afterward. Well, perhaps she could sit here to peel the potatoes, and then Blanche could bring in the wood for the stove even if Miney didn't want her attempting to put wood in the firebox. She'd manage, she had to because there was no one else. Well, the Lord had seen her through these times before, so she had no doubt He'd see her through this time as well.

Miney was busy baking bread. She usually baked only once a week, on Saturday mornings, but there had been extra men this week since the weather had been hot and dry, and they had been busy putting up hay. The barn was already full, and there was a huge stack north of the far driveway.

"Blanche, do you suppose you could set a washtub out in the sun and put some water in it for your pa? I just know that since he'll be sweaty and dirty from working in the hay, he'll want a bath, and I do dread to have him take it in that awful cold well water."

"Just a minute, Ma. I'm working on my embroidery, and I've almost finished this flower."

"All right, only don't forget."

"I won't, Ma, honest, I won't."

By the north kitchen door stood a wooden windmill that had been put up the summer Blanche was two. The wooden enclosure around the pump often served as Millie's bathhouse, since when he came up at night on days like this, he often went into the well house, pumped a tub of water, and took a bath. Miney often offered to give him a teakettle of hot water from the kitchen to at least take some of the chill off the water, but he always laughed at her suggestion. Said the cold water was good for his blood. The only concession he would make was to let a tub of water be set in the sun to warm somewhat. She never did get used to this practice, and the thought of that cold water made her shudder, but Millie minded not in the least. In fact, it seemed to be a source of pride for him that he was man enough not to need the coddling of warm water like a woman.

What a beautiful July morning! The air was warm, a gentle breeze languidly stirred the leaves on the huge, ancient cottonwood, and the sun shone brightly on a serene world. Perhaps the weather lent a sense of well-being to Millie that had prompted him to offer to drive Mina and the children to church and Sunday school.

He knew Miney would have liked for him to dress up in his good clothes and attend services with her; however, he hadn't felt all that generous. Besides, what made men think they were any closer to God sittin' in some man-made building, listening to some long-winded preacher talk about the sins of man? Now, out here in God's world of grass, trees, birds, and animals, now that's where a body could feel close to God with His sun's rays warming a man's body and His blue sky, dotted with fleecy tufts of cotton, the only roof over one's head. Yup, it didn't take a heap of know how to appreciate the world God had given us, and he didn't need any gal-dang preacher telling him how he should live.

Millie had been brought up to labor for what he wanted, to respect his elders, to be honest, and to respect the rights of others, so what else needed to be taught? He didn't rightly care about all those people who lived so long ago. It was the people who lived now who interested him because they were the ones who affected his life. Besides, he knew more than one man who sat piously in church every Sunday, but during the week was the biggest skinflint that could be found anywhere, always trying to put it over on his neighbors in any deal. Church for the likes of them was to cover up the sins committed during the week. Well, God was not to be fooled, and they'd get their comeuppance come judgment day.

"Miney, aren't you and Blanche ready yet? You daren't blame me if you're late for church," Millie called from the seat of the surrey where he held the team, as they stomped and jangled the bit, impatient to be off.

"We're almost ready. Is Ralph with you?" she called.

"Rate's been sittin' here just like you said, waitin' for you wimmen to get done primping."

"Blanche, do stand still, or I'll never get your hair braided. Pa's driving us today, and we don't want to make him wait."

"But, Ma, you pull."

"If you'd stand still so's I could do it like I ought, it wouldn't pull, missy. There. Where's my pocketbook? Let's be on our way."

Blanche ran out the door ahead of her mother and clambered up into the high back seat of the surrey. Miney noted with satisfaction what a nice-looking vehicle the surrey was, and Millie always had a good-looking driving team—ones that showed some spirit—and the harnesses were nicely trimmed.

Miney sat next to Blanche, reminded Ralph to sit down, then exclaimed, "Oh, Millie, I forgot my new hymnal. It won't take but a minute."

As she started for the house, Blanche exclaimed, "Ma, what's that on your dress? It looks all sort of funny."

"She's right, Miney. Your dress looks wet."

"Land's sakes, how could that be?" She turned her head and twisted so she could somewhat view her backsides. It did look wet, and it looked dark.

"Blanche, stand up." Blanche complied. "Turn around so's I can see your hindside." Once again Blanche did as she was told. "Oh, no. Her dress is ruined. Just look at it, Millie. Whatever it is, it came from the surrey seat, that much is certain."

Millie put a tentative finger on the leather seat and then brought the finger to his nose. "Oil. Harness oil. But how in the world—"

All eyes turned on Ralph, who was standing on his knees in the front seat peering into the back, his solemn eyes wide and guiltless.

"Rate, do you know where Pa keeps a jug of oil?"

Rate nodded his head affirmatively.

"Can you show Pa the jug?"

Millie lifted him down from the seat, and off scampered Rate to the shed.

"Here," he called. "You keeps it here."

Millie turned the jug bottom side up, and only a faint trickle of oil ran out.

"What happened to the oil? Did you put it on the seat?"

"Millie, he couldn't have done it. He's too small to lift that jug, let alone when it was full of oil," came from Miney, who had followed them.

"Well, *I* certainly didn't do it. Ugh! That smelly, dirty, old oil. He'd be enough of a dunce to do it."

"That will do, Blanche. I don't recall asking for your opinion. Now, boy, come here." Ralph stood in front of his father. "What did you do with the oil?"

"I taked it. Seats were hard. I oilded them," he stated proudly.

Miney started to sputter, but Millie stopped her by saying, "Well, last week he watched me oil some harness, and I told him it was to keep the leather from getting hard, so I guess he didn't know any better, but I reckon he's got to be punished. Rate, that was a bad thing you did. Look at Blanche's and your ma's dresses. Do you see that? I'm going to give you a tanning for being naughty. You are never to touch harness oil again without asking me first. Do you understand?"

Millie picked up a thin piece of board and proceeded to use it on Ralph's behind. The boy whimpered a little, but didn't actually cry. Millie was proud of his small son since he took a licking like a man. Ralph was to have two more lickings from his father during the growing-up process.

Miney was more upset over the episode than her husband. Not only had her best dress, as well as Blanche's, been ruined, but she had had to miss church. Miney's Sunday was not complete if she had to miss services. She liked singing in the choir. Somehow, when she raised her voice in song, it made her feel much closer to God. She had always felt thus, even as a little girl. She could remember staying over at Lorin's when Lorin and Norm were first married; she had started singing in bed, and Lorin had crossly told her to quit, saying that when she sang in bed, the devil danced over her head. This had somewhat mollified her for a spell. She certainly didn't want the devil dancing over her head. In fact, she feared any thought of the devil being in close proximity to her. However, the more she pondered the situation, the more certain she became that God would not tolerate the presence of the devil when she sang His songs of praise, whether she was in bed or not. She felt sure that God looked with favor on her because she liked to sing His praises as well as talk to Him in prayer. Somehow, music had made her troubles seem lighter as a child, and even now, church music could soothe her soul and bring a feeling of peace.

She wished Millie would go to church with her, but the last time she had mentioned it, he had given her to understand that the subject was closed. Knowing how set in his ways Millie could be, she realized that he had meant what he said. Seemed strange though when Mother and Father Setterington had been such churchy people and this being the only segment of his life where Millie flaunted his parents' wishes, for she knew his waywardness was a source of irritation to them. They expected such behavior from John, but not from dutiful Millie.

Ma and Pa had both attended church regularly, so she had grown up accustomed to attending church as a family unit. Why, Pa had even hauled all the timbers when they had built the church in 1875, even though he had only one horse and had had to haul them one at a time. Well, Ralph would be brought up to attend church regularly, so's maybe when he was grown, he'd still uphold the Sabbath by going to church.

Not that Millie wasn't a good man; she guessed he was better than some who sat in church each Sunday. Leastways, Millie was no liar; Father Setterington had seen to that. As long as he lived a good life, perhaps it didn't matter if he didn't attend church. Of course, he was a believer—or was he? Now that she thought about it, she wasn't entirely certain Millie did believe in God; she had simply assumed that he did. Goodness, what if Millie didn't share her faith in one supreme being? She had never really thought of that possibility before. Why, then they would never be united in heaven for all eternity. Perhaps she had better start praying a little harder and see if the good Lord would bring about a change in Millie. She felt that if He wanted to, He could certainly make Millie want to go to church. At any rate, she intended to ask.

Lavina and Mina sat in the parlor on a rainy afternoon. They had just returned from the Ladies Missionary Society meeting, and Vine had asked Miney to sit a few moments before going home.

"Mina, Rate and I were discussing Blanche staying with us again this year, and we've decided she simply cannot sleep in that back upstairs bedroom. We had really never given it much thought before, but supposing we had another fire, there'd be no way anyone could ever get up there and get the child out. I don't know why we never thought of it before. It just makes me shudder to think of what might have happened. Rate never thought of it either."

"Where did you plan for her to sleep?"

"We'll just put a single bed in our room. There's plenty of room, and I'm sure it will work out quite satisfactorily."

"Of course, Mother, if that's what you think best."

"I do, Mina, and so does Rate."

This ended the discussion, if one could call it that. Often any verbal exchange with Lavina was likely to be somewhat one-sided with her views being freely given, but with little attention given to the thoughts of the other person. Such was the case now, but Mina had become quite accustomed to having her mother-in-law brusquely brush aside any comments Miney might have regarding any subject. In the second year of their marriage, Miney had had an attack of St. Vitus's dance, which she had felt certain had been brought about by the frustrations of trying to cope, not only with marriage itself, but with the domineering personality of Lavina.

Mina had never fully realized the relationship that existed between Millie and his parents. John had been the one to rebel against them any way he could, while Millie could never quite bring himself to oppose his father in thought or deed very often, and to her knowledge, he had never really asserted himself with his mother. Miney had found that hearing people talk about the stiff and unbending Lavina was an entirely different matter from becoming one of her family. Yet, Mother Setterington could be one of the kindest persons to someone who had had a stroke of bad luck. She was always the first there to offer help or a basket of groceries or to gather clothes for the needy. A mighty strange mixture. Miney sometimes wondered what Grandmother and Grandfather Reynolds had been like to have begat the likes of Lavina. It was difficult to imagine her as a young girl, falling in love, having and loving babies.

When Blanche had been told of the new sleeping arrangement, she had silently said a prayer of thanks. No more going up that scary old stairway so far away from Grandmother and Grandfather. She knew their bedroom was huge compared with what most people had. As one entered the door, their bed was to the left; against the opposite wall stood the dresser and chest and wardrobe, which left plenty of room for Blanche's single bed to the right of the door. This arrangement was much more suitable, but being a true Setterington, Blanche never let on that this situation appealed to her far more than the upstairs bedroom.

Now that Ralph was going on three years old, Miney decided it was time to start teaching him that he must remove his hat when he entered a building. It wasn't that Ralph minded removing his hat, it was simply a matter of not remembering to do it. In some way, Miney was forever bringing his attention to the fact that he still had his hat on his head.

This particular Sunday, Ralph had followed his sister through the large double doors into the church. He looked so nice in his little red suit with the matching hat. Miney hesitated a moment, giving the lad a chance to observe the amenities. However, when Ralph continued down the aisle, hat on head, Miney reached forward and tapped him firmly on the shoulder. Rate looked around at his mother, noted her stern visage, and then smiled in remembrance.

He hurriedly doffed his hat, twirled it around his head, and yelled at the top of his lungs, "Hurrah for McKinley."

Miney stared aghast.

Blanche looked back, suppressed a snicker, and continued on to Grandfather's cushioned pew.

Miney quickly recovered her aplomb, grabbed Ralph by the hand, yanked him down the aisle, and gave him a not-too-gentle shove into his seat as she noted her mother-in-law's look of displeasure. She held her head high in spite of her embarrassment. She could just feel the eyes of the congregation following them to their seats, and she knew some of the people were chuckling to themselves. Millie and his bright ideas! Just wait until she got home.

Ralph looked at his mother's face and gave her a charming, wide-eyed, innocent look. He knew from the scowl he received that he had displeased his mother, and he supposed if they had been any-place but in church, she would have tanned him good. He guessed he shouldn't have yelled, but Pa had always thought it funny when he swung his hat and hurrahed. Must be it had something to do with being in church. He had often wondered why everyone always looked so solemn and no one talked to his neighbor, just sat quietly except for the singing and the reading. Grown-ups sure were hard to understand.

True to her word, Miney had no more than stepped in the door of the house when she started berating her husband.

"Milford Setterington, just you guess what your son did in church today."

"Miney, I haven't the slightest idee, but I can see that whatever it was, it riled you plenty."

"Well, you know how I've been teaching him he must remove his hat?" Millie nodded. "Today, he forgot as usual, so I tapped him on the shoulder. Just you guess what he did then."

"He didn't. I guess he did. He must have hurrahed for McKinley." Millie's face was expressionless, but his eyes twinkled.

"That is exactly what he did, and it is all your fault."

"My fault? Never told him to do it in church, did I?"

"I don't suppose so, but apparently you never told him not to either. You're the one who thought it was so funny. Well, it certainly wasn't funny in church."

"I'll bet it got plenty of smiles, if not a few out-and-out chuckles." Millie laughed.

"I don't think it one bit comical."

"Oh, Miney, don't take it so serious. No harm's done."

"Your mother didn't take it any too kindly either, although I suspicion Father didn't mind all that much. Men! Sometimes you can be so exasperating."

Miney flounced off to change her dress as Millie chuckled to himself. He'd never dreamed the lad would pull such a stunt. Bet it had taken folks by surprise. Rate sure had a knack for doing the unexpected, and Miney might just find out that this was only the beginning—at least that was the intuitive feeling he had at this moment.

Cash Waldron had arrived on time for his usual Wednesday evening visit with Frankie Keenan. Millie often teased the young couple about their "intentions" and about the long hours spent together; therefore, he was not completely surprised when he came out of the bedroom in the morning to notice Cash just unhitching his horse from the hitching post. Shoes in hand, Millie went out on the porch and good-naturedly called out to Cash.

"Since you've been here this long, whyn't you help me with chores and stay for breakfast?"

Looking somewhat abashed for a moment, Cash grinned ruefully then, taking the bait, answered, "By golly, Millie, that's a good idee. You won't mind if I give old Dandy a bag o' oats, will you? He's probably tired from standin' here all night."

"Help yourself. Poor horse probably wonders what is goin' on. 'Course there's us humans that are doin' some wondrin' too," Millie said pointedly.

"Jest you never mind. Don't tell me you 'n' Miney didn't do no sparkin' afore you got hitched."

Cash's thin, angular face creased into a grin.

"On my honor," said Millie solemnly.

"Don't josh me, Milford Setterington."

"Cash, my ma would've skinned me alive if I'd ever been out this late with Miney. Didn't make any difference how old I was. Ma had her rules, and they were to be followed to the letter."

Millie chuckled as he and Cash headed for the barn, Cash leading Dandy to put him in the barn with a ration of oats.

At breakfast, Millie started to tease Frankie. However, Frankie was in such good spirits, nothing he could say bothered her at all, she just had a good-natured retort to everything said.

"Millie, if you'll quit jawing long enough, I've got something to tell you and Miney. Cash and I have set the date for our wedding," she announced.

"Well, by golly, it's about time," came from Millie.

"Frankie, how nice. When?"

"The twenty-fifth of next month."

"Goodness, Frankie, that soon?"

"Why, yes, Miney. You don't object, do you?"

"Of course not. I'm happy for you, only I'll not like having to break in another girl to my way of doing things."

"Well, Cash and I talked about that too. I could come in by the day once or twice a week. We're going to be living with his folks for a while, so it won't be like I was havin' to keep house all by myself."

"That would suit me fine."

"Miney. Uh…Cash and I want to ask you something. Don't we, Cash?"

"Reckon we do."

"Well, Cash and I, we was wondrin' if we could be married here at your place?"

"Here? Land's sakes, I suppose so, but why?"

"Well, you and Millie are like family. I love the children, and oh, Miney, I'd just feel better about it. Do give it some thought."

She could have added that the house where her mother and stepfather lived was so tumbledown and in need of repair, she certainly did not want to be married there. That would leave Waldron's, and yet, it was customary to use the bride's home.

"No need for that. Is there, Millie? Of course you can be married here. Can't they, Millie?"

"If that's what they want."

Both Frankie and Cash sighed in relief. Both of them counted Millie and Miney as their best friends. To be sure Frankie worked for them as a domestic, and Cash broke driving horses for Millie, but they had more than an employer-employee relationship.

The next Saturday night, Blanche spoke with her usual candor.

"Bet Frankie's beau is coming tonight, isn't he, Frankie?"

"Well, yes, but how'd you know?"

"Oh, I just knew. Fire's going in the parlor, isn't it? Every time Cash comes callin', there's a fire in the parlor. Ma, how come they don't stay out and talk to us? They always go in there and shut the door. What they got to say they don't want us to hear?"

"Blanche, you stop pesterin' Frankie. Why, no young man wants to come courting with an old married couple and a nosy little girl listening to everything they say."

"Well, I expect old Dandy gets mighty tired of waiting for Cash 'cause I know he stays awful late."

"All right, Miss Know-It-All, Cash and I are going to be married next month right here in this house, and then you won't have to wonder any more."

"Honest, Frankie?"

"That's right. We decided Wednesday while you were at your grandmother's."

"I suppose that's nice, but I'm not ever going to get married," stated Blanche emphatically.

"You'll sing a different tune in a dozen years or so." Millie laughed.

"No, I won't, Pa. I don't care much for boys. They are just a nuisance and always do mean things to us girls."

"It seems like that now, Blanche, but things will change. Perhaps some nice young man like your pa will come along."

"I don't think so, Ma. There's no one like my pa," she said, crawling up on Millie's lap and cuddling up to him in an unaccustomed display of affection. Since she had started school, she often felt she was too grown-up to sit on anyone's lap very often.

Millie beamed and snuggled his daughter in his arms. She sure was an observant little gal. She also liked to tease. My, how he loved her.

A month before election, the price of wheat had risen from sixty cents to eighty cents a bushel due to reported shortages in foreign countries. For some reason, the farmers were convinced this was a result of the good work of the Republican party, and they stood more solidly behind McKinley than ever; and on election day, they helped push McKinley into office by a large margin. Millie was well satisfied and looked optimistically to the future.

On Wednesday evening, the twenty-fifth of November 1896, Cassius Waldron and Frances Keenan were married by Rev. D. D. Martin, with W. W. Brainard and Ora A. Martin as witnesses, in Miney's parlor.

Blanche had observed the simple ceremony with interest. There had been only a handful of friends and a few family members present, two of whom were Frankie's brothers, Merval and Jim. Frankie's mother had come, but her stepfather had shown no interest, so had failed to accompany his wife.

Even at such a tender age, Blanche noted the striking difference in the brothers. Merval was neatly dressed, hair neatly cut and slicked down, not a strand out of place, and he had such a nice, polite manner, a quiet way of speaking; then, there was Jim. Today was the first time Blanche had really ever seen Jim dressed up, if you could call it that—his suit was ill-fitting and rumpled; his hair, although combed, looked dirty and greasy; his hands, while clean, looked unkempt because of the broken, dirty nails. He looked ill at ease, as if the effort to clean up for his sister's wedding had not been quite worthwhile. Blanche wondered if Frankie noted the difference in her brothers and if she cared. However, from the look on Frankie's face, she probably hadn't even noticed because she seemed more concerned with the bridegroom than anyone else. Getting married sure had a strange effect on people, thought Blanche. She wondered if Pa and Ma had been like that on their wedding day.

With the arrival of winter also came the season for sickness of various sorts. Blanche had been ailing for a number of days, so Mina had finally taken her to Doc Brown. He had given her some tablets to give the girl, not really telling Miney just what was wrong, if indeed he actually knew. Blanche was already in her nightgown sitting on her father's lap when Miney came with the tablet and a glass of water.

"But, Ma, I can't swallow a tablet. I just know I can't."

"Well, if you can't swallow a pill with water, I know how you can." Miney disappeared into the kitchen for a moment, the cupboard door opened and closed, and then she returned. "Here, Blanche, try this. I've put the pill in this piece of peach, and when you swallow the peach, you'll swallow the pill too."

Blanche looked at her mother skeptically.

"It won't work," she stated flatly.

"Come now, give it a try because I know it will."

Blanche dutifully put the piece in her mouth, wallowed it around, then swallowed. She immediately put her hand to her mouth, extracted something, and said somewhat smugly, "Here's your old pill."

Millie had sat quietly through all this procedure. Now, without a word, he tipped his daughter over, used his large, heavy hand on her up-ended bottom several times, then once more sat her upright on his lap. Blanche was crying loudly, half from pain, half from anger.

"Now, young lady, you quit your caterwauling and take that pill."

Blanche knew from the tone of her father's voice that if she didn't comply with his wishes, she'd get a harder licking next time. She quickly took the pill, drank some water, and was amazed at the ease with which that little old tablet slipped down her throat. Millie acknowledged it by a bear hug, and Miney gave a sigh of relief that the battle was over. She knew Millie had a heavy hand, and while she often switched Blanche's legs, she never resorted to a real, honest-to-goodness licking, so she had actually suffered with Blanche even if she had been put out with the child.

Miney enjoyed doing dishes when Blanche was home, not because she had help, but because she and Blanche always seemed closest then. They talked of many things, and Miney did enjoy talking. She found some of her daughter's observations amusing while others were astute and showed that Blanche was advanced for her years.

This evening was no exception. Blanche had recounted much of the week's activities. She liked school and was a good student. Sometimes, she seemed older than her classmates.

"Ma, Georgie came to visit Grandma this week."

"That was nice. I think Ma misses having him around. He used to spend more time with Ma and Pa than he did at home. Lorin was always glad to have Ma take care of him."

"He's kind of funny though."

"Funny? You mean full of fun?"

"No, I guess I mean *different*. I hadn't seen him for a long time, so I was glad to see him. He was sitting at the kitchen table eating a piece of pie. Well, I came up to him and put my arms around his neck. Ma, his face got all red, and he almost choked on his pie. Then, he gave me this queer look and says, 'Blanche, don't you ever do that again.' Golly, Ma, I hadn't meant no harm."

"Of course you hadn't, dear. It's just that Georgie doesn't know how to handle affection. Lorin is a rather odd person even if she is my half sister. Why, I don't think she ever hugged or kissed him when he was a baby even. Lorin just isn't the affectionate type. Poor Georgie was simply embarrassed."

"You mean Aunt Lorin never hugged or kissed him when he was little? You hug and kiss Ralph sometimes."

"I know, although sometimes Ralph thinks he's getting too big for such things. But yes, Lorin really didn't even like Georgie when he was first born. That's why Ma and Pa sort of raised him. Lorin just never wanted him around. I guess having a grandmother love you isn't quite the same, so in some ways, Georgie is different. I'm sure he likes you, but any display of affection would make him uncomfortable."

"Ma, I'm glad I know you and Pa love me," Blanche confided. "Golly, even Grandmother gives me a hug now and then. 'Course she usually yells shortly after."

Mina laughed at that remark.

"Well, you at least know that all of us love you even if Grandmother does yell."

"Poor Georgie."

"I don't suppose it is as hard on a boy. I've always felt it was lucky Lorin didn't have a girl."

"I'd not like it much if I had no one to love me," said Blanche. "Guess I'm pretty lucky."

Blanche was home for the weekend and as usual was bubbling over with stories to tell her mother about the activities in school.

"Ma, did you know that we sing ever morning before our studies start?"

"Do you now?"

"Well, first off we pledge allegiance to the flag. It hangs in front over the blackboard. It took us a while to get it memorized, but now every one of us can say it. Then, we have a prayer, and then we sing. This is usually the first, second, and sometimes the third and fourth graders."

"What do you sing?"

"Oh, lots of things. They's all in the Knapsack. Only, Ma, sometimes we don't always know the tune very well, and we can't read all the words, so Mr. Brown takes it a line at a time and teaches us while Mrs. Brown plays the piano."

The Knapsack was a small, soft-covered book in which were printed the words to many, many songs. A few of the patriotic songs were already familiar to the children, and quite a number even knew some of the words. Other songs would give the title, and underneath it might have "to the tune of America" or some such familiar tune. The children loved this time of singing, and while some of them perhaps had difficulty carrying the tune, their childish voices rang out lustily and clearly quite filling the entire room.

"Ma's glad you enjoy school so much. But what about your reading and writing?"

"Teacher said I was getting better at making my letters every day. I hardly ever need help with my words. Guess I like doing my sums best of all. I'm usually the first one done," she said proudly.

"But are they always correct?"

"Well, most of the time. Sometimes I miss one," she admitted.

"Then don't be in such a hurry. You must be careful to have them right even if it does take you a little longer."

"Yes, Ma. Did you know that before school is out, we get to use pens for penmanship?"

"You do?"

"Yes. Mrs. Brown told us yesterday. Guess she thought of it because on Friday it is time to fill the inkwells from that big old jug for the next week. She said that it wouldn't be long before we'd need ours filled just like the older students'. I can hardly wait."

Goodness, the child surely did enjoy her studies. She did very well too, and the work was coming easily for her. That was indeed a blessing. School had always been easy for Miney, and she had thoroughly enjoyed the learning process. However, while Millie had learned easily enough, he had not had her zeal for learning something new. If it had to do with ciphering, Millie excelled, if not, he sometimes failed to apply himself. From Blanche's actions, the child was most assuredly enjoying herself learning.

Miney watched as her daughter scampered off to play. She was such a pretty child, a very willful child to be certain, but she had such lovely fine hair and beautiful dark eyes. Miney was extremely proud, and she knew that she was certainly glad the good Lord had seen fit to give her this daughter.

Of course, Ralph was a dear little boy, she thought somewhat guiltily. Now that she had him, she guessed she didn't even mind that he was a boy—well, not very often anyway. It was just that he got into so much more mischief than Blanche, but Millie assured her that it was simply the way of little boys.

The church was packed. Even the classrooms on both sides of the center pews had been opened and people were sitting there. It was always thus when the Baptist Church gave their Christmas program. Even those who attended services rather sporadically throughout the year showed up now.

Mina worried about Ralph. He had a short piece to speak, and she just knew he'd have stage fright when he saw all those faces peering at him. How humiliating it would be. Last year Jacob had forgotten his lines, and his mother had been so embarrassed whilst the crowd had twittered with laughter. Now, she knew just how Emily had felt.

Mother Setterington had taken Ralph aside just before they left the house, and Miney had no idea what she'd said to the boy. She only knew that Ralph's eyes had taken on a glow, and he'd drawn himself up straight as if he were trying to look years older than the three that he was. My oh my, she wished the program was over. She looked at the clock: seven fifty. Time to get the youngsters lined up for their entrances so's the program could go off as smoothly as possible.

Miney and some of the other Sunday school teachers began to create some semblance of order out of the reigning chaos. When the children realized that zero hour was approaching, they quieted down with only a few admonishing remarks needed to bring a few older boys into line. A little girl started to snivel. Miney moved quickly to comfort the child. Something like that was extremely catching, and soon, the whole row of youngsters would be bawling.

Ralph was the eighth child to recite. Thank heavens for that. The program started. Mary gave the welcoming address and did wonderfully well, but then, she was older. Next came a little girl, and she raced through her lines like a house afire. That was almost as bad, in Miney's opinion, as forgetting. Lawsy, Ralph had recited his much better than that at home. The girl ahead of Ralph was singing "Away in a Manger." She had a sweet voice, Miney noted.

She straightened Ralph's collar and smoothed his skirts. She supposed she'd have to start putting him in pants soon, but he did look nice tonight. His dark hair was neatly combed, and he lacked that mischievous look she had come to know so well and dread. That was worth a sigh of relief.

The girl finished and left the stage.

Ralph walked calmly out, bowed to the audience, flashed a smile at someone, and began. Miney peeked out to see if Mother Setterington was noting her grandson's impeccable manners. Her eyes widened in surprise, and she took in a startled gasp of breath. Good heavens! There sat prim, staid Mother Setterington very calmly holding up a banana. The light dawned. Now she knew what the furtive conversation had been about. Of all things! Mother was bribing Ralph. She glanced back at the boy; his piece was nearly finished, and he was reciting loudly and clearly and with meaning, just as she had taught him. Well, bribe or not, she'd not have to be ashamed of him this night.

There. He finished, made another bow, but what was he doing? Instead of going off to the side as he should, he walked deliberately to the front of the stage, jumped off, and ran to his waiting grandmother; the appeal of the banana had been too much. The crowd burst out laughing even if they were in a house of God. Well, she supposed it could have been worse. Besides, she couldn't entirely blame the boy. Mother Setterington had been at fault too. Miney had never been one to bribe a child into good behavior, but then, it wouldn't matter to Lavina Setterington whether her daughter-in-law approved or not.

Anyway, she couldn't dwell on it because the program had to keep going. Miney had to play the piano for three little girls from her Sunday school class besides help keep everything moving. She'd give it some thought later, no doubt, but other things were more pressing now.

That same evening after Ralph and Blanche had both been tucked in bed, Miney recounted the evening's events to Millie.

"Your mother was to blame for him jumping off the stage like that. He only did it because he wanted that banana she was holding. Then, she sat right there and let him eat it. In church, mind you. Why, she would not tolerate anyone else behaving so in the house of the Lord."

"No harm was done, Miney. 'Ppears like it was a good notion Ma had. Kept him from getting stage fright, didn't it? Besides, the way you tell it, folks thought it was funny, and they no doubt needed something to tickle their ribs. I wouldn't have minded that."

"Millie! You encourage the boy by your always laughing at his antics. It happened in the house of the Lord, and even if it was just a Christmas program, he has to learn respect."

"Don't be so serious. Rate's only a little boy as yet, and there's time enough to set on him. I wouldn't give a nickel for a boy who didn't have a little get up and go."

"You want him to be a rapscallion," she accused.

"Not at all. I just want him to be all boy. Girls were meant to be dainty and well mannered, but boys were meant to be—well, just boys. Besides, Rate will do fine. He's a good lad, Miney. You ofttimes judge him too harshly."

"Well, maybe," she admitted. "If I do, it's just because I do so want him to be a credit to the name of Setterington. He has a lot to live up to," she said softly.

Millie patted the hand she had tenderly placed on his shoulder. Things were looking better. Miney had come to care for the boy—perhaps not with the love she had for Blanche, but she no longer resented him, of this he was certain. It gave him a feeling of tenderness toward this woman who was his wife. He knew she was not always content with her lot in life, but even if she wasn't, she was not a chronic complainer. True, she sometimes berated him for something Ma did, but he didn't mind because he realized Ma never considered what someone else wanted.

Funny thing, though, hardly anyone ever disagreed with Ma. Sometimes he'd like to tell her to go chase herself, but one just didn't talk that way to Ma. He'd learned that quick enough as a boy. Why, he recollected the time John had had the audacity to sass Ma when they was in the store. Ma had grabbed John's wrists in her stout hands and had pummeled him in the face with his own hands until his nose was good and bloody. John hadn't dared fight back even though he was a large boy. Ma's temper was something to be reckoned with, and one simply didn't cross her no matter what the provocation. It had made no difference to Ma that he and John had growed to be men. She bossed them anyway.

'Course Ma even bossed Pa a good share of the time, but Millie had always felt that Pa let her do this because, for some reason, he enjoyed it. "Now, now, Vine," he'd say when Ma started complaining too much. "You'd best not get so overwrought. You know it's bad for your health." They'd both chuckle, and that would be the end of it.

Pa knew how to handle her all right. No one could ever accuse Horatio Setterington of being a hen-pecked husband, that's for damned sure. Pa just seemed to know when being thoughty paid off, like the time when he brought Ma that fancy set of silver—the forks engraved with the whole name of *Setterington* instead of just an initial and the pearl-handled knives. Well, Pa had given them to Ma and said offhanded like, "There, Vine, that's your laundry bill for a spell." Ma had been complaining of late because even when working in the field, Pa always wore those ruffled white shirts that had to be starched, and it took forever to iron them. Ma had said there wasn't no sense in him wearing white shirts because other men didn't. Pa hadn't argued the matter with her at all. In fact, Millie didn't even remember Pa taking the time to answer. Now, Millie wondered if Pa had planned on buying the silver afore all this happened, or had he done it because he knew it would stop Ma's complaining. With Pa, it was hard to tell; he was a mighty crafty person and had a way of being able to manipulate people unbeknownst to them. Yessiree, Pa was quite a man. Somehow, thinking of his father made Millie feel inadequate; however, he vowed he would always keep trying to measure up to Horatio Setterington.

Although the Baptist Church had had their Christmas program and party on Christmas Eve, Lavina expected Millie and John, each accompanied by his family, to join her, Horatio, and Ruby at her house on Christmas Day for a special dinner and gifts afterward. This year was no exception, so while Miney still felt miffed with her mother-in-law because of last night's episode, she knew there was no way short of death she could gracefully get out of appearing at her in-laws' for dinner, and that did rankle Miney clean through; so, if the stove lids rattled more than usual as Miney prepared breakfast, it was because she was still more than slightly piqued. Mother just never once considered anyone else's wants, simply did as she pleased about everything and expected all to pay homage to the queen.

Miney fumed.

Ralph had looked like such a darling little boy, but for Miney, the whole performance had been spoiled when he jumped off the stage to run to his grandmother. Best not think of it any more right now, she thought as she jerked the knife down through the loaf of bread, making much thicker slices than the thin, neat slices she usually made. She slammed the plate onto the table with such force it would surely have broken had it been china instead of the enameled, everyday ware.

Since Santa had paid his usual nocturnal visit while the two youngsters slept soundly, breakfast turned into a rather hurried affair with the children in such a hurry to enter the double doors to the parlor where the tree stood. Millie had been in there to tend the fire, but it had been truly amazing how a man of his girth could slip through such a small opening, and although both Ralph and Blanche had craned their necks, they had not even so much as been rewarded with a glimpse of the tree. Christmas was certainly an exciting time.

When the children had finished the very last morsels of their breakfast, Millie opened the parlor doors, and both came running. The stockings had been hung on the doorframe nearest the tree, and it was to them the children went first. Both stockings, the heavy, long woolen ones they wore in winter, were filled with candy, cookies, and fruit. Rate popped a candy in his mouth and headed for the tree with Blanche close behind. There were small toys for each child. Ralph was particularly interested in a bright-red, hard rubber ball. Blanche had a new book, now that she was beginning to read, and a nice new pencil box, like the one she had been eying in Van Deusen's General Store.

Each child had an article of clothing from Millie and Miney. Blanche had a petticoat with real lace insertions, which Miney had spent a great deal of time making. There was a shirtwaist for Ralph to go with his red suit. Miney and Millie exchanged some small gift, usually something needed. This year, Millie received a new mustache cup and Miney a new bone hook large enough to use when she crocheted rugs to put here and there on the wooden floor.

The children kept busy until it was time to leave for Lavina's. The day was clear, sunny, and somewhat mild. Miney saw to it that the horsehide robe was tucked in snugly around their legs. She and Blanche carried muffs, which kept their hands comfortably warm; the men had lined mittens. The wind in their faces—as Old Mikey moved along, snorting and blowing, acting much younger than his years—soon turned their cheeks a rosy red as well as the tips of their noses. The sparkling snow glared into their faces and made them squint their eyes against the brightness. What a glorious day!

They were the first to arrive at Lavina's; John and Grace were notoriously slow at getting around, or perhaps they were simply in no hurry to spend their time with John's family. There were times when such occasions became rather strained because it was very evident Lavina did not approve of Grace. Sometimes, Grace's jovial nature, which often made light of a barbed remark, irritated Lavina to no end. At least she had never objected to Miney, for which her daughter-in-law was eternally thankful.

They were in for the surprise of their life when they entered Lavina's parlor. Instead of the usual large, nicely trimmed tree, there were rows of clothesline draped across the room just above head level, and on these lines, clothespins pinned a spectacular array of presents. It was a rather bizarre sight and astounded everyone. Even the children were speechless.

When the reason was learned, it seemed that Horatio had not seen fit to go chop a Christmas tree on the exact day Lavina wanted it. Her wishes thwarted, she had simply shown her husband that with a little ingenuity, she had handled the situation quite adequately without being dependent on him. Horatio had roared with laughter when he first observed what his wife had done; however, it was the first and last time he failed to get her a tree on the designated day.

CHAPTER 7

❖❖❖

Rate sat listening to his grandfather and father, who were discussing some business matters. The boy didn't understand much of what was being said, nor for that matter was he particularly listening to the words; he was merely absorbed in the steady intonation of the male voices as he watched his grandfather with admiration. Rate worshipped his grandfather, but he also feared him. There was a quality of humor about the deep-set, dark-brown eyes that went unnoticed by the lad; he saw only the sternness of line in the sharply molded features, the shock of graying hair, thinning on top, and the slightly wavy chin whiskers, neatly trimmed and streaked with gray; there was a certain wiriness beneath the surface here, a strength coiled and waiting for a time to be used, and Ralph sensed this.

Millie was a larger man, standing taller, weighing more, but he stood no straighter than his father, and the larger allotment in size still did not make him the commanding figure that was Horatio Setterington. In truth, Millie not only had respect for his father, but also realized that his father possessed the strength of no ordinary man.

The Setteringtons were a large, well-proportioned breed of men, stronger than average, slow to anger, yet with an obstinacy that sometimes was their undoing; they were careful not to show their emotions whether it be love, sadness, anger, hate, or even happiness. The only clue was in the depths of their eyes, for in an unguarded moment, an astute observer might catch a glimpse of their innermost feelings before the mask slipped carefully into place and this moment of weakness—for such it was considered by them—passed.

Ralph became aware that both men were looking at him.

"Rate, how'd you like to take a ride with me this afternoon?" asked Horatio.

"Can I, Pa? Can I?" There was exuberance in his voice.

"Best go ask your ma, boy, and see what she says."

"You just tell her that Grandfather is going to Bannister this afternoon, and you want to ride along," put in Horatio, never doubting that this settled the matter; and, of course, it never occurred to Miney to say no to her father-in-law. She had tried only once, the time before Blanche had started school, but the long battle had ended in an ignoble defeat, and nothing else ever seemed quite as important to Miney again.

It was in the early spring of the year, the time when the days warmed somewhat, the roads thawed, the wagon and buggy wheels cut deeply into their elastic, bottomless surface; then, the weather became cold once again, freezing the roads into a myriad of ruts that made travel anything but pleasant.

Ralph had been quiet, as befitted a small child, on the ride to Bannister and had watched the countryside with interest. Nevertheless, even a well-brought-up lad does get bored after a certain amount of inactivity. Ralph would have liked to ask his grandfather some questions, but that severe visage did nothing to encourage the small boy. Finally, he began to fidget on the seat as the team picked their way slowly over the rutted road. At last he could remain quiet no longer.

"Grandfather, is we gonna drive this slow all the way? I thought you said they's a fast team, and that Little Mac really likes to go."

"In a hurry, Rate? Now, boy, you just stop and think about the roads a minute."

At that moment, the side curtain of the buggy came loose, slipped, and fell with a crack like the sound of a whip. The team, jittery because of the enforced slow travel, jumped forward as one unit, and, in spite of Horatio's steady and strong hands on the lines, took off down the road with the buggy swaying dangerously from side to side.

"Here, boy, hang on to me," Horatio yelled as he braced himself and tried to bring the runaway team under control.

Ralph clutched his grandfather's coat with all his might. His legs were too short to brace himself in any way, so he bobbed around like a cork on a stream. Finally, the horses began to tire, and Horatio brought them to a near walk once more. His forehead was wet with perspiration not only from the exertion, but from the anxiety. As the horses slowed to a walk, blowing and wheezing from their run, Ralph looked indignantly at his grandfather.

"Well, I didn't mean for you to drive that fast."

Horatio burst into hearty laughter, put his arm around his grandson's shoulders, and remarked, "Nor did I, Rate, nor did I."

Later, when relating the incident to Millie, Horatio declared, "If I hadn't had the boy with me, I'd never have stuck with it, Milt, I'd have jumped for sure. I never thought I'd get them stopped before that buggy turned over. It's a wonder Ralph wasn't thrown out. The Lord certainly took good care of us today. I was so busy with that team, I didn't even have time to pray, but He took care of us anyhow. Believe me, I'll thank Him in my prayers tonight."

Miney only heard Ralph's excited version of the ride. She held her son close for a moment and thanked God he was safe. She guessed she did care for Ralph because it gave her a queer sort of constriction around her heart when she thought how nearly his outing came to ending in tragedy. A body just never knew what might happen. Who would have thought that as capable a horseman as Father Setterington would have had a team get out of hand? Well, as Millie was wont to say, all's well that ends well.

Not long after the runaway incident, Millie approached a subject that had been on his mind for some time. Miney was doing some sewing at the time, and Millie sat contemplating her as she bent over the sewing machine he had given her a short time ago.

"Miney, just when are you going to put Rate in pants? He's past three years old now, and you've dressed him like a girl long enough. Most others have their sons out of skirts long before this."

"I've been thinking of it, Millie, honest, I have. I know I'm not as handy as I could be when it comes to sewing, but I've been meaning to ask Lorin if she would help me."

"Well, you do just that. It is fine for Blanche to look like a lady, but how's Ralph to act like a boy with those danged skirts swirling about his legs? Come summer, he'll be climbing worse than last year, and you hollered all the time then because he was always tearing those infernal skirts. And another thing, it's high time you quit putting those goldurn sunbonnets on him. Those were made for women, and I'll not have you make a sissy out of the boy."

"All right, Millie," she sighed, "as soon as I finish these bloomers and petticoat for Blanche, I'll try my hand on some pants. I'll have to get some material the next time we're in town, and I'll get him a straw hat this year. I don't want to have him blackened by the sun. He has such a pretty, white complexion."

"Nice for a girl," muttered Millie, but he said no more to Miney on the subject.

It was true, Mina had been putting off dressing Ralph like a boy. Ma had spoken of it to her when Ralph had turned three, but Ma was anything but the pushy type and had made no issue of it when Miney had given her a rather noncommittal answer. Now, thoughts were tumbling through her mind like water flowing through a rockstrewn riverbed. Millie had just spoiled her day with his subtle ultimatum that she start dressing Ralph in pants. In her heart, she knew Millie was right; a boy should be dressed in pants before his third birthday, and she had simply been procrastinating. Perhaps she still harbored some slight resentment because Ralph was a boy instead of the girl she had wanted.

She hated making men's clothes. Mary and Lorin had always laughed at her because they were of the opinion that sewing was sewing, and it didn't really matter what the garment was—dress, shirt, or pants, since each required the same amount of proficiency with a needle. They told her that anyone who could crochet and embroider so beautifully could certainly learn to sew equally well. Anyhow, she guessed the time had come for the metamorphosis because when Millie had that set look to his face, he wasn't about to be put off.

Miney had a flash of thought. Before she took Ralph out of dresses for good, she'd have his picture taken in his red suit—she was certainly partial to that outfit. Millie tended to think pictures were a waste of money, but this time she'd not be put off, she'd have Ralph's and Blanche's picture taken, and Millie could just keep still about her wasting money. With that thought in mind, Miney smiled a small, secretive smile and continued with her sewing. She was so pleased with herself, she even started to sing as she worked.

True to her word, Miney summoned her courage and, instead of asking Millie, simply told him she intended to have the children's pictures taken. With his usual unpredictability, Millie voiced no objection whatsoever, said he thought it was a good idea.

Ralph did look like such a darling. If only they could catch the mischievous twinkle in his dark-brown eyes while the face had an angelic look of innocence. Blanche looked so grown-up, prim, staid, almost afraid to smile, such a sweet child who was growing up faster than Miney liked to admit.

Miney had had pictures taken of Ralph and Blanche together; then, she had decided on a picture of each alone. Blanche's had been a close-up, a bust only, while Ralph's had been taken with him standing on a wicker chair, his hand resting on the back of the chair. Millie could perhaps demand that she dress him like a boy, but she could always have the picture to remind her of how nice he looked in his raspberry red suit.

She hung the two portraits in her parlor. They never failed to bring a nostalgic look to her eyes and a small, wistful smile whenever she looked at them.

As she had promised, Miney did buy material and enlisted Lorin's aid in the actual making. Goodness, pants certainly were much more of a bother to make than dresses. It took her several weeks to complete the job. A full grown man's pants were so much easier—especially for one the size of Millie. If Millie wondered at the length of time, he kept his thoughts to himself.

Begrudgingly, she guessed Ralph did look better in pants, and she knew from Millie's look of satisfaction that he was well pleased. Of course, there was one drawback. Since he was no longer hampered by those silly old skirts, Ralph could run faster, climb higher, and get out of sight much more quickly. My, but that boy did enjoy life. Just seemed as though he was a constant worry. Miney decided she would be glad when he was older so's he wouldn't be so much trouble.

Miney loved flowers. In the summer, there was a vase of fresh flowers on the buffet or dining room table or both from the time of the first daffodils in the spring until frost blackened the blooms of the annuals. Usually, if she suspected a frost was imminent, she picked as many blooms and buds as possible. Somehow, to Miney, the house never looked quite as cheery and friendly without a vase or two of her favorite flowers.

A few days ago, Ray Sawyer had spaded the flower beds south of the house to the west of the porch. Ray was such a congenial young man, medium height, lean, wavy blond hair, and laughing eyes the color of blue cornflowers. He had the most infectious grin and just always seemed to be good-natured. Miney had been well pleased with the careful job he had done; besides that, he had raked half-rotted cow manure in with the topsoil, so Miney was sure her flowers would do especially well this year.

A day or so after Ray had done this for Miney, he happened to overhear Blanche asking her mother if she could have a flower garden too.

"Now, Blanche, I've no time to be weeding a bed for you since I have enough of my own to tend to. I suppose I could spade you a small place and give you a few seeds if you promise to take care of them yourself."

"Oh, I will, Ma, honest, I will. Can you do it today?"

Miney was busy kneading bread dough.

"No, I don't have time today. Perhaps tomorrow."

Before Blanche could raise any objection, Ray stepped into the kitchen and spoke to Blanche.

"I've got a little spare time, Blanche. Come along and show me where you want it dug up. It's all right, isn't it, Mrs. Setterington?" he asked, flashing a smile.

"Of course, Ray, if you want to bother."

"It's no bother, ma'am. Besides, the little one does want it so badly. Blanche, I'll go get a spade and meet you south of the house. You have the place all picked out."

"Oh, I will, Ray. I surely will."

The little girl clapped her hands and dashed for the door, her pigtails bobbing as she went.

When Ray appeared, he found Blanche carefully surveying the scene. Her mother had a space for flowers from the west end of the porch all along the side of the stone cellar. She guessed that left her the front of the narrow porch on each side of the steps. She consulted Ray, and he felt sure this was a likely place for a flower garden. Very methodically, he began to turn the earth over, spadeful by spadeful.

"Blanche, I forgot to bring the rake. Can you get it from where it hangs in the woodshed?"

"'Course I can."

Blanche ran around the house, through the gate, and on to the woodshed. She had a little trouble getting the rake off the hooks it hung on; but in short order, she was back at Ray's side. She watched as he carefully smoothed the dirt, making a nice, fine seedbed in the rich, black soil.

"You think you could finish doing this?"

"Well, I've watched you, so I reckon I know what to do," was the reply.

Ray gave Blanche the rake, then disappeared around the corner of the house. Blanche was so busy raking, patting an errant lump to break it up, and then raking again, she did not hear Ray return.

"Here, Blanche. See what I brought for your flower garden."

Blanche peered into the pail, sniffed, and then looked up at Ray.

"That's manure," she stated.

"That's right. I brought it to work into the soil. It will make your flowers grow better."

"Not much, you're not," she said, her eyes blazing. "I won't have that stuff in my flower beds. I'm not going to have my flowers all stunk up," she declared vehemently.

"But, Blanche, that's what I did for your mother. It makes the flowers grow better. Honest, it does."

"I don't care, Ray Sawyer. I'm not having that stinky mess in my flower garden. You can just take it back where you got it from."

"All right, you're the boss. I'll take it away."

Ray chuckled as he moved off. For a child, she sure had a mind of her own. Sure was comical. Why, when she made her mind up to something, she sure wasn't going to let anyone change it for her.

Blanche acquired seeds from Miney and followed her mother's instructions for planting them to the letter. When the seedlings were large enough, Miney patiently showed the girl how to tell the difference between the flowers and the weeds. Blanche tended her garden carefully; she watered it when the weather became dry and pulled the weeds as soon as they put in an appearance. If her flowers were less sturdy than her mother's, and if they had fewer blooms, she said nothing. Perhaps down in her heart she realized Ray had been right, and Miney's flowers thrived because of the manure, but she was not about to admit it—at least not out loud. Blanche was a Setterington in many ways.

Mina sat in a rocker, which she had drawn out on the north porch, a large enameled pan on her lap full of the first peas of the spring, a pail on her left to receive the pods as her nimble fingers shelled them. The pods were plump and full with tender green peas.

Miney was content with her world just now. She looked across the yard to the barn with its gable roof and pile of manure just outside the south horse stable door. The sheep barn stood to the south and west, then the small granary, the chicken coop and woodshed with the icehouse behind that. Along the drive, the picket fence kept the stock in as they came to the house for water from the tank fed by the creaking, wooden windmill.

Rate appeared from somewhere and stood at his mother's side, where he absently reached over, plucked a pea from the pan, and popped it into his mouth.

"Ma, you got teeth, haven't you?"

"Well, of course I have." She laughed. "Whatever made you ask such a fool question?"

"I was just wondrin'."

He paused, ate another pea, then ventured, "Then how come Pa don't have no teeth?"

"Goodness, Ralph, your pa had his teeth pulled years ago. They were bad and nearly fell out."

"How does he eat?"

"You see him eat just like I do. Somehow, I don't think anything could keep your father from eating." She chuckled. "I've never seen a man who likes food any better than he does. I've always wondered how he managed steak, but it just never seems to bother. However, that's why he always uses a sharp knife and cuts his corn off the cob, so that was one thing he couldn't quite manage without teeth."

Ralph digested this bit of information along with a few more peas.

"Whyn't he have store-bought teeth? Don says his grandfather has teeth that he can take out."

"I don't know, son, but I guess your pa just never felt they'd be worthwhile."

Ralph started to ask another question, thought better of it, and scampered off.

Mina watched him go, stopping momentarily with her work. Land's sakes that boy did have a bump of curiosity big enough to choke a horse; he was always full of questions of some sort. In some ways, he was so old for his age. If only he wasn't always getting into mischief, but then, from what others said, boys were like that just because they were boys.

Crops were ahead of schedule because of the unseasonably warm weather accompanied by an adequate amount of rain. Millie had gone to town one afternoon to get some parts for the cultivator since the corn was already tall enough to start cultivating. He had decided the old shoes needed replacing.

When he returned, he had a basket on his arm; and the brown, silky head of a pup could be seen sticking out.

"Blanche, Blanche. Come here and see what I've got," he called from the porch.

Blanche came to the door, took one look at her father, and emphatically stated, "You're not my father."

"Why, what do you mean?"

"You're not my father," she repeated in a determined tone. "My father has a mustache, and you don't"

Millie started to laugh. "Don't you like me without it? I thought I looked right nice." He put a finger up to his bare lip.

"No. I don't like it. Ma, come and see. Pa's shaved his mustache off. Just see how dreadful he looks."

"Millie, you did do it. I never thought you really meant to."

"How do you like it?"

"I'm not sure. You look so different, and you've worn one for a long time."

"Well, he's not my father anymore," said an indignant Blanche.

Millie chuckled at his daughter's haughty look.

"Here, Blanche, I almost forgot. I brought you this pup. Here, take him."

"No, thank you. I don't take presents from strangers."

And with that, she turned and marched back into the house, head held high.

Millie burst out laughing. "Don't that beat all, Miney, my own daughter disowning me. I had thought she'd like the pup, but I know her set ways, and she'll never want him now. Well, little fellow, guess you're just stuck with the rest of us. Now, be honest, Miney, do I look that bad?"

"It's not that you don't look all right, it's just that it's so different. She'll get used to it. Guess you won't be needing that mustache cup I got you last Christmas, at least for a spell."

Millie put the team away and sat scraping the hardened sweat from a horse collar when he looked up and saw Ralph standing just inside the stable door eyeing him. Millie gave no indication that he knew the boy was there, but continued with his work. Rate spoke no word, watched him a moment more, then scurried to the house.

He came into the kitchen where Miney was peeling potatoes for dinner.

"Ma, who's the new hired man in the barn?"

"What new man? There's no one there but your father."

"Yes, there is. I was in the barn playing, an' I see him sittin' in the horse stable. He was cleaning a collar with his jackknife. Honest, Ma. I really did see him."

"Lawsy, Ralph, that had to be your pa."

"No, it weren't. He didn't have no mustache. Pa's got a mustache. I'd know if it was Pa," he finished lamely.

Just then, Millie stepped into the kitchen.

"Am I your pa?"

Ralph turned and eyed the newcomer. He stepped a step closer to his mother, then said, "Uh-uh. Pa don't look like you."

Millie burst out laughing. "Rate, come here. Do I look that different without a mustache?"

"Pa? Is it really you?"

"Of course, boy."

"I liked you better when you had a mustache." Ralph peered up at his father, displeasure showing on his face.

"Well, dang it all, Miney, my own kids disowning me. Beats all, don't it?"

Thus Millie decided that he would grow back his mustache and not shave it off ever again.

Millie had fully understood his daughter. It was several days before she treated him in a normal manner, and the pup, given the name of Grip, never did hold any attraction for her. Perhaps it was the circumstances of his arrival, but whatever the reason, Blanche cared nothing for the pup, nor did Millie for that matter. He had no patience to train a dog to be of any help around the farm. His firm belief that a dog only made more work was often verified since he never quite understood how to teach a dog to help handle livestock. What help Grip was, at times, was simply a result of the dog's own instinct. Ralph liked the dog well enough, but he was too young to teach Grip; besides, Millie had brought the pup home for Blanche, so Ralph always thought of Grip as belonging to his pa and his sister.

It was a warm, sunny, lazy type of day. Mina had hurried through her morning chores with the idea in mind to go calling in the afternoon. Blanche was at Mary's, and she did get lonesome with only Ralph for company. Unless he was looking in books, that boy was usually doing something outdoors, which she supposed was just as well. Leastways, he got into less mischief outside, or perhaps it simply didn't show up as quickly. Now and then, Millie wondered what had happened to a hammer or saw, and while he usually found it sooner or later, he felt sure his young son was responsible for its disappearance.

When the dinner dishes were finished, Mina changed her dress, made sure Ralph had clean hands and face, and set out for Edwin Knight's to see Emma. It was a mile walk, but such a pleasant day to walk, not too warm, and the meadows and wheat fields were such a lovely shade of green. Mina did love early summer. Spring was likely to be too wet, but now, everything was growing nicely, and it was once more dry underfoot.

The afternoon was passing quickly with the two women chatting amiably. The clock struck four, and Mina realized she must soon take her leave. Ralph had sidled up to his mother and, after a moment of indecision, stated, "Ma, I'm hungry."

"Ralph, you will have to wait until we get home. You know that."

"Oh, Miney, of course the lad is hungry. A growing boy like him gets hungry quicker than we do. Let's see now, Ralph, what can I give you? Would a cookie do?"

The boy looked puzzled and hesitated before he answered.

Turning to his mother, he said, "Ma, what's a cookiedo?"

Both women burst out laughing, and Rate looked even more perplexed.

"Land's sakes, Ralph. Emma just wanted to know if you'd like a cookie to eat."

"Oh, boy, I sure would."

Still laughing, Emma got up from her chair.

"Come with me to the kitchen then, and you can sit at the table to eat your cookie."

Emma's cookies were thick and large, and Ralph munched contentedly. He wondered what his mother and Mrs. Knight had found so funny. Mrs. Knight sure had a strange way of asking a boy whether he wanted a cookie or not. He didn't think there was anything funny about it. Women certainly were strange at times. Well, if there was ever a next time, he'd know what she was talking about when she said "cookiedo." At least she made right good cookies, maybe not as good as Ma made, but then, Ma was just an awful good cookie-maker.

Her molasses cookies were the best he'd ever eaten. Sure was nice to have a mother who was such a good cook and could bake good too. He guessed he was a lucky boy. Guessed it didn't even matter all that much if Ma did like Blanche best. If only he could figure out just why Ma didn't care much for little boys. He pondered the situation while he finished the last bits of his cookie.

"Ralph, are you almost done?"

"Yes, Ma."

"Good. We've got to be on our way if I'm to have your father's supper on time."

One thing about Millie, he was hardly ever late for meals, which really made Miney's task much easier. She knew some of the women complained because, even though they rang the dinner bell or supper bell, their man stayed in the field as long as he wanted, leaving his wife to do her best to keep the meal warm without entirely spoiling it. No, Millie liked to eat too well to ever be that inconsiderate. If, for some reason, he was not going to be able to be on time, he was always sure to let her know. Mother Setterington's training, no doubt. Mina could imagine that quite likely a boy who couldn't be on time for a meal at Lavina's table just might have had to skip that meal entirely.

Mina was buying groceries at the general store, which was owned by Milo Van Deusen. It was located on the south side of Main Street between Downey's Hardware and the jewelry store operated by H. T. Blank. Rate had been wandering around the store past the pickle barrel, the cracker barrel—they always bought their crackers here because the other store sold kerosene and Mr. Van Deusen didn't, so his crackers never tasted of kerosene—and he'd made two trips by the candy jars. Sometimes, Ma gave him a penny to spend, but today she hadn't, and he wasn't sure he should ask for one. Ma was always awful close with money.

Finally, he came up to his mother and said, "Ma, I'm thirsty. Is it all right if I get a drink?"

"Where are you going to get a drink now?"

"At the back of the store. There's a water pail and dipper."

"Is it all right?" Miney asked the clerk.

"Sure. You go right ahead, Ralph."

The boy needed no more encouragement. He took off on the run, and the next thing they heard was a thud, *bump, bump, bump,* and a child's crying.

"Ralph," cried Miney, hastening in the direction he had gone. No Ralph was to be seen, but there stood the water pail by the ominous gaping hole where a stairway descended into the basement. From the depths came sobbing.

"Ralph! Ralph! Oh my goodness, he's fallen down these steps. Ralph, are you all right?" asked Miney as she started down the steep stairway.

Milo pushed past her and, in a moment, returned with the small boy in his arms. Rate's face was streaked with dirt, the skin was scraped along one temple, and his clothes were awry; other than that, the lad seemed little worse for wear.

"Goodness, Ralph, you gave me a fright. Here, let Ma wipe your face. Are you sure you're all right?"

"I…I guess so. My head hurts here."

"I should think it would. You'll have a bump like as not where the skin is broken. Whatever happened?"

"I stubbed my toe and just fell."

"Milo, there should be a railing around here. It isn't safe like it is." Miney's tone was reproachful.

"Usually we have the trapdoor closed during business hours, Miney, but I've been bringing stock up to replenish the shelves. I'm thankful he's not hurt badly."

"So am I. You'd best not be wandering off anymore, Ralph. Then, you won't be getting into trouble."

"But, Ma, I'm still thirsty."

With that, everyone gave a relieved chuckle. Mr. Van Deusen escorted Ralph back to get a drink while Mina finished making her purchases.

When she related the incident to Millie, she voiced her opinion that it was not all the lad's fault, and she felt it was negligence on Van Deusen's part to have an open stairway in the first place. She'd make certain that the next time she went into the store, she'd check to see if the trapdoor was closed before she let her son go rambling around the store by himself.

Millie sighed indulgently. Since no great harm had been done, he couldn't see making all that fuss over the episode. Like as not the boy would have worse happen before he was a man grown.

And how right Millie was!

Ralph knew something exciting was in the air; he had known this for weeks, but he wasn't sure just what it was. For one thing, Blanche had been home all this while, and he'd heard her complaining to Ma about not being able to stay at Grandmother's last Sunday after church. When she stayed there, she got a chance to play with Fern Wooley, who was in her grade at school, or maybe Gracie Albaugh or Pearl Tuttle. Ma had said something about Grandmother being too busy with wedding plans to be bothered. Blanche had pouted the rest of the day, which Ralph thought was funny.

Blanche usually did pretty much as she pleased, staying with Grandmother and Grandfather to go to school and always staying overnight there on some pretext or other. Well, for once, they didn't have time for her; now, maybe she knew something of how he felt when much of the time Grandmother ignored him. Why, he had never been allowed to see all the rooms of the house. He knew about what Blanche called the doll house, but he had never been allowed to climb the ladder to enter it.

He was as terrified of his grandmother as he was of his grandfather, but while he worshipped Horatio, he was more in awe of Lavina. She was a commanding figure, being tall for a woman; broad-shouldered; rather stout around the waist; stern, coarse features that seldom smiled; graying hair that had once been quite reddish; cold blue eyes; and a voice that always held a note of authority. Here was none of the love and warmth a small boy would have welcomed. True, she sometimes would slip a silver dollar down his shirtfront when she and Grandfather had been visiting, and a whole dollar was a heap of money. Still, he'd have liked it better if she'd not been so cold and had done things for him like he heard other boys tell about their grandmothers.

He wisht sometimes she'd have offered him an orange, or better still, a banana from the silver dish that always stood on her buffet filled with fresh fruit. Once he'd asked Ma why they never had fruit like Grandmother's and had been told in no uncertain terms there wasn't money for such fancy things. Now and then, Ma might buy a banana or an orange apiece, but not often. They only ate the fresh fruit that was in season or what Ma had been able to can during the summer and fall. 'Course he never had dared ask Grandmother for a piece of fruit; hard tell what she'd a done, but he knew Ma would have whacked him for sure. He just bet Blanche got to have those things when she stayed there.

'Course, it wasn't too long ago that Grandmother had set Blanche in her proper place. Ralph laughed to himself as he recalled the incident. He and Blanche had been spending the afternoon at Grandmother's, and true to form, they had started bickering over something. Now, Grandmother hadn't liked this a little bit and had said, "Ralph, you sit in that chair and, Blanche, you take this one. You can sit there and look at each other and think about learning to get along without squabbling." Ralph had hastened to do his grandmother's bidding, but Blanche, being a mite spunky, had said, "I'll not sit in any old chair because of him. It was all his fault. I'll just go and see my grandmother Smith, I will."

Grandmother had looked like the wrath of God and had stated clearly and firmly, not even raising her voice, "Blanche Lenore Setterington, you will do no such thing. You will sit in that chair until I get good and ready to let you get out. And in the future, young lady, you will not sass your grandmother."

Grandmother and granddaughter had stared into each other's eyes for a moment that seemed an eternity to Ralph. Blanche had drawn herself up proudly and was very tempted to defy Lavina, but there was something in those intense eyes that made the child realize here was a will stronger than most, and she had better comply with her grandmother's order.

When Blanche turned and flounced over to the chair, Ralph had wanted to snicker, but the look on Grandmother's face stifled it before it even got started. Anyway, it did his heart good to see

Blanche put in her place for once; still, he couldn't help wondering why they all liked her best.

Ralph finally understood that his aunt Ruby was getting married to Mac. He didn't see why this was something to get so het up about. Seems he'd heard someone say they thought Lavina had given up hopes of Ruby ever catching a man, whatever that meant. Anyway, it sure was causing a commotion. Aunt Ruby was all right, he supposed; at least she acted as if he was just as good as Blanche. She still didn't hold a candle to Aunt Lorin, who liked him best. Seemed like it was a lot of fuss and bother just so's a woman could live with a man. Oliver McQuistion didn't impress Rate very much, and he'd heard Pa say he couldn't figure out what Ruby saw in the man since he'd never amount to much.

Blanche had been excited when she had learned that Aunt Ruby had set the date for her wedding to Mac. It was to be the fourth of August. Of course, she hadn't reckoned at all the furor it was to cause.

She had been to her grandmother's the day after Ruby and Lavina had gone to Owosso to buy the material for the wedding dress. How beautiful the material looked. Blanche was somewhat awed by it and could not resist lightly touching the brocaded satin. Grandmother had laid the material out on the dining room table and had pinned the pattern in place. Blanche sensed her grandmother's absorption with her work and had watched quietly from a chair in the corner. Finally, Lavina looked up at her granddaughter and spoke.

"Blanche, I just dread cutting into this material. I'm so afraid I'll make a mistake. I'd much rather have hired a seamstress, but Rate complained about all the expense, so I decided to make the dress myself. I used to turn a pretty fair seam, but I've not sewn on anything this lovely." Heaving a big sigh, she said, "Well, no use putting it off. Right now, I wish we had picked a simple pattern instead of one with a train, and there is the long veil too."

Blanche could think of nothing to say. It was the first time in her life that she had ever seen her grandmother show any indecisiveness. She watched as Lavina began to cut along the edge of the pattern. Grandmother usually looked stern, but right now she looked worried. Blanche even felt a little sorry for her.

Blanche lay on her bed pouting. She had known for weeks when Aunt Ruby was getting married and that Grandmother had saved money by making the wedding gown. Blanche had seen the finished product of the beautiful white, brocaded satin, and she was sure it would make Aunt Ruby look very beautiful. When they had been making plans for the wedding party and had mentioned flower girl, Blanche had felt certain this honor was to be hers. She was Aunt Ruby's only niece except for Uncle John's Frieda, who was only four months old, so it was only fitting that she be the one. My, wouldn't it be nice to be part of a real wedding. However, Grandmother had taken her aside and explained, "Blanche, your best dress is that little challis dress with the pink flowers, and it really isn't suited for a flower girl. Now, Fern Wooley has a silk dress that is much more appropriate, so we've asked her. We do have a rather important job for you. You are to stand at the head of the stairs and show the people where to put their wraps."

Well, if Grandmother wanted Fern just because Fern had a silk dress, she didn't care. Who wanted to be in any old wedding anyway. Important task, my foot. Who'd have wraps in August? Maybe Fern would get sick. At least the possibility was a pleasant thought.

The day of the wedding came, and Ralph was anything but enthused about having to get all dressed up when he'd rather have been out playing. Ma wouldn't let him voice his opinion and shushed him up when she'd stood him on the stove hearth, which made him just the right height so's she could wash his ears really good. Why'd mothers always think a boy's ears got so dirty anyhow?

There had been an early morning rehearsal for the wedding. Fern had been there with her hair still done up in rags so she could have long curls. Everyone left and would return only a short time before the ceremony—that is, everyone but Fern. When Lavina found her sitting where someone had put her to be out of the way, Fern was sent home to get bathed and changed. Mrs. Wooley didn't get the necessary ablutions made soon enough for Fern to return in time for the ceremony, which Lavina would not allow to be delayed for even one minute, flower girl or not. Blanche was secretly very pleased over the situation although she kept her thoughts to herself. She considered this some sort of justice.

Lavina never spoke a friendly word to Mrs. Wooley from that day on since Lavina was certain that had Mrs. Wooley felt the wedding was of sufficient importance, she could have had her daughter there at the designated hour. It was not often Lavina's wishes were thwarted.

The ceremony had been completely dull, and Ralph had fidgeted in his seat. Ma had scowled at him, and he'd had sense enough to stop. Now, they had all gone to Grandmother's for the wedding dinner they'd called it. Rate figured it was more like supper, but he didn't care what they called it as long as they ate. He was hungry.

The house was decorated with flowers, and there was a table set for Uncle John, Aunt Grace, and Ward; one for the bride and groom; Harry Squair, who was the best man; and Bertha McLaren, who was the bridesmaid; one for Grandmother and Grandfather; Elder Whitaker, his wife, and two lovely daughters; and he guessed Mac's folks; then one for Pa, Ma, Blanche, and himself. They'd all got sat down when Uncle John, whose table was way over in the sitting room, hollered, "Hey, Milt, what's these things? Rooster's eggs?"

He held up an olive that he had speared on the tines of his fork.

"Danged if I know, John. Could likely be judging from the size."

Grandmother had been speechless. Aunt Ruby looked furious. Ralph snickered, and Ma said sharply, "You hush." Uncle John and Pa were the only ones who seemed to think it funny although Rate thought Grandfather's eyes looked merry, like he was enjoying something. Rate hadn't known then what the things were, but he tasted one out of curiosity, and he figured whatever they were, they had been well worth putting on the table.

Elsie was one of the more-fortunate small villages in the respect that they had an opera house, owned by Van Deusen, which was located on the south side of Main Street, almost a block east of the grocery store.

Rate overheard his mother and father discussing it one night.

"Millie, have you read the notices for the next play at the opera house?"

"Ummm."

"Millie, are you listening to me?"

"What's that, Miney?"

"Just as I thought. You haven't heard a word I said. Do you know what is playing next Saturday at the opera house?"

"Can't say as I do."

"Harriet Beecher Stowe's *Uncle Tom's Cabin*."

"Hmmm."

"Millie, do you think we could go?"

"To a play? Whatever for?"

"Well—well, to enjoy it. You read the book same as I did, and now we could see live actors play the parts."

"Thought you didn't hold with actors and such."

"I usually don't. But this is different. Will you take me?"

"I guess if you've your heart set on it, we might. What do you think Ma and Pa would say?"

"There you go, afraid to do anything unless your parents approve. At Ladies Missionary Society, the women were discussing it, and your mother actually said they might attend. Seems she's read the book and thinks the subject matter is all right for folks to see."

Millie seemed relieved to hear this.

Miney, while glad he had so readily given his consent, still felt somewhat irritated that his first concern had been whether or not his parents would approve. If only Millie were just a mite more independent. Of course, some of the entertainment produced at the opera house was hardly what good Christians should be interested in, yet there were some programs she was sure were all right. Now, this one was based on a very prominent book that dealt with that abominable practice of slavery. Mina felt certain it would be worthwhile.

Miney had wondered just how well-behaved Ralph would be at a stage play since he sometimes fidgeted in church, and this would require that he stay seated much longer. She needn't have worried. There was enough activity on stage to hold his rapt attention. Once, he had stood up in his seat so he could see better over the lady with a rather large hat sitting in front of him.

Someone yelled, "Down in front."

Blanche turned to give a scathing look at the man who had hollered, then turned to her little brother and said, "Ralph, just you stand up if you want to. You paid just as much for your seat as he did for his."

It was Monday afternoon, and Blanche had gone with her grandmother to the depot to meet Aunt Ruby's train. Ruby was coming from St. Johns, where she and Mac lived since their marriage in August. She wanted to help Lavina with last-minute preparations for Christmas, which fell on Wednesday this year. Mac had to work, so he could not come until the afternoon of Christmas Eve.

Lavina was in a particularly affable mood, which Blanche found more than a trifle out of character. She attributed it to the fact that her grandmother hadn't seen much of Aunt Ruby since the wedding and now was looking forward to having Aunt Ruby spend a few days with her.

Aunt Ruby was loaded down with parcels, so both Lavina and Blanche helped carry them to the waiting cutter.

Back at the house, Ruby turned to Blanche.

"Blanche, how old are you now?"

"I was eight in July."

"That's what I thought. Tell me, do you still believe in Santa Claus?"

"What do you mean 'still believe,' Aunt Ruby? Of course I believe in Santa. He brings me presents ever year."

"Just as I thought. Mina wants you to be a child forever. You're certainly old enough to know the truth. Blanche, there is no Santa Claus. Your mother and father give you those presents."

"Oh, no, Aunt Ruby. Santa brings them 'cause I get presents from Ma and Pa besides. And he always puts something in our stockings, Ralph's and mine."

Ruby patiently explained to Blanche how it was all accomplished. Finally, the young girl said no more and went off by herself to wait for her father, who was coming to take her home. Her serene visage belied the turmoil inside.

She still wasn't absolutely sure Aunt Ruby wasn't spoofing. However, Aunt Ruby was not one to tease like Pa and Uncle John. Well, she'd ask Ma when she got home because she knew that although she might hedge just a little, her mother would tell her the truth.

Blanche was right. Miney did try to evade the question, but when she discovered her daughter was not about to be put off, she admitted that Ruby was right.

That night, when Blanche went to bed, she shed a few tears. Never again would Christmas seem quite so wonderful. She resented the fact that Aunt Ruby had seen fit to enlighten her and never quite forgave her aunt for so abruptly destroying her child's world.

Miney, on the other hand, was angry through and through. Ruby had stuck her nose into something that was none of her business, and Miney intended to tell her so. While Miney might be in awe of her mother-in-law, the same did not hold true for her sister-in-law. It was true that Miney had felt that this would probably be the last Christmas for Blanche to believe in Santa, and as such, Miney had expected it to be rather special. At around nine, the children at school began to talk, and usually a child began to ask too many questions. Ruby just had no right to interfere. She was becoming another Lavina, and Miney wasn't certain the world was ready for that.

When she expressed her thoughts to Millie, he shrugged his shoulders and said, "Ruby gets more like Ma every day. She thinks the world was made for her to run. You can't undo what's done, so you'll just have to make the best of it. Perhaps you can get Blanche interested in playing Santa for Ralph."

Miney did enlist Blanche's help in filling Ralph's stocking, and Blanche still hung hers because, of course, Ralph would still expect Santa not to overlook his sister. Blanche guessed it was fun because she knew her small brother would be excited. Oh, well, being eight and a half meant she did have to grow up a little, Blanche thought as she gave an audible sigh.

Mina's thoughts were still in a turmoil, and she sighed wistfully as she watched her daughter; she still resented the fact that Ruby had been the one to spoil this Christmas. At least Blanche had made the best of the situation, and as long as her daughter was happy, Miney was content.

Millie was certainly right. Ruby became more like her mother every day.

Heaven help us all, thought Miney.

Chapter 8

The year 1898 heralded a national crisis. On February 15, the battleship *Maine* blew up in Havana Harbor. All the ill feeling toward Spain came to the fore, and the entire country blamed the Spaniards for the death of the men aboard the ship. McKinley, probably influenced by an enraged and warlike American public, demanded Cuban independence. Spain refused. Congress went so far as to recognize the independence of Cuba and authorized the use of US military power to oust the Spaniards from Cuban soil. In retaliation, on April 24, 1898, Spain declared war.

"I tell you, Miney, this war broods nothing but ill will. We got no business sticking our nose into what shouldn't concern us."

"I thought it did concern us. What about the *Maine?*"

"Tarnation! No one knows for certain what did happen to it. Hardly seems likely the Spaniards would be that ignorant as to blow up one of our battleships, especially when it's anchored in their own harbor. No sir, war's just a waste of money and men."

"Well, then, President McKinley should have stopped it."

"Can't rightly blame the president. It was Congress that said they recognized Cuba's independence. Some of them are looking to line their pockets with money from war contracts. Such a waste. War is all wrong. It wastes lives as well as money. It's the poor man who gets to fight, while the rich man only gets richer. It just isn't right at all."

Rate sat at the supper table listening to his parents talking. Blanche was home, and while he was always told children were to be seen and not heard, she was allowed to enter into grown-up talk some of the time. They especially listened to her when she came home on weekends during the school year. Oh, well, he guessed he could understand that since she always had lots of news, but there were times when he'd liked to have asked questions, yet he daren't.

"Pa, have you ever heard of houses being lighted by something called electricity?"

"There's been some talk about that. Some man by the name of Westinghouse built some sort of contraption by Niagara Falls that folks say makes electricity, and some folks have it for lights in their houses. It'll never last. Why, I've read that that there electricity goes on wires from place to place. It just don't seem right, putting up a lot of poles to string wire on."

"My teacher says that someday all of our houses will be lit by electricity. Grandfather said he'd have to see it work first, and then, he might be interested."

"Lots of people have tried lots of things that didn't work. Just like that there horseless carriage, those things they call automobiles. From what I hear, they are a lot more trouble than they're worth. At least a body don't never have trouble starting a horse"—he chuckled—"unless he's balky that is."

"But, Millie, men always keep improving things. Just think how the binder saves you so much work, and ours is a better one than your father had."

"True, Miney, the one Pa and Grandfather had was a wire-tie affair, but still it was certainly a great improvement over using a scythe and cradle. However, I still say that man can only improve things so much, and I don't think automobiles and electric lights will ever work out. Just mark my words."

Blanche didn't say any more for the way Pa had said those last words, gave no doubt that the subject was closed. However, Blanche was inclined to believe what she had heard in school, and Grandfather had thought the whole thing was possible. Just imagine, they said that with electric lights, you pushed a switch and a light came on, you pushed another one and the light went off. No more stinky, old, kerosene lamps to fill, no more smoked-up chimneys to wash each morning, no more wicks to trim, or if it was a gas lamp, no more having to be careful not to break the mantles or having to pump it up so's there'd be light.

The whole idea seemed very wondrous to a young girl.

Rate hadn't paid a great deal of attention to this talk. He had no idea what electricity was, and he didn't really care. He went to bed shortly after the lamps were lit in the wintertime, so he didn't much care what kind they were. He'd heard some men and Pa talking about these horseless carriages before, and they didn't sound all that great. He liked horses and couldn't see what was wrong with them. How could a boy pet a machine? And it sure wouldn't come when he called. Of course, he didn't suppose they kicked like some of the horses Pa got when he traded. Still, there hadn't been many whose stall Rate had not dared enter.

Rate had been trying to amuse himself and as yet had found nothing he wanted to do. As he sat on the steps of the north porch, a small kitten came edging cautiously up to him and finally crawled up on his lap. Ralph had absently stroked the small furry bundle. Then, he began to move his finger and laughed to himself as the kitten batted at his finger with her paws. However, he soon tired of this.

Next, he went to the toolshed, carrying the kitten in one arm, and procured a length of binder twine from the grain binder. He returned to the porch, set the kitten down, and proceeded to tie one end of the twine around the cat's neck. A few moments later, he put the other end of the twine over the door handle of the kitchen door and pulled it enough to raise the kitten off the ground by the string around its neck. He gave the kitten a push and watched it swing back and forth, clawing and scratching as best it could against the ever-tightening twine around its neck.

Just then, the present hired girl, Sarah Perkins, came onto the porch. She noted what Ralph was doing. With a cry of, "You stop that," she yanked Ralph away, released the poor kitten, and then bent Rate over her knee to paddle his backsides.

"You wicked little boy. What were you trying to do? Choke that poor little kitten to death?"

"'Course not. I was only pretending the kitten was a clock. I didn't mean to hurt it, honest."

"What is going on?" asked Miney from the doorway.

"Ma, Sarah licked me," Ralph stated indignantly.

"Land's sakes, Sarah, whatever was he up to now?"

"He near killed a kitten, that's what. Had this here twine tied around its neck, the tuther end tied around the doorknob, and was swinging that poor kitten back and forth like this."

She demonstrated with the twine just how the kitten had been moving. As always, her movements were quick and jerky.

"Why, that knot was gettin' tighter an' tighter. Wouldn't have been no time at'all afore that poor kitten would have choked to death, an' him just standin' there laughin'. I sure did wallop his backsides, Mrs. Setterington, but he deserved it."

"All right, Sarah, you go back to your work. I'll settle this with him."

Rate looked at the wrath in his mother's face and wondered if he might get a licking from her. He eyed her suspiciously, waiting for her to make the first move.

"Well, now, Ralph Setterington, whatever made you do such a thing?"

"I dunno, Ma. I didn't intend to hurt the kitten. I like kittens. I was just pretending it was the pend'lum on a clock."

"A clock! But goodness, Ralph, how'd you like to be tied up by your neck?"

"I-I-I guess I wouldn't. I didn't know the twine would get tighter either. I didn't mean to choke her."

He was almost in tears. Miney sensed the boy was truly sorry, and she felt certain he had not done such a thing out of cruelty. Her tone softened somewhat as she continued.

"Let that be a lesson to you. After this, don't you do anything without first asking yourself if anything or anyone is going to be hurt by what you do. You hear?"

"Yes, Ma."

Golly, he had never intended to stir up such a fracas.

Mina returned to her work shaking her head as she thought, *That boy just always finds something to do that's wrong. Good thing Sarah found him before the kitten died.* Miney had always liked cats, so she felt a little more upset over his antics today than usual. She did believe he hadn't lied when he told her he hadn't meant to hurt the kitten. Ralph liked animals too much to maliciously harm one.

It was the middle of May, and the spring planting was progressing nicely. Millie had broadcast a piece of oats north of the barn where last year's corn had been, and now the field looked fresh and green. The field south of the house was partly plowed for the corn they would plant come Decoration Day. There had been sufficient rain so the timothy fields were already lush with renewed vegetation. Of course, no one realized better than Millie just how quickly what started off as a productive year could change into a particularly adverse year—drought during the summer months, an overly wet season at harvesttime. The farmer was completely dependent on the forces of nature for his livelihood. Sometimes, his hours of backbreaking labor went for nought.

Millie came into the house with an expression on his tanned face that bordered on anger. Miney looked up from her patching, noted his angry countenance, so held her tongue and waited for him to speak.

He struck his fist in the palm of his hand.

"Durned fool kid. If that isn't the most foolish thing I've ever heard of. Can't talk any sense into him no matter how I try. Wants adventure, excitement, to see far-off places, and the list is endless. Just won't listen to reason."

"Whatever are you talking about?"

Millie stopped his pacing and looked at his wife as if seeing her for the first time.

"It's that Ray Sawyer. That's what I'm talking about."

"What has he done? Ray's such a fine young man. I've never known him to shirk his work."

"'Course he don't shirk his work. He's one of the best hired men we've ever had. Well, he and that Lona Huffman, they went and enlisted in the Army, that's what he's done."

"Oh, Millie. Whatever for?"

"Blamed if I know. I've talked till I'm blue in the face to change his mind. You know how I feel about war, Miney. Nothing but a complete waste, and they've never solved any problems yet, only made more. I'm so angry, I could take that young whelp by the scruff of the neck and shake him until his teeth rattle. Only it wouldn't do a whit of good."

"When do they leave?"

"The end of next week."

"So soon? Blanche is going to be upset, I can tell you. She thinks the sun rises and sets in Ray. He's always doing something for her."

"I know. We'll all miss him. Don't suppose I'll have any trouble finding another hired hand, but it is a shame to lose such a capable one for just plain foolishness."

With that, Millie turned on his heel and stalked out of the house.

"Ma, Ma, guess what Ray is going to do for me?" shouted Blanche as she came running into the house. The screen door closed with a bang.

"Blanche, for heaven's sake, do be a little more ladylike. Now, what is it you wanted?"

Blanche tried to control her enthusiasm. "I just wanted you to know that Ray told me he was going to put up a swing after tonight's chores. He found a length of rope in the barn, and he says it's long enough and strong enough."

"Now, Blanche, have you been pestering Ray? You know both he and your pa will be dead tired. They'll have spent a long day in the field."

"Oh, no, Ma. Ray vol…vol—"

"Volunteered?"

"That's it. He volunteered without my even asking. 'Course he knowed I had asked Pa if I might have a swing. And, Ma, I do want one ever so much."

"Well, I suppose Ray wants to do it, or he wouldn't have suggested it. He certainly is a nice young man. If only he hadn't joined the Army. He won't be with us much longer, you know."

"I know. Ma, I'm going to miss him." Her face saddened, and tears welled in her eyes. "I don't know why he wants to leave us. Pa's never had anyone work here who is as nice to me."

"Perhaps his leaving is one reason he wants to get your swing up. It will give you something to remember him by."

That evening, after chores, Ray shinnied up the cottonwood tree with a length of rope coiled over one shoulder. He swung up onto the first limb, which had conveniently grown horizontally away from the trunk for some two feet or so before stretching skyward. Ray cautiously removed the rope and knotted one end to the limb only a few inches from the trunk. As he wound the other end around the limb, he looked down to judge the distance the loop of the rope was from the ground.

"Blanche, you sit on the rope and see if it is high enough. Now remember, when we put a board on it for a seat, it will be a little higher. Of course, you are a growing girl, so you don't want it too close to the ground."

Complying with his instructions, Blanche managed to sit on the rope. Ray drew it higher until her feet barely touched the ground.

"There, sweetie. Be careful getting out." He knotted the rope securely, slid down one side to stand once more on the ground. "Now, Blanche, we have to make a seat. I know there's a board in the woodshed, but I have to cut it to the right length."

Blanche tagged along and watched as Ray sawed off a fifteen-inch piece from a board eight inches wide. Next, he cut a notch in each end, and back they went to the dangling rope. Ray placed the seat in position, the notches holding it in place; it was higher than he thought, but he felt it would suffice.

"Oh, Ray, it looks wonderful." She jumped excitedly and clapped her hands. "Can I try it?"

"Of course, that's why I made it. Here. Let's see if you need help."

Blanche backed up to the swing, and the board promptly swung away from her body.

"Look, Blanche, grab the rope up higher. Now, give a little jump and then lower yourself onto the seat." She tried and failed. "Try it again. It takes a little practice. There. That's my girl. Now, I'll give you a swing."

Ray pulled her forward and then quickly released her. He stepped behind her and pushed her higher and higher. Millie and Miney came to the doorway as they heard her squeals of delight. When she got out, she ran to Ray, and he picked her up in his arms to receive a bear hug and a somewhat shy kiss on the cheek.

"Thank you, Ray. It's the best swing anyone ever had."

"Well, thank you, little princess. Just don't you forget who put it up for you when I'm far away."

"I'll never forget you," she said solemnly.

It was Saturday morning when Lona Huffman came by to pick up Ray and his belongings. Rate wasn't all that interested in the boys leaving, but he was absorbed with watching the colt Lona had tied to the hitching post. It was hitched to a light cart. For the first few minutes, the colt stood quietly, then he began to step sideways, toss his head, back up, put his head down, just anything he could think of to do. He tried to turn around; while he couldn't exactly maneuver this, he did manage to tip the small cart over on its side and become entangled in the harness and the rope used to tie him to the post. Ralph thought it was funny watching the young men work to extricate the colt and set the cart to rights again.

Blanche had seen nothing humorous in any of the activity. Ray had picked her up and given her a big hug. She just knew he was the nicest young man she would ever know, and she felt like crying because he was leaving—only he was so cheerful, it was hard to be sad for long. At least she smiled and waved until he was out of sight; then, she disappeared into her room where she shed tears profusely to assuage the hurt.

Blanche had moped around for several days after Ray and Lona left. Miney surmised what was wrong although the girl said nothing. She spent hours swinging, or often as not, just sitting in the swing, her hands holding the ropes, with her head tipped to the side resting on her hand—a dejected little creature indeed. Miney had tried to enlist Blanche's aid in baking cookies or kneading bread, something she usually wanted to help do, all to no avail. Blanche remained completely unresponsive and didn't even get angry with Ralph when he teased.

Since Sarah had promised to stay for a spell with an ailing relative, Miney had Ethel Putman come in two or three days a week, but she always went home come evening. Ethel noticed the young girl's preoccupation, so she mentioned it to Miney. Upon being told the reason, Ethel asked if she might try to do something to cheer Blanche. She had Miney's wholehearted approval.

The next day that Ethel came, she hurried with her cleaning and then approached Blanche, who was once again sitting listlessly in the swing.

"Blanche, your dolls are beginning to look awfully seedy. Why, if I was their mother, I'd say they need some new clothes."

"But, Ethel, I can't make them any. I don't know how."

"Well, now, supposing I teach you. Look. I've even brought some scraps of material which will do right well."

Blanche slid out of the swing to come peer into the sack. "Oh, Ethel, such pretty colors. When can we start?"

"No time like the present. You decide which color for which doll."

Miney was forever grateful to Ethel for the way the young woman made doll clothes for Blanche's dolls. It kept the girl interested for several days, and with the true resiliency of the young, Blanche no longer mourned for her friend. She even began to speak of Ray again; she was proud to know someone who was in the Army. When one day she had a letter from Ray, she bubbled over with joy.

Rate knew his father had cut logs last winter that hadn't been used in the stoves because they were still piled by the sheep shed. It had seemed odd to him, but they had also served as a place for him to play. As long as he didn't knock any of them down, he knew Pa didn't care if he crawled around on them. Now, it seemed he was finally to learn what was to be done with them because Pa was loading the logs on the wagon. Ralph watched his father from a safe distance. He'd liked to have asked what Pa was going to do, but experience told him that Millie was too busy to be bothered by a small boy's questions.

Millie finally threw the last one on the wagon, paused to wipe his brow on a large red bandana handkerchief, looked at Rate, and said, "Whew! Oak is mighty heavy wood. I can see that you're wondrin' what I'm going to do. Just supposing you climb up on the wagon, and I'll show you."

"But where are you going?"

"Never mind. You'll see. Don't you want to go?"

"Oh, yes, Pa. I'll go."

"Get up there then."

Rate climbed hastily onto the wagon box while Millie picked up the lines and climbed up beside the boy. He clucked to the team and drove up to the house.

"Miney," he called and, when she appeared at the kitchen door, added, "Rate's going with me. We'll be back in plenty of time for supper."

Not waiting for her reply, he slapped the lines and turned the team north out of the driveway.

His destination was the stave mill at Bannister where he figured he'd get a good price for this load of oak that had lain and seasoned all these months. Millie thought perhaps Rate would benefit from watching the men make staves. The lad was never any trouble when Millie took him along, and Millie was sure he'd like the outing.

As he glanced at his son, the thought crossed Millie's mind that Ralph seemed small. Well, maybe it was because Millie wasn't that used to young ones, but it didn't seem that Rate was as big as he'd been at the same age. He didn't look much like a Setterington either except maybe around the eyes. His nose and face resembled Miney, not that Millie minded because he thought she was a mighty fine-looking woman. However, he did hope the boy would be at least as large as Pa. It would seem odd if there was to be a "small" Setterington. Uncle Albert's boys, John and Willie, had always been large for their age and were growing into tall, broad-shouldered, heavy-set young men much like himself. Oh, well, there wasn't a dadblamed thing anyone could do about it. Still, it didn't keep a man from wishing. Besides, how could he impress Pa if his son was small and weak?

Now that the lad was almost five, Millie would have liked another child. However, he knew better than to even mention his desire to his wife. She constantly reminded him that since they had both a boy and a girl, they were fortunate indeed and needed no more children. He knew Blanche had never quite liked having a little brother, but Rate now, he'd get a lot of enjoyment out of another boy in the family. No, best he count his blessings and leave well enough alone. Miney was just not the type of woman to have a whole brood. Seemed odd too since both her ma and her pa had liked children so much. Why, Mother Smith always enjoyed having youngsters around, and the neighbor children would drop in to pass the time of day since Doc died and she lived alone. She was always quick to have a cookie for a little visitor, and they never were afraid of her.

'Course, Mother Smith just looked a lot more pleasant and friendly than Ma. He couldn't really imagine a young child dropping in to pass the time of day with his mother, and yet, she had enjoyed having children of her own. Just whatever way you looked at it, women were hard to understand. Miney was really a good wife, and he had no real complaints. He knew she felt their intimate life was only to be tolerated, not enjoyed, but he guessed that was the way a proper-brought-up woman was. Leastways, she seldom complained.

It was only a few weeks since Millie had moved the small, old granary to the north eighty. He had decided to build a larger one, along with a toolshed on one side, to meet the growing needs of more tillable land. Millie was busy sharpening a hoe on the grindstone. The round stone wheel fitted into a stand and could be turned by a person who sat on the seat and pushed the pedal. He looked up when a young man approached. Millie looked the newcomer over skeptically. Must be about twenty; his clothes were old and patched although they were clean. His shirt was faded to a near gray; the material looked thin from wear. The pleasant face was thin and boyish, the frame sparse and wiry.

"Mr. Setterington?"

"Yup. What can I do for you?"

"I was told you owned that building north of here across from the Garretts."

"That's right."

"I was…I was wonderin' if me an' my wife could rent it for the summer?"

"What for?"

"To live in. We've only been married for a few months, and I've not been able to get steady work. Some of the farmers hereabouts said I could work for them a day or so at a time. I'd like to be close by since we don't own a horse."

"But it's only an old granary. There's no water, no nothin' except a floor, four walls, and a roof."

"I know. We don't have much furniture either. There's a hole to the back where we could put a stovepipe out. We'd manage, Mr. Setterington. Mr. Garrett said we was welcome to fetch water from their place."

Millie liked the cut of the young fellow. He had an honest, clean look. Must be really down on his luck if he was willing to live in those primitive conditions.

"Tell you what. I didn't get your name."

"Luke. Luke Black."

"Well, Luke, it sure isn't much. I'll let you stay there for a dollar and fifty cents a month. How'd that be?"

"Gosh, Mr. Setterington, that ain't hardly enough. I can pay what it's worth." He drew himself up proudly. "Me an' my Mary, we ain't askin' for charity. I reckon to pay my load."

"Realistically, boy, it isn't worth much. Nope, a dollar fifty suits me fine."

The young face broke into a wide grin.

"Thank you, Mr. Setterington. It sure is a deal." He grabbed Millie's hand and pumped it vigorously. "Yessir, it's a deal."

The next day, Luke and Mary moved their meager belongings into the building.

Susie Garrett confided to Miney that she had watched from across the road and then had gone over with a loaf of freshly baked bread. She had noted a beat-up, old bed, a battered dresser, a rickety kitchen table, a couple of straight-backed chairs, and the cookstove. Some boxes served as cupboards. However, she was quick to add, the tablecloth was spotless, and although the quilt looked worn and scarcely serviceable, it was clean. The girl looked younger than her husband and was a shy, sweet little thing. She had been grateful for the bread, said she wasn't all that good at baking yet. Susie explained that she had invited Mary over to watch the next time she baked. Susie had a generous nature, and Miney was certain she would give Mary pointers on how to bake good bread.

Several days later, Miney missed Ralph. She called and called, but got no response. Millie had not seen the lad, and Blanche volunteered that the last time she had seen him, he had been playing by the oak tree at the edge of the north drive.

Miney had a hunch. Ralph had been consumed with curiosity about the young couple who had moved into the old granary across from the Garretts. He had wondered how they got along with no windows, only a sliding door, no water and no toilet. Miney had explained as best she could. She told him that Millie and Ezz had given Luke some old scrap lumber to build some semblance of an outhouse; they carried their water from the Garretts, and she did suppose it was pretty bad not having any windows because she was certain the flies really swarmed through the door, which was usually open since it was the only source of daylight.

Recalling this, Miney set off down the road. Just wait, if that child was there, she'd make certain he would never want to run away again. The angrier she got, the faster she walked.

Sure enough, there was Ralph sitting in the doorway talking to the young woman who sat beside him. Miney found herself a switch from a patch of brush along the roadside, near the rail fence, then continued determinedly.

Rate looked up with some misgivings. Ma sure did look mad. Then, he spied the switch in Miney's hand. He jumped up, said a hasty goodbye to Mary, and started for the road. Miney made a quick feint and caught him. She hastily explained the situation to the startled girl and then started Rate for home, switching his legs as he went. Miney also made it perfectly clear to her small son that he was never to run off again. He was to ask permission. As Ralph moved faster, so did Miney, and the switch moved with regularity. His bare legs were covered with red welts by the time they reached the house. Now, to add insult to injury, Miney made her son sit in a chair to give him time to contemplate his misdeed.

Rate had sobbed most of the way home although mostly from anger. Now, he wiped his tearstained face with a grimy hand, leaving a streak of dirt down the side of his face. He sat in silence, staring indignantly at his mother. Miney was tempted to laugh. He did look comical. However, he just had to learn that a lad of four and a half was not old enough to go traipsing around the countryside by himself. She knew he resented his punishment. Well, perhaps he had learned his lesson—at least she fervently hoped so.

"Ma, ain't I never gonna be old enough to take my own bath? I bet Don Sherman don't have his mother washin' him."

"Well, land's sakes, I suppose you could try. But don't you dare splash water all over the floor, and you make sure you scrub yourself to get clean. Your ears always need extra work."

Miney had brought the washbowl into the kitchen and had filled it with warm water from the reservoir. She had tested it with her finger and found it to be just right so had started to lather up the washrag while Rate finished getting out of his clothes.

"Just look at your dirty feet. I am behind with things as I still have a little bit of hem to put in in Blanche's dress. All right. Get washed, and don't forget to dry yourself well before you put on your clean clothes." With those directions, Miney left to finish her sewing.

Rate surveyed the situation somewhat skeptically. He knew he'd better get himself clean because he was sure his mother meant to inspect almost every inch of him looking for any spot he might have missed. Well, no use to sit and ponder; he might as well get started. He had already stripped off his clothes, so he dipped the washrag into the warm water and did his own lathering. Golly, but his feet were the dirtiest, guess he'd start there. He took the washbowl off the chair very carefully, set it on the floor, sat in the chair, and put one foot in the water. He took the soap and began to scrub. When that foot looked much cleaner, he wiped it dry, noting the black marks on the towel, and washed the other foot. Well, that much of him was clean. What was it Ma had said about behind his ears? Guess he'd tackle that next. He sure was proud of the good job done on his feet.

"Ralph, how are you coming?"

"Just fine, Ma."

Guess he'd best hurry afore she thought she had to come for a look-see. Now, how was a boy supposed to know if his ears were clean since even in the mirror he couldn't see them lessen he had eyes on the side of his head. Boy, Ma had stood him up on that cookstove hearth from the time he could remember, just to dig at his ears and behind them. Didn't seem as though she'd ever worried that much about Blanche's ears. It was some small consolation that he was now getting big enough so he could stand on the floor. Somehow, it seemed more befitting his age even if he did have to suffer the indignity of having his mother wash him. Maybe if he showed her what a good job he could do, she'd not bother with him anymore. He heaved a sigh. Somehow, he just felt as though she'd still not trust him to do the job. Mothers were peculiar about some things, he guessed.

Mina was indeed in a hurry. It was Saturday and their regular day for doing next week's grocery buying. She also had an appointment at the church to practice for tomorrow's services with Cap and Flo Rummel and Richard Fizzell. For some time now, the four of them had been furnishing special music about once a month. In fact, they had even been asked to sing at other meetings around town. Folks had been quite generous with their praise. Of course, that was just because most folks couldn't sing harmony like the four of them did. She didn't really remember how they'd got started, but it was rewarding. Miney did love to sing, and she thoroughly enjoyed singing in church.

Whether it was because she was indeed pressed for time, or whether Ralph had done a respectable job of washing himself, he was never sure, but at least he had passed one more milestone in his life. Never again was his mother to bathe him. To be sure, there were times when he had to stand inspection, ears were checked as well as hands and wrists because somehow she found that small boys often considered their hands as the palms only. Still, he couldn't help feeling proud that he had one less thing for which to depend on his mother. It seemed only right since there were so many chores she had considered him big enough to do.

Millie had been awakened during the early morning hours by his wife's restless moving in bed. At first, when he had roused with a start, he had thought he had slept beyond his rising time of four thirty, and had felt slightly annoyed. He was a man who prided himself on being able to wake up at the same time each day, summer and winter, without the use of an alarm clock. He had often voiced the sentiment that he "wouldn't have an alarm clock in his house." As far as he was concerned, they were an unneeded contraption. However, he quickly realized that Miney was sick.

"Miney, what ails you?"

"It's my stomach, Millie. I've taken some of that medicine the doctor gave me, but I'll never be one whit of good to anyone today. Whatever will we do with men here to feed?"

"Blanche will just have to do the best she can. It isn't as though it was threshers, there won't be but five extra."

"But, Millie, she's only a child. Won't you see if you can get Lena? Or perhaps Frankie could come."

"She'll manage. Now, you try to rest and don't worry. You know you are only worse when you're upset. It will all work out. You'll see."

Mina often had these spells with her stomach. Sometimes, the pain was almost constant, and her stomach felt on fire. The medicine helped, and a very bland diet returned her to normal although it usually resulted in one whole day of bed rest.

Lucky it was that Blanche was home for the weekend. Sarah Perkins, who often stayed on as the hired girl, had been let go elsewhere as things were kind of slack until butchering time. Ethel Putman, who was not really a very strong person, had been helping some, but she was not due back for two days. Ralph could give his sister help with running errands, and he could certainly help with the stove. They'd manage.

Millie called Blanche earlier than usual. When she came downstairs, albeit somewhat sleepily, he explained the situation.

"Blanche, your ma's laid up with her stomach complaint today, and I've got five extree men coming to cut wood. It will be up to you to get the meal. Your ma's got the baking done, and she can tell you what to have since we bought everything in town yesterday."

"But, Pa, I can't cook good enough for menfolk. I only help Ma, I've never cooked anything without her being there to watch me.

Mostly, I just set table and things like that while she does the cooking. I never cooked meat or made gravy. I just can't do it."

"You'll have to. There's no one else."

"Pa, I just can't do it with no help. Honest, I don't know enough," came the imploring reply as the young girl looked into the set face of her father.

"Blanche, are you a Setterington?"

"'Course I am, Pa, you know that, but—"

"Then stiffen your spine, girl, and act like a Setterington. You'll do what needs being done."

Blanche felt a sinking feeling. She knew Pa would not try to get any help from the neighbor women. He considered her old enough and knowledgeable enough to take care of the situation. Why oh why did Ma have to have one of her spells today of all days? Still, she did feel sorry for Ma because she knew her mother was always in a deal of pain, and it would be several days before her eating could return to normal.

Ma was never one to complain about not being able to eat the things she cooked for the rest of the family either. Blanche loved her mother dearly, and if not always a thoughtful daughter, she did have her moments of considerateness. She peeked into the bedroom and saw her mother's drawn face; she knew Miney would prefer not to have to answer a bunch of questions, and yet, how was she supposed to do everything all by herself without asking questions?

If only Pa wasn't so blamed set in his ways. She bet Mrs. Garrett or Lena Clark or maybe Mrs. Sherman or even Mrs. Hiers would have put aside their own work to help out a neighbor. But would Pa ask? Not him. Be independent, depend on no one but yourself, ask no favors—more than once she'd heard him expound these views. Well, it didn't help his young daughter even a little bit; and right now, Blanche felt very, very young, inexperienced, and more than somewhat discouraged. However, she angrily brushed away a tear that had begun to trickle out of a corner of her eye, squared her shoulders, heaved an audible sigh, got a pan, and started to the cellar for potatoes—she knew it would take a large amount, and my, she did peel slowly.

Whether the men found the meal to their liking, they ate heartily. Blanche had done her best and had tried to bother her mother as little as possible with questions. If the meat was a little tough, the gravy more than a little lumpy, the potatoes boiled to such a degree of doneness that they broke into pieces when speared with a fork, and the squash a little soupy because she hadn't been able to drain it all that well, the men made no comment. Even Ralph kept a civil tongue in his head and found no fault, seeming to sense that his sister had been called upon to do a task that was greater than one of her tender years should have been asked to perform.

Millie was proud of his young daughter although he failed to tell her so.

Rate listened as his mother and father discussed the expected apple crop.

"Miney, I don't ever recall all of the trees bearing like they have this year. There's a heap more apples than will keep in the cellar. Ed said we was welcome to put some up in their basement, but I figure even that wouldn't be enough."

"What do you intend to do? I hate the thought of them going to waste. I've made enough crabapple and snowapple jelly to last us this year and part of next. I've canned sweet apples and applesauce until I'm blue in the face. Still, it seems a shame not to use them."

"You know I just sold that oak, so I reckon I'll go to the cooper shop and buy a couple of barrels and have some cider made."

"Milford, I don't want you drinking hard cider. You know I don't approve of spirits."

"Oh, it will keep a long time if I wait until the weather is getting nippy before we have it made. Besides, a couple of barrels won't last long. There will be men here again to help cut wood, and I'm sure they'll be glad to help drink it. We can always keep some to make vinegar too. There's still going to be a pile of apples left, so I think we'll pit them this year."

"That's a lot of work, but I guess it is worth it."

After Millie left, Rate asked his mother what Pa had meant by "pit them."

"He'll dig a hole in the ground to keep them in. They'll keep good until spring that way."

Somehow, this didn't quite make sense to Ralph. What good was it going to be if the apples were covered with dirt? He guessed he'd just have to wait and watch while Pa was doing the work. Pa was always telling him to keep his mouth shut and his eyes open to find out something.

First, Millie dug a large pit west of the cellar, next he lined the hole with straw. Then, Ralph watched as his father and Charlie picked apples and dumped crate after crate of the shiny red apples, flecked with white, into the hole. When the hole was nearly full, they covered the apples with a thick layer of straw; on top of that, they forked a layer of horse manure brought from the barn, and then they covered the whole thing with dirt. Rate had watched the process with interest. He never did know why they put in the horse manure, but there must have been a reason, he figured.

Millie spoke to his son as he threw on the last shovelful of earth.

"Well, boy, there's a lot of good eating covered up there. There will be pies and applesauce and baked apples and apple pudding and apples just for eating. I can see you don't quite believe it, but just you wait and see how nice those apples will be come February or March. The way you like baked apple, you'll be mighty glad we put them away, just you wait and see."

"Won't they freeze when it gits real cold?"

"Nope. They'll be just as nice as they are today. An apple keeps best when they're cold, yet not cold enough to freeze."

During the winter months, Ralph began to wonder if Pa intended to eat the whole crop of apples by himself. They had stored a goodly number of crates in the cellar, and when Ralph watched them stacked away, he'd wondered if they'd even bother to uncover those in the pit since it looked like they had enough apples for the whole countryside. However, Millie would often take a pan from the kitchen, disappear into the cellar, and come back with eight or ten apples; he'd sit in his rocker and begin to pare apples. He peeled them tissue paper thin, starting at the stem, going round and round, seldom breaking the peel until he reached the blossom end. To Rate's utter amazement, night after night, he watched his father devour apples, the last one seeming to be as tasteful as the first. Now, Ralph liked baked apples, he liked them in pies, he liked applesauce, but he never cared much for an apple out of hand.

The Thomas house across from the athletic field was under quarantine. Their two young daughters had come down with the dreaded diphtheria. The whole village was deeply concerned. No one knew with any degree of certainty how the disease was spread, but they did know that children were most often afflicted, and that it was nearly always fatal.

Miney knew the family and had remembered them in her prayers each night. Goodness, what if her own two children lay sick of the awful disease? How her heart went out to the Thomases.

Millie, Miney, and the children were driving to town to do the usual week's shopping. As they neared the Thomas property, Miney turned to give instructions to Ralph and Blanche.

"Now, when I tell you to begin, you are to hold your breath until we get by. Don't want you breathing any of that contaminated air. Do you understand?"

Both children solemnly shook their heads.

"Now! Hold your breath. Millie, drive faster, or they won't be able to hold their breath long enough."

Millie touched the horse lightly with the whip, and she broke into a fast trot.

"That's better. We're almost by. Just a little more."

Both children's faces were turning pink with the effort, and they clasped their hands over their mouths in an effort to do as they had been bidden.

"There. Now, you can breathe."

Blanche and Ralph alike gulped air, and their chests heaved with the effort to fill their lungs. Goodness, if they were going to have to do this on the way home, they both hoped Pa would drive a little faster. Ma sure would have been mad if they'd caught their breath before she told them to do so.

A few days later, Blanche learned that both small girls had died; and since they had had diphtheria, they had had to be taken out at midnight when there would be little likelihood of encountering anyone and quietly buried. Poor little tykes, not even a funeral, no one but the mother and father to lament their passing. It made Blanche feel very sad.

Sometimes, Blanche wondered why God did as He did. What had those tiny girls done to have deserved such a death? Certainly they were too young to have been sinful. Had He been punishing the parents? If He intended to take the girls at such an early age, why had He given them to Mr. and Mrs. Thomas in the first place? Somehow, it did not seem at all fair. Blanche knew that her mother would have been upset if she had known her daughter was questioning the will of God. However, Blanche did not always find that she could blindly accept Miney's explanation that "God has His reasons." Perhaps when she was older, she would understand better; although for the time being, she had a lot of unanswered questions, and she didn't dare ask anyone for an answer.

CHAPTER 9

Rate was absorbed in watching his father. Millie had cleaned and oiled his ten gauge shotgun and was now in the process of loading a supply of ammunition for the next day's hunting trip.

"Pa, why you doin' that?"

"Just keep your mouth shut and your eyes open and you'll find out."

So he asked his father no more questions and was careful not to get in Millie's way.

Millie took the brass shell casing, pushed out the old primer and inserted a new one, poured in a measured amount of black gunpowder, shoved in the wadding, poured in what looked to Ralph like small BBs, then put in another piece of wadding. Rate wondered if it was hard work. It didn't look like much when he saw Pa do it. He would've liked to have asked his father how he knew the amount of gunpowder needed, only he daren't. He didn't think Grandfather hunted, so Pa must have learned it somewhere else. He also wondered what would have happened if a body put in too much gunpowder.

As if in answer to his unasked question, Millie explained, "Now you see, Rate, you use only this much gunpowder. Too much is dangerous, and not enough doesn't give enough distance to do a whit of good. I always measure it carefully so's my shells are all loaded the same. Some fellows aren't that particular, and then, they wonder why their shells don't always fire right."

Millie was still loading shells when Mina reminded Ralph it was high time he was in bed.

Rate dreaded going away from the warmth of the fire to a freezing, drafty bedroom and a cold bed. He had liked it better last year when he still slept downstairs. When the wind had blown real hard from the northeast during the year's first heavy snowstorm, there'd been a pile of snow on the floor by his bed, and he'd been too sleepy to notice and had stepped in it with his bare feet. Now, that was something to bring a fellow awake in a hurry, let me tell you. He'd learned his lesson, and now he didn't budge from under the covers until he had properly surveyed the scene.

At night, he always undressed upstairs, but come morning, he grabbed his clothes from off the chair and hightailed it down the stairs as fast as his legs would carry him to dress by the warmth of the stove. Sometimes, he tried covering up head and all; but then, he'd felt like he was going to smother, so he'd had to poke his nose out from under the heavy quilts. At least the feather bed would squish up around his body, and the corn husk mattress made a pleasant squeaking sound as he shifted his weight, so when he finally got settled, it wasn't so bad.

It was that first shock of the cold flannel sheets that usually woke him up even though he'd been awfully drowsy by the fire downstairs. However, at times like these, he thought of the farm he'd one day have, or the hunting and trapping he'd do when he got a little bigger. Someday, Pa was sure to buy him a rifle and maybe even a shotgun. Someday, he'd raise horses, not running horses like Grandfather raised or the pacers and trotters, Hambletonians they was called, like Pa raised, but good solid workhorses, and he'd not trade his all the time; he'd keep two teams, and they'd be matched, maybe strawberry roans or blacks with a white blaze or perhaps dapple gray, he wasn't sure which.

It didn't take long for thoughts like these to induce sleep, and Ralph slept the peaceful sleep of the very young, no worries or cares beset his slumber, and if he dreamed, they were the pleasant dreams of youth.

Rate had been restless all afternoon and had kept watch out of the north window hoping to see a wagon coming along the road. There hadn't been enough snow yet for anyone to get out sleighs or cutters for travel. He'd seen the Garretts go by with the buggy and Tabors, but no wagon as yet.

Millie had gone off early that morning with Clayt Sherman and a couple of other neighbors to go in north of Bannister hunting rabbits. Ralph knew the men intended to sell them to the butcher shop in Elsie. From hearing his parents talk, he guessed the man was paying a mighty high price for rabbits, and they didn't even have to be dressed out. This was the part that had sounded good to Pa since he had never liked skinning rabbits any too well. Rate hadn't thought it looked like much of a job when he watched Pa skin out those two that he shot last week. Anyway, it seemed to Ralph that Pa had been gone a tolerable long time.

It was just before dusk when he finally saw something moving along the road.

"Ma! Ma! I think I can see Pa coming. Leastwise it looks like Cap and Mage."

Miney came to look out the window.

"Land's sakes, Ralph, how can you tell anything at this distance? I don't believe it is your father although I had certainly expected him before this."

"Yes, it is, Ma. See, that's Pa driving."

"Well, perhaps you're right."

"Can I put my coat on and go out to meet them?"

"You put on your overshoes, coat, hat, and mittens, and then you wait in the driveway. No farther. You hear?"

"Yes'm."

Miney knew that by the time Ralph got dressed, Millie would likely be ready to turn in the yard anyhow, if it was Millie. At least she wouldn't have to worry about Ralph getting in the way.

Ralph had been right, the team was Cap and Mage, and it was his father's hunting party. Ralph was waiting by the driveway when they drove in. Millie stopped the team, grabbed his son under an armpit, and easily swung the boy up to sit on his lap.

"Look at that, boy. Did you ever see so many dead rabbits in all your life?"

Ralph peered into the wagon box, which, to the lad, looked almost full of the brown furry bodies.

"Pa! Did you fellows shoot all them?"

"Reckon we did, Rate. Just wanted to tell your ma we was going to drive right on in to Elsie to get them off our hands."

"Can I go too, Pa?"

"You'd best stay here as that wind is getting mighty raw, and a wagon isn't like a buggy with side curtains. Jump down and tell your ma I'll be a little late for supper. That's a good lad."

Miney had come to the door just as Millie dropped Rate to the ground.

"Millie, what a load of rabbits! Why, I never in all my born days thought you'd get so many."

"We had mighty good luck. Why, the rabbits were thicker than fleas on a dog. We're taking them on in to Lafe's right now, so I'll be about an hour late for supper."

With that, he clucked to the team and was off.

"Ralph, shut that door," Mina called to her son. He had stepped into the house, but stood with the door wide open watching the wagon move onto the road.

"Yes, Ma. My, but that was a lot of rabbits, wasn't it? Pa should get an awful lot of money, shouldn't he?"

"I don't quite know about that. Just you remember that whatever they get is divided four ways."

"Why?"

"Because there is Clayt, Ed, and Guy as well as your pa, and they all get a share."

"But it was Pa's team and wagon, so shouldn't he get more?"

"Goodness, Ralph, what a businessman you'll make. Pa drove, but the others would have done the same, so he doesn't get any more than they do."

"Don't seem fair," muttered Ralph.

"Sometimes a body does things for his neighbors without thought of getting paid. That's the Lord's way of doing things. We must be generous and kind. I'm sure your pa never even considered he had more coming than the other men."

Well, if that was the way things were, it must be all right. He guessed Pa must have known it was share and share alike when he said he'd drive. Rate forgot that he hadn't thought the division was fair when Millie came home because he had two new horse blankets and was in exceedingly good spirits.

"Miney, I never figured we'd have such good luck. I didn't have quite enough from the rabbits for what Tom was asking for these blankets, but we dickered a while, and since I wanted two, he let me have them at my price. All in all, it was a good day. A good day's hunting, the fun of being with friends, two new horse blankets, and a mighty fine meal to end the day. Sure makes a man glad he's alive," said Millie with a satisfied grin.

Rate thought the new blankets looked mighty fine. Pa had said for some time now that he needed new blankets to use on the driving horses; he would then use the present blankets to replace a couple of the stable blankets, which were getting worse for wear. The barn was just too drafty to let the horses stand without being blanketed. That way, they grew such a winter's coat of hair, when used for even light hauling, they would sweat. That was one quick way to get a sick horse.

Miney had driven the buggy into the long shed behind the Baptist Church. The rigs drove in from the east side and could drive right on out the west, so it only afforded the protection of a roof. Unless the wind was blowing hard, the horse kept quite comfortable in its blanket. Besides, services didn't last all that long.

Rate sat primly by his mother during the first part of the church service, but now he became restive. He fidgeted, and Miney scowled. The minister droned on and on; because Ralph didn't understand what was said, his mind wandered, and his eyes roved around the church looking for something to hold his interest. He sneaked a look behind him and recognized one of Elder Whitaker's daughters. The girl smiled at him. He turned back around to face the front of the church, but in a moment, he had taken another peek; the young miss held her Bible in front of her face and then peeked at him. Rate snickered.

Miney observed what was going on, so she turned Ralph around in his seat, admonishing him for his behavior. She ended with an ultimatum. "If you so much as turn around once more during this service, I will take you out and give you a licking. Is that clear?" she hissed.

Ralph nodded. Ma looked kinda mad. He'd only been looking at that girl and she at him. Ma sure was persnickety about some things.

Time dragged. Ralph squirmed. He looked out from under straight, dark lashes and scanned his mother's face. He tentatively turned in his seat, then thought better of it and sat straight once more. Well, maybe one little glance. Cautiously Ralph turned around and peered over the back of the seat. Once more the girl peered around her Bible at him, and once more he giggled.

The next thing he knew, he was being yanked out of his seat, down the aisle toward the back of the church, almost faster than his short little legs could carry him. Miney went through the double doors into the vestibule where she stopped and yanked Ralph around to face her.

"What did I tell you, young man?"

"I don't remember," he said, his jaw set in that peculiar stubborn way that reminded her so much of Millie.

"Perhaps this will jog your memory."

Miney turned Ralph over her extended leg and proceeded to paddle his backsides hard enough so the palm of her hand hurt.

Anger made him cry.

"Now you hush your crying. We are going back in there, and you are going to sit and behave like you should. Do you understand?"

"I...I...I guess so," he gasped in between sobs.

"Then stop sniveling so we can go back in."

Rate wiped his eyes with a fist. Miney noticed and stooped to wipe his eyes with her hankie. He stared at her defiantly for a moment, then dropped his chin and looked at his toes.

"Ready?"

A mollified small boy nodded his head affirmatively.

Back through the doors they went. The Whitaker girl kept her eyes demurely down and pretended not to notice as Miney and Ralph settled themselves once more.

Miney had noticed the girl when they entered the pew. Perhaps Ralph hadn't been completely at fault, but he did have to learn that there was only one acceptable mode of deportment when in church, and the sooner he understood that, the better off he'd be. He had to learn respect when he was in the house of the Lord.

A few weeks after the hunting trip, the land was covered with several inches of snow. There had been a real cold snap, and the millpond had been frozen by Thanksgiving. Some of the boys had ventured out skating already, being careful to avoid the channel. The covering of ice where the main course of the river ran was particularly deceptive; it looked like the millpond, but the boys knew that it was only a thin scum and would not support a person.

Blanche had watched the skaters for a while. It looked like such fun to go skimming over the ice. Right then, she knew what she wanted for Christmas. Ice skates, that's what. Guess she'd just have to mention it to Ma this weekend.

It was while doing the supper dishes on Friday night that Blanche had an opportunity to speak to her mother about skates.

"Ma, do you suppose I could get a pair of ice skates for Christmas this year? Fern says she's getting some and so is Gracie and Lulu. Zella and Hazel already have some. If we all have skates, then we can go to the millpond after school. Sometimes, they even skate there at night because some of the boys bring wood and build a giant bonfire."

"Well, I suppose it is a possibility. Guess I hadn't really thought about girls wanting to skate. They didn't in my day, you know."

"It is supposed to be ever so much fun. If I can get the skates, I won't ask for anything else," she bargained.

"At least not now." Miney laughed. "Somehow, I can't imagine you wanting only one thing for Christmas."

"Oh, Ma. You're just teasing. Besides, I know you'll get me some clothes. You always do."

"Well, you always need them, don't you?"

"I wasn't complaining. I like anything you get me."

Blanche gave her mother a quick hug and a soft peck on the cheek. Miney felt a sudden surge of love for this daughter of hers. She was perfection personified in Miney's adoring eyes. All those fears before Blanche was born were for naught. She had been so certain she could not love a child, and Ma had just said, "Just wait and see. Ma knows." Well, Miney had been wrong and her mother right. She certainly did love her daughter—and even her son, she hastened to think a little guiltily. Yes, Ralph was loved too—not as much, but he was loved.

Sarah Perkins came back to work for Mina when the butchering time came. Millie butchered a hog, so there was sausage to make, hams to cure and smoke, bacon to cure, slices of pork to fry down then place in ten-gallon crocks and seal with lard, lard to render from the trimmings of fat, headcheese to make; and Millie wanted pickled pig's feet, ears, and tail.

Both Mina and Sarah worked countless hours.

Miney hated the smell of fat trying out of the fat chunks of meat, which were in a rather shallow tin in the oven. Still, lard made such good pie crusts and other baked goods, she guessed it was worth it. She guessed she'd even make some fried cakes as she'd have plenty of lard for the deep fat frying. Of course, Millie tended the fire in the smokehouse for the hams and bacon. He used hickory chips, which made the best flavored meat.

Shortly after the huge sow had been slaughtered, Millie butchered a cow. He sold half of the meat; however, there was still plenty for Miney to can, and then she cooked up the bones and made vegetable soup to can. They left a sizable piece from the hind quarter hanging in the cellarway so they could have fresh round steak for a while. It would remain partially frozen in this weather, so there was no question of it spoiling.

December 10, 1898, saw a treaty between the United States and Spain. The country as a whole heaved a sigh of relief that the hostilities were over, and the men in service could return to their homes. Most of the common people cared little that Spain had ceded the Philippines to the United States to the tune of twenty million dollars and that we now had Puerto Rico and Guam or that Spain had given up all claim to Cuba. What Millie was more concerned about was that the war had cost over five thousand American lives. True, only a small percentage of these had been battle casualties; disease and food poisoning had caused the rest. However, Millie looked at it this way: a man was just as dead whether it be from typhoid, dysentery, or a bullet, and the whole thing had been a ridiculous waste of men and money. He cared little that we had acquired new territories; he felt we had enough trouble at home without taking on more problems than we could handle. As he often said, "It don't pay to bite off more than you can chew."

Miney watched her husband coming to the house, his head down, looking pensive and sad, his movements mechanical, not noticing anything around him. Goodness, thought Miney, something dreadful must have happened. Yesterday, he was so jubilant when he learned the war was over at last. What could have happened to change him so completely in such a short space of time?

As Millie entered the kitchen, Miney spoke.

"Millie, whatever is the matter? You look as though you've lost your last friend."

"Well, Miney, I purt near have. I just came from Clayt's, and he heard up town this morning that Sawyers had just had a telegram from the War Department. Ray died the ninth of December from food poisoning. Don't that beat all, Miney? Day before the treaty, and he has to die."

"Oh, Millie, how dreadful. Where was he?"

"Somewhere in Cuba, I guess. I didn't pay that much mind. All I know is that a fine young man lost his life a long ways from home for no worthwhile reason. Wars be damned! They take the best of our youth under the guise of being patriotic when it's only politicians sitting in Washington who get us into these fracases."

"His poor parents. What about Lona? Have the Huffmans heard from him recently?"

"Last I knew, he was all right. 'Course that don't help because it takes a while to learn what's happened."

"What about Ray's body? Will it be sent here so he can at least be buried with friends, where his mother can tend his grave?"

"Don't know. Guess Clayt didn't have that much information."

"Blanche. Oh, my goodness, how am I to tell her? Thank the Lord she is home and not at your mother's. Honestly, Millie, your mother just never learned to be tactful. I'm glad she's home, only I scarcely know what to say."

"You'll think of something," came the toneless reply as Millie went back outdoors.

Miney's thoughts were in a turmoil. How could she tell Blanche that Ray was dead? Why, only a few weeks ago Blanche had had a short letter telling her that he hoped it wouldn't be long before he came home. She guessed war had not turned out to be the romantic adventure he had envisioned. Poor lad, if only he had listened to Millie, but then, the good Lord must have had some purpose even if mere mortals couldn't understand.

"Ma, why are you looking like you might cry? You do have tears in your eyes," accused Blanche.

"I've just had some very sad news. Come here, sweetheart, Ma has something to tell you."

Miney sat down in a chair, and Blanche came to stand in front of her mother. As Miney took the child's hands in her own, she absently noticed that Blanche was growing much taller.

"What is it, Ma?"

"Your father just found out that Ray Sawyer died a few days ago."

"Oh, no, Ma. That can't be so. It just can't be so. Not Ray."

"Yes, Blanche, I'm afraid it is true. Sawyers got a telegram today. He died of food poisoning."

"Food poisoning. What's that?"

"Well, it comes from eating food that's partly spoiled, I guess. Seems that Cuba is a lot different country than these parts, and they had an awful time feeding the troops. Mr. Huffman said once that Lona said half the food wasn't fit to eat, but it was eat what they got or go hungry."

Why didn't Blanche cry? Show some temper? Do something but just stand there? Miney felt ill at ease. She knew this had come as a shock to the girl, and she also knew how much the girl adored Ray.

"Ma, what do they do about a funeral?"

"I'm not quite sure. I think his body will quite likely be sent home."

"Oh," came the listless reply.

Blanche extricated her hands from her mother's, turned, and went upstairs to the cold solitude of her bedroom. She crawled under the comforter even though Ma frowned on this. Beds were made to sleep in at night, not lie on during the day, Miney often said. However, Blanche wanted to be alone to sort things out. Ray was dead. Ma had said so. Good-looking, well-mannered, fun-loving Ray. She had never seen him angry, nor had he ever been grouchy, always so good-natured. It just didn't seem right. Here, she'd been looking forward to the time when he might work for Pa again. Now, he'd never work for Pa or anyone.

He and Lona had been together. Ma hadn't mentioned Lona, so he must be all right. Why couldn't it have been Lona instead of Ray? She knew that was a wicked thought, but her hurt was so deep she didn't even care. Must be God wanted Ray in heaven, but she wondered why. She felt like crying, only no tears came as she stared unseeingly at the wall, her back to the room, nor did she hear her mother as Miney quietly slipped up the stairs to peek in the open door at her daughter.

Blanche seemed so small huddled under the covers of the large bed. Miney assumed Blanche was asleep, so she went back down the steps as quietly as she had come. Little did she realize how hard the young girl was struggling to come up with some sort of reason for Ray's death.

Blanche bitterly resented Ray losing his life in such an ignoble way. He had been deprived the questionable glory of dying in battle; however, to Blanche, it would have lent some dignity to his death. As it was, he died of food poisoning, which had to be someone's fault. Nothing was fair. Maybe when she was older, she'd understand, only right now, she was angry with the whole world and even angry with God.

In due time, Ray's body was returned to Elsie for burial.

Once again, Blanche and her grandmother had a battle of wills. Ray's funeral was to be held at the Methodist Church on an afternoon of a school day. Right at this time, there was nothing more in this world that Blanche wanted than to be allowed to attend Ray's funeral. However, when she approached her grandmother, Lavina dismissed it as being too trivial a matter to warrant Blanche missing school. No matter what her granddaughter said, Lavina was not about to be swayed one iota. Blanche could do Ray no good now that he was dead, and missing an afternoon of classes could hurt Blanche. The matter was settled.

Blanche seethed. She contemplated leaving school at lunchtime and going to Grandma Smith's until time for the funeral. Still, she had never yet openly defied her grandmother. She knew that while Ma might want to take her side, Pa would certainly side in with his mother. A body would think that when they got to be as old as Pa, they'd not have to cater to their mother, but for some reason, Pa always did as his mother wanted. Besides, if she hid at Grandma Smith's—and she was sure Grandma would take her in—then Grandmother would be mad at Grandma. There was no solution. That domineering old woman just always had her way. Well, someday, Blanche knew she'd be old enough to assert herself. She was not going to grow up jumping every time Grandmother snapped her fingers.

Right then, the child strongly resembled the grandmother she resented so much. Little did Lavina realize that by her dictatorial manner, she was alienating her granddaughter's affection. A day would come when Lavina would wonder why Blanche would brook no advice from her grandmother.

Millie, Miney, and Ralph attended the services. Rate was not all sure what was going on. He knew Ray had died, but all they saw was a flag-draped coffin, so it seemed very impersonal to him. The words of the minister were hard to follow, so he gave up and was simply glad when everyone filed out. Ma had cried a little, but he knew men didn't cry, although Pa did look kinda sad. It was a relief to him when they left the cemetery and headed for home.

Ralph lay whimpering in bed, half asleep and half awake, trying to be grown-up and not really cry loud enough to wake his mother. Finally, the pain became more than he could bear quietly, and he began to cry in earnest. In a few moments, Mina called from the stairway door.

"Ralph, what is that crying all about? Are you sick?"

"N-n-n-no, but I got an awful leg ache," he managed in between sobs.

"Again? My land, but you've had more than your share just lately it seems. Well, come on down, and Ma will see what she can do for it."

Rate came limping down the stairs, his cheeks streaked with undried tears.

"Which one is it?"

"Both of them, only this one hurts worse," he said pointing to his left leg. Mina sat down in the rocker drawn up close to the stove and took the boy on her lap; she covered him with a quilt and began rocking. She rubbed the errant leg while Rate continued to sob. Finally, Millie called from the bedroom.

"Miney, what ails the lad?"

"He's got another one of those leg aches. Do you suppose you could get a kitchen towel and wring it out in cold water for me?"

"Reckon so."

Millie got out of bed and hurried to the kitchen. In a few moments, he returned with a towel dripping wet.

"Here, Rate, stick that leg out here."

Rate pushed his foot and the lower portion of his leg from beneath the cover.

"Got to do better than that, boy, and get your nightshirt up so it don't get wet."

Ralph stuck his foot way out.

"Ow! Ow! Oooooooooh," he cried out in pain.

"Oh, Millie, look what the child's done. He stuck his foot on the stove. Can you see if it is burned much?"

"Wait till I turn up the lamp a mite more. He surely did. It's going to blister for certain and right on the ball of his foot too. Well, here, we'll wrap his leg, and then I'll get some butter for his burn. It'll help, only it's going to be mighty sore come tomorrow."

Poor Rate, first a leg ache and now a burned foot. One thing was evident, his foot hurt him so much, his leg didn't seem that important anymore. Mina rocked him a while longer, and when his sobbing ceased and he became drowsy once more, she carried him upstairs and tucked him in bed.

Lawsy, he was getting big to lug around. That child certainly had been plagued with leg aches of late. Some of the older women said they were just growing pains. Well, she for one would be glad if he ever got over having them. Couldn't rightly blame the boy for crying out so when he got burned either; of course it hurt, poor child. Goodness, she bet he'd never be able to walk on that foot come tomorrow, which was likely to lead to difficulties since Ralph wasn't always one to take to being idle. Well, perhaps he'd like to be read to. Too bad he hadn't started school yet so's he could read for himself. Mina was sure—what with the way he always listened so attentively when she could spare a few moments of her time to read him a story—he'd take to reading like a duck takes to water.

Millie had been right. Rate's foot boasted a blister that protruded a good inch above where the sole of his foot should have been, so the boy didn't do any more getting around than was necessary. He could no more put a shoe on than anything, and even one of his father's wool socks didn't feel all that comfortable, but Miney was afraid he'd take cold if he was to go barefoot on the drafty floor; therefore, he wore the sock even if it did bother, and he knew enough to know that complaining would not alter the situation one iota.

This Christmas Ralph received a storybook, *Children's Christmas Chats* from his grandma Smith. Ralph loved to get books although he could not yet read. He loved when his ma would read to him. She would hold him on her lap so that he could look at the pictures while she read. These moments weren't as often as he would have liked 'cause his ma's lap was usually occupied with fancy work of some kind or mending. Blanche would sometimes read to him. Yet other times she would start reading, only to close the book and say, "I don't have time to read right now. Guess you'll have to read it yourself." (Knowing full well he couldn't read.) Ralph wouldn't show his disappointment since he could look at the pictures and make up his own stories.

From their parents, Blanche received the much-wanted ice skates while Ralph received a beautiful sled, his very first. However, he was to learn that a sled was not just a toy. Millie split kindling where he and one of the hired men had used the crosscut saw to cut foot-long lengths from the logs brought up from the woods; it now became Rate's chore to haul the kindling for the kitchen stove. These pieces were small enough for him to handle easily. He had to pile it just outside the kitchen door, leaning it against the house, so it was readily accessible to his mother. He also hauled some of the larger blocks of wood, which were for the dining room stove, but many of these were larger than a small boy just turned five could handle, so Millie still did most of this.

Some days, Ralph almost wished he'd never been given a sled because, childlike, he got sick of having so much wood to haul. On the nice sunny days, it wasn't so bad, but when the wind blew, and it seemed as if his nose, toes, and fingers turned to icicles, he hated the job. Of course, it never occurred to him to complain. He knew that a body had to pull his share of the load in this old world, and he guessed Pa had decided hauling wood was his share.

Still, he did wonder sometimes just what Blanche did to earn her keep. Of course, when she was home on the weekends, she did occasionally help him haul wood. They'd tried to be so careful of the new sled, trying very hard to place the wood down gently so it didn't scratch that brand-new finish; it had been such a nice red and blue and green design. He had to admit that Blanche tended to be more careful than he. However, it almost always ended with their squabbling about who was doing the most work. Rate felt that Blanche should have done it by herself since she was gone all week, and he had to do it by himself all those days.

Sometimes, Miney threatened both of them with a licking if she heard just one more word about who was doing the lion's share, whose turn it was to haul the sled, or whether they had hauled enough for the day. Blanche was usually in favor of quitting one load shy of what Ralph wanted to haul. Perhaps it was just that she never quite wanted to do anything exactly the way Ralph wanted it done. She did rather enjoy bossing him around, and now that he was older and resented it more, her enjoyment increased tenfold. Blanche liked a good healthy argument, and she was secretly glad that at times Ralph showed considerable spunk.

A fine, powdery snow had been gently falling for some hours now. Blanche came stomping into the back door of her grandmother's house, her coat glistening with an accumulation. Her cheeks were rosy from the cold. She dropped her skates in the corner nearest the door, then turned to shake her hat outside the door.

"Blanche, close that door! It makes a terrible draft."

"Yes, Grandmother. I was just shaking the snow off my hat," she explained.

"Goodness, Blanche, you look half frozen. Is it really worth all that just to ice-skate?"

"I'm beginning to wonder. My ankles are so weak they turn in, then out, then in again, and I have a terrible time. Fern can go pretty good now and so can Gracie although Lulu isn't much better than I am. I hate having the others be better. Honest, Grandmother, I try so hard."

"Just you never mind. It hardly seems a ladylike pastime to me anyway. Why, if you fall down, I suppose your skirts sometimes fly up?"

"Sometimes they do," she admitted.

"Are there boys skating where you skate?"

"Not really. They go off by themselves, and sometimes they skate up the river channel. We girls just stay on the pond. If only my ankles weren't so weak." She sighed.

Blanche tried in vain to learn to skate. Somehow, her ankles just never seemed to get any stronger. After a few weeks, she gave up. Since her friends always wanted her to go with them, she walked with them to the river. There was a large log at the edge of the ice where the skaters usually sat to put on their skates. Here, Blanche sat and half froze while her friends skated. Sometimes, she wondered why she went with her friends just to suffer all that discomfort. Partly, she guessed, because it was better than spending those hours hearing her grandmother find fault with her.

Rate soon learned that he had still another job with the arrival of the sled. For some time now, Millie had paid the man who ran the Star mail route from Elsie to the post office, which was one mile west by the feed mill and cheese factory, to leave his mail in a box up on the corner as had some of the neighbors. Once before, Millie had sent Ralph to fetch the mail, but the boy had come home empty-handed, explaining to his father that the wooden box perched on top of a wooden post was too high, and stretch as he might, he couldn't quite reach into the box far enough to get the mail. Now, the sled solved that problem nicely. Rate could walk to the corner dragging his sled and use it to stand on, whereupon he could reach into the box with ease.

Rate had heard Pa talking to Ma about something called Rural Free Delivery, which he hadn't really understood. However, from the way Pa explained it to Ma, Congress in Washington had passed some sort of law that meant the mail would be delivered to the farms just like it was to the houses in the cities. He wisht they'd hurry up and get around to doing it so's he wouldn't have to trudge to the corner most every day in spite of the weather. Why, one day it had been snowing and blowing like all git out, and Pa had just said, "Rate, hadn't you best be gettin' the mail?" He'd known right then that no matter what, he'd be expected to fetch the mail lessen Pa had been to town or to one of the neighbors and had come by the box himself. Some of the time, there wasn't even anything in the box, and he'd make the trip all for nothing. Pa had just laughed when he'd complained and said the walk did him some good. Well, if being half frozen was good for a person, he supposed it had.

Blanche had been standing in front of the glass case in Grandmother Setterington's sitting room covertly gazing at the beautiful china dolls encased there. How she did long to hold one even if only for a moment or two. There were three of them. Their features were dainty and the silk dresses gorgeous.

Just then, Lavina came into the room.

"Blanche, what are you doing?" she demanded.

"Just looking, Grandmother."

"Mind that you keep your fingers off the glass. I don't want it full of finger marks."

"Yessum. Grandmother—please, could I hold one just for a minute?"

The young girl turned a wistful face to her grandmother.

"Now, Blanche, you know those were your aunt Pearl's dolls. She was my oldest daughter, and she died when Ruby was just little. Why, I've never even let Ruby play with them. I had wanted a girl so badly—Rate had his two boys, and I wanted a girl. We had had a girl between your father and Uncle John, but she only lived a very short time. Pearl was such a beautiful child, brown eyes and auburn hair, such a lovely complexion. I'll never understand why God took her from me," she mused to herself. She fell silent a moment, then continued, "I'm sorry, Blanche, I'm so afraid you might break one. They are all I have left of my little girl, you see."

Was that a tear in Grandmother's eye? Goodness, thought Blanche, she had never seen her grandmother look quite so sad. She wondered if Grandmother had hollered and complained at everything Aunt Pearl did. Must be not. It was very difficult to imagine Grandmother Setterington playing and laughing with a little girl, but perhaps she had been different once. 'Course, she never found much fault with Aunt Ruby, not like she did Pa and Uncle John. Maybe it was just that she liked girls best.

"But, Grandmother," beseeched Blanche, "I'm not asking to play with them. I just wanted to hold one for a few minutes, and then you could put it straight back."

"Blanche, what did I just say?"

"I know, that you're afraid I'd break one. Bet if Aunt Pearl were alive, she would have let me touch one," muttered Blanche.

"Well, there's no way to prove that," said Lavina. Blanche, engrossed as she was, completely missed the sadness in her grandmother's voice.

No use even looking. Blanche knew she would never get to touch one of Pearl's dolls, and it did seem a shame. They looked lonely in their glass case with no little girl to hold and cuddle them.

*****

"Ralph, pay attention and turn faster."

Mina was in the midst of doing the washing, and it was Ralph's job to turn the wringer for her. It seemed a never-ending job, and besides, he was sure this was woman's work. Mina had the clothes in the tub of hot water where she'd been scrubbing them on the washboard, pausing now and then to rub a little more soap into a particularly dirty spot; now, she was ready to wring the clothes out and put them in the rinse water. Ralph had started turning with a will, only now he had slowed to almost a standstill.

"Aren't we almost done?"

"We'd have been done already if you'd only turn that handle as you should. Goodness, child, at this rate we'll never get done."

"But, Ma, my arms is tired."

"Hurry and get finished, and you can rest until I get the clothes rinsed. There, that's better," she added as Ralph, using both hands on the handle, began to turn it faster.

He hated this job more than anything. It wasn't so bad on towels and small things, but the heavier clothes made the wringer turn hard. Worst of all was Pa's overalls or his swanky. He was glad they didn't wear heavy underwear the year around since it turned hard too. Ma's and Blanche's dresses weren't quite so bad. He sure was glad washday came only once a week. He'd be glad when he went to school so's he wouldn't always be available to help. 'Course there'd still be all those weeks in the summer, and he supposed Ma would think he could give her a hand then. Well, when he got big enough to do fieldwork, he bet he'd not have to help her. He'd be helping Pa then.

Rate was out in the front yard rolling himself a huge snowball when he heard the jangle of sleigh bells and the sound of a fast-moving team. He looked up to watch his father's team, hitched to a set of sleighs, go running by both driveways with no sign of his father anywhere. He debated a moment over whether he should go in the house and tell his mother what he had seen. Just as he'd made up his mind she should be told, he noticed a horse and cutter coming along at a fairly fast clip. Even though it was a single horse, the thills were off-set, so the horse traveled in the track made by the runners of the sleigh. He watched with interest and noticed Pa was in the cutter.

"Boy, did you see our team go by here?" Millie shouted.

"Yes, Pa. They was really going."

"They'll tire afore too long," Rate heard his father explain to his companion.

Later that day at the supper table, Millie explained the incident to Miney.

"I had driven the team up to throw on the grist just like I always do. I hadn't fastened the lines as they usually stand good, and they'd have stood this time if it hadn't been for the noon whistle. Seems like a steam engine always has a good whistle if nothing else. Anyway, when that thing blew, they took off like a scared rabbit. I was on the platform and had no chance to stop them. Well, Jack was there and said he'd take me to see if we could catch up with them. If the truth's to be known, I'd expected to find the sleigh overturned somewheres and the team all tangled up, if not hurt. They made the corner all right and were almost to the township line. Guess they just got tired of running. The sweat was running off of them, and they were blowing pretty hard when we pulled up. They were meek as lambs while we went back after the feed. Got them rubbed down and blanketed as quickly as I could. Figured to give them some hot bran after I finish eating so they won't take a chill."

Miney didn't comment, but she did wonder why it was Millie could never take the time to tie a team. Seemed that for the little time it would take, it could save a lot of lost time and effort. This was not the first time Millie had had a runaway team.

With the first real hint of spring, the frost being driven from the ground by an increasingly warmer sun, it was time to open the pit of apples, and just in time too. Millie had finished the last of the stored ones and was glad there was to be no interruption in the availability of apples to eat. Blanche had been rather impressed with the truly fine-looking apples Millie had brought into the house, hinting that perhaps an apple pie might go good for supper.

"Ma, can I have one to eat?"

"May I."

"I'm sorry. May I, please?"

"If you want. Here, polish it off with the towel."

Blanche started to eat the apple with relish. My, it sure tasted good. When she went into the dining room, Rate looked up, solemnly watched her a moment, then asked, "Is that apple good?"

"It really is. It's just as good as those were when Pa picked them in the fall. Want one?"

"Naw. You know what makes them so special?"

"What?"

"They were packed in horse manure. That's what you're tasting."

"Horse manure! You're joshin'. You're just trying to make me sick so's I can't eat."

"Ask Ma or Pa, they'll tell you. I oughta know. I watched Pa bury them. Horse manure. That's what it is."

Blanche looked at her apple skeptically. The look on her face shouted that she no longer found the apple delicious. She looked at her smiling little brother.

"I think you're horrid. I will ask Ma. I don't believe you one little bit, Ralph Setterington. You just like to pester me."

With that she returned to the kitchen, where Mina was beginning to pare apples for the pie Millie hankered for.

"Ma, Ralph says these apples were packed in horse manure. That's not so, is it?" she asked hopefully.

"Well, partially. They are packed in straw first and then the horse manure. Don't rightly think it hurts the apple if that's what you're afraid of. Tasted good before, didn't it?"

"Yes," she admitted. "But do you mind if I peel the rest of this? Ralph thinks it's funny, but that's just because he don't ever eat an apple unless it's cooked."

I'll get even with him one of these days, she thought as she proceeded to peel the rest of her apple. 'Course, it had tasted good, and if no one had mentioned horse manure to her, she supposed she'd have eaten the whole thing, and it wouldn't have hurt her at all. It was simply the thought of it now. Still, he hadn't been very nice, and she'd make him sorry somehow.

This had been Blanche's week to stay with Grandma Smith, and as usual, she hated to see the week end. It always seemed as if the time flew by in such a hurry when she stayed here, and the time was interminable when she stayed with Grandmother and Grandfather. Grandma was never demanding, just never complained, and seemed to be glad she had her granddaughter for company. If she disapproved of something Blanche did, she merely very quietly made a suggestion, like the one a few days ago.

Blanche had been out in the yard skipping rope when she had noticed a redheaded woodpecker fly into one of the maples by the street. She had stopped skipping and had stood quietly watching the little fellow as he pecked out a tattoo in search of a meal. When he finally flew off, she ran into the house to tell her grandmother what she had seen.

"Grandma, you'll never guess what I just saw."

Mary paused in stirring the soup simmering in a large kettle.

"No, Blanche, I have no idea. What did you see?"

"A woodpecker. That's what. He had a red head and was just peckin' away at that big maple."

"That's nice, dear, but after this, don't call it a woodpecker as that sounds rather vulgar and unladylike. After this, call it a *tree peck*. It sounds so much better."

Tree peck! Good heavens, where had Grandma come up with such a name? Oh, well, she supposed elderly people sometimes had strange notions. Now, how did *tree peck* sound more ladylike than *woodpecker*? If it had been Grandmother Setterington, Blanche would have told her that in school they were taught to call them redheaded woodpeckers. However, Grandma Smith was such a dear old soul, she wouldn't want to hurt her feelings in any way, so she merely replied.

"All right, Grandma. I'll try to remember. My, that smells good. I'll be glad when it's time for supper because I'm near starved. Is there something I can help you with?"

Mary smiled at her lovely granddaughter and said, "It won't be long. I'll call you when it's ready. Now, you go and have fun. I'm not so old that I can't cook and set table for two. Grandma likes to see you enjoy yourself. You will have a lot of years for work, so enjoy being a young girl."

*****

Miney was standing at the stove turning the pieces of beefsteak in the large iron skillet. The dish of potatoes was boiling merrily although the pan with the squash hadn't even started to simmer. Oh, well, it didn't take long for squash to cook when it was cut up small, so she expected all to be done at the same time. She was sorry that this was the last of the winter's squash although she was pleased at how well it had kept. Blanche had been tending to getting the table set. Now, she stood watching her mother.

"Ma, did you know you're a lot better cook than Aunt Lorin?"

"Guess I hadn't given it much thought. Where did you get that idea anyway?"

"When I stayed with Grandma last week, Aunt Lorin invited me over for supper. Honestly, Ma, she pounded that poor steak with a hammer until it was just full of holes before she dipped it in flour to put it in the fry pan to fry. Why does she do that?"

"I expect it makes it more tender."

"You don't pound ours like that."

"No, but that's why I have it sliced thin. If it is too thick, it always seems to be tough."

"Well, then, we had plain boiled potatoes and her salt-rising bread, and that was all. She didn't have any vegetable, and she didn't even make gravy. How come Aunt Lorin don't eat butter?"

"Lawsy, I'm not sure. Lorin has always been rather notional about what she could eat and what she couldn't. Like she won't eat anything but salt-rising bread—carries a slice or two with her any time she is going to eat away from home."

"Ma, don't you think Aunt Lorin is peculiar?"

"I suppose in some ways, but then, all of us have our peculiarities. I suppose that to her some of the things we do are peculiar. As for her cooking, she has never liked to cook, so I guess she does only as much as is necessary. Sometimes, I don't think she has an abundance of money to shop with, and they don't have their own eggs, meat, milk, butter, and flour like we do. Some years Lorin doesn't even have a garden."

"Well, I'd rather eat at home. Next time she invites me, I'll think of some reason I can't. Grandma is a good cook, and although she never cooks much meat at a time, she always has vegetables or fruit. It all depends on the time of year," Blanche explained.

Miney chuckled. She was sure her daughter meant exactly what she said. Funny thing about Lorin, she could bake and cook as well as the next person, if she was so inclined. Take her salt-rising bread for instance. There wasn't a soul around who could bake a better loaf. 'Course it wasn't everyone who liked salt-rising bread.

Now, if Lorin had asked Ralph over for supper, she surely would have had cookies or even a pie for dessert since she knew Ralph's weakness for sweets. Sometimes, it rankled just a mite when Lorin was rather obvious about liking Ralph best. In fact, sometimes Lorin even had the nerve to accuse Miney of showing partiality. Grudgingly, Miney admitted Blanche was her favorite, but she just knew she never showed it. In this respect, Miney was like an ostrich with its head stuck in the sand, she saw only what she wanted to see. She even ignored the obvious, that the older the children got, the more Millie favored his daughter and often blamed Ralph for things Blanche had done. Neither she nor Millie were ever to admit their preference for Blanche showed even though the whole town knew it and, as a result, had a great deal of empathy for Ralph.

Ralph had been standing near the north window watching his father and Lou Clark, Ed's brother. Since the men just stood there talking, Rate quickly grew bored and returned to play with his spool, which Millie had rigged with a matchstick and a rubber band in such a way that when wound up, the spool was propelled across the floor. Then, he heard Lou leave, and he looked out the window again.

"Ma! Why's Mr. Clark leading Mikey behind his rig? Pa didn't sell him, did he?" He hurried to the kitchen where his mother was just finishing the breakfast dishes. His face was creased with worry.

"Goodness, Ralph, I'm sure your father didn't sell Mikey—at least I don't know why he would."

At that moment, Millie came in the door from the porch.

"Pa, did you sell Mikey?" demanded Ralph.

"'Course not. Where'd he get that fool notion?" he asked his wife.

"He saw Lou leading Mikey away."

"Oh, that. Well, Rate, Lou needed an extra horse to help haul the milling machine, boiler, and engine from up on the Ridge. He's moving it down near the depot in Elsie. Mikey was the best I could spare since he will hitch in with any horse and not cause any trouble. Satisfied, boy?"

Ralph nodded his head.

"I like Mikey. He's pretty, and he's quiet."

"There's those that would disagree with you. There's an old-timer's saying that goes:

> Four white feet
> A blaze down his nose,
> Knock him in the head
> And feed him to the crows.

Guess that description fits Old Mikey."

"I like him anyway, and I don't want him knocked in the head or fed to any crows," was the indignant reply.

"I agree. He's a good old horse, and we're likely to have him a while yet, although you must remember that Mikey is getting old."

Ralph digested this bit of information as he returned to his playing. Mikey was a shiny black with four white stockings and a generous white blaze on his face going from high up between the eyes to the end of his nose, wide enough to cover the nostrils. Ralph thought him quite handsome, far prettier than the less-showy bays with no markings. He hoped they had Mikey until he was old enough to drive him.

Rate had been watching the procession coming down the road. There was a covered wagon with several people walking beside it, most of them dressed in buckskins. He knew they were Indians from the Isabella Reservation at Mount Pleasant. Early each spring, they came along the back roads to the villages selling baskets, beaded work, leather goods, axe helves, and hammer handles that they had made during the winter months.

"Ma," called Ralph from the north porch.

"What is it now?"

"Are you going to buy anything from the Indians? There's a band almost at the driveway."

"I do want a new grocery basket if they have one the shape and size to suit me."

Miney had been kneading bread dough. She wiped her hands on the dishcloth, then stepped to the washbasin to hastily wash them. She was already at the door when the group arrived in the front yard.

Miney loved to look at the beautiful baskets they had to offer. They had several that would meet her needs. They also had one that caught her eye because it was just the right size for a sewing basket. Miney had asked the price of nearly everything, and the spokesman of the group had patiently and politely answered all her questions. While she was debating as to whether she should spend the money, Millie put in his appearance and, without any ado, said he would buy an axe helve.

"Miney, do you need anything?"

"I need a grocery basket. This one is just what I wanted. I was kind of looking at these round covered baskets. They would be nice for a sewing basket. Still, I don't know as I should spend all that money."

"Miney, if you want it, get it. You know you couldn't get a like quality anywhere else for twice the money. Make up your mind so I can pay them."

"All right. I'll take both baskets."

Millie gave the Indian the money, Miney went back into the house with both baskets, and the Indians went on their way smiling their thanks.

"Women. Rate, if I hadn't come by, your ma would have kept them here a half hour trying to make up her mind whether she should spend that little bit of money. Never saw anyone who hates to part with a penny like your ma. I suppose being frugal is all right, but sometimes, she just gets carried away with pinching the pennies. We've always had enough that your ma can buy what we need and even get a few frills now and again."

Millie sounded miffed, which surprised Ralph because his father was never one to share his thoughts. Perhaps there would be more days like this now that he was fast becoming a man.

Rate was inclined to agree with his father. Ma sure could be a tightwad. Not that she never gave him money, because she always did. Each week one of his parents gave him money to spend in town. It was just that Ma always gave less than Pa. Even Blanche complained that Ma never gave her as much as Pa did. Well, at least when it came to money, his mother seldom showed partiality.

He guessed Ma had not had much to spend as a young girl, and she just never got used to the idea that they were more affluent now and could afford these things. Pa had always had money—he may have had to work hard to get it, but Grandfather had almost always been generous with his family.

Chapter 10

Ralph had supposed that his chore of hauling wood would stop as soon as the snow was gone and he could no longer use his sled for this purpose. In this he had been partially right. For a while, at least, Millie had done the lion's share with Ralph carrying only a few armfuls. However, once the spring rains were over and with it the mud, Millie remedied the situation by buying Ralph an express wagon. While Rate was glad to have a big wagon, he wasn't that enthused at the return of his daily chore with no more help from his father. He'd be glad when he got old enough to do fieldwork, but then, the thought occurred to him that there still wouldn't be anyone to haul kindling, so it didn't look as if he'd ever get rid of the chore. At least during the summer months, it took a lot less wood each day.

Another thing. He was always having to help churn butter. How he hated that. Blanche was forever getting out of taking her turn it seemed, or she had some excuse not to churn as long as he did, but he was never let off. Why, he bet he could be near death's door, and Ma would just holler, "Ralph, time for you to churn butter, and mind you keep busy. You know full well we'll never get butter if you don't keep turning that wheel."

Maybe it was the shape of the churn he didn't like. He'd seen Lena churning one day, and their churn was tall and narrow with a plunger that went up and down, and he bet it got butter faster too. Now, theirs stood on an iron stand and was like half a barrel with a top that had to be fastened down with a clamp, and when the wheel turned, the barrel rolled over and over. Sometimes, the cream was so thick it stuck in one place and wouldn't drop down, so then Ma would add a few drops of hot water, and he'd have to get busy. Round and round and round, *slosh, slosh, slosh*; it was the most monotonous thing he could think of doing. If he even stopped to rest, no matter where Ma was in the house, she'd call, "Ralph, you'll never get butter that way. Now, get busy."

Sometimes, he wished they didn't even need such a thing as butter, but he had to admit that when he was eating a thick slice of warm, freshly baked bread with plenty of butter on it, he'd almost say that it was worth all the arm-tiring work. He rather liked watching Ma work the butter in the big wooden bowl with that large curved wooden paddle. Seemed she knew just how to pat and work the golden butter to make the last bits of buttermilk work to the surface to be drained off. Then, she'd salt it, work it some more, then pat it down in small brown crocks, cover it with paper, and store it in the cool cellar. The buttermilk, for the most part, went to the hogs unless Grandfather was there, and then, he always wanted some to drink.

'Course there was one day when there'd been a little excitement to break up the monotony. He'd been in the kitchen turning away when Ma came to check the churn. Somehow, she hadn't got that clamp fastened down right, and on the very first roll, the lid had flopped off, and there went all the cream into a pan of cold water that set under the churn waiting to receive the butter when it came. Of course, it ran the pan over, and there went half-churned cream and water all over the floor. What a mess! Ma had been frightfully upset, so he'd not dared laugh. Sure had ended his churning chore for that day. It brought to mind that Pa was always saying, "No great loss without some small gain," but in this instance, Rate figured the gain was right near monumental indeed.

Tomorrow was Decoration Day, and Rate wanted to go see the parade. He'd asked Ma about going, but she hadn't said much, so he still didn't know if they were to go or not. He knew all his friends' folks were going to the celebration. Folks set a big store out of paying tribute to all those who had fought and died in our wars.

It was called Decoration Day because everyone took flowers of some kind to the graves of loved ones. He knew that Ma and Grandma Smith would put a bouquet on Great-Grandfather Barnes's grave as well as Grandfather Smith's. Likely Grandmother would put flowers on the graves of her four children who had died.

The cemetery always looked nice on this special day, the lawn freshly mowed, the flowers, and most of all the flags on the graves of the veterans. Somehow, it looked pretty, like a person's last resting place should. Now, if Blanche wanted to go, maybe then they could. Guessed he'd sort of approach her on the subject although he'd have to be careful, for if Blanche felt he really wanted to go, she'd want to stay home like as not.

Whether it was because of Blanche, or whether, like everyone else, it was because Millie simply decided to take the day off, Rate had no way of knowing, but they went. He was impressed with the Civil War veterans, some of whom were certainly getting on in years, but there they were, resplendent in their dark-blue tunics, the buttons gleaming, and the light-blue trousers. He noticed that here and there a uniform hung slackly on a sparse frame, the man a withered caricature of what he had once been; then, there was an occasional tunic fair bursting the buttons, and he bet that underneath, the pants had been altered with a gusset, but the men had one thing in common: they held their heads proudly and walked with a military air.

He picked out old Charley Dodge, who often worked for Pa; Sam Packinham and Andrew Call, each with a peg leg; and Charley Clement, who worked at the school. Charley Clement had been the one who had spent almost two years in Libby, a Confederate prison. He'd heard Blanche tell that if the kids at school asked him why he had fought, he'd growl, "To preserve the Union."

There were a goodly number of Spanish War veterans too, but Ralph wasn't all that interested in them. He liked the special blue of the Yankees. He'd be glad when he got to study about the Civil War in school. He had heard Ma say that her father, Grandfather Smith, had gone off to war for a little while, but he'd only served as a doctor. Ma, being a girl, hadn't been all that interested, and she couldn't remember much about what her father said, if anything, about the event. Grandfather had died just before Blanche was born, so Rate never did know much about it. He supposed he could ask Grandma Smith, but seeing as she was just a woman, he was sure she wouldn't be able to tell him much.

'Course, some of the men didn't care to talk about it either. A couple of times, he'd asked Charley Dodge a question, but Charley had put him off not really saying anything. Anyway, they sure had looked nice in those blue uniforms. He sure was glad we were still one country. Still, there was an awful lot he didn't know, and he'd welcome the chance to learn more.

While Ralph had been completely engrossed in the military parade, Blanche had been filled with thoughts of the dead they were honoring. She couldn't keep her thoughts from turning to Ray Sawyer, who just a year ago had been so alive and enthusiastic about life. She vividly remembered the evening he had put up her swing. These thoughts brought tears to her eyes, which she angrily brushed away. No use to think about Ray now. He was lying here in this cemetery even though he was too young to die. Blanche decided then and there that she hated war. Maybe there wouldn't be any more wars—at least this was her fervent prayer.

*****

Ralph and Blanche were both unable to contain their excitement. Miney had just told them that come Wednesday, they were going to Chicago to visit Aunt Mary and Uncle Jap. Blanche especially had missed Aunt Mary although she had been only six when her aunt and uncle left Elsie.

Only recently had Jasper moved to Chicago, taking his family with him. He had taken a job working on the streetcars. Ralph didn't even remember his aunt or his cousins. Lelah was Blanche's age, and the girls had been congenial playmates before they had been separated. Blanche was ecstatic about seeing her favorite aunt and Lelah while Ralph was excited because it was to be a long train ride.

Rate watched Miney pack them a lunch, check the valises to be sure nothing was forgotten, and then, they were finally ready to leave. Aunt Lorin was taking them to the station. Rate had not reckoned on the tiresomeness of watching mile after mile of woods and farmland pass by the window to the steady clackety-clack of the wheels, the occasional shrill whistle of the engine, or even the brief stops at some small station or a water tower to take on water. They changed trains in Durand with a minimum of confusion and almost no waiting. With a child's impatience, Rate was ready to eat before they hardly got started. He scowled his displeasure when his mother told him that he must wait.

Green meadows, green wheat fields, the tender green growth of oats, brown fields that had received this year's planting of corn—all too much sameness to hold Rate's attention for long. Therefore, it was no small relief to Miney when the swaying of the car finally lulled him to sleep. He looked rather uncomfortable huddled in the corner by the window. She gently pulled his head toward her until it rested on her lap; that was much better. By the time he awoke, they could have their lunch, and hopefully, he'd be good until they reached Chicago.

Mary and Jasper Sickels lived near Lincoln Park and the zoo, which was one of the first places they took their visitors. Ralph was intrigued. The children rode on an elephant in a brilliantly colored howdah. The lumbering steps of the animal filled them with laughter, and even the grown-ups laughed to watch the expression on the children's faces. What impressed Ralph most was a large, circular cage filled with monkeys. He laughed at their antics and had to be literally dragged from the scene.

The next morning when all were discussing what should be done to entertain the visitors, Ralph promptly stated that what he wanted to do was go back to the monkey cage. Well, it was too far for him to wander completely by himself, so Frank, Mary's only son, was delegated to take him there, which was not completely in accord with Frank's idea of fun. Hattie, the eldest daughter, would have been glad to take Ralph anyplace he wanted to go, but she worked in a tailor's shop and could hardly miss work for such a trivial matter.

Getting Ralph away from the monkeys was like pulling teeth from a chicken. It got to be a joke with the adults that all Ralph wanted was to watch the monkeys, but with Frank, Lelah, and Blanche, it became downright disgusting. They failed to see anything remotely humorous about it.

One evening, Millie and Jap left the house for a walk. They ambled over to Water Street, where many shops were filled with all sorts of produce. On impulse, Millie bought an entire stem of bananas, shouldered it like a sack of grain, and headed back to Mary's. Amid cries of delight from the children, he pounded a nail into the side of the porch and hung up the stem. Millie stepped back with a grin and said, "Well, what are you waiting for? Dig in."

Ralph, Lelah, and Blanche quickly broke off a banana. Frank, being somewhat older, took his time since he didn't want to seem so childish. Even Hattie edged over and broke off a banana although she asked her mother and aunt Miney if she could get one for them.

Lelah later confided to Blanche that they didn't often have bananas to eat since her ma said they were frightfully expensive, so she just knew it was Uncle Millie's idea. Blanche beamed with pride when Lelah told her what a nice man her father was. Of course, Blanche knew Pa was pretty nice, but it sounded good to have someone tell her so. She guessed she was a pretty lucky girl to have such nice parents, and even if Ma was close with money, she knew they sometimes had more of life's pleasures than Aunt Mary's family did.

"Ma, are you almost done washin'?"

"This is the last bits. As soon as we get these wrung out, we'll be done. Why'd you want to know?"

"Can I use your tub of wash water?"

"Whatever for?"

"I want to give Maggie a bath."

"A bath! Now, Ralph, that pig won't take kindly to any bath, I can tell you."

"But, Ma, she's awful dirty. I'll manage, and then I'll empty the tub, honest, I will."

Maggie was Ralph's white pig that he was raising because the sow had farrowed so many she couldn't feed them all. She'd lost two, and then Millie had given this one to Ralph to see if it could be saved. Getting plenty to eat had made the difference, and the pig was growing nicely. She followed Ralph around almost like a dog. Ralph had noticed that Maggie's white skin was getting extremely dirty, so he had decided that his mother's wash water would be just the thing in which to give Maggie a bath.

"Well, I suppose if you want to bother, it makes no difference to me. Just make sure you leave the tub clean and take care of it."

"I will, Ma, I will."

Ralph set off toward the barn calling his pig. Soon, soft grunts were heard from the horse stable, and here came the pig, ambling out of the south door. She made no protest when Rate came up to her and picked her up. She'd probably been hoping for food, but if this boy wanted to carry her around, it didn't seem to bother any. Now, when Rate put her in the still-warm, soapy wash water, it changed the picture completely. Maggie squealed in horror. A half-wet pig isn't the easiest animal to hold on to, but Ralph grabbed her by the front leg and held on with the tenacity of an English bulldog.

"Maggie, you stop it. Just quit your squirming, and it'll be over afore you know it. I'm going to scrub you whether you like it or not."

Ralph scrubbed with an old scrub brush until her hide under the white coat of hair fairly shone. He supposed he should have had an old rag to dry her with, only he hadn't given it that much thought beforehand. Drat that pig anyhow! She sure had splashed him up plenty. Who'd have thought she'd have fought the water with so much fervor when she was so quick to lie down in a mud puddle?

He finally finished and turned the ungrateful pig loose to watch her amble off snorting and grunting her disapproval with each step. She took a direct route to the horse manure pile outside the south horse stable door; having reached it, she wallowed and rolled, and none of Rate's indignant yells deterred her one mite. His lovely white pig looked worse than when he started. It was enough to make a preacher swear, but he knew Ma'd switch him for sure if she heard him, and sometimes, it was uncanny the way she knew things.

Dumb ole pig. Just wait till next week. He'd show her.

This procedure was to continue weekly until the pig became of sufficient size that the boy found her too much to handle. Rate had been determined that just once he'd be able to keep her clean after her bath, but that pig continued to thwart him like clockwork. She even got to the point where Ralph was certain she knew the days of the week since he could catch her easily on any other day, but come Monday, she did her best to elude him, and the older she got, the harder she was to corner and catch.

"Aw, Ma, must I go with you?"

"Didn't I say so? I'm not leaving you home alone, and you know your pa won't be back before suppertime. Now, wash your face and hands like I told you, and mind you don't wipe all that grime on the towel."

Ralph sauntered slowly to do his mother's bidding. He had been outside playing, and he hated being interrupted. After all, he'd been on a safari. He wasn't quite sure what a safari was, but he'd heard Pa talking about someone going on one in a place called Aferka, and he knew it had something to do with hunting wild animals.

The thought of stalking a lion intrigued him. He could hardly wait until he was old enough to get a rifle, but Pa had said he had to wait until he was twelve for a gun of his own; as it was, he made do with a long slingshot. It wasn't much, just a triangular patch of leather with long strings attached, but he had practiced by the hour, fitting a stone in the leather, whirling the slingshot around his head, and then, releasing the string that had a knot tied in it at the right time so the stone left just when it was in line with the target.

Now, all that had been interrupted because Ma wanted to go gadding. Well, he supposed he'd better get washed like she said, or she'd likely swat his backsides. Wasn't as if there'd be any boys to play with either, only John who'd likely be napping since he was just a little fellow. Oh, well, Ezz was building a new house, and they were framing it in, so's he guessed he could watch the men at work while Ma and Mrs. Garrett talked. After all, a boy didn't find much to his liking in wimen talk.

Ralph and Mina set off down the road for the next neighbor's farm. Ezra Garrett and his wife, Suzie, lived in a log cabin yet, but Ezz had finally started the new house. Some said Ezz was tighter than the bark on a tree, or he'd have built Suz a house a lot sooner. Suzie could hardly wait for the house to be finished, and Mina didn't blame her. Mina had lived in a log cabin when she was very small although she didn't really remember much about it because they had soon moved to the house where her mother lived now. At least she and Millie had never had to live in a log cabin.

Her house hadn't always been a house, so Millie had told her. The upright had been a barn and had stood up on the southeast corner of the property, next to the line fence. That had been when Father had first acquired the land. In fact, where the house now stood, Millie said had been nothing but swamp, and although the lumber had been cut off some of it, the stumps hadn't been cleared out.

Millie remembered the work to dig the ditch across the farm. In fact, much of it had been done right through the stand of timber, and what a lot of trouble all those roots had been. Each farmer had been assessed so much ditch to dig, and Millie had had to work partly on the next farm. The ditch gave them drainage, so they had been able to drain the building site, and after that, the barn had been moved, and Father had had it remade into a house.

The first crop in the south field had been wheat. They had simply plowed with a jumper plow, which was so designed that it just "jumped" right over the roots instead of getting hooked on them like a regular plow, and sowed the wheat around the stumps. When it came harvesttime, they had to scythe and cradle it, which had been an awful lot more work than a binder. It took one man to swing the scythe, which was no easy task, and then another to pick up the grain from where the cradle deposited it, tie it into a bundle, and then another man to put the bundles into shocks. Millie was lucky he didn't have to harvest grain that way now.

Then, Mina remembered their first year in the house. They had been married in November of 1885, the twenty-sixth to be exact, and had moved in. My, that had been a cold winter, and since there were no porches, and the foundation was open in places, the floors had been frightfully drafty. Millie had had to work diligently to keep firewood for the stoves. The next year, they had put on the porches and had fixed the place up a bit, and now with the new kitchen, it was really a place to be proud of.

Suzie deserved a new house, and Miney was glad for her.

Ralph scuffed along, his bare feet and legs browned from the hours spent in the sun. His gray pants came almost to the knee, and his shirt was a red polka dot that Mina's sister, Mary, had made for him. Ralph liked the bright color. Ma always picked out such dark drab colors for his clothes, mostly because they didn't show the dirt, she said. He supposed that was right, but anyhow this was a pretty nice shirt that Aunt Mary had made, and he was grateful to her. His straw hat was pushed back on his head so that his dark hair showed from under it along his forehead. He stopped to pull a timothy stalk and started chewing on it.

Goodness! Ma sure walked slow; ifn he'd been by hisself, he'd sure been there long afore this. Ma wasn't one for talking with him, so he daren't voice his thoughts for fear of being told to hush. Sometimes, he'd liked to have asked her questions, only she never quite had the time to answer him. 'Course now, if Blanche wanted to know something, that was a horse of a different color. Ma always seemed to have time for Blanche. 'Course Blanche didn't vex her near as much as he did, he had to admit. However, there were times when he got blamed for picking on Blanche when all's he was doin' was payin' her back for something she'd done. Blanche was a sneaky one, and Ma never caught what she did to him, but he never told. Ma wouldn't have believed him anyway. 'Sides, it was much more fun to get even on his own.

Blanche was gone a lot, even during the summer, because she was always having to be to Grandfather's and Grandmother's or Grandma Smith's. That was so she could have some girls to play with, she said. Well, guess she did like being with Fern and Gracie more than just being by herself. He guessed he sometimes missed her; he had to admit it was dull without her to tease.

Ralph stood by the screen door of the cabin watching the men working on the house.

"Ma, can I go out and watch the carpenters?"

"Can you keep out of their way and not pester them with a lot of questions?"

"Yes, Ma. I promise."

"All right, but don't you go away so I can't find you when I'm ready to go home."

Ralph went out the screen door, but in a matter of seconds, he tore back into the cabin. Mina was about to admonish him, only Suzie was speaking, and she hated to interrupt. In a few moments, Ralph went out the door again and again rushed back into the room. On the third sally, Mina could contain herself no longer.

"Ralph, come here and sit down. You can't be running in and out like that. What ails you anyway?"

"But, Ma, that old turkey-gobbler, he won't let me out of the house. He chases me somethin' fierce."

"Miney, the boy's likely right. That gobbler is a mean one. Where's Ezz? He can chase him away for you."

"Haven't seen him," said Ralph, "and that old turkey won't let me find him either."

Suzie came to the door and shouted, "Ezz—ra! Ezz—ra."

"Comin', Suz," came from the new house. "What do you want?"

"Can't you do something about that old gobbler? He won't no more'n let Ralph stick his nose out the door."

Ezz chuckled. "What's the matter, Rate? Old Samson a bit too much for you?"

"He jes comes right after me," Ralph explained.

"Wal now, we'll fix that, I reckon. Here you be, Rate. Take this stick, and ifn he does come after you, give him a right good whack."

"All right, Ezz. But won't I hurt him?"

"I doubt if you'll even hit him. It will likely scare the daylight out of him, so's then he'll leave you alone."

Looking somewhat braver than he felt, Rate sauntered outside keeping a wary eye on the huge turkey-gobbler who was strutting about his domain like a dignified monarch. Finally, Samson decided Ralph had gone far enough. Wings outspread, he charged. Ralph waited, then struck. He missed, but Samson, startled by this unexpected turn of events, turned with a squawk and ran. Ralph quickly seized the advantage and, stick in air, took off in hot pursuit of the now thoroughly frightened turkey. Around the new house to the north side of the driveway, they dashed. They were approaching a rail fence, so the gobbler took to the air and settled on the topmost rail. Ralph came nearer, certain now of being able to soundly whack this feathered adversary. Before he could strike a blow, the defiant turkey gave a loud gobble and pounced on this would-be foe. The suddenness of his attack knocked the boy to the ground while his wings beat a tattoo on the boy's body. When Ralph's cries finally brought aid, Samson seemed content to walk stoically away, his anger vented with the assertion of his superiority over a mere lad.

Ezz was the first to reach the boy, but Miney and Suzie had been alarmed by the cries for help and were close at his heels.

"Well, Rate, I reckon you should have left well enough alone. You hurt, boy?" asked Ezz, standing Ralph on his feet.

"Naw," he answered, bravely wiping an errant tear on the sleeve of his shirt.

"Ralph, whatever happened?" asked Miney. "Are you all right?"

"Yes, Ma. That old turkey flopped me good, and I never even got a chance to hit him once, he was just that quick."

"Is that all? Goodness, but you gave me a fright. Can you stay out of trouble for a little while, or do I have to make you sit in the house with me?"

"No, Ma. I mean I'll be all right, lessen that gobbler comes around again."

"I don't think he'll bother the boy anymore today, Miney. Tell you what, Ralph, ifn he does, we'll give you an invite to help eat him. How about that?"

"He's so mean, he'd probably be awful tough, but I guess I'd like it anyway."

Shortly after their trip to Chicago, Millie had commenced work on a granary. It was to have a floor a couple of steps from the ground with bins, there was an upstairs where things could be stored, and to the south, a toolshed. The men worked hard, and by the time wheat harvest was at hand, it was almost completed. The doors hadn't been put in place, but at least the bins were ready to store this year's wheat crop whenever the threshing rig came around.

Ralph had been playing with Grip, and the dog had followed the boy up the stairs to the second floor. Rate soon tired of playing up there, but when he came to leave, the dog could not be enticed down the steps. No matter what Ralph did, Grip stayed at the top of the steps whining and taking on, afraid to attempt descending. The dog was too large for the boy to carry, so finally, Rate walked off in disgust. When Grip realized Ralph had actually left and he was alone, he ran to the open space, which was waiting to receive a window. As he peered down, he could see Ralph moving off toward the barn; he gave a yip, circled once, ran toward the opening, and jumped out. He ki-yied when he hit the ground and limped off toward the house, nor did he stop when Ralph called to him. The dog crawled back under the house and refused to come out.

On the second day, when Millie wondered at the supper table where Grip was, Ralph did not volunteer any information; he wasn't quite sure if his father would have done anything or not, only he wasn't about to find out. After all, he really wasn't to blame because the dog was too dumb to come back down steps he had already climbed. Rate had never expected the dog to jump out the window opening. However, he was mighty glad when on the third day, Grip came out, hungry, thirsty, and a little stiff, but otherwise seemingly all right.

*****

When Blanche's birthday came near, Millie asked his daughter what she'd like for a present.

Her answer had been, "All the oranges I can eat."

"Oranges?" laughed an astounded Millie.

"Yes, Pa. I do love oranges, and just for once, I'd like to have all of them I want. You know Ma hardly ever buys any, and Grandmother is always stingy with hers."

"Blanche. That's no way to talk about your grandmother," admonished Mina.

"Well, it's true," countered Blanche.

"I don't know. Oranges are danged awful expensive. You think you're worth all that much?"

"Oh, Pa, you're just teasing."

"We'll see. But mind you, I'm making no promises."

The Fourth of July was cause for another celebration; it had been only a little over one hundred years since the United States had won a hard-fought battle for independence from Great Britain. Even folks like the Setteringtons, who were of English heritage, approved of being independent from a mother country far across the Atlantic. Indeed it was a day worth celebrating in this new nation, and folks who labored diligently six days a week for a minimum of ten or twelve hours a day welcomed a chance for a respite from their endless toil with a day's festivities, the getting together with friends.

Blanche could hardly contain herself; the Fourth of July was her favorite time of year. Besides, since it was the day before her birthday, she always pretended all the festivities were in her honor.

Miney had packed a picnic lunch: cold fried chicken, rolls that she made only on such special occasions, slices of ham, pickles, canned sweet apples, garden lettuce with sugar and vinegar, chocolate cake and fresh raspberry pie. Rate was almost as interested in the lunch as anything else.

Each of the merchants had a rather crude wooden stand on the boardwalk in front of their establishment with small items and trinkets to sell. The Ladies Missionary Society had cajoled, or coerced, or both, until their husbands had helped with the making of ice cream. It had been the woman's job to cook the mixture of cream, eggs, and sugar while the job of breaking up the ice, packing it in the freezers along with coarse salt, and turning the crank to freeze the mixture, fell to the men. A nickel bought a huge helping of the delicious ice cream from a stand run by some of the young married women.

The restaurants had stands with lemonade standing in huge wooden tubs. Chunks of ice, brought from the icehouse, had been washed clean of sawdust and floated in the tubs to keep the lemonade cold. If, in the final stages, it tasted a little watered down, no one seemed to notice. At least it was cold.

In the forenoon, there had been horse drawing contests with teams pulling stoneboats loaded with stones. The teams were divided into classes by weight and had to have an official weight slip from the local mill before they could be entered. There was always a baseball game between the Elsie Independents and some neighboring town in the afternoon.

Ralph had been interested in all these activities, but what appealed to Blanche the most was the merry-go-round. First of all, she loved the brightly colored saddles on the black, white, brown, or gray horses, which tilted forward and backward like a rocking chair while the merry-go-round turned round and round. A section of the floor lifted up, allowing a horse to be led into the center and harnessed in place. Then, the horse started walking in a never-ending circle, turning the merry-go-round as it went. Of course, the other delightful feature was the calliope-type music, which played the same song endlessly all day long. Blanche loved it. However, she often felt sorry for the poor horse and was glad to note that the man had two or three extra ones and changed the horse every hour or so depending on how busy he had been.

Usually, there was a band, and this year was no exception. They played all the old favorites, many of them Civil War songs. The Declaration of Independence was read by Miss Kate Finch, a young teacher who taught the seventh and eighth grade at the village school. Her family had been among the first to settle these parts.

Millie, like most of the farmers, would have to go home to do chores. The family always stayed at Horatio's while Millie went home since he would return to see the fireworks, which were set off after dark. This was only the second year Elsie had had such an event, and old and young alike enjoyed the rather brief display. There was only one more big event for the afternoon. The crowd was already assembling along the main street in readiness.

Millie knew all about this next event. It was to be a horse race from the west village limit to the main four corners of town. In fact, Millie felt certain he knew who'd come up with the ten dollars prize money. He and Ward Thomas had been wishing they had a horse to enter when Millie had had a brilliant flash of thought: Pa had this racer that was really fast, but he knew that even if Pa would want to, Ma would never let him enter one of his horses in a race, especially one for a purse of ten dollars, and where there would undoubtedly be plenty of betting on the outcome. Well, he and Ward had cooked it up between them to just sort of borrow Pa's mare for a spell, like from just before the race until shortly after. They would then return the mare to the barn with no harm done, only he'd certainly be five dollars richer because he and Ward would split the winnings since Ward was to ride her.

Everything was working fine. Millie had slipped away for a short time, long enough to get the mare and help Ward get her saddled. That mare seemed to sense something was in the wind because she pranced and danced and was just rarin' to go. He and Ward had chuckled to themselves knowing a win was practically in the bag.

Now, back at Ma's, he'd been somewhat astounded when Ma had suggested they all sit on the front lawn and watch the race. Ma, of all people! He didn't ever remember her showing any interest in horse racing before. Oh, well, perhaps she wouldn't recognize Pa's horse. He was sure that Horatio wouldn't volunteer any such information.

They hadn't much more than got out by the street when they heard shouts, the pounding of many hooves and knew the race had begun. Millie scarcely dared look. He glanced surreptitiously at his mother out of the corner of his eye, then at his father standing so innocently interested, then back at the race. Here they came! It wasn't even close. Dancer was out in front by two or three lengths and showed no slackening of speed as she went by. When the roar went up from the finish line, he knew who'd won and felt a moment of elation before he glanced back at his mother.

Lavina did not smile, but looked steadily at her husband. Finally, she gave him a withering look and said scathingly, "Rate Setterington." With that she turned and stalked into the house.

Milford looked at his father rather skeptically, but when the crinkles began to show around his father's eyes, he breathed a sigh of relief.

Rate clapped his son on the shoulder and said, "No harm's done, boy. Your ma will simmer down after a bit." As an afterthought, he added, "'Twas a mighty fine race Dancer ran. However, your mother will never believe I wasn't in on it, so there's no use to deny it." His face clouded for a moment, then broke into a smile as he chuckled. "My, but a good race is a fine thing to watch. Ward really did her proud." There was a note of pride in his voice since to Horatio, good horseflesh was one of the most beautiful things in the world.

Millie felt the burden lift from his shoulders. Just went to prove that there never was a time when he could put something over on Pa. Ma sure had looked mad clean through, and he bet she didn't get over it for a spell either. Still, Ma was kinda peculiar; while she had always ranted at him and John, she seldom raised her voice to Pa. If you gave the matter much thought, his parents were well-matched. Both had a whoppin' big stubborn streak, both were domineering and tended to be more than a mite opinionated, so he guessed any argument they might have had would have been a draw anyway. Still, it did take some of the glory out of winning the race because Ma was blamin' Pa for the whole thing. Like Pa said, no use to try to explain. Ma had always interrupted any explanation he had given as a lad when something went wrong with "Excuses, excuses, excuses. That's all you ever think of is excuses. They just don't hold water with me." Trouble was, Ma meant just what she said. Oh, well, it was done; he'd be five dollars to the good as soon as he found Ward, and Pa had been pleased. It wasn't often Millie felt that what he did pleased his father. The Lord knew he never gave up trying.

Blanche had been on pins and needles all afternoon just waiting for her father to come home from town. She wondered if Pa would get the oranges. Mmmmm, she could just taste them. She guessed she liked oranges better than any other fruit she could think of at the moment. Peaches were awfully good, but she guessed they were second best. Seemed a shame that oranges didn't grow in the North like apples did; she could just envision a whole orchard full of orange trees. 'Course, she guessed she should be glad the stores had oranges at all. There was a time, Ma said, when no one in Michigan could have oranges, bananas, grapefruit, and such because there wasn't the trains to get them here. Perhaps she was lucky after all.

It was late afternoon when Millie came home from town. Blanche rushed out the door at the first sound of the buggy wheels in the drive, then because she didn't want to appear quite so anxious, she slowed her steps and continued down the steps toward the drive in a most ladylike manner. Millie had driven up to the house, then from the buggy, he picked out a huge cloth sack and held it out to Blanche.

"Here, daughter. Here's your birthday present from your ma and me."

"Oh, Pa, oranges! Are they all oranges? Ma, just look what Pa brought from town." She headed back into the house with her oranges. "Ma, may I eat them now?"

"You certainly can't eat all of them now. You may have one before supper."

"Let the child be, Miney. She wanted oranges, and she's got oranges, so let her eat as many as she wants," interrupted Millie as he followed Blanche into the house.

"But, Millie, she'll make herself sick. I just know she will."

"Well, let her. You aren't going to be that hoggish, are you, Blanche?"

"'Course not. I'm just going to eat and eat. I'll save some for tomorrow though. Here, Ralph, do you want one?"

Ralph was taken by surprise by his sister's generosity. It wasn't often she felt this benevolent toward him. He declined, saying it was her birthday present. My, all those oranges must have cost Pa a fortune, and Pa wasn't usually one who spent money in a frivolous way. Now, if he spent all that on Blanche, maybe he'd offer to let Ralph pick out his own birthday present. Bananas. That's what he'd ask for if he ever got the chance. 'Course there were lots of times Pa and Ma did things for Blanche, but his turn never seemed to come. Maybe this time would be different.

That Blanche was so funny; she ate oranges until Pa told her they was coming out her ears, and then she even took a couple to bed with her. Girls were mighty silly at times.

CHAPTER 11

It was Sunday morning and time for the chore of driving flies out of the house. Mina hated this job, but how else was one to rid the house of flies? Seemed that July and August were the worst months, when it was hot and dry after a wet spring, and this year seemed to be a really fertile one for flies. Why, when it was going to storm, they clung to the screen door in swarms and crawled in every little crack and crevasse. Of course, every time Ralph went in and out, he let in at least a dozen it seemed. Blanche wasn't near as bad, for of course, she stayed put much longer at a time than her brother.

Miney had finished drawing all the shades in the house, and now she handed dish towels to Blanche and Millie. Blanche came from the bedroom, Millie the kitchen, while Miney took the parlor, and Ralph stood by the north dining room door ready to open the screen at his mother's command. Here they came, waving the towels, and the flies swarmed ahead of them.

"Ralph, get that door open."

"Yes, Ma."

"Now, you be ready to close it as soon as we get these flies out. We don't want them coming back in."

Ralph did as he was bidden, and when the last flies flew past, he slammed the screen door with a bang.

"Goodness, Ralph, I didn't mean for you to take the door off the hinges. There, that's done. Now, you and Blanche hurry and get ready for church. We're a little late, so don't dawdle."

Flies were just something everyone accepted as inevitable, Miney included. Neither she nor Millie stopped to consider that it was only a few yards from the back door to where they slopped the hogs, and my, how the flies did swarm about the sides of the feeding troughs, which were covered with remnants of swill and sour milk. Then, the cattle came almost to the back door to drink from the large tank by the creaking wooden windmill. Of course, not much farther away was the sheep barn, still partly full of manure because Millie had been too busy with other things to get it hauled out yet, and then there was the barnyard, which always seemed to be wet where the manure piles had stood.

The horse stable and cow stable were kept clean, but there was always a calf or two tied on the barn floor, and the litter simply built up around them. Really, a farm was a fly-breeding paradise. They had screens for some of the windows and screen doors, but nothing ever seemed to fit quite as snugly as it should, and those flies could always find a place to crawl into the house.

The first of the week, they kept busy with a flyswatter, and it wasn't so bad. However, come Sunday, the flies were pretty thick once again. It wasn't as though they were the only family with this problem because they weren't. All the neighbors had the same chore on Sunday morning, and until someone came up with a better idea of how to control the fly population, this method would suffice.

The threshing rig had come and gone, and now, there was a big bin on the south side of the granary full of dark golden kernels of wheat. Ralph had been glad to lend a hand shoveling the grain back in the bin from where the men dumped their sacks at the front. He had liked the feel of the cool grain coming up between his toes; and when he sank above his knees, he had pretended he was sinking in quicksand. He'd heard Grandfather tell about someone getting caught in quicksand, and if there hadn't been two men to help him out, the man would have died. Ralph had thought about that for days and wondered how it would feel to have his body being slowly sucked down, not being able to help himself, until his mouth and nose went beneath the surface and filled with the sodden, slimy sand.

Anyway, it had been great fun playing in the bin of wheat, so a couple of days after they had threshed, for want of something to do, he had clambered into the bin to play. Millie had found him there and had sternly told him the wheat bin was not meant for him to play in, and he had shown Rate where his antics had thrown some grain out onto the granary floor. Ralph couldn't understand why it mattered that much when they had a whole bin full, but he had not argued with his father.

The very next afternoon, he had once again been bored with life and could think of nothing to do to keep himself busy. He started thinking about how he liked the feel of the cool grain on his bare feet and legs, and before he knew it, he found himself back in the bin once more. The thought did occur to him that he would be in trouble if Pa caught him, but then, Pa had gone back to the field right after dinner, and he shouldn't be up afore suppertime. Rate was having a glorious time when he looked out the doorway—the doors had not been hung as yet—and spied his father headed his way. Cripes! He had better get out of there fast. He swung over the side of the bin, went through the door to the toolshed, ran out of the toolshed door, smack-dab into the waiting arms of his father. Rate's heart sank. Pa scowled something fierce as he held him at arm's length.

"Boy, didn't I tell you just yesterday you were not to play in that wheat bin?"

"Yessir."

"Then, I guess you'll just have to take what you got coming."

He moved off a few feet to pick a two-by-two picket from the fence around the driveway. Ralph looked at the picket with misgivings, but he said nothing. Millie gave his son a good shellacking, hard enough to turn the boy's backsides black and blue for a few days. Ralph made no outcry although a few tears slipped down his cheeks to be hastily wiped off on his shirtsleeve. This was licking number two for the growing-up years.

Millie hitched the team to the wagon, which was loaded with a few bales of hay. Horatio had asked him to bring the last of it into town. The new cutting of hay was already stacked by the barn waiting for the arrival of the hay baler.

Timothy hay to feed the nation's horses was a good money crop for farmers. All those horses stabled in the cities consumed tons of hay each year, and the farmer was the supplier. Millie always sold his crop as soon as the baler left, but he kept enough bales to furnish hay for his father's horses. The hay for his own livestock was mowed away in the barn for convenient use during the winter months. Millie only baled what he intended to sell for ready money.

He and Ralph started off at a brisk trot for Elsie; they turned east onto the Ridge Road and had just passed Sherman's when they met a man driving a pair of bays on a rather rickety-looking wagon. Ralph hadn't known the man although his father seemed to recognize the farmer since they both drew up their teams.

"Nice-lookin' team you got there," observed the man.

"Yup. They're good workers, steady and not too old either."

"How old be they?"

"Look for yourself. Make it a practice to let a man do his own looking," said Millie.

The man fastened the lines, climbed down, and proceeded to examine Millie's team. He looked at their teeth, he checked their feet and legs; in fact, very little escaped his eye. Millie sat relaxed on the wagon, seeming to pay little attention, but Ralph noted his father looked rather critically at the other man's team.

"How'd you like to make a trade, Millie?"

"Sam, you make me a good enough offer, and I just might be interested."

"Fifty dollars. I'll go fifty dollars."

"I said a good offer. You know that team of yours has at least eight years on this team. They could use a little more weight to be in fit condition. That off one has a collar sore." Millie knew he could heal this in short order with blue vitriol and rest.

"Well, maybe you're right. I'm not sayin' they be that old, mind you. Tell you what. I'll go seventy-five. Cash money. Got it right here, only we got to trade right now."

Millie seemed to ponder the situation. Rate watched with interest. He knew his father had bought this team at a sale as Millie had said "for a song," and that much sounded like a good deal to him.

Finally, Millie said, "Make that an even hundred cash, and I'll do it. You'll be getting the best of the deal, I'm thinkin', but I'll take a chance."

"Sold. Let's get 'em switched. We can change harness one at a time."

"Let's see the money first."

"I've got it all."

The farmer counted out the money, and they proceeded to change harness and teams right there in the middle of the road.

As Ralph and Millie continued on their way, Millie spoke.

"Let that be a lesson to you, boy. When you trade, always get boot money. Know someone who wants a second team who'll be glad to get this one since they don't want to pay for a prime young team. I know I'll get as much or a mite more than I gave for that other team, so I'll have made a hundred clear profit. Yessir, boy, it is always wise to trade if the boot money is good enough. 'Course it helps to have an eye for horseflesh too. Now, Pa is the one who knows horses. I'm not near as good at judgin' a horse as Pa, but I'm a sight better than John. You could give him the best team in the world, and by the end of the week, he'd have nothing but a pelt of feathers. Somehow, John always gets took." Millie chuckled.

Ralph tried to digest this scrap of advice tossed out by his father. Pa sure was some businessman. Bet not many people ever swapped horses right in the middle of the road. He'd heard his grandfather complain because his uncle John just never seemed to learn about horses. 'Course, there had been a time or two when he had seen Grandfather point out some minor flaw that his father had failed to see. He guessed there just wasn't a more astute horse trader around than his grandfather. Rate made up his mind that he would try to learn as much as he could about horses so he would be like his father and grandfather instead of like Uncle John. Golly, wait until he saw Curly Sherman and told him about this. Bet Mr. Sherman had never swapped a team like that. Ralph's pride in his father grew by leaps and bounds.

Ralph had already hauled wood for the day. That was one thing in favor of hot weather, it didn't take near as much kindling for the cookstove since Ma kept only as much fire as she needed to cook the meals. If it was a baking day, it took more, but she hadn't used what he'd stacked up yesterday, so it had taken only one wagonload to finish the job.

He couldn't rightly make up his mind what he should do for the rest of the morning. Pa hadn't given him any special chores, and he was tired of playing catch with himself. He had gone to see Curly, but had been told that Curly had gone to town with his father, so Rate had sauntered back home. Since Blanche had stayed over to Grandmother's yesterday, he couldn't tease her.

He ambled toward the granary where Pa had been doing some painting. Since they had just finished building the granary, Pa was in a hurry to get the new wood painted before we started getting fall rain, he'd said. Yup, there was Pa, bent over stirring a big, five-gallon pail of red barn paint. Rate watched him a moment, noticing just how enticing Millie's backsides looked where the overalls stretched tightly over his buttocks. Rate picked a picket out of the fence, moved nearer his father with careful steps, then whack! Ralph hit Millie a resounding blow, square on his posterior end. Rate laughed as Millie jumped, then realized he had better make tracks.

Out around the granary he went, by the sheep shed, and down the lane. Now, Millie was just a mite slow to follow since he took the time to pick up a gallon pail of paint and a brush; then, Millie, paint pail in one hand and brush in the other, took off after his son. Some of the paint spilled a little and splashed on his striped overalls, but Millie didn't seem to notice. He was intent on the small figure scurrying along in front of him.

Rate must have known that even with a sizable head start, his father could surely outrun him. However, he kept going as fast as his legs would carry him. They were almost to the bridge when Millie caught up with his son. Since he had transferred the brush to his left hand, he grabbed Ralph's arm with his strong right hand, lifted the boy off the ground, and plunked him down on the top rail of the lane fence. He spoke not a word, chuckled to himself, and proceeded to paint Rate's bare legs and feet bright red. One thing about Millie, he never did half a job on anything, so when he finished, Ralph was red from knee to toe, with no patch of white skin showing any place. With still no word to the boy, Millie sauntered off as if this was the most usual thing in the world—painting a small boy who hadn't dared wiggle.

Ralph sat a few moments on the fence looking at what a sight he was. He felt like crying. How was he ever to get that paint off? He knew Ma would holler at him even if it wasn't all his fault. She would likely switch his legs good since Ma sure did cotton to switching as a way of punishment. It's a wonder she hadn't killed that poor little tree south of the house, she'd broken that many switches off it. 'Course she would jaw at Pa too, not that it would do any good.

He started back for the buildings, the fine black dust from the lane sticking to the wet paint, making his legs and feet a dirty, grimy mess. Luckily he hadn't got any on his pants. Why, when Pa had started, he'd wondered if Pa was ever going to quit. He could just picture being red from head to toe, so he'd been mighty thankful when Pa had stopped.

As he came around the corner of the sheep shed, the hired man, old Charley Dodge, who had been in the Civil War, spied the boy.

"What happened to you, Rate? Did you turn Indian?" He laughed.

"Naw. I just couldn't outrun Pa, that's all. Someday I'll get even." He took a huge burdock leaf and scrubbed down the side of his leg. It came away tinged with red, but had actually made little difference to his leg. Then, he took a handful of sand and scrubbed it along his leg with the same result. The paint clung tenaciously to his skin. "Ma's going to yell something fierce if I don't get this off," he commented with a worried frown.

"Got any old gunnysacks around?"

"I guess so. Why?"

"You jest go fetch one, and we'll see what can be done 'bout that there paint."

Ralph soon returned with a torn gunnysack and watched as Charley wet a large corner of it with turpentine.

"Now, Rate, you scrub yourself good. When you've got the paint off the best you kin, use some of your ma's soap and lather up good with warm water from the reservoir. Think that'll git most of it. Now, git busy afore it gits any drier."

Ralph set to work with a will. That paint sure did stick something awful. He scrubbed with the turpentine until he felt as though the skin would come off along with the paint. He supposed Ma would be in the kitchen, so's he wouldn't stand a chance to sneak a washdish of water without her knowing it. Well, maybe if he got the most of it off, she wouldn't holler at him. After all, it was Pa's idea. He certainly never dreamed Pa would do such a thing, but one never could outguess Pa. Too bad he hadn't been able to outrun him, but then, there'd be another day.

Hay baling time was always a time for an extra hand around, so Millie hired Jim Keenan. Usually Jim only worked for him by the day and always spent his nights elsewhere. This time, Jim moved into the small upstairs bedroom with Ralph being shuffled downstairs to the front bedroom.

The first morning when Miney went up to make Jim's bed, she let out an exclamation of disgust.

"Bedbug! A bedbug in this bed."

The bedding flew as she hastily gathered up the sheets, pillowcase, and light quilt. Downstairs she went and onto the porch. She stalked back upstairs, grabbed Jim's battered old valise, a pair of pants and shirt from off the chair, then down the stairs once more. Clothes and valise all went into the yard. Next, she hauled the cornhusk mattress down the stairs and out into the hot sunlight.

When Millie and Jim came up for dinner, they found the bedclothes soaking in a tub of hot water, Jim's clothes in the yard, and an extremely determined woman barring their entrance to the house.

"Jim Keenan, I found a bedbug where you slept last night, so your belongings are over there. I've gone all over that room with kerosene in hopes if there was more than one, I got them. Oh, Millie, just imagine. Bedbugs in our house."

"I'm sorry, Miney," said Jim. "But what harm's a little old bedbug?" he teased.

"Sorry! Well, you should be. Look at all the work you've caused me. There's no sense for anyone to be so dirty as to have bedbugs, Jim Keenan. I certainly am not going to have a house full of bedbugs from having you here. From now on, you can just sleep in the granary."

"The granary? Aw, Miney, ain'tcha got no heart?"

"None at all. Granary, that's where. There's an old bed in the upstairs that you and Millie can set up, and you can sleep there. I'll not have you bringing any more bedbugs into my house. Now, you hurry and get washed since I've got dinner ready to set on the table."

Jim shook his head good-naturedly as Mina went back into the house slamming the door as if to punctuate her words.

Millie and Jim moved over to the washbasin sitting on a bench by the pump to the cistern at the southeast side of the porch. Most families had a rain barrel to catch their soft water, but Horatio had put an underground cistern to the east end of the porch, which caught the rainwater coming off the eaves. During the warm months, the men always washed up there instead of in the house.

For a week after this incident, Miney checked the bedroom each day. The second day, she found another lone bug so repeated the kerosene treatment and continued to air the mattress. Since no more bugs were found, after the smell of the kerosene left, Ralph returned to the upstairs bedroom while Jim spent his nights on the second floor of the granary; it mattered not in the least to him since all he asked for was a roof over his head, good meals—and Miney certainly provided those—and a few dollars' pay each month.

Rate kept watching up the road in expectation. Last night, he had heard Pa tell Ma that the baler would be here tomorrow, and she would have some extra hands to feed. Rate had seen them bale hay before, yet he was always fascinated by the process much the same as he was fascinated by the threshing rig.

Yup. Here it came. He knew better than to get around in the way. Pa was just not one to fool around when it came time to get work done. He kept his distance as the machine came into the drive and set up between the two large stacks of hay east of the barn by the north driveway. The scales set to the south of the drive and would be used today although the baler carried its own set of scales for when they set up in a field where there were no scales available. Such would be the case when they moved to the north eighty from here.

Now that they were ready to go, Ralph came over to watch. Six horses were harnessed in place to walk steadily in a circle, round and round, turning the driveshaft, which set the baler in motion. A man methodically pitched forkfuls and shouted "Bale!" when he had thrown in enough hay for one bale. Another man put in a divider so the second bale was begun.

Two men, one on each side of the machine, sat there to punch the wire into a hole where it came through and was used to tie the bale. The wire-tied bales were huge. As they came from the chute of the machine, two men dragged them to the scales where they were weighed, the weight recorded on a split four-by-four wooden tag, and the tag inserted under the wire to be held firmly in place. These bales averaged three hundred pounds each, so they were not something one man could toss around. The elevator paid for the hay by the ton as well as the fee for the baler, but each bale had to be weighed because some townspeople bought only a few bales at a time from the feedstores. The bales were immediately loaded on wagons, so Jim Keenan and Jake Finch could haul them directly to town.

Baling time was worse than threshing time as far as Miney's work was concerned. The five men who arrived with the baler would stay right here until the baling was completed, usually in four or five days. Millie might have to provide stable space and feed for six horses, but the man who owned the baler saw to taking care of them.

The men slept in the barn, so they were there for breakfast, dinner, and supper, along with Millie and Jim. Now cooking for seven hungry men for breakfast was no small task. For dinner and supper, it made nine extra since two more men came in to handle the bales from baler to scales, along with Jake. Seemed as though it took forever to do the dishes even if Blanche was there to help.

One thing was certain, they didn't get a lot of variety. Breakfast was fried eggs, fried bread, and coffee. Dinner was plenty of boiled potatoes, some sort of meat and gravy, creamed string beans from the garden or perhaps some lettuce with vinegar and sugar, bread and butter, coffee and pie. Supper consisted of the leftover potatoes cut up with leftover meat diced into them for hash, some sort of cooked vegetable, bread and butter, perhaps some canned fruit, cake, and coffee. The men didn't care all that much about variety—they wanted plain food and plenty of it. Bread, meat, and potatoes were what they appreciated most. The other things were just extra trimmings, which placed Miney a little above the average cook.

Although Mina was frugal in many ways, she always set a good table for hardworking men. It always pleased her when some of the men would take the time to tell her how good the meal was. Seemed like it made the effort more worthwhile. After all, she did get completely worn-out having to feed so many extra hands for so many days. However, it was just one more task with which a farmwife had to contend.

Rate had seen fit to ask his father if he might ride with one of the men into town, so when Jim left with the first load, Ralph went along. He liked sitting up on the bales. They smelled good. He guessed he still liked the smell of freshly mowed hay the best. Why, when they had first finished haying, he had teased to sleep out in the barn. Ma had been quick to say no, but Pa seemed to understand boys better, so he'd said, "Miney, let the boy go. I've slept in a hayloft afore this, and I can't rightly see where it hurt me." Ma had sighed and said, "Well, if your father says so, I guess it has to be all right." Yup, there were times when Pa was a lot more likely to let him do what he wanted. He guessed women were just natural-born worriers.

It had been one of those extremely hot August days, the sky a cloudless blue, and hardly a breath of air stirred the leaves on the trees; all had been quiet except for the droning of a few insects, when Rate came bursting into the house where Mina sat with some patching.

"Ma, one of Pa's old sows is in the cornfield. I tried to git her out, but she won't even budge for me." Now, the field south of the house was planted to corn, and a good-looking piece it was. "Where's Pa?" he added.

"Lawsy, Ralph, I don't hardly expect your pa till near supper-time. What shall we do? That sow will kill herself eating green corn, not to mention the havoc she'll wreak knocking it down. My oh my." Mina headed for the door to survey the scene. "Ralph, where's Grip? Maybe he'd get her out. Grip," she called. "Here, Grip."

In a few moments, the dog sauntered around the corner of the house clearly wondering what anyone wanted with him on such a hot afternoon.

"Ralph, now you take him with you into the cornfield so's he can see the sow, and then tell him to get her. If we're lucky, maybe he can get her out of there. Do you know where she got out?"

"Yup. There's a hole in the fence over yonder where a rail is busted."

"Well, she ought to remember where she got in there, I expect. See what you can do."

Ralph and the dog went down the fenceline to the hole where both of them crawled into the field.

"C'mon, Grip, I can hear that old sow over this way."

The dog followed the boy willingly, and sure enough, there was the hog gorging herself on the corn and knocking down twice as much as she could eat. Pa sure was gonna be mad over this.

"See her, Grip. Fetch, boy, fetch."

The dog perked up his ears, looked expectantly at the boy, then at the sow, but made no move.

"Fetch her, Grip. See that there hog. Now, she's got to be got outta here. Like this, see?"

The boy started to run in the direction of the hog. She raised her head while chewing noisily on the cob of corn protruding from her mouth; then, she noticed the dog, turned, and ambled off at a slow walk. Now, Grip seemed to get the idea because he barked and started in her direction.

"Good boy, Grip. Take her outta here."

The dog barked again, and the sow took off on the run. Rate watched dog and hog disappear down a row of corn and then became aware that his mother was calling him to get back to the house. Boy, old Grip sure was makin' that sow move. He just wondered how much more of Pa's corn they was knocking down.

There went that danged sow right by the hole she had come through, and she acted like she'd never seen it before. Ma was worrying now as the sow passed it for the second time. Who'd a thought she'd be so dumb 'specially with ole Grip right after her. He'd bite, she'd squeal, and then, off they'd go for another circle through the corn. Finally, they were out of sight for a long time. Then, here come that old sow right up to the fence where they was standing, and she dropped right there, pantin' somethin' fierce. Grip didn't look as if he was any too anxious to run anymore either. He tried to worry her with a few half-hearted barks, but that old sow just lay there panting.

"Grip. Grip. That's enough," cried Miney. "Oh, my, that poor thing is like to die of heat prostration. Oh dear, whatever shall I do? I know, I'll get a pail of water to help cool her off."

Mina hurried through the house to the well and in a few minutes returned with a pail brimful of cold well water. She carried the pail over to the fence where she sloshed it through the rails all over that heaving hog. Ralph watched in awe as the sow shuddered convulsively, stiffened her legs, and then went limp.

"Ma, what's wrong? She don't act right. Whyn't she get up when you doused her?"

"I-I-I don't know. She looks dreadful strange. She's not panting anymore."

"Is she...is she even breathin'?"

"Goodness, I think so. I hope so."

"Her sides aren't moving like they was," Rate observed.

Just then Grip moved closer, took a nip at a leg, and the sow didn't move; he moved up to grab an ear, and the sow didn't move. Rate reached through the fence and lifted a leg, let go, and watched it drop limply back into place.

"Oh, no," exclaimed Miney. "Ralph, I think she's dead. Whatever will your pa say?"

"What'll I say about what?" asked Millie from the door of the house, having returned sooner than Miney expected.

"Millie, I-I guess I killed one of your sows," started Mina, and then she began to cry.

Upon being questioned, Ralph related the incident to his father, who patted Miney on the shoulder and said, "Never mind, Miney. What's done is done. I'll get her buried whilst you're getting supper. She'll bloat dreadful fast in this hot weather, so the sooner it's done, the better."

Rate would've liked to have asked Pa why the sow had died, but he sensed this was not the time to ask his father questions. The ground was hard and dry, and the sweat ran off Millie's face in rivulets as he worked diligently. Rate watched the entire proceedings with interest. The thought crossed his mind that Pa was burying an awful lot of good meat, or so it seemed to him, but he supposed Pa knew what he was doing. Still, it did seem odd that they didn't dress her out—must be something with the way she died. Maybe he'd understand better when he was older.

September soon rolled around, and Ralph was to start school this year. The night before school started, Millie called Ralph over to stand in front of him and told his son that if the teacher ever found it necessary to give him a whipping at school, he could be mighty certain he'd get the second one when he got home. Ralph looked at his father's stern face and knew that Millie meant exactly what he said. Gripes. That meant he had better be pretty darned careful for when Pa whipped, he sure didn't spare the rod. What made Pa think he'd get whipped at school anyway? He was lookin' forward to learning, and he guessed he knew how to behave.

The schoolmistress at Stafford was Miss Edah Silvernail. When Blanche first met her, the girl had been hard put not to snicker because Edah reminded her of a bird sitting on a fence since her dress was much longer in the back than in front, so it looked like tailfeathers. Besides, she was slender to the point of being skinny, and her features were rather rough-cut.

Although Blanche still stayed in Elsie with either Grandfather and Grandmother Setterington or Grandma Smith to attend the village school, no such suggestion had been made for Ralph. Of course, he was expected to walk the mile and a half regardless of the weather, for after all, he was a boy; since Blanche was a girl, this was too much to expect of her. However, Salina Clark up on the Ridge seemed to do it without any trouble. If Ralph thought anyone was showing partiality, he made no comment, nor did he hold it against his sister. In fact, he guessed he wouldn't have wanted to go to Elsie to school since his friends were neighbors. He and Don Sherman got on right fine even if Burl, who was a year younger, was always in the way. Naw, he guessed he was plenty satisfied with things just the way they was.

School wasn't half bad either. Ma had taught him some of his letters, so he had a head start on some of the others. He could count and write his numbers to ten too. While he liked learning to cipher, it was reading that interested him most. He had always wondered just how growed folks knew how to put letters together to make words; he'd often looked at books, studying the words carefully, trying to make out what they meant. It was always nice when Ma had time to read to him, but now, he was learning to read all by himself. Someday he'd be able to read growed-up books, and he could hardly wait for that time to come.

Dinner was almost finished, and while Rate felt almost full, those small boiled onions with white sauce sure had tasted good.

"Ma, is there any more onions left?"

"Well, there's a few." She scraped the dish. "There's more than I thought. How many do you want?"

"All of them. They sure tasted good," he said, smacking his lips.

"Oh, Ralph, I don't know. There's more than you'll likely want. Besides, maybe your pa would like some more."

"I'll eat them, honest, I will. I want another big dish just like I had in the first place."

"Let the boy have them," said Millie as Miney looked at him undecidedly.

"Well, all right, but be sure your eyes aren't bigger than your stomach," said Miney as she emptied the bowl into his dish.

Ralph started eating with a vim, but about halfway through, he slowed down, another mouthful, and he stopped altogether. After sitting a moment contemplating the situation, he finally said, "Ma, I'm full. Do I have to finish these?"

Millie, who had been watching his son, fully realized Ralph was already stuffed, and yet, he had to learn, so Millie said quietly, "Boy, eat your onions."

With a sidelong glance at his father, Rate dug in. He cleaned his dish just as his father said. However, he had also learned his lesson well. Never again was he to ask for seconds when he was already rather full no matter how good something tasted.

*****

Ralph tried to sneak quietly into the house and place his round tin dinner pail on the kitchen cabinet without being seen. Luck was not with him today. Just as he had carefully set the dinner pail down without so much as a tiny clatter, he turned to see his mother watching him from the dining room doorway.

"Ralph, what have you been up to now?"

"Nuthin', Ma. I just got home from school."

"I can see that. Little late, aren't you? Where'd you get the grime on your face, and look at your clothes. Ralph, did you get into a fight?"

"Well, sorta."

"What do you mean sort of? Either you got into a fight or you didn't."

Rate heaved a sigh.

"I got into a fight," he admitted.

"With whom?"

"Aw, that Naegle kid. He was bragging because he can run faster than I can and was calling me turtle, so I pasted him one. Then, he hit me back, and afore I knowed it, we was on the ground. I was gettin' the best of him when Miss Silvernail came out and hauled us apart. Then, she made us stay after school awhile."

Millie had happened in as his son was describing the fight.

"See, Millie," accused Miney, "he's just a chip off the old block. Your mother tells how you and John always fought. I don't want my son to be such a ruffian."

"Boys will be boys, Miney, lessen you want him to grow up to be a sissy. Don't appear that he came out too bad. Leastways he doesn't have a black eye. Don't look like he had a bloody nose either. What more can you ask?"

"Men! I'll never understand one if I live to be a hundred."

With that, Miney pushed past Ralph to return to the dining room. She muttered to herself as she went, "Why do fists always have to settle an argument? Why can't they be more civilized? Didn't Christ teach us to turn the other cheek? Sometimes, I don't think Millie ever got past the Old Testament."

Millie winked at his son, the crinkles around his eyes deep-set with merriment.

"Well, boy, did you learn anything today?"

"Sure did, Pa. It's better not to get knocked down, but if you're down, it's a lot better bein' on top."

Millie laughed heartily.

"Rate, just remember, if you can't avoid a fight, be sure and get in the first lick. Don't never back away from a fight, but don't go around askin' for one either, and don't pick on those smaller than yourself. I won't tolerate a bully."

"Oh, no, Pa. I'd never do that. 'Course, right now at school, I'm about the smallest one. Next year, I'll be bigger than any old first grader though."

Millie chuckled at this logic. He left the kitchen while Ralph raided the cookie tin. Gosh, for a minute he had thought Pa might be mad, but he guessed Pa remembered what it was like to be a young boy. Ma sure had been upset. Guess he'd better get his face and hands washed before she yelled at him again. Then, he'd get right to his chores, and maybe by suppertime, she'd feel in a more congenial mood.

*****

Ralph peered cautiously in the kitchen door. No sign of Ma anywhere, so he slipped quietly into the house. With him, he had a green tree branch a little over two feet long that had one end sharpened to a point. He stepped noiselessly up to the cookstove, but try as he might, the lid clattered a little as he lifted it off. Darn! Oh well, no time to worry now.

He had no more than stuck the end of the stick into the coals of the nearly burned-out fire when a voice hissed, "What do you think you're doing? I'm going to tell Ma."

Rate jumped, then gained perfect aplomb and answered rather nonchalantly, "Go ahead. See if I care."

"You know Ma doesn't want you messing around in her kitchen. What are you doing anyway?" Blanche added, her curiosity showing.

"Nothing a girl would understand."

"I would so. Why are you burning that old stick?"

"Keep your mouth shut and your eyes open, and you'll find out."

"Now, you sound just like Pa."

The end of the branch had burned just a little. Ralph surveyed it critically, decided it would do, replaced the stove lid, then spoke to his sister.

"If you want to see, you'll have to follow me."

"Oh, all right. If you aren't going too far. I might still tell Ma," she threatened.

"Then, I won't show you."

Whistling somewhat tunelessly, he moved out the door.

In spite of herself, Blanche found herself following him out to the orchard where there were a goodly number of green apples on the ground. She watched as Rate stuck an apple on the end of the stick, whipped it through the air, and sent the apple flying.

"Is that all? It certainly doesn't take much to amuse a boy."

With that observation, she returned to the house.

Girls sure were silly. Well, he hadn't really expected her to be overly enthused about his game, but it was fun whether she thought so or not. He could really whip an apple a considerable distance, and the more he practiced, the more accurate he got.

Girls just never understood anything that wasn't connected with cooking, sewing, or fancy work. Now, he couldn't understand sitting for an hour or so embroidering on some dresser scarf. 'Course, it had been kinda funny when Blanche was first learning. He remembered how Ma had said Blanche's fingers were all thumbs, and Blanche had pricked her finger; and while it bled, she cried. Still, Ma had been awful patient with her. She showed her and showed her, and when Blanche's thread got all knotted and tangled, Ma had just laughed and commented that she didn't see how a body could make such a mess out of something.

Blanche hadn't given up at all. She'd just kept right at it, and if Ma took out some of her stitches, she just put them right back in, and it wasn't long before Ma was telling her what a good job she was doing. Ma, being a perfectionist, wasn't one to give praise unless it was due either.

That was one thing about Blanche, she just never admitted she couldn't do something. He guessed Ma was right when she accused her of being an awful lot like Grandfather.

Ralph, Blanche, and Miney sat in church with Horatio and Lavina in what was known as the Setterington pew. The pew was located to the right side of the podium and resembled a box at the opera since it was cushioned in a rich dark velour and was the only one so extravagantly covered in the church. Rate wiggled a little as the minister started giving his sermon. He guessed he liked having the cushions to sit on since they were a lot more comfortable than those hard wooden seats. Ma always scowled fiercely if he wiggled during the sermon. Sometimes, if Blanche sat by him, she'd pinch him and make him squirm. While he daren't do anything back right then, he had his ways of getting even. He never tattled on his sister, he just used his own methods of retaliation.

The minister was really getting all het up today since his topic was "the wages of sin is death." Rate didn't quite understand what was being said, but Grandfather kept nodding his head and saying "Amen," so he guessed Grandfather agreed with what the preacher said. He'd asked Ma 'bout it one day, why Grandfather often did this, and Ma had said it was to show that he agreed. Grandmother didn't say anything, simply sat there poker-faced and only nodded her head.

Sometimes, Grandfather acted as though the preacher was talking just to him, and Rate wondered if he would ever get big enough to understand what was being said. Right now, all he knew was that if one wanted to have eternal life, a life after death, which he supposed meant going to heaven, he sure as heck didn't want to sin. He supposed those people who drank in the saloons were sinners, and he knew that it was sinful to lie or cheat or steal, but he wasn't sure if this covered everything or not.

He wondered if card-playing was sinful. He was mindful of hearing Ma tell how when Blanche was little she'd really embarrassed Ma something awful. This had happened before he was even born. It seemed that Blanche and Mina had gone over to Grandfather's after church. Well, Blanche had one of those little cards they often got in Sunday school, and she had gone up to Grandfather and asked, "Grandfather, is this a pedlow card?"

Grandfather had then asked, "Blanche, do your parents use pedro cards?"

Blanche had answered honestly, "They plays with cards."

Miney had just entered the room in time to hear Grandfather say, "Blanche, your parents should not be playing cards of any sort."

"Father Setterington," interrupted Miney, "if you want to know whether Millie and I play cards, why don't you ask one of us? It is not right for you to question Blanche since she is only a child."

"All right, Mina. I will ask it of you. Do you and Milt play cards?" asked Horatio, his black eyes boring into the fierce blue eyes of his daughter-in-law.

Miney held her head a bit higher and said, "Yes, on occasion we do play cards. At Grange meetings they usually play after the business meeting." It wasn't often Miney felt this brave around her father-in-law.

Horatio had stared at her a moment while Miney struggled not to let her eyes waver and fall. Just this once she would stand up to him. She found it easier since Lavina was not in the room.

Finally, Horatio had spoken although not unkindly.

"Cards are the devil's advocate, Miney, take my word for it. Most things start small, but that's all the foothold the devil needs. I hope in the future you and Milt will find it in your heart to refuse temptation. Remember 'Get thee behind me, Satan,' and do just that. A person must be strong to withstand the temptations of the devil."

Well, what else was Ma to do? She half promised Grandfather that she wouldn't play cards again. Must be card-playing was a sin, or Grandfather wouldn't have been so insistent on the matter. Rate knew that he'd never seen his folks play, although at Grange meetings at neighbors' houses, the menfolk often played and occasionally some of the women. It had looked like a lot of fun to him, and he wasn't sure just where the devil fitted in. Guess he'd understand when he was older.

While he had been pondering the situation, the sermon ended, and everyone rose to sing the closing hymn. When he slid out of his seat, he stepped on Blanche's foot knowing she couldn't do a thing about it without drawing Ma's attention. The hymn was "Rock of Ages," and Ralph raised his voice in song, his face a picture of innocence.

CHAPTER 12

Birthday time for Ralph rolled around, and he hadn't forgotten what Blanche had had for her present, so he waited like a babe in a nettle patch, hoping that Millie would ask him what he wanted for his present. Two days before the eventful day, Millie spoke to his young son.

"Rate, what's the day after tomorrow?"

"Saturday."

"Is that all?"

"It's my birthday too," he ventured.

"Is it now? And what would you be liking for a present this year?"

"Bananas," Ralph almost shouted.

"Bananas! Whatever for?" Millie laughed.

"To eat. Blanche got her oranges, and I'd like bananas. They's the best eating of anything. Can I have them, Pa?"

"We'll see. Can't tell you for sure and spoil the surprise, now can I? I'd thought maybe you'd like a new slingshot or something, but no, you want bananas because Blanche had oranges."

"Not because Blanche had oranges, but because I like bananas," he clarified.

"Well, have it your way."

The morning of Ralph's birthday dawned crisp and cold even though the sun shone pleasantly enough. Ralph wanted to ask his father whether he had decided on his birthday present, but he daren't. All he could do was keep busy and hope Pa would go to town after dinner. Pa and Ma had bought groceries yesterday when they went to bring Blanche home from Grandma Smith's. He knew of no reason for his father to go to town again. Rate got around and hauled wood right after breakfast while Millie was in the barn cleaning stables and doing the rest of the chores. Ralph was on tenterhooks waiting to see what his father intended. The thought crossed his mind that perhaps they had bought some small article for him yesterday.

Shortly after dinner, Millie left for town. Not a word had he said to Ralph before he left, and if he noticed that the boy hadn't eaten a very big dinner, he didn't say anything.

"Why do you keep watching out the window? Bet I know. You think Pa's going to bring you some old bananas just because he brought me oranges."

"Well, he didn't say he wouldn't," countered Ralph.

"Didn't say he would either," jeered Blanche. "What makes you think he'll spend all that money on you? Bananas are frightfully expensive, I heard Ma say so."

"I dunno. Pa just might."

"When he doesn't, just remember I told you so."

Perhaps Blanche was right. Pa never had said he'd get them, but the fact of the matter was, Pa hadn't said he wouldn't. At least Rate could still hope, even if Blanche had thrown a wet towel on his thoughts.

It was late in the afternoon when Millie and the cutter turned into the yard; already dusk had fallen, and crane his neck as he might, Ralph could get no hint of anything Pa had with him. He never gave a thought to the weather being only about fifteen degrees above zero, so if Millie did have fruit in the cutter, it most certainly would be covered with the horsehide robe. He watched apprehensively as his father drew the team up as they reached the house.

"Rate! Well, boy, where are you?" bellowed Millie.

"Here I am, Pa. What do you want?" Rate called from the doorway.

"Just wondered if you was about."

Millie climbed out of the cutter and reached back for something. As he turned around, Ralph's eyes nearly popped out of his head.

"Pa," he said in awe. "You did it. You brought me bananas. Oh, Pa."

"Don't just stand there, boy. Let me in the house so's I can set them down."

Ralph eyed his father in wonder. Millie had not bothered with a measly few bananas, oh, no, he had brought home a whole stalk of them.

"Well, Rate, you just gonna stand there looking?" Millie laughed as he stood the stalk against the wall.

"Do I get to eat all I want?"

"They're all yours, so I reckon so."

"Millie, he'll get sick," put in Mina.

"That's what you said about Blanche and the oranges, and she never got sick, now did she?"

"No, but you know how Ralph likes bananas. What if he doesn't know when to stop?"

"Then he'll get a bellyache. Miney, just keep still and let the boy be."

Ralph was still gazing at the bananas. Why, there must be more'n a hundred. Well, maybe not that many, but my, there was an awful lot of them.

"Ma, can I start eating?"

"Your father says so. Just you mind you don't get sick to your stomach, and don't try to hog them down. No one is going to take them away from you."

"I won't. Here, Ma, don't you want one?" Ralph broke off the first banana and offered it to his mother.

"Thank you, Ralph, but you had better have the first one."

"But I want you to have one, and Pa, and here, Blanche, don't you want one?"

"I guess maybe I will. I think Pa got you more bananas than he got me oranges."

"What did you expect, Blanche, a whole tree?" chuckled Millie.

"Of course not," she snapped. Then, she added in a more modulated tone, "Well, maybe it just seems like more." She took the proffered banana somewhat hesitatingly, wanting it…and yet not wanting it.

Goodness. Now, who'd have thought Pa would have bought all those bananas for Ralph? Bet they cost more than the oranges. Somehow, she just hadn't thought Pa would be that foolish. Ralph sure was going to act smart just because he got what he wanted for once. Oh, well, at least he wasn't selfish and had wanted to share with everyone. Sometimes, Pa was just hard to figure out. There were times when he acted as though Ralph was really the cat's meow, yet, when it really counted, she knew she always came out best.

Pa never said anything to her if she shirked her work, yet he never let Ralph get by without doing his. 'Course, part of this was because she was Ma's favorite, no doubt about that, and that was just because she had had the good fortune to be born a girl. Grandma Smith had told her that one day when she had been lording it over Ralph, and Grandma had peered at her through those steel-rimmed glasses, and the tone of her voice had made Blanche just a little ashamed of herself for teasing her brother. After all, she was more fortunate because Ma and even Pa most always favored her, and it really wasn't very nice of her to throw it up to Ralph. He couldn't help it because he was born a boy, but somehow, she didn't think Ralph would have liked being a girl even if he could have had a choice. Nope, she was sure he was entirely satisfied being a boy.

Ralph had been standing by the window watching the huge flakes of snow drift lazily to the ground. It was pretty when it came down like this, and besides, there wasn't much else to do at Grandmother's except be quiet and not bother the grownups that is. As he stood there, he absentmindedly kept wiggling a tooth that was getting mighty loose and near the dropping-out stage.

"Rate, what are you doing?"

"Just looking out the window, Grandfather."

"No, I mean what's that you've got in your mouth?"

"Oh. A loose tooth. See?" He opened his mouth to display a slightly askew tooth.

"Come here, boy. I can't see it from clear over there."

"Uh-uh. If I do, you'll pull it."

"Now, what would I pull it for?" Rate eyed him suspiciously, mulling over in his mind his grandfather's question. "Well, Rate, what's taking so long?"

The boy finally edged over to his grandfather and stood in front of him with a somewhat wary look.

"Open up and let's see that tooth." Rate obediently opened his mouth, and Horatio peered at the small baby teeth. "Is this the one?" he asked as he tentatively touched the wobbly tooth.

"Uh-huh," acknowledged Ralph with his mouth still open.

Just then, Horatio gave a little shove with his finger, and Ralph hollered. "You pulled it, just like I knowed you would. You pulled my tooth," was the indignant accusation.

"No, boy, I simply pushed it out. There's a difference." Horatio chuckled. "Now, doesn't that feel better already?"

The boy was angry, and he scowled his displeasure, but he dared not view his thoughts aloud. He felt his grandfather had tricked him, and it hurt his manly pride. Horatio sensed the lad's struggle to keep to himself the thoughts that were churning inside. To make amends, he gave the boy a silver dollar telling him that that was a pretty good price for a worn-out tooth. Rate thanked him for the money, while underneath he still seethed. Next time, he'd know better, and he'd listen more carefully to how Grandfather worded what he said.

Usually, the only gift Blanche had for her mother at Christmas was one she had made at school or something Pa had bought to come from all three of them. This year was going to be different. Several weeks ago, she had noticed an advertisement on a soap wrapper at Grandmother's that for ten soap wrappers and fifteen cents, she could get a sugar spoon. She had asked some of her girlfriends about wrappers, and in a few weeks, she had had the necessary amount of wrappers as well as the money. Then, she had waited impatiently for the package to come in the mail; she had had it sent to her in care of Grandmother so there would be no chance of her mother opening the package by mistake.

When it finally arrived, Blanche was delighted. The small fluted bowl of the spoon was gold in color while the handle was silver; Blanche thought it was beautiful and could hardly wait until the day of gift-giving arrived.

To say that Miney was surprised at Blanche's gift would indeed be an understatement. She was almost as delighted as the young girl. It was certainly a gift she would treasure all her life. It graced Miney's table every day, and Blanche was truly proud of her accomplishment.

Rate too was pleased with Christmas. Ma and Pa had bought him a new slate to take the place of the old one, which had been Ma's and had a crack diagonally across it, making it difficult to use. The new one had four usable sides; it was like having two small slates, but they were hinged together so they could be folded for storage in the desk or spread out for use. Of course, a body didn't have to spread them out; they could be kept folded and written on both sides, or they could be turned to bring the used sides together, and the clean sides were then ready to be written on. Rate was sure his was quite the nicest slate anyone had in school.

*****

Millie had finished cleaning the cow stables and had put the cows back in the barn. He stood for a moment watching them eagerly eat the fresh hay he had just forked into their mangers, the wooden stanchions creaking in protest as the cows strained against them to reach what looked to be a choice morsel the farthest from their reach. Well, that was done, and there'd be nothing more to do today until time for chores at night.

He was in hopes Cash Waldron would be over in the afternoon for a game of checkers. Somehow, he and Cash never did seem to get tired of checker playing. Sometimes, Miney asked him how they could get any pleasure from it when they'd sit for hours at a time, hunched over the checkerboard on their knees, neither speaking, intent upon the moves to be made. Wasn't that just like a woman? 'Course a woman would never be able to keep her mouth shut for that long a time. Many's the time when Miney got to rambling on, he felt he just had to shut her up, so he'd say, "Miney, keep still." He knew it hurt her feelings, but her chattering just rankled sometimes. Now, he and Cash did their talking at other times; during a game was no time to let senseless talking divert their concentration.

As Millie came by the horse stable, he heard Rate's voice yelling, "Get off my foot, Mage. Get off my foot."

He stepped through the doorway into the stable, and there was Ralph, standing in the stall alongside Mage, whacking the large bay horse with his felt hat, yelling at the horse who stood very unconcerned, not moving a muscle.

"What's all the screeching about?" asked Millie suppressing a laugh.

"Pa," came the relieved reply. "I can't get Mage to move off my foot. I can't pull it out either. He just won't move no matter how I hit and shove."

"Rate, use your head for something besides a hat rack. Reach down, grab his fetlock, and tell him to heist. When he does, move your foot, then let him put his foot back down." Rate did just that, and on the command "Heist," Mage obediently lifted his foot. "See how easy that was. If you're going to work with horses, you've got to get a little horse sense yourself. Remember that, boy."

"Yes, Pa."

Easy enough for Pa to say, but Mage hadn't been standing on his foot either. 'Course Pa's idea had worked. If Mage wasn't so dumb, it would never have happened. The other horses never seemed to step on him, or if they did, they moved just as soon as he gave them a shove and told them to get over. Boy, his foot didn't feel any too good either. Mage sure was heavy enough, and it felt as if the dumb animal had leaned toward him, thereby putting extra weight on that foot. Well, he'd know what to do next time, if he was unlucky enough to have a next time.

Nineteen hundred! The change of a century. While large cities like New York, San Francisco, St. Louis, and Chicago celebrated this change with more than the usual festivities for New Year's Eve, in the small villages like Elsie, the passing of one century for another went virtually unnoticed. The farm folk could see no cause for exuberance. A man who had to be in the barn early to care for livestock had little time to be spending the night celebrating anything. Not that they didn't like a little diversion now and then, but there were more appropriate times to their way of thinking. Let the city folk squander their time and money. The farm folk couldn't afford to be that frivolous. What if one went to bed and the year was 1899, and upon awakening, it was 1900? One day or one year was pretty much the same—some better, some worse, with a man doing honest labor to provide for his family just as the good Lord intended.

The snow was gone, but the ground was still partly frozen, although the days warmed enough to give hint that warmer weather would soon be on hand. Ralph had spent a portion of the afternoon with his grandfather getting wood from the north eighty. Since the stoves still devoured a considerable amount each day, Grandfather said his woodshed was getting too low for comfort, and he'd get the wood before the roads turned into a mire of mud. That night at the supper table, Ralph related the events to his father.

"Pa, do you know how to tell when you get a full load on that springboard like Grandfather's?"

"I reckon when it's piled a certain height."

"Nope. That's not the way Grandfather does it. We kept throwing on wood, and then he'd pick up the back wheel. We'd throw on some more, and he'd do the same thing. Well, when he couldn't lift the wheel, he said he guessed that had better be a load, and we pulled out."

At that, Millie burst out laughing. "Leave it to Pa to have some gimmick like that. Guess he knew how much that driving team of his could pull without too much effort. See, Rate, you learned something."

Rate nodded his head, only he wasn't too sure just what he had learned. He'd heard Pa and Guy Sherman talking one day, and they'd said that Rate Setterington was a heap stronger than most men, so unless he got to be as strong as his grandfather, it wouldn't do any good to judge a load that way.

Pa had once said that Grandfather was stronger than either he or Uncle John. Why, he told of the time when his pa was young, there'd been a dance at Elsie, and two strangers had come by. These two had decided to break up the dance, but before they got started, Grandfather had hit the one who'd been full of all the big talk. The man dropped like a felled ox, and for a while, they thought he was dead. Grandfather had said that if the man ever came to, he'd never hit another man as long as he lived. Then, Pa had chuckled and said he guessed that didn't hold for him and John since Pa had always whipped them when he thought they needed it.

Ralph had wanted to ask his father just what it was that he and Uncle John had done that Grandfather had felt they needed to be whipped. He guessed maybe he shouldn't interrupt, but he'd try to remember to ask Pa some evening after supper when sometimes Pa felt like talking about the days when he was just a kid. He was five or six years older than Uncle John, so he'd had plenty of work to do.

Rate also wondered what his grandfather had been doing at a dance since he knew that both Grandfather and Grandmother looked upon dancing as something evil and were quite outspoken in their views on the subject. In fact, dancing was cause for a rather serious breach between them and Uncle John. It seemed that when there was work to be done, Uncle John's feet always hurt and he felt miserable, but let him get wind of a dance somewhere, and he'd be there for the first squawk of the fiddle until the last. Aunt Grace was just as bad. She loved to dance, and when she played the piano, instead of it being the sedate, pious church music, she played other more rollicking tunes like the ones Ralph had been given to believe were played in saloons. Bet back in the old days, Aunt Grace could have made a mighty fine dance hall girl.

Of course, Grandmother and Grandfather never failed to voice their disapproval, but Uncle John, unlike Pa, paid no attention to his parents' objections. In fact, he seemed to maliciously enjoy having them know that he danced whenever and wherever he could. Perhaps John deliberately flaunted his sinful ways—for to Horatio and Lavina, they were indeed sinful—as a means of getting even for some of those boyhood whippings he had resented so much and for the times when his mother and father had tried to interfere with his way of living when he was already a married man, making his own way in the world.

Certainly John and Milford were not one bit alike. Millie never crossed either of his parents, not even to take his wife's part in some rather minor disagreement. Because Millie was desperate for parental approval, he could never bring himself to disagree with his parents' wishes, and while he perhaps secretly admired John's spunk, he let it be known that he did not agree with his brother's lack of respect for Horatio and Lavina. In fact, from the time of being boys, this had been a bone of contention between the two.

It was only a few evenings later when Millie, chores done, a satisfying meal under his belt, felt like expounding somewhat on his early life. Rate had started the ball rolling by asking, "Pa, how old was you when you came to Elsie?"

"Well, boy, I was two years old. Don't recollect much about the journey myself," he added with a chuckle. "Your grandfather and your great-grandfather John Setterington came here to Elsie in 1867. They opened a general store and run a livery stable right there on the south side of Main Street, west of where Van Deusen's grocery store is now. I don't know as I know what made them decide to leave Canada or why they came to Elsie, but they did.

"Grandfather had told Pa that whenever he wanted to go back, they'd settle up right then and there. Well, one day in 1871, Pa was cultivating corn in north of where they built the school. He owned a whole section there, and Grandfather owned a section to the east. Grandfather sent word to Pa that he wanted to take inventory right then because he was going back to Canada. Pa had to drop everything and do like his father wanted. Didn't make any difference that Pa had been smack-dab in the middle of a job. When Grandfather wanted something done, he wanted it done then. There used to be a high board fence between the livery stable and the store so's the horses could get a little exercise. It was my job to take those horses to the creek north of town each day for water. I wasn't very big then, but I had a pony to ride, and I guess the job could have been a whole lot worse."

Rate figured it didn't sound too good to him. He bet some of the horses gave a lot of trouble, so he ventured, "But, Pa, didn't they sometimes run off?"

"Not usually. We had one old mare that kind of lorded it over the rest, and she was dependable. She'd have gone there and back by herself, I think, and the others sort of followed her. If we got a new horse in, it might cause some trouble, but somehow me and that old pony managed. Guess the horses knew it was their only chance for a drink, and once they'd had their fill, they were content to come back to their hay and a ration of grain."

Millie paused a moment, then went on to explain, "Our first home in Elsie burned. Don't know just what caused it, but I presume sparks from the chimney. Sometimes, chimneys weren't put up as good as they ought, and this could have been one of those. I was about twelve when Pa decided to build kitty-corner to the west of your grandma Smith's. At that age, I was considered man enough to handle a yoke of oxen, so Pa sent the hired hand and me to fetch a load of shingles from Potter's mill. Jake told me when we left, 'Now, Millie, when we come back, watch your oxen, for they'll be dry.' Kid fashion, I hadn't known what he meant, only I didn't ask any questions either.

"On the way home, I went to sleep up on top of the shingles. I knew the team would follow the wagon ahead of us. Well, sir, I didn't wake up until that wagon was going down the embankment to the river. It tipped over and scattered those shingles all down the slope and ended in the river. I went into the river with shingles on top of me. Thought I'd like to drown, but Jake hauled me out. Then and there, I knew what the hired hand had meant. I should have unhitched the oxen back down the road apiece, led them to the river for a drink, and then hitched them up again. Those oxen had been mighty thirsty, and they'd just taken the shortest route to water.

"By golly, by the time we got the load set to rights again, it was nigh unto morning. In fact, I got home just in time to set down to breakfast. Believe you me, I was beat. Pa didn't say much except I was given to understand that my chores still needed doing. I knew right then and there that sleep or no sleep, Pa intended me to do my day's work just the same. When I kept busy, it wasn't so bad"—Millie chuckled—"but if I sat down, I'd almost fall asleep."

"Your father certainly wasn't very understanding," volunteered Miney.

"I don't know as I'd say that, Miney. I suppose he felt it was my own fault, and I guess it did teach me something. I lived through it, so no harm was done."

Millie was always quick to defend his father from any criticism, no matter how insignificant and small. However, Rate was inclined to agree with his mother. He could just visualize the stern look on his grandfather's face reminding Pa there was chores to be done. Grandfather certainly had his own ideas about how to bring up boys. Shirking work didn't enter into the plan not one little bit.

Ralph had heard his father and his grandfather talking about a barn raising on some property just outside of the village that belonged to his grandfather. He'd heard the older men talk of such things, but there hadn't been any around this neck of the woods since he'd been old enough to be interested. He was in hopes Pa would let him tag along and watch this one. He figured he'd wait until that very day to ask permission; otherwise, Pa'd have too long a time to think about it, and then, he'd likely think it was no place for a small boy.

Pa had stopped in on their way home from town one afternoon, and Rate had seen the piles of lumber, and he had watched a man using a broadax. The axe had looked funny to him at first with its crooked handle, but when he saw the man deftly square off a beam from what had once been a round tree trunk, he could see the wisdom behind it. My, but there was a lot of lumber. The shingles had been piled to one side along with the wide boards, which he supposed would be siding, only there was a lot of other pieces, which he had no idea what they were designed for. He had hoped fervently that Pa would let him come to watch so's he could find out where they went.

He'd heard Ma and Grandmother and Aunt Grace talking about feeding all those men, so he knew Ma would be busy all day too. Like as not they'd expect he and Blanche to go over to Grandma Smith's. Not that he didn't like to go there, 'cause he did. Grandma always had cookies for him, and she smiled a lot. If he did get into some little mischief, she never seemed to mind awful much. He guessed she must be getting awful old, and she had been poorly of late, but she still was always good-natured and glad to see him. Besides, she usually took his part when he and Blanche disagreed. He guessed she liked him just as much as Blanche or even a mite better. She was sure some different than Grandmother. But even if he did like going there, just this once he'd rather stay and watch the workmen. Maybe he should ask God to give him a little help. Ma always said that if we prayed in Jesus's name, God would answer our prayers. Well, he guessed he'd put it to the test.

The day dawned sunny and bright. Millie was in exceptionally good spirits, so as everyone was bustling about getting victuals packed in the buggy, Rate brought up the question foremost in his mind.

"Pa, can I stay with you and Ma and watch the barn raising?"

"I don't know, boy. Think you could stay back out of the way? The men will be too busy to have a boy underfoot, and you could get hurt."

"Millie, hadn't he better go to Ma's along with Blanche? I'll have no time to keep my eye on him and neither will you."

"The lad might learn something. Tell you what, Rate, you can stay, but the first time I have to speak to you, off you go to your grandma's."

"All right, Pa. I promise I'll look out, honest, I will. See, Blanche," he hissed, "you said Pa wouldn't let me 'cause I was too young. Lot you knew."

"Who'd want to stand around all day watching some old barn being built anyway? Bet I have more fun. I might even get to bake cookies, and just see if I bring you any."

"And I suppose I'll care."

"You two hush up and get in the buggy," ordered Miney. "Your pa is coming with the wagon and team. Hurry now, I don't have all day."

What Rate didn't know was that Blanche had already seen more than one barn raising, so it wasn't the novelty to her that it was to him.

What in future years would be the Schenck place was bustling with activity. Horatio had bought the place from his brother-in-law, Lem Bingham, and since it had no barn, he had decided it would increase the value of the property enough to go through the bother of building one before selling the place. Men and rigs were arriving in droves. More women joined Miney, Lavina, and Grace in the tent erected for them. Men working hard had ravenous appetites, and the women were starting early. They knew there'd be a steady stream of men for coffee and a plate of food or a piece of cake or pie, and since not all would be working at the same time, they'd eat in shifts.

Rate watched the swarm of men with interest, each man intent upon some job, each seeming to know what he was to do. One man, the master carpenter, was everywhere at once, issuing orders and supervising construction. Rate watched the assembling of the bent on the ground. The beams had been notched so the others slipped into place and were pegged with a cylindrical wooden peg, which had to be driven into the bored-out hole. As Ralph watched the bent, which was to be the east end of the barn, taking shape on the ground, he began to wonder just how they'd ever get it upright and in place. Guess maybe he now understood what "barn raising" meant, for if they built all that stuff laid out on the ground, somehow, it was going to have to be raised into place. Boy, supposing one side was longer than the other? Somebody sure had to know what they was doin'.

In a shorter time than he had thought possible, the bent was finished. Now he'd find out how they'd get it up. From somewhere, there came a lot of ropes. The ropes were tied to the topmost beam of the bent, the center one strung through a pulley on what he later learned was called a gin pole. It was a tall pole set in the ground in what was to be the inside of the barn. Some of the men carried pikes, which to the lad looked like something out of medieval history, since they were long, stout poles with a spike at the end. With no instructions given, each man seeming to understand his job, the men assembled along the bent, one row on a side.

Ralph watched in awe as the men who were to handle the ropes started taking up the slack, and then began pulling in earnest to "Heave! Heave! Heave!" in steady rhythm. Slowly and surely, the top of the bent began to rise. As it neared its upright position, the men with pikes began to push and brace, giving it the support needed to stay in position. When it was upright, ropes to the east and ropes to the west were snubbed around metal braces driven diagonally into the ground.

In the same manner, the next bent was put into position, and Ralph watched as the men skillfully pegged timbers linking the two bents securely in place. He sensed, rather than saw, the ripple of relief that spread through the workers when this task was done. The addition of the second bent lent stability to the structure.

All right, now he knew how they raised this much, but they still had the rafters to be put in place. The thought occurred to Ralph that someone sure had to be pretty bright to know how to do all these things. The lad realized once again that adults knew a lot about many things. My, but he did have a lot to learn. Pa sure was smart. Rate had watched him, and he seemed to know just what to do and when.

Ralph watched the other bents raised into place, propped, and supported; next, he watched as the ridgepole and rafters were raised and nailed into place. He thought the men who crawled around on these rafters were very brave, and he wasn't at all sure he'd have liked their job. After the roofboards were in place, the job of shingling didn't seem all that bad.

By late afternoon, much of the barn was completed. Of course, it was a rather small one, not nearly the size of the barns built on farms. There was still part of a side on which to finish putting the siding, and the doors still had to be made and hung, and the roof wasn't quite finished, but it was nothing that a small crew of men working together would have any trouble finishing.

Toward the end, Ralph had begun to get restless, and he'd liked to have asked Ma when they was going home, but he daren't. He also knew better than to hunt up his father to ask him. He had seen a few men and rigs leave, but he supposed since it was Grandfather's barn, it was more than likely that Pa and Ma would be one of the last to leave. He was still glad he'd come. Bet Blanche hadn't learned half as much as he had today.

School was almost over for the year, and Ralph was looking forward to vacation. Still, he guessed he'd sort of miss having so many friends to play with. He liked playing anti-I-over. At noon hour, they'd choose up sides, and then one group would go on one side of the woodshed, one group on the other. Someone would roll a ball over the peak of the roof to the other side yelling "anti-I-over." If a person over there caught the ball, they ran to your side, trying to touch as many of your players with the ball as they could while the two teams changed sides. If you got caught, you had to change teams. Sometimes, one team would get down to only one or two players. Rate was getting pretty good at catching the ball when it rolled off the roof, only he couldn't always catch someone from the other team because he wasn't all that fast at running.

'Course, he'd liked it in the winter when they'd played fox and geese in the snow. The older boys played prisoner's goal, but they wouldn't tolerate the smaller children playing with them—said they only got in the way. Well, next year he'd be bigger, and he just knew he'd be able to run faster, so maybe the big boys wouldn't laugh at him for being small and slow.

CHAPTER 13

Rate sat on the porch idly toying with a stick, his thoughts engrossed with the litter of pups he'd seen yesterday. Don Sherman—better known as Curly—his best friend, had told him Wally Hiers's bulldog had whelped a few days ago, and sure enough, when he went over there, Mr. Hiers had let him look at the silky, wiggling mass of puppy flesh, so entwined it was hard to tell which head went with which body, legs, and tail. One pup, a little larger than the rest, had been snoozing fitfully, his belly obviously full, and his littermates crawling over his topside bothered him not in the least. Rate had wanted to pick that one up in his hands; he could almost feel the silky smoothness of the close-fitting puppy hair, and his fingers itched with longing.

Mr. Hiers had said they were too little to be handled, and old Maudie wouldn't take kindly to someone picking them up while they were so little; however, the longing in his heart didn't seem to go away.

Rate wanted a pup.

More than anything, he wanted that contented little fellow who didn't get disturbed even if his brothers and sisters did crawl all over him. He'd asked Mr. Hiers how much they cost, and he had told Ralph he would sell him a pup for a dollar and a half.

"Might's well be five," Rate said aloud. "Pa wouldn't let me have a pup—he says dogs are more bother than they're worth, and since Grip disappeared some time ago, he likely wouldn't want another dog. And I don't have more'n a few cents anyhow."

He sprang up and dashed into the house unmindful of how he slammed the door and dashed upstairs to his bedroom. He dug down into a drawer for the box in which he kept important things.

He dumped the contents on the bed. There were a couple of shiny stones, a porcupine quill, a jackknife with one blade broken, some string, some nails, a rivet or two, a pencil stub, a ring from a horse's harness, and two pennies. Ralph stared at the pennies. It would take 148 more to have the price of a pup, even if Pa would let him have one.

Once more, he sat down disconsolately. Golly, a boy needed a dog, something he could call his own, something to love that would love him in return. There just had to be a way.

That night at supper, Rate announced to his father, "Maudie, Wally Hiers's bulldog, had her pups, Pa. I went over an' see 'em today. They sure are the nicest pups I ever see."

"Well, now, are they? What made them so special?" asked Millie, his eyes twinkling.

"They…they…well, they was nice and fat for one thing, and ole Maudie, she's takin' awful good care of them, an' this one ole fella is bigger'n all the rest."

"They aren't very old, are they?"

"No, Pa, they're tiny yet. Just got their eyes open a day or so ago. Ole Maudie didn't want nobody touchin' them yet, so's Mr. Hiers said I couldn't hold one. When they get bigger, he's gonna let me," he stated proudly.

"Ralph, you aren't to make a nuisance of yourself," put in Mina.

"I won't, Ma. Mr. Hiers, he told me I could come over anytime I liked. Honest, he did. Pa, could I have a pup?"

There, the words were out. To be sure, this wasn't quite as he'd planned it, but still, he'd got the question out. Now, he waited breathlessly for his father to answer.

Millie watched the face of his young son and saw the unspoken pleading in those brown eyes, which were so like his own. He forced himself to refrain from allowing a smile to creep to the fore as he seemed to ponder a moment, then asked, "Will Wally just give you the pup?"

"Not… not exactly. He wants a dollar and a half for one."

"Boy, do you have a dollar fifty?"

"No, Pa, but I thought—"

"You don't have a dollar and a half? Just where did you expect to get the money to buy this pup? Money doesn't grow on every bush as you well know."

"I have part of it," Rate volunteered.

"Well, Rate, just how much do you lack?"

"A dollar and forty-eight cents."

At that, Millie could contain himself no longer; he burst out laughing. Rate did not share his father's humor, and his downcast eyes gave hint that he would have shed tears if he could have managed to be alone.

"Millie, don't tease the boy. This is important to him," chided Miney. "Ralph, did you have a plan for the rest of the money? A dollar and a half is a lot to ask for."

"I know, Ma."

"Not a dollar and a half, Miney, a dollar and forty-eight cents." Millie chuckled again. "Tell you what, boy, since your ma seems to cotton to the notion of you having a dog, perhaps she'd be willing to pay you to pick strawberries. There's quite a patch on that south forty. What do you say, Miney?"

"I hadn't given it much thought. I hadn't intended to go traipsing clear over there for strawberries when I'll likely have all I can take care of right here. Do you think we could sell them?"

"I'll ask next time I go to town. Seems like one of the stores could use them, if not both."

"If we can sell them, I guess I could probably pay Ralph a cent a quart for the picking."

"Hear that, boy? I think you can consider you have a job."

Ralph's face beamed. It was like the sun breaking through a dark storm cloud and shedding its quick, bright light upon a hopeful world. The supper he had been pushing around on his plate began to disappear as his appetite miraculously returned.

He hated picking strawberries, but when the drudgery of the job was balanced against a pup of his very own, the scales most certainly tipped in favor of the pup. At this moment, Rate truly believed there was no job he would not have tackled with a vim since he would be allowed to purchase a pup with the money.

Picking strawberries was not the greatest job in the world; in fact, it was rather backbreaking work—the hot sun beating down mercilessly, making one feel a little like a roasting pig except there was no one to turn the spit, so the picker gets overdone on one side. Be that as it may, Rate was sure a cent a quart was a fair price. That meant he had to pick 150 quarts of berries. Well, 148 if he took into consideration that he already had two pennies. Then, the awful thought came to him like a blow to the head. What if there weren't that many strawberries? A hundred and fifty quarts was an awful lot of berries, that was for certain, so supposing he still didn't have enough money?

Maybe Ma would help him out if he did some extra chores for her. He couldn't rightly think of what, but there must be something he could do for her, and maybe she'd give him a nickel. But no, Ma was awful close with money. Besides, it was only a little short of a miracle that she had not only consented to let him have a pup, but had almost volunteered to help him get it. No, he could expect no more help from that quarter. Ma always said if you had a problem of any sort, you should take it up with the good Lord in prayer. Well, it seemed he now had a problem, so he guessed he'd better ask God to make sure there were 150 quarts of strawberries in that old patch. God had sure enough seen that he got to the barn raising, maybe He'd think a pup was important too.

That night, Ralph's sleep was beset by dreams. He held a brown wiggly puppy in his arms while the pup's little pink tongue proceeded to wash his face, and its needle-sharp teeth nipped at his ear. He awoke and, for an instant, wondered what had happened to his pup. Then, he remembered. He didn't have a pup; he could buy one if he could earn the money—the gigantic sum of $1.50—to pay Mr. Hiers.

"Please, God, please help me," he murmured as he drifted back to sleep.

*****

"Ma, when's Pa coming back from town?"

"I don't rightly know, but I expect he'll be here by suppertime. That man just never misses a meal," she added.

"Do you suppose he'll remember to ask about selling the berries?"

"If he told you he would, he will. Now, stop fretting. Your moping around won't change a thing. Why don't you just go outdoors and play and get out from underfoot?"

"Can I have a cookie first?"

"Here, take one and leave."

My land, but that boy had been a nuisance ever since he'd wanted that pup. He hadn't really teased Millie to find out if they could sell the strawberries, he knew better than that, but the question had been there, unspoken on his face each day, patiently, although solemnly, waiting for his father to make a trip to town. Well, Millie had left right after dinner, and for once, Ralph had expressed no desire to go with his father. She supposed that while he was anxious to know, he had a fear that neither of the stores would want to buy strawberries. Poor lad, that pup was certainly the most important thing on his mind right now. She knew Millie would never give Ralph the money if the stores wouldn't buy the berries. She wouldn't want to give him the money outright, and he already did most of the little chores for her that he was capable of doing, so she had no ready solution. In fact, she too was apprehensive, wondering if the boy was going to get what he already considered "his" pup.

A light rain had begun to fall, so Ralph came back into the house to play. He commented to his mother that Pa should be home most anytime, but knowing that she had begun supper, he wisely stayed out of her way.

When Blanche came downstairs to take the cheesecloth off the table, put the plates in place, put the flatware around, and do the things young girls were supposed to do to help their ma, she hissed, "What makes you think you need some old dog anyhow? Bet no one wants to buy strawberries. Why, most everyone has their own."

"Not the ones who live in town, and not even all the farm folk. I heard Mr. Fizzell say they weren't going to have any this year, so why wouldn't folks buy them?"

"Maybe they don't have the money. Not everyone can buy just any old thing they want, you know. Bet you don't get a pup."

"Bet I do. Just wait and see. I'll show you, and when I do get him, you better watch out, or if you kick my shins, he'll bite you."

"Ha! Lot you know. Any dog of yours would be too dumb to do anything."

Drat it all. Blanche was probably right. He'd never be able to earn the money. He sat down by the south door where he could keep watch of the road and could see his father approaching long before the rig reached the driveway.

"Ma, Pa's home. Shall I go help him take care of the team?"

"You stay right here in the house. It's raining quite hard now, and one person getting wet is enough. Like as not he'll have to have a change of clothes when he gets in the house. Besides, it won't take your pa long, and then you can find out about the berries," she added kindly.

Rate looked at her in wonder. How in thunderation had she known what was on his mind? He certainly had been awful careful not to say one word about strawberries or pups even if that was about all he'd been thinking of just lately. Sometimes, mothers were a wonder, and sometimes they were awful nice to have around.

He guessed his ma was kind of special even if she did favor Blanche. Lot he cared. Pa liked it 'cause he was a boy, and who'd want to be a silly old girl anyhow?

Millie came in shaking himself like some huge dog.

"Gettin' mighty wet out there, Miney, but we do need the rain. Things was gettin' awful dry. Wouldn't hurt a bit if it kept this up all night."

"Here, I brought you a dry shirt. Almost looks as if you need dry trousers too."

"No, this will be fine." He slipped into the dry shirt, quite unmindful that his underwear was damp too. "Something smells good. Don't know why, but a good rain always whets my appetite."

"A good rain or anything else. Milford Setterington, you always have an appetite for two men."

"Now, Miney, would you want to feed some persnickety soul who didn't do justice to your fine cooking?"

"Oh, sit down and stop soft-soaping me. I know how much you think of your stomach."

The meal was nearly over when Rate brought up the subject foremost on his mind.

"Pa, did you find out?"

"Did I find out what, boy?"

"'Bout the strawberries," he explained patiently.

"What about strawberries? Looks like there'll be a good crop this year," he added, the crinkles around his eyes showing.

"Millie, don't tease," chided Miney.

"Pa, didn't you ask like you said you would? Can't we sell strawberries anyplace?"

"Oh, that. Well, I spoke to both stores, and either one will take all we can bring in. They'll pay us eight cents a quart too. So, boy, now all you have to do is get them picked."

"Golly, Pa, that's just great. They'll be ripe soon, won't they?"

"In a couple of weeks or so, they'll start turning, unless we get too much cold weather."

Rate felt as if the weight of the world had been lifted from his shoulders. He just knew he'd get that pup now. He guessed he'd better start thinking of a name for him since it had to be extra special, for this was an extra special pup. The pup would be his, all his, and he'd be the one to teach it lots of tricks, and he'd take his dog with him everywhere he went. His dog. My, but those words had a nice ring. Something that was to be his very own and not shared with anyone.

A few days later, Ralph listened with interest as Millie and Cash Waldron discussed a colt.

"Millie, I've broken and trained a lot of colts for you, but this one has me stumped."

They were leaning on the gate watching a sleek-looking bay cavort around the barnyard. Muscles rippled under the glossy coat. He watched a leaf glide to the ground, ears forward, a wary look in his eye, then he danced away on dainty feet.

"In what way? He appears all right to me."

"Most of the time he is. Most of the time he handles as nice as an old mare, but then he explodes, and I mean just that. Once he's over it, he settles back down and drives like a dream. No, sir, Millie, you'd best get rid of him as soon as you can."

"Badger Jay! Come here." Millie whistled. Obediently the colt trotted over to the fence, nuzzling his nose in Millie's outstretched hand. "Seems gentle enough, Cash. Sure it isn't just that he's a mite more frisky at times?"

"It's more than that. I've handled too many horses not to recognize a bad actor when I see one. You'll have nothing but trouble with him, mark my words. Seems a shame as he is a beauty."

"Think I'll try driving him for a spell and see for myself."

"Don't say I didn't warn you."

Millie did just as he told Cash; he hitched up the colt, and on the first outing, all went well. Badger Jay drove as steady as anyone could wish, just as though he'd been driving for years. However, this proved to be the lull before the storm.

Mina and Millie were going to town, and Ralph asked to be dropped off at Sherman's. When Millie brought the buggy around, Miney asked, "Isn't that the colt Cash told you not to drive?"

"Ye-es," admitted Millie, "but I drove him day before yesterday, and he behaved like a charm. Cash always did tend to be somewhat pessimistic."

"Millie, he kind of scares me. I wish you'd taken one of the others."

"It'll be all right. You'll see."

Miney hesitatingly got into the buggy. Ralph handed up a large basket of eggs to his mother and then hopped onto the back.

"All set, Pa." And with that, they left the yard at a brisk pace.

"See how well he moves, Miney. This one paces naturally. We never had to put the training hobbles on him once. He's a mighty fine animal. Someone will give me a good price for him."

"The sooner, the better," muttered Miney, a worried furrow between her eyes.

They turned the corner east onto the Ridge, and as they neared Sherman's driveway, Millie pulled the horse in to stop. The buggy had not quite stopped when Rate jumped off. Then, he heard his mother scream. Badger Jay was releasing all his pent-up fury in the only way he knew—head down, heels flying—with Miney holding her basket of fragile eggs up in the air, saying, "Do something, Millie, do something."

"I'm trying, I'm trying. Whoa! Whoa, there." His hands were steady on the lines, his words soothing yet forceful. "Steady, Badger Jay. Steady, boy. There now." The animal quieted, and off they went; Millie was looking as though nothing unusual had happened, but Miney's face was drained of all color, and she was busily mopping her brow with a white handkerchief, which quite matched her face.

When Rate explained it to Curly, he said, "Ma sure did look funny holding that basket of eggs just inches above Badger Jay's flying feet yelling at Pa to do something, and all the while Pa just sat there calmly talking to the horse like nothin' was wrong at all. Bet Pa never drives Badger Jay again when Ma is going with him."

"Wasn't you scared?"

"'Course not. I knew Pa could handle him," he boasted.

"Wisht I'd a got here in time to see it," came the disappointed sigh. "Suppose he'll act up when they come back by?"

"Naw. From what Cash says, he's likely to drive all right for days, but then he'll explode again. Sure seems a shame, him bein' such a looker an' all."

Millie was never one to admit he was wrong or that he had possibly made a mistake in judgment, so he was not about to admit that he had misjudged the colt, and Cash's observations had been more astute. He sold Badger Jay as soon as possible at a ridiculous price if one was to judge only by the appearance of the colt in the stall or pasture. However, he had told the man what to expect, since Millie was one of the more honest horse traders. It was not his fault if the buyer had felt Millie was exaggerating because Millie obviously didn't know much about horses. Millie was to learn that in a few months' time, Badger Jay had had two more owners. A born outlaw? No one knew. Millie secretly felt he was lucky to be shed of him although he would have denied having such thoughts had anyone bothered to ask.

Blanche had gone with her grandmother to spend the week with Aunt Ruby. Mina had been giving it thought for some time now that she would like to go visit her sister Ettie in Traverse City. Now seemed as good a time as any because if there ever was a lull in her work, it was now. Ethel Putman could come in by the day to get Millie's meals while she was gone. There wasn't likely to be a hired man until haying season.

After talking the matter over with Millie, it was decided Miney and Ralph would leave on Tuesday. When Lorin heard of it, she mentioned it to Georgie, who promptly wanted to come along. Mina wasn't all that enthused because her nephew sometimes seemed to be even more peculiar than her half sister. So far, he hadn't held a steady job but worked here and there—he was between jobs now. He would quit a good job when he got a little money ahead and then not work until he was broke again. Miney often wondered where he got this trait since Norm always worked although he did spend a lot of what he made on drink. Well, maybe it would be handy to have a young man along to help with the valises, and he could perhaps help look after Ralph. That boy was just not one for sitting quietly for very long, and he had the biggest bump of curiosity she had ever seen. He wanted to know how everything he saw worked. 'Course Millie was rather strict with the lad, so Ralph seldom got in anyone's way, and he didn't pester with a lot of questions; however, not much escaped his eye.

She just knew he would become bored long before they reached Ettie's, so maybe if they had a few minutes' stop someplace along the line, Georgie could take him into the depot just to give him a chance to stretch his legs and a change of scenery to boot.

Although Miney was right and Ralph had become bored, he was less trouble than she had imagined. Of course, it had helped immensely when the conductor had taken a liking to Ralph and had taken him on a tour of the train, even going into some of the other cars. Ralph had excitedly told his mother every incident on the excursion. Then too he had been shown where the watercooler stood at the back of the car, and it was simply amazing how often he worked up a dreadful thirst—almost as if he was in the middle of the Sahara. Naturally, being the outgoing child that he was, he smiled at the other passengers as he sauntered down the aisle and even said hello to some; so on about his third trip, some of them struck up a conversation. He came back all excited because one rather elderly lady had given him a cookie while another had produced a piece of stick candy—his favorite, wintergreen—which he elatedly showed his mother.

"Goodness, Ralph, I thought I had taught you better manners. Don't you know that you are not to accept gifts from strangers?"

His face fell for a moment, then he said brightly, "But, Ma, they aren't exactly strangers. That made the third time I see 'em."

"*Saw*, not *see*."

"Saw them."

Miney laughed at his logic.

"Aunt Miney, there's something in what he says. Besides, this really isn't like meeting some stranger out in the open. Those old ladies think he's cute, and you'll have to admit he doesn't hang back like some youngsters. He's always got a ready answer."

"You're right there, Georgie. I guess there's no harm done. Ralph, did you mind your manners and thank them properly?"

"Oh, yes, Ma. I 'membered, just like you taught me. They even told me their names. The candy lady was Mrs. O'Hare, and the cookie lady was Mrs. Evans. They aren't going as far as we are," he confided.

It had taken the entire day, but they finally arrived in Traverse City. Ettie had not come to meet them, but her husband, George Curtis, along with their sons, Glen and Free, was there when the train pulled into the station. Glen was nearer Blanche's age, so Ralph rather looked up to him just because he was older, and yet, even though Georgie was much older than either boy, Ralph did not look up to him as someone he would want to be like. Free, although nearer to Ralph in age, was too quiet and had little to say, so Ralph made no attempt to get acquainted with this cousin.

The next couple of days passed quickly. Ralph liked Aunt Ettie just fine. She was kinda small like Grandma and rather plain looking, but she treated him right well. Uncle Doc—George had once been a practicing physician although he was now an attorney—was exceptionally nice. During the evenings, he took the boys places and certainly did much to make Ralph's stay enjoyable. Ma, he guessed, was having a good time just visiting with Aunt Ettie, who was her own sister, not a half sister like Aunt Lorin and Aunt Mary.

Ralph had known that Aunt Ettie had a telephone because he had been nearby when Uncle Doc had called. The thought of being able to talk to someone who was so far away intrigued the lad. He mentioned this to Glen. Thus it was that the next day when Aunt Ettie sent the boys downtown on an errand, Glen stopped into the drugstore and asked the clerk if he might use the telephone. He gave Central the number of his home and, when his mother answered, explained the reason for the call.

Then, he gave the phone to Ralph.

"Aunt—Aunt Ettie?"

"Yes, Ralph. Where are you?"

"We're at a drugstore," he almost shouted.

"Ralph, it isn't necessary to holler. I can hear you perfectly well."

In a more modulated tone, "I can hear you too, Aunt Ettie. My, this sure is something. Just think how far away I am."

"Yes, Ralph, I know. The telephone is a marvelous invention, isn't it?"

"Oh, my, yes. Glen says I gotta go now. We'll be back shortly. Bye, Aunt Ettie."

Gee whiz, he'd talked on a telephone. Why, Aunt Ettie had sounded almost like she was standing right beside him. He'd known her voice right off. Goodness, just wait until he got home and told Curly that he had used a telephone. There were quite a number of them in use in the village, but thus far, not many lines had been strung into the country. Sure was amazing how a person's voice could go over the wire. Someone had to be powerful smart to have figured it all out.

*****

"Mina, where's that boy? Just lately he's never around when I want him. Where's he go all the time? He does his chores then ske-daddles off so fast I can't catch him to do anything else."

"Why, Millie, every day he's been going over to that south forty to check on those strawberries. I thought you knew."

"You mean he traipses clean over there every day just to see those strawberries? No, I never dreamt that was what he was doing. What in tarnation for?" Millie looked completely perplexed.

"He's making sure they're getting ripe. Now, don't laugh, he is absolutely serious. He's afraid they'll get ripe early and he will miss a few quarts. Millie, that pup is all he thinks of. I've never seen a child so obsessed with anything."

"Well, I'll be darned. When he gets his heart set on something, he really goes whole hog, don't he? Think he'll stick to pickin' so he'll earn enough money?"

"If there's enough strawberries, Ralph will pick them. He may get sick of the job, but the thoughts of that pup will keep him going. I'm certain of that. My only concern is what will happen if there isn't 150 quarts. Do you realize what a disappointed young lad we'll have?"

"Let's not cross our bridges afore we get to them."

Miney knew there was no need to pursue this line of questioning because she would get no further opinion from Millie.

She pushed back a stray tendril of hair with the back of her hand. The palms were flour-covered where she had spread a thin coating on the board in preparation to roll out cookie dough. She paused a moment, watching her husband return to the barn. His shoulders were broad, his stride long; he was a powerful man who actually enjoyed physical labor, but a man extremely set in his ways. She knew he had set forth the criteria by which Ralph was to get a pup, and in no way would he alter any of the conditions. His stubborn English heritage would not let him pamper his son in any way nor give help where he deemed it unnecessary. No, poor Ralph would have to earn his dog with no outside help except God.

Ralph and Miney had spent a lot of anxious hours all for naught. The strawberries flourished. There was ample rain, and when the berries were large, a warm June sun softly kissed them to a deep-red, sweet-tasting and juicy. Ralph picked with a will. He zealously counted and recounted his growing pile of money. The nearer he came to the goal, the more he worried whether there would be that many quarts.

As all things must come to an end, so must the season for strawberries, and with its close came the pup to the Setterington household. Ralph christened him Bruno, and while no one exactly appreciated the first few nights when the pup howled his loneliness, he settled in quite well.

If anyone noticed that Rate often slipped a piece of meat from his plate to the pup wiggling under his chair, they said nothing. Actually, the pup was exceptionally well-behaved in the house as though he knew with a certainty that any infraction of the rules would result in him being cast outside quicker than a body could say *scat*.

Blanche had been wanting a bicycle for several weeks since some of her school chums were getting bicycles now that they had the same size wheel front and back and were much easier to handle than the old-fashioned kind had been. She had mentioned it to Pa and Ma, rather hinting that she could even ride into town as they weren't always too keen on her driving because some of the driving horses Millie kept were a little on the skittish side. Honestly, they never thought she could do anything unless it was connected with work. Ralph had been driving since he'd started school, and he wasn't even tall enough to throw a harness on a horse yet, so Pa always did that. Anyway, they were always afraid she'd get hurt just because Pa had known a family whose little girl got dragged by a runaway horse—seems she'd tied the lines around her waist so's she wouldn't drop one—and she'd been killed. Well, Pa said he didn't want anything like that to happen to his daughter. Actually, Blanche felt that her mother was behind the whole thing. Ma always seemed to worry about her, but she sure put up with a lot from Ralph without worrying.

Anyway, she'd broached the subject of a bicycle hoping for one for her birthday. Ma had been anything but enthusiastic, but Blanche felt that was just because Ma was so all-fired close with money. She'd tried to be extra nice to her father, knowing that he would be the one worth winning over.

Whether all of Blanche's thoughtfulness paid off, or whether Millie had intended to get her a bicycle all along, she never knew. However, her birthday did bring her a nice, new, shiny bicycle. For once, what Ma and Pa gave her far outshone any other present. She had the book *Jessica's First Prayer* from her grandmother, and Grandfather had given her a five-dollar gold piece, but it was the bicycle she appreciated most. My, it was beautiful. She could hardly wait until she could learn to ride it well enough to ride into town to show it off to her friends. She was certain it was the nicest one she'd ever seen.

Blanche had not reckoned with the condition of the roads when she had envisioned riding a bicycle into Elsie swiftly and easily. The Ridge Road was a rather sandy affair, and where the wheels of the buggies and wagons went, there was usually a rut, not always the straightest since often the horses sort of picked their own way, and the next team just naturally followed the same tracks. Blanche was to learn that between the wheel tracks, it was too soft, and the hard, narrow bike tires sank in far enough to make it virtually impossible to pedal. Trying to follow the ruts was almost as bad.

Besides, if she rode into town, Ma was sure to think of something she needed from the general store, so Blanche had to contend with a basket hanging on the handlebars, swinging back and forth, making steering more difficult and sometimes whacking her on the knee.

Then, there was the gristmill hill. Just as she crossed the long wooden bridge, with its board sides, which slanted across Maple River, Blanche always began to pedal furiously, hoping to gain enough momentum to enable her to make the hill. It was always the same. Even though she stood on the pedals and put all her weight on them, just shy of the top, she came to a standstill. Somehow, it always rankled to have to get off and walk the rest of the way. She hated to be bested at anything.

Of course, coming down the hill on the way home atoned for the ignoble ascent. She'd take her feet off the pedals even if it didn't look ladylike and let the bike fly. It was glorious! Down the hill, around the curve, and then quickly start to pedal to get over the bridge and up the incline to make the turn by the cemetery. Somehow, this always made the ride home exciting, which in turn made the whole trip worthwhile.

It was election year once again, and Ralph had often heard his father and other neighbors talk politics when they met in town. Sometimes, he hung around to listen, but much of the talk was too deep for him, so he usually wandered off a ways to look in store windows or hang by his legs from a hitching post or to look over the teams and driving horses tethered along the street. My, some of those horses sure were pretty, and those fancy harnesses! He sure liked all those shiny buckles, the white rings, and the bridle rosettes.

Politics was a big issue once again. McKinley received the Republican nomination without any difficulty, and this time his running mate was to be Theodore Roosevelt, governor of New York. Teddy was a nationally known figure since "Colonel Teddy" had received a notoriety of sorts at San Juan Hill during the Spanish-American War.

Since the depression had ended in 1897, the Republicans were a strong force indeed. The best the Democrats could put up as an adversary was the already oncedefeated William Jennings Bryan with Adlai Stevenson for vice president. The Democrats had opposition to imperialism and the gold standard as a platform, whereas the Republicans upheld the gold standard. The Republicans also had prosperity on their side. McKinley's "full dinner pail" speeches did much to keep the support of the nation.

Millie and the neighboring farmers were no exception. They basked in the rising prices for grains and all farm commodities. They were not about to gamble with some new ideas in the White House when the present ones seemed to be doing much to improve their station in life.

Mina sat by the south dining room window doing some mending. Seemed as though there was always something wrong with Ralph's clothes—a missing button, a three-cornered tear, a torn suspender, just anything to keep her busy with a needle.

Of course, Millie was right near as bad it seemed. That man not only lost buttons, but they often got torn off where he caught them on something, so they always took a little of the cloth along with them. Miney disliked patching more than she did the original sewing, and she had no love for that.

She wished she could have been working on the rug she was crocheting, since she really did love to crochet. Time always slipped by rapidly when she was doing something she thoroughly enjoyed, and it did drag at times like this. She laid the shirt down in her lap a moment and looked out the window. Then, she chuckled. My goodness, that boy certainly enjoyed his pup.

Ralph took off running, and the pup chased after him as fast as the short legs would propel the fat, little body, yapping as he went. Then, Ralph dropped to the ground, and the pup tried to lick any part of his master's exposed body he could reach, and judging from the sounds, his needlelike teeth sometimes found a bit of flesh to grab since Rate hollered, "Bruno, you stop that. Don't be so rough. And don't you grab my pants. Ma will be awful mad if you tear them. Now, stop it. You hear?"

Miney laughed again. She guessed Rate never intentionally tore his clothes, but things just always seemed to happen to that boy. He attracted trouble like honey did flies. She had thought his most troublesome years would have been the baby years when there had been all that extra washing, or the toddler time when he had gotten into everything; but now, she wasn't all that certain. Still, he was a lot of help to her.

Blanche could help if she wanted to. She always dusted and helped with the dishes, and she could now iron some of the flat things—that is, unless they were starched; but she was gone a lot, and when it came to churning butter, well, she hated to do that as much as Ralph did, and they were forever squabbling over whose turn it was. In the summer, she helped feed the baby chicks or ducks or geese, if they raised any. Still, if a body was to be perfectly honest with oneself, Ralph was often more of a help than a hindrance and perhaps a mite more helpful than Blanche, Mina thought grudgingly.

Mina smiled as she thought of her daughter. Blanche was growing prettier all the time. She was tall, slender, with such a smooth, creamy complexion; her dark hair was fine and thick, and her brown eyes were so dark that at a distance, one couldn't see the pupils. Millie's had never been that dark, but Father Setterington was the one with the black eyes. Perhaps in some ways Blanche reminded her a little of her father-in-law; she certainly had a big dose of his stubbornness and pride. Well, if life would only be as successful for Blanche as it had been thus far for Horatio Setterington, she would be a mighty lucky girl.

One day, Blanche asked her mother what Grandfather did for a living. Blanche had been giving this a lot of thought for quite some time. She recollected that he had once owned a livery stable and general store, a furniture store and funeral parlor, but now he owned no business, and yet he seemed to have plenty of money. Not that he or Grandmother squandered any, but they could buy whatever they took a notion to.

Mina explained to Blanche that Horatio loaned money, and people paid him interest on the loans; he also bought farm property or city lots that were being sold for taxes throughout Clinton County and some in Gratiot and Shiawassee County, which he sold for a tremendous profit; he also raised running horses.

This bit of information impressed Blanche—the fact that owning money could earn you enough to live in quite as comfortable a manner as her grandparents did. She knew Horatio often came out to the farm to help Pa with some of the work, but it was because he liked to work and not because he had to. He often remarked that a man got soft if he just sat around. Grandfather certainly wasn't soft. He was twenty-three years older than Millie, but he still could match his son in the field.

Blanche knew that Grandmother had a hired girl come in by the day to do the cleaning and laundry. She felt that Lavina did the cooking simply because she enjoyed cooking, and she prided herself on her baked goods. Remembering, Blanche felt that Grandma Smith made much better cookies, and Ma's pies were better, but Grandmother did make awful good bread.

Grandmother not only had her own hired help anytime she wanted help, but Blanche had heard Ma and Pa talking about that ever since Aunt Ruby and Uncle Mac were married, Grandmother had paid for a hired girl for Aunt Ruby. Uncle Mac made nine dollars a week as a bookkeeper at Masons, and that didn't quite allow the luxury of hired help. However, Lavina was not about to let her only daughter do all her own housework, and if Mac couldn't afford it, Lavina could. Horatio had not objected to the situation although it probably would have made no difference if he had. Where her daughter was concerned, Lavina was even more unmovable than was usual. There had been some talk of Aunt Ruby and Uncle Mac moving to Big Rapids because Uncle Mac had the offer of a job in a bank. Maybe then they could afford their own hired help.

Blanche decided a person could do a lot worse than pattern himself after Rate Setterington. Pa resembled him in looks although he wasn't as clever in business, partly she guessed, because he was softer and let his heart rule some of his dealings. She guessed that even though she was a girl, she would like to be as astute about business as her grandfather.

Once again, Jim Keenan was back to help with the haying. Like as not, his brother, Merval, would be here at least part of the time too. Millie liked hiring the brothers since they were both good workers and never slacked off on any job they were set out to do. Jim was an exceptional man with a team, but while Merval lacked his brother's ability with horses, he more than made up for it in his quickness in the field.

Ralph was chatting with Jim while the latter spliced one of the small ropes used in the barn during haying.

"Jim, don't you never go home?"

"Nope."

"You still got a ma and pa, haven't you?"

"Well, Ma's still alive, and I got a step-pa. I ain't seen 'em for quite a spell. If Ma comes to visit Frankie, I allus go to see her if I can. Missed her last time though."

"Whyn't you ever go home?"

"Rate, it's like this. Me an' my step-pa, we don't see eye to eye. I weren't much of a kid when I left home for good."

"Don't your step-pa like you?"

"Don't reckon I know. Don't recollect my own pa, but I allus figgered he wouldn't have whupped me like my step-pa did. S'pose I asked for some of it, but I allus figgered he delighted in whuppin' me. Anyways, I got a good laugh the day I left home for good."

"What happened?" asked Rate.

"I'd been out huntin', an' I wuz comin' back to the house. By the back door stood this swill barrel where we dumped garbage an' such to use when we slopped the hogs. Well, a neighbor's cow stood there with her head down in that barrel. I pulled up my gun and filled her backsides with buckshot. She let out a beller, an' in her hurry to get her head outta that barrel, she somehow got it caught on her horns. Wal now, she couldn't no more see where she was gain' than a bat in bright sunlight, so she just took off blindly. I thought she looked funnier'n hell until I saw she was headed straight for our privy. She hit it smack-dab in the middle, an' over it went. She had busted the barrel off, so now she took off for home. It was then I heard the screechin'. Seems like old man O'Hare, my step-pa, had been sittin' in that outhouse, and he was lettin' loose with a string of cusswords to fair curl your hair. Wal, Rate, I figgered I had better make tracks, so I just turned and left. Ain't never been back."

"But, Jim, how'd he get out?"

"Damned if I know. But I wasn't about to wait and find out. I was only about fifteen, and he'd have near killed me. He was just lucky it didn't fall on the door. He'd have had trouble crawlin' out a hole," Jim stated laughing. "No, I don't reckon Ma's had too easy a life with him an' his temper. She's allus had to work hard, and they've allus been dirt poor. I'm just glad Frankie got out of there. It's a lot harder on a girl not to have nuthin' than it is for boys. 'Sides, I like not stayin' in one place too long. Workin' for your pa is fine, but after a while, I'm ready to move on. Don't know if I'll ever want to settle down."

Rate decided he was glad he didn't have a step-pa 'cause he sure didn't want to leave home. Maybe Ma and Pa did favor Blanche, but they were good to him in lots of ways. Why, he always had spending money each week even if sometimes Ma only gave him a penny. Whenever Pa went to town, he got to ride along, and sometimes, Pa would buy him a stick of candy without him even askin'. He liked things just as they were.

The haying season was almost finished. The last two days had been unbearably hot as only a cloudless July day can be. The men had soaked their shirts in short order as the sweat poured out of their skin much as water goes through a sieve. The horses were frothy wet where the harness laid, and small rivulets of water ran down their sides. They moved with methodical slowness needing to be urged to go from one haycock to another, content to wait while the men pitched the hay onto the wagon. Millie had cut this field two days ago, and it had cured fast enough to be raked yesterday. He had used a dump rake to put three swathes from the mower into a straight line, and the two hired men had pitched them into cocks to make it easier to pick up today.

Mina was even more uncomfortable in her kitchen than the men were in the field since the only breeze there was came from the south, and none of it relieved the additional heat from the cookstove in the kitchen. Well, the men had had a good midday meal; there had been six extra hungry mouths, but since the men had their own chores to do, they'd go home for supper. Therefore, she made up her mind that their meal was to be warmed-up leftovers. There was enough of the beef roast left, she'd slice that cold; she'd warm up the boiled potatoes and gravy, they'd have leaf lettuce from the garden with sugar and vinegar, and she'd open a jar of peaches—she still had a few jars left—and there was pie enough for Millie and Father Setterington and Ralph. She and Blanche could do without, or if Blanche wanted, she'd have to split a piece with Ralph. They'd have milk for the children and cold tea for the three grown-ups.

With a sigh, she sat down in the rocker by the south dining room door to take a moment's respite. Wouldn't you know it, what little breeze there had been had died down, so she absently picked up a cardboard fan, a means of advertising from Van Deusen's grocery store, and gently fanned her face. She wondered where the children were. Blanche was no doubt upstairs doing some embroidering; she had started a pair of pillowcases, and that girl just never was content until she finished something. Ralph would be somewhere around the barn or riding on one of the hay wagons. Millie might even be letting him drive a team on the wagon. She'd heard Ralph ask his pa about it after dinner, but she hadn't heard what Millie's answer had been, if indeed he had bothered to give one.

That was one of Millie's traits that never failed to irritate her, his being so closemouthed and never taking the time to answer her questions or discuss things with her. Like as not any discussion they were to have about folks in general was pretty much one-sided and often ended by Millie saying, "Miney, keep still." Those words always raised her ire partly because she knew that any further attempt to draw her husband into conversation would meet with stony silence and partly because she hated being spoken to in that tone of voice. Her own father had been much more voluble and had often recounted some humorous incident at the supper table. Not so with Millie. To him, a meal meant a time to replenish his stomach's needs, and hardly a place for a great deal of conversation. On occasion, by the time he was down to his dessert, he might talk some, but Miney always suspicioned that was just to prolong being at the table for the extra piece of pie. That man was a bottomless pit when it came to devouring food.

When the menfolk trooped into the house for supper, Miney was putting the last of the victuals on the table. As Horatio walked by the kitchen cabinet, he noticed a pan half full of milk that had clabbered solid in the heat.

"Mina, are you going to throw this out?"

"Yes, Father, I was. It was only milk from yesterday, but even with the cellar, it is hard to keep in this weather. It was sour this morning, and just look at it now, clabbered solid."

"But, Mina, it is still good to eat. Do you mind if I have some?"

"Of course I don't mind. I just never thought of anyone wanting to eat it," said a flabbergasted Miney.

She watched in awe as her father-in-law spooned a sizable helping onto his plate and, immediately after grace, set in with a will to devour the soured milk. Millie seemed not to notice, but the children watched wide-eyed with disbelief as their grandfather ate with gusto. From the looks on both of their faces, one could safely assume the dish did not appeal to them. Since Millie paid no heed, Miney presumed he had seen his father eat clabbered milk before. Oh, well, she guessed it wasn't going to hurt him any, only she knew for certain that what he didn't eat would get fed to the hogs.

Horatio had left for home, but before he had taken his leave, Ralph heard him say, "Milt, I'm glad that was the last of your hay. It's too hot, and there's something in the air. Doesn't even smell right."

Rate sniffed the air, but all he could smell was the smoke from the chimney and the carcass of a chicken that had died a couple of days ago, around which those big green blowflies were swarming; he knew the next day it would be crawling full of fat white maggots.

"You're right, Pa, something don't feel quite natural. It's mighty still tonight, and even the robins have shut up and aren't calling for rain anymore. Don't know quite what to make of it."

"Nor I, Milt, but I don't like the feeling."

Ralph asked Millie about it after his grandfather left, but Millie only said, "It's something I can't put a finger on, boy, but mark my words, something is going to happen."

That night, before Millie went to bed, he went out on the south porch to look at the still somewhat lightened sky. A man who arose at four thirty each morning went to bed these summer months before total nighttime darkness shrouded the land. He stood for a few moments gazing intently to the southwest, looking for clouds above Sherman's woods. At this time of year, any sudden, severe storm was more than a little likely to come from that quarter; however, he could see nothing unusual in the softly illuminated sky where the rays of an already setting sun still unveiled a light cloud cover.

"Miney, something's brewing. I feel it in my bones."

"What do you mean?"

"I think we're in for bad weather, a hailstorm, a cyclone, hard thunderstorm, or something."

"I don't see anything unusual," said Miney as she came out to stand beside him, slipping her arm around his waist. "Still, the hogs were scratching their backs today, so it could likely rain."

Ignoring her remark, Millie muttered, "I don't like waiting for the unknown, so I wish it would hurry up."

The black, ominous clouds hung low as they swirled and fought for position, first one on top, then another seemed to take its place as if stirred violently by an unseen giant hand. Mina had been nervously watching out the south door, noting the roll of thunder like the beat of distant tom-toms, sometimes an incessant rumble summoning nature's mighty forces for an attack on puny Earth. She remembered Millie's prediction of last night, and she wished he would get home before the storm broke, knowing full well that he was powerless to change the will of God, but it would make her feel easier to have his stalwart frame seated in his chair, nonchalantly watching the foreboding signs.

Nothing ever flustered Millie. He firmly believed what would be, would be, so there was no use to fret. She didn't know if she wished she could be more like him or not. She knew she often worried, and yet, it made not one whit of difference in the outcome. Millie was wont to scoff at her fears, so she usually tried to hide her feelings, but sooner or later, she could keep still no longer. Now, she had to control her emotions as best she could, for there was no cause to alarm the children. Ralph sat on the floor contentedly playing with Bruno. The pup knew something was amiss because his mind seemed to wander, and Ralph had to repeatedly urge the pup to retrieve the ball he was throwing.

Ralph certainly did take an interest in that pup. Bruno had been fetching a ball for several days, and Ralph was now trying to teach him to roll over. It made no difference to him that Millie had told him the pup was too young. Ralph knew this was the smartest dog God ever created, so he wanted the pup's education to start early. At least the pup was keeping Ralph occupied, so he apparently paid no attention to the heralding of a storm. Not that he'd have been afraid—he was too much Setterington to ever admit fear.

Goodness, it did seem that both he and Blanche took after Millie's side of the family much more than they did hers. Pa and Ma had been so much easier going and not nearly as stiff-necked and proud. 'Course, they'd never had as much either, but they had been mighty good parents, and she loved them both.

Here came Blanche. If she had noticed the black clouds, she certainly didn't act worried. Blanche might be petrified, but her dignity would carry her through, and no one would be able to detect any fear in her speech or actions—once again the Setterington pride.

The wind was starting to blow in strong gusts.

"Ma, should Ralph and I put the little chicks back in their coop? It looks dreadfully stormy."

"Oh, land's sakes, yes. I'd forgotten that we had let them out for the day. Ralph, you leave Bruno here while you help Blanche. Oh dear, do hurry."

The children left to find the settin hen with her brood of twelve chicks. They had raised a corner of the A-frame coop to let the mother hen wander. Much to their relief, the hen had sensed the offing of a storm and had returned to the safety of the coop with her chicks settled comfortably under her wings. They carefully put the corner down and hastened to the house, and only just in time because the first large drops of rain began to pelt the ground furiously.

"Ma, did you get the windows closed?"

"Yes, Ralph, I did that while you were outside. I wonder where your father is?"

"Comin' like a streak o' lightnin'. Just look at him travel," marveled the lad.

Ralph was right. Millie had let the team have their head, and the wagon, loaded with bags of grain, bounced wildly on the rough road. It seemed the team wanted to be home as much as Millie did. He pulled the wagon onto the barn floor; closing the big barn doors proved to be troublesome as the wind was now increasing in velocity, and it took some effort to fasten them in place. Miney noticed that Millie lost no time in getting the horses unharnessed and turned out, stopping to close the granary door on his way to the house. The rain still held off, the large drops not having been enough to lay the dust.

"Millie, I'm glad you're home," greeted a relieved Miney.

"So am I. I didn't relish getting soaked to the skin. I think that this wind is going to blow up a good rain, and I'm not sure what else. It's too danged hot and too humid."

"Guess you were right last night. Goodness, Millie, the windows are rattling, and just look at the trees."

Miney had looked out to see the box elder south of the house trying to touch its topmost branches to the ground. The poor old cottonwood creaked and groaned as did the stalwart elm behind the woodshed. Even the sturdy house seemed to tremble, perhaps in fear of the furious hand who guided these massive forces.

"Millie, are we going to be all right?"

"Don't fret none. It will soon blow by. A wind this strong can't last," was the optimistic reply.

"Pa, the door came loose off the corncrib," volunteered Ralph. "Boy, look at it rain!"

The rain had finally come. Sheets of water, driven by the wind, swept across the countryside. The barn, hardly more than a hundred yards away, could scarcely be seen. The crackling of lightning increased, the thunder tried to outdo itself with each rumble louder and longer than the one before. Blanche and Ralph watched in fascination, hardly noticing that Bruno kept close to Rate or to Millie, going from one to the other; Miney couldn't help showing her anxiety, and when one loud report seemed exceptionally close, she jumped and cried, "Millie, did anything here get hit?"

"I don't think so," he replied, looking out the north window to see what he could of the buildings. Just then, a loud, sustained, agonized screech reached their ears.

"Pa, there went a limb off the cottonwood!"

"I see it, boy. We were clean lucky. It missed the house completely."

"Oh, Millie, is it ever going to quit?"

"Reckon so. Most storms do, don't they?"

"I mean before it blows down some of the buildings."

"Well, you didn't say that. I think the worst is over. At least the wind is dying even if the rain hasn't let up any."

"Pa, look at the corn," came from Blanche. "It's all tipped."

The field south of the house was planted to corn, which had been its knee-high by the Fourth of July, but now, it looked sick indeed. The fury of the wind had tilted the young plants, so they leaned at an angle of close to forty-five degrees. The leaves hung limply like a hound dog's ears.

"It'll straighten up some, Blanche, but it sure don't look good now. Just knew that hot, humid air would bring some foul weather sooner or later. Just be glad nothing worse come of it. I've seen the time when we had hailstorms that stripped all the leaves off the corn. Think we can consider ourselves lucky this time."

The storm finally abated, the wind no longer blew with ferocity, and the rain fell softly and gently; the sun finally peeked through the clouds, and across the sky was as beautiful and perfect a rainbow as one could wish to see.

"Ma, come look," called Blanche. "See, isn't it pretty?"

"Yes, Blanche, it is. Must be that the storm is over for certain. God paints a right pretty rainbow, doesn't He? Millie, what are you fixing to do?"

"Thought I'd take a gander and see what damage was done besides this cottonwood. Rate spoke of the door off the corncrib. I hope we didn't lose any shingles off any of the roofs."

"Ralph, where do you think you're going?"

"With Pa. I want to see too."

"There's no need to have both of you getting wet shoes, so you stay right where you are."

Ralph looked his displeasure, but said nothing. He stood on the porch and watched as his father headed for the barn.

A survey showed that except for some small branches off the elms and box elders, the door off the corncrib, and the large limb off the old cottonwood, they had no major damage. Millie felt they were lucky.

When he learned that in some places barns and sheds had been blown down and trees uprooted, he was indeed thankful their losses had been so minimal. Mina was just plain relieved and hoped there was not going to be another storm like this one for a good long time.

CHAPTER 14

Miney was in a hurry. She lifted the iron lid of the cookstove and peered in with an exasperated sigh. "I just knew that wood was too damp to burn like it ought," she mumbled to herself. She removed the lid and poked the small sticks of kindling with the poker. As if to pacify her at least temporarily, the fire began to burn a little brighter. "Suppose I might just as well add another stick so it can be drying out."

Doing this, she then set the kettle filled with potatoes into the place where the lid should have gone. It would mean a blackened pot to clean, but there was no time to brood over that now. At the rate the fire was going, dinner was going to be late since the meat had hardly started to sizzle, let alone fry good; and if there was anything she didn't like, it was half-fried meat. No, sir, she wanted hers well-done with drippings to make nice brown gravy.

Mina checked the potatoes. At least they were beginning to boil. Must be that last stick of wood hadn't been as wet as the others.

"Blanche, it's time for you to get the table set."

"All right, Ma. Do you want me to cut the bread too?"

"Well, I don't know." Miney knew that the slices Blanche cut were often lopsided, starting with a nice narrow slice but ending with a width of nearly an inch. Still, how was the girl to learn? "Go ahead, but try to cut straight down through the loaf like I've shown you."

"I do try, only it just never seems to come out right," she lamented.

"Oh, I'll need milk for the gravy."

"Do you want me to go get it?"

"I think I'd better. That pan was really full, and I'm afraid you'll spill it. Goodness, here comes your father already. Well, he'll just have to wait for once. Guess it won't really hurt him any, although I suppose he's most dying of hunger now."

Miney turned the meat in the pan—it was frying well enough now, checked the potatoes and found they had a ways to go yet; then, she left for the cellar.

In a matter of moments, a shrill scream pierced the air. Millie dashed into the house, Rate tight at his heels, and as the next scream came, they dove for the cellarway door.

"Miney, what on earth is the matter?"

"Oh, Millie," she half sobbed, pointing toward the south wall. "A snake, a big snake, coiled up in the pan where the milk should have been. It just looked at me a minute, and then it slithered away. It was this big." She held her arms as far apart as they'd reach. "And it was this big around." She used her thumb and forefinger to measure the diameter of a silver dollar.

"What color was it?"

"A malted color, sort of mottled. What was it, Millie?"

"Just a harmless old milk snake. Your screaming probably scared him worse than he scared you. There, it's all right," he said clumsily, patting her shoulder. "You know a milk snake never hurt nobody. Don't quite know how he got in though."

"How'd he get in the safe? And into my pan of milk?"

A safe was simply a screened-in, portable cupboard with shelves for storing perishable food. The door was standing ajar, and there set the gray enameled pan, empty of its contents, mute testimony as to the presence of an intruder.

"It was a whole pan full too," wailed Miney.

"Now, Miney, no great harm's done." He sniffed, then asked, "Do I smell something burning?"

"Oh dear, my meat. Or is it the potatoes?"

Miney rushed up the stairs to salvage the midday meal.

Rate had watched the entire episode silently although he found it a trifle humorous. Ma wasn't usually one to get that scared over an old snake, but it sure must have taken her by surprise. He wondered if the snake had found a hole in the stone wall and had left by the same way or if it would show up another day in the cellar. Much to

Miney's relief, the snake disappeared, and it was as though the episode had only been a bad dream.

Blanche had remained at the top of the cellarway steps. She hated snakes with a passion. My, but she felt she was to be eternally thankful that she had not been the one to go fetch the pan of milk. Just supposing she had been the one to open the safe and find that ugly head, with the flicking tongue and beady eyes staring at her. She shuddered, her arms covered with goose bumps, and she felt cold all over. She fervently prayed that the snake was gone for good. She didn't care if Pa did say they were harmless, she hated them, and they gave her a creepy feeling. She wasn't about to admit that the feeling was akin to fear, she simply knew she never wanted to have such an encounter. In fact, she and Miney were both so upset that they ate very little. However, both Millie and Rate remained undaunted, and the food disappeared as usual before their voracious appetites.

A harmless old milk snake was of no concern to Millie or Ralph. These snakes were a frequent visitor around the barn. Millie supposed they ate mice and rats although some people swore the snakes milked the cows, so if they had a cow that was off on her milk, they laid the blame on the poor snakes. Sometimes, when pulling straw for bedding from the huge stack behind the barn, with the hooked tree branch worn smooth and shiny from use, it was not uncommon to pull a snake out with the straw.

In some parts of the county, there were still a number of rattlesnakes, but Millie hadn't seen one on his own farm in years. Why, he'd mind hearing Dave Watson tell about when Dave first settled on his farm, they had a lot of marsh grass to put up for hay. The rattlers were so bad they had to wrap the horses' legs with burlap bags to protect them from the snakes. Hadn't been completely safe for the men either, but they had worn high tops and kept a mighty close watch on what they were doing. Millie had to admit that he had a healthy respect for a rattlesnake and wasn't exactly sorry there had never been but a straggler or two left on his farm. 'Course, he supposed womenfolk were different, and he couldn't blame Miney for being upset. Like as not it was the unexpectedness of it since Miney wasn't usually that easily excited.

Blanche had gone with Millie to the neighbors. Now, for some reason, she was driving home in the light springboard wagon by herself, for Millie was nowhere to be seen. When she pulled into the yard, the pup, Bruno, ran yapping toward the wagon. Just before Blanche halted the team, the pup got too close to the back wheel. When it struck him, he limped off yelping his indignation and pain.

Ralph came bounding off the porch, and the pup, sensing this was going to be a sympathetic person, limped ki-yiing to his master.

"Blanche, you've cracked his hide! Just look. You've cracked his hide."

Ralph took hold of the pup's loose skin, pulled it away from the body to show his sister, looking at her accusingly.

Blanche climbed down from the seat of the wagon.

"Oh, Ralph, he's all right. Bruno's hide has always been loose like that. Honest."

"Tweren't neither. You've cracked it. Here, Bruno, poor fellow. Why'd you run over him?"

"I didn't mean to run over him. He just ran right under the wagon."

"You could have stopped," he accused.

"I'm sorry. Here, Bruno."

The pup had quieted with all this attention and now ambled over to Blanche to lick her outstretched hand.

"See, Ralph. He's all right. I didn't do it intentionally. You're going to have to teach him to stay out of the way."

"Are you sure he's all right?" the boy asked as an errant tear slid down his cheek.

"Of course. See, he doesn't even limp now, and his hide isn't cracked one bit."

"Well, if you're sure."

Ralph picked the pup up in his arms and headed back for the porch with Bruno trying his best to lick his master's face.

Goodness, thought Blanche, Ralph sure was concerned about his pup. Who'd have thought the pup would be that dumb anyway. At first, she had been afraid he was hurt badly. Now that she knew he was all right, it was rather comical. Cracked hide indeed. Bruno's skin had always been so loose, you could always get a good handful. Poor Ralph, he really did love that pup, and she was thankful nothing was really wrong. She wouldn't have wanted it on her conscience to have seriously hurt Bruno. Besides, she kind of liked the pup too. Even Pa seemed to like Bruno, so the whole family would have felt badly if he had been killed.

She guessed young boys just needed a dog to grow up with. Ma had even taken an interest in the pup and had shown Ralph how to teach him some tricks. Ralph had really been very patient and had taught him to sit up and speak. Ma said that when Bruno got a little older, Ralph could teach him to roll over, sneeze, say his prayers, and read the newspaper. Ralph just never doubted his mother one bit since he knew Bruno was of exceptional intelligence.

The dog was easy to teach, and between Ralph and his mother, they not only had a well-behaved dog, they had one who enjoyed showing off in front of an audience. He also enjoyed the tidbits Ralph sometimes gave him for a job well done.

Because Grandma Smith was feeling poorly, Millie had a telephone installed so Lorin could call Miney if she was needed. It took several days for the phone company to get the poles set and the phone installed; of course, even though they now had a telephone, the children were not allowed to use it. In Miney's mind, it was for adults only, and then only used when absolutely necessary. She never considered calling someone just for the sake of talking; besides, she didn't have time to waste.

When school started, Ralph had a new teacher, Barbara Hess by name. He didn't much mind. Miss Silvernail had been all right although she never laughed much. Blanche said she looked like a bird perched on a fence, and he often thought of that when he looked at her. Still, she'd always been nice to him. Now, Miss Hess smiled a lot more and often came out on the playground to supervise the youngest children. They loved her.

She even tried to make the rather drab schoolhouse look pretty by putting up pictures appropriate to the season. The windows had been built high, and when students were seated at their desks, they could not look outside. Of course, this had been intentional since the students were there to learn, not to gaze at the countryside. Anyway, she had some pretty pictures she put up all around the classroom. Sure brightened it up. She also said she'd asked the school board to replace the recitation bench since it was rough, and if a child was to slide along it, he might pick up a sliver. She wanted one with a seat that folded up like their desks.

Ralph was glad to be back in school. He liked learning new things. He worked hardest at learning to read because he wanted to get big enough to read books like Blanche did.

November came, and with it, election day. The people of the growing new nation turned out in remarkable numbers to make their choice. Once again, as a nation, they turned to the Republican party and reelected William McKinley as their president, and with him, Theodore Roosevelt became the vice president. For the second time, Bryan had gone down in ignoble defeat. Prosperity had made a very worthy opponent, and McKinley was the one who had prosperity on his side. The deck had been stacked in his favor from the onset.

Millie and his neighbors were exceedingly pleased with the election outcome. They foresaw continued prosperity for farm families. Prices for farm commodities had been holding steady, and they attributed this to the Republicans; they forgot that grain failures in Europe and other parts of the world had improved foreign trade, thereby creating a demand for these same commodities. People often believe only what they want to believe, and Millie was no exception. He was confident the good times would continue, and at least in this respect, Millie was much like anyone else—he enjoyed work, but he also enjoyed a just reward for his labor.

Christmas that year was even more special to Ralph. Since he was learning to read, Aunt Mary sent him some books as did Aunt Ruby. To be sure, he could read only a few words here and there, but he was assured that by the time school was out in the spring, he would be able to read them with ease. At least they had some pictures, so he could enjoy looking at them. Besides the books, Grandmother and Grandfather gave him a blackboard that stood on a frame. He'd never seen one like it; there was even a box of chalk.

Grandfather immediately asked Rate to do his sums and nodded his head in approval when the lad did the simple addition quickly and correctly.

Anyway, Rate figured he had been mighty lucky this Christmas. Of course, he hadn't got the ice skates that he had wanted so badly, but he did have some money that he was saving like a veritable miser. 'Course, Ma never gave him much at a time. Fact was, she'd only give him a penny to spend on Saturdays, and some of the time he just felt he had to spend it.

Wieners—how he did like wieners, and a penny was enough to buy one. Now, if Pa was to give him money, he'd like as not give him a whole nickel, so that way he could buy a wiener and have four cents left to put toward his skate money. Trouble was, just lately Ma usually beat Pa to it, and if Pa went to give him money, she'd always say, "I've already given Ralph his spending money." Sure. One measly old penny, yet he didn't dare complain.

It was one Saturday in January when Rate's grandmother found him counting his small cache.

"What are you doing, Ralph?"

"Counting my money, Grandmother. So far I've got thirty-eight cents."

"What are you saving all that money for?"

"I want some ice skates."

"Ice skates? Where will you go skating?"

"At school. At noon hour, the fellows go to the river to skate. Most everyone else has skates," he explained.

"Even those who are your age?"

"Yep. Curly Sherman got a pair for Christmas."

"Is it safe to be on the river?"

"Where we go, it is. Farther north, just afore the bridge, is the rapids, and that don't ever freeze over, I guess. But where we go, it is safe enough."

Lavina nodded and continued on to the kitchen where Miney was busy baking.

Before she left for home, she called her grandson over to her.

"Ralph, can you carry this basket of eggs out to the cutter for me?"

"Yes, Grandmother. Soon's I put on my coat."

Ralph followed his grandmother to where his grandfather already sat in the cutter. As he handed the basket up to her, he felt something round and cold being pressed into his hand. He opened his palm, and there lay a shiny silver dollar. Eyes wide with wonder, he glanced up to say, "Th-th-thank you, Grandmother. Oh, gee, thanks a lot."

"Be sure and put it towards those skates."

With that they moved off. Ralph was certain his grandmother had smiled at him fondly, and even those cold blue eyes had looked warm. Oh boy, a dollar and thirty-eight cents. Why, that was nearly enough to get the skates. Maybe he'd be lucky enough to have them before the winter season passed.

My goodness, who'd have thought that Grandmother Setterington would have given him money just because he wanted some skates. Must be she did like him after all, for every once in a while, she'd do something nice when it was most unexpected. If only she didn't look so stern all the time. Of course, she often had a smile for Grandfather, but children just seemed to bring out her sternness. Even Blanche said she didn't smile much, and everyone knew she thought Blanche was quite the nicest one around.

His thoughts turned to his grandma Smith. My, but she was different. She just seemed to like children. Look how she'd taken care of Georgie when he was little; everyone said it was because Aunt Lorin was scared to handle him when he was small. Of course, this was long before he was even born since Georgie was a lot older'n Blanche even. Anyway, he'd heard Ma laugh and say Lorin held Georgie at arm's length, afraid to hardly touch him. Seemed funny that Aunt Lorin hadn't cared all that much for her own boy, but yet, she was always saying that she wished she had a boy like Ralph. Mighty strange. She had always been good to him and even treated him as good or better than Blanche. Ma had always said that Lorin never liked Georgie until he was older. 'Course Uncle Norman had always drank a lot and had changed jobs often, so maybe that had something to do with it too. Anyway, all the grandchildren liked Grandma, but he bet he liked her best.

Rate knew his mother was extremely worried about Grandma Smith because he had come into the kitchen, rather quietly for a change, and had found her crying as she sat peeling potatoes. She had hastily dried her eyes on her apron when she noticed him, and when he'd asked her what was wrong, she'd said that she was all right and nothing was the matter.

But he knew differently.

Grandma had been poorly of late, and he and Blanche had talked about how it was so much harder for her to get around, her movements were much slower and more calculated. Blanche had told him it was because Grandma was getting awful old, and when folks got that old, their body began to wear out. At least that was what Grandma had told Blanche.

He wondered why it had to happen to such a kind person as Grandma. Just didn't seem fair to him. She had been seventy-six on January 30. He had asked Ma what year that meant she'd been born in, and Ma had said 1825. The year made it sound awful old indeed, and he knew that seventy-six was older than his other grandmother.

Then, last night, Aunt Lorin had called. Ma hadn't said much to Pa in his hearing, but he knew from her part of the telephone conversation that Grandma had had a bad spell and that Aunt Lorin was going to spend the night with her. Tonight, it was to be Ma's turn, so she was hurrying to have an early supper and had told Blanche that she could do the dishes by herself. It still got dark quite early since it was only the first of March, and Ma wanted to be there before dark. He didn't think Pa was driving her, and he knew Ma disliked having to drive a horse after dark.

No one mentioned the word *dying*, but he had a hunch his grandmother hadn't long for this world. It made him feel depressed, the very thought of not having Grandma's kind, homely face to watch as she told him some story, not having her warm cheery kitchen to visit and her cookies to munch; he liked to watch her knit, since Ma never did, and the clicking sound of the needles was a soothing, comforting sound.

Mary Smith had always made the heavy black woolen stockings they wore in the wintertime. In a world where Ralph's wants always came in second, his sister's always given priority, it was little wonder he enjoyed the unselfish, kindly, little Scotswoman who did not have it in her heart to show any favoritism.

Of course, Ralph knew that Grandma tired easily, and he supposed she was ready for her home in heaven since then she would be shed of this tired, aching body and would be reunited with her loved ones. This last thought gave him some consternation. Since Grandma had been married to a man named Elisher Fuller, Aunt Lorin's and Aunt Mary's father, he wondered if she'd be reunited with him or with Grandpa Smith, who was Ma's father. Things like that were awful hard to understand, especially when one was only seven years old. He expected he could ask his mother, but like as not, it would only make her feel badly, so he guessed he'd better not.

Ralph was right. Mary Barnes Fuller Smith was tired; her poor body was no longer functioning properly, but even though she sensed that death would soon be a caller, she kept her thoughts calm and serene, comforted by the passage in the Bible: In my Father's house are many mansions. She would now have the wondrous eternal life that God's Word promised. She had no apprehensions, no anxieties, and the only regret she had was the prospect of leaving her daughters and grandchildren. She loved them dearly. Yet, it was inevitable. Hers had been a good life, and she thanked God for all the favors He had bestowed. If there had been any moments of doubt, any days of darkness, He had guided her safely through the storm and had seen her in the midst of the fold once more. This worldly life had become an unwelcome burden. Mary began to long for release.

Thus it was that on Tuesday evening, March 12, 1901, Mary Smith left this world quietly as she slept. The look of peace and contentment that heralded the transition was noted by both Miney and Lorin, who sat at her bedside. Mary had happily gone home.

Blanche and Ralph were told the following morning. Even though both of them had known for several days that this would likely be the outcome of Grandma's illness, it made the reality no easier to bear. Ralph didn't say a word but sat on the floor pushing a toy in an abstract manner, while he used his shirtsleeve to wipe a tear that now and then managed to sneak out from the brimming eyes. Even though he knew boys weren't supposed to cry, he wished he could resort to tears.

Blanche went back upstairs to her room. Ralph knew why. He knew Blanche would be crying out her grief in the solitary confines of her room. That was Blanche for you. She never wanted anyone to know that she ever cried over anything. Rate knew because he sometimes sneaked upstairs and caught her with her head buried in her pillow to muffle the sounds. For some reason, he had never told on her, and much of the time, no one else guessed she had been crying.

Ralph correctly understood his sister's actions. Blanche had gone upstairs to bear her grief in solitude. Her beloved Grandma Smith was dead. No more would she be waiting with open arms to assuage Blanche's grief over some confrontation with her grandmother Setterington. No more could Blanche sit in her warm, cheery kitchen eating some of Grandma's delicious cookies. All this was gone, wiped out in one brief instant. One moment Grandma had been alive and the next she had been with God. Blanche felt more than a little resentful that God had chosen now to take her grandma home. Didn't He know how much she, Blanche, needed her? Didn't it make any difference to Him? Ma always said that God knew best, and we must never question His wisdom. Well, what was she to think? Right when she needed her grandmother, God took her away.

Of course, she thought begrudgingly, Grandma had been feeling poorly for the past three or four months. Why, all this school year, Blanche had tried to be much more of a help and, since Christmas, hadn't even been able to stay with her, but she'd still stopped in after school because Grandma was always so glad to see her. If God had been a mind to, He could have made Grandma feel better. Perhaps Blanche had not prayed hard enough for her grandma's good health, and perhaps the prayers had not been all that regular. This made her feel a twinge of guilt. Maybe God would have left Grandma here to provide Blanche with the comforting love she so longed for if only she had prayed more diligently. With these thoughts, she cried as if the tears would never stop.

Ralph only remembered going to Ray Sawyer's funeral, and since Ray wasn't relation, it was hardly the same. Now, he was unnaturally solemn, fully realizing the gravity of the situation. The rooms of the house were packed. Grandma had had a lot of friends. No one was paying any attention to him. Ma was crying softly as the minister began the service. Even Pa looked sorrowful, and he was sure he'd seen Grandmother Setterington hastily dab at her eyes with her lacy handkerchief. Aunt Ettie, Aunt Mary, and Aunt Lorin were crying in turns. Blanche sat staring straight ahead, and he just knew she was fighting to keep back the tears. He paid little attention to what was being said. No one needed to tell him that his grandma was a mighty fine person—he already knew that.

At last, there was a final prayer, and then the people began to file out. Since they were family, they were the last ones to leave. Now, to the cemetery, and then it would be all over.

The black hearse, drawn by black horses, moved slowly and steadily west on Pine Street as the church bell tolled mournfully. It was only a block to the village cemetery. The hearse turned into the solitary drive situated in the center of the cemetery. Rate knew Grandma's lot was on the north end, right by the drive, because he'd been there with Ma to put flowers on Grandpa Smith's and Great-Grandfather Barnes's graves. He could see the mound of dirt and the opening while they waited for the pallbearers to bring the casket and place it over the opening. While the wind was cold and raw, the sun did peek from behind the clouds as the minister stepped to the head of the casket for the final words and prayers.

Soon, it was over. Rate watched as the coffin was lowered into the cold, bleak earth, but turned away as the men began to shovel the dirt from the pile onto the casket. Somehow, that act made it all seem so final, the thud of the half-frozen clumps striking the wood. He hated that sound. He was more than glad to move away, back to their carriage, and begin the ride home.

It was several days after the funeral when Blanche asked her mother what was going to happen to Grandma's house. Somehow, it was important to her not to have strangers cluttering up her grandma's house with its simple, homey furnishings.

Mary Smith had owned a small farm, some lots in the Tillotson Division besides the house where she lived with two lots and a barn across the street. Her four daughters—Mary, Lorin, Ettie, and Almina—were to share equally in the estate. On the counseling of his father, Millie decided some town property might be a good investment. Miney passed this bit of information on to her daughter, who felt much relieved. Grandma's house was to be theirs, and even if Grandma couldn't be there, she could sit in the house and remember the good times.

Therefore, by the time it was all settled, the farm and the lots being sold, it was decided that for two hundred dollars, Millie could buy the house and lots across the street.

Blanche finally had the courage to speak her thoughts to her mother.

"Ma, I'll just never understand why God took Grandma. I enjoyed her so much, and I feel kind of lost knowing she isn't there for me to talk to anymore."

"Blanche, Ma was ready to go. Don't fret, child, God knows best. Ma had been in much more pain than she ever let on, and now, she has no pain. She missed Pa an awful lot these past few years, and I'm sure she was glad to see him. I know you will miss her. I'll miss her too. I've never known anyone kinder or more mild-mannered. Why, she just never lost her temper even when we were children, and Ettie and I did get into mischief now and again. She'd chide us or scold a little, but I never remember a switching. Even with Pa's boys, she was loving and kind. I sometimes wish I was more like her, but I guess I'm more like Grandfather Barnes, too outspoken and opinionated to always get along. Leastways that was what Ma always said. He died before I was old enough to remember."

"But, Ma, why didn't God see that we needed Grandma?"

"That is a very selfish thought. You should be asking yourself what was best for your grandma. Do you think she would choose to live here in pain when her husband was waiting for her to join him in heaven? Not to mention her own mother and father and, I believe, sisters and a brother."

"I-I-I guess not. But didn't Grandma love Ralph and me? And Georgie? And Aunt Mary's family?"

"Of course she did, sweetheart. She loved all of you dearly, but, Blanche, seventy-six is a lot of years to have lived. Remember Ma had had a hard life. She was born in New York State, you know, came to Michigan in a covered wagon when Mary was just a little tyke. Her mother was dead, so her father came with her and her husband. Now, a covered wagon isn't the best mode of transportation. Guess probably Ma walked a good share of the way—that's one reason her feet always gave her trouble. It was already the first of November when they got to Vernon, and then, her husband just dropped dead. Pa lived in Vernon, and his wife was dead. He had four boys to raise, the youngest being Lorin's age. Since both of them needed someone, they started keeping company after Ma's year of mourning. Then, after she married Pa, he decided to come here to live.

"Why, the house I was born in was just a log cabin a block south of the main four corners. I remember that much. Ma worked hard all her life, and I expect she was just plumb wore-out. Oh, she never complained, but that was just Ma. Besides, dear, we are not to question why God does what He does. I'm not even sure that when our time comes, we will ever understand why He did things as He did. Don't suppose it really matters. The only thing that matters is that we lead the kind of life He expects of us, and then salvation will be ours, and we will one day all be together in heaven."

Blanche mulled these words over. She guessed Ma was right, and she was glad she knew Grandma was safe and happy in heaven. However, the ache in her heart was still there, and she knew it would be for some time to come.

Goodness. Blanche certainly was getting to be spunky and opinionated. Imagine questioning why God had done something. Miney hated to admit it, but at times like this, that stubborn streak of Blanche's reminded her of Mother Setterington. Oh dear, why did Blanche have to take after her? Well, perhaps it was just her imagination. Still, the older Blanche got, the more she had a mind of her own.

March had been colder than usual. Winter seemed determined not to relinquish its hold on the land. The sun managed to shine feebly on some days, but its efforts seemed too puny, and the snow still covered the ground with the only bare spots being on an occasional hilltop.

April was heralded in by fierce cold blasts instead of the usual warmer breaths of spring. The prolonged cold made lambing season more difficult than usual. Try as hard as he might, the number of lambs disowned by their mothers kept growing. An ewe is an especially unnatural mother; let her lamb get separated from her while it is drying off, and nothing you can do will make her accept the lamb and let it feed. Quite the contrary. She will butt and kick the lamb unmercifully each time it tries to suck, so the poor creature slowly starves. Often when giving birth to twins, she will accept one, but not the other.

This year, Millie had brought more than one lamb, looking more dead than alive, to the house in a wooden crate to set it on the oven door for warmth. It was always a little amazing how life seemed to return to that tiny body, which looked to be all legs, when it had become sufficiently warm. It didn't take much to put a nipple on a bottle and give the lamb warmed cow's milk. Their soft, high-pitched bleats filled the kitchen each time they became hungry. When they gained strength, they were taken back to the barn. However, they had to be fed four times a day for the next month or so if they were to live.

Millie decided Ralph was old enough to take on the responsibility of raising lambs on the bottle. He'd done right well taking care of the white pig. It was good for the boy to learn some responsibility at an early age. He'd been helping Miney for some time now what with the churning, carrying firewood, and turning the wringer; however, he'd never had anything to do that had to be done in the morning before school, but the lambs would have to be fed then. Millie would have to tend to the midday feeding, but Rate could feed them after school and before he went to bed. The boy was seven, so it was time for more chores. It was true he'd helped with the horses for a spell now, so Millie was sure he could take on the bottle-feeding of a few lambs.

When the final tally was in, Ralph had seven lambs to raise for which Millie had told him he could have one of the lambs as his pay. This seemed like a good proposition to the boy. Besides, he liked the soft woolly creatures and felt sorry for them because their mothers would have let them die.

Rate always had a soft spot in his heart for any young animal, wild or tame. He always felt badly if something died and was at a loss to understand his father's seemingly unfeeling acceptance of the way of life—some things lived and some died no matter how a person worked to make them live. All his life Ralph was to dislike losing an animal even though he knew he had done all humanly possible to save it from death.

Blanche prevailed upon her parents to let her drive to school for a few days since Grandmother and Grandfather wanted to go visit Aunt Ruby. It had taken some doing, but Blanche had finally convinced both parents and grandparents that she could certainly be trusted with such a reliable mare as Topsy.

It rained most of the night, but with the coming of dawn, the rain ceased, although the clouds were black and scudded ominously across the sky. They hung so low that Blanche felt hemmed in as she started for school. Golly, maybe it hadn't been such a brilliant idea to drive to school this week; she could have stayed with Fern Wooley, only Blanche had failed to inform anyone that Mrs. Wooley had extended the invitation. She shivered. The wind was still cold. Sure didn't seem like April. When she crossed the river, she noted the rain of last night had swollen the artery considerably; it wasn't far from reaching the bottom of the bridge.

Mr. Cooley at the gristmill had been watching the river. It was still rising. A couple of inches more, and it would reach the planking of the bridge. Giving the matter some thought, he decided the village should be told in the event there was someone who had to go west to get home. That old bridge wasn't all that good anymore, and if the water kept rising, it wasn't going to be safe. In fact, the turbulent, swirling river just might take it out, or at least destroy the middle portion.

Blanche was busy writing a theme for English when someone came to the door and spoke to the teacher.

"Does anyone here have to go home west over the gristmill bridge?" asked the teacher.

Blanche raised her hand.

"But, Blanche, I thought you stayed in town with your grandparents."

"Not this week, ma'am. I drove."

"Goodness, child, then you had better hurry. The river is rising fast, and they are afraid the bridge might go out."

Blanche left immediately. She ran most of the way to Grandfather's, taking the shortcut through Grandma Smith's backyard. She was half crying as she got Topsy, who seemed to move at a snail's pace, out of the barn and hitched to the buggy. She didn't even take time to close the barn door, she just clambered into the buggy, picked up the lines, and started for home. Try as she would, she could not get Topsy to hurry. She even hit the horse lightly with the whip, but after a few yards at a slow trot, Topsy dropped back to her rapid walk. Time seemed endless. Blanche just knew she'd never make it to the river in time.

After what seemed an eternity to the frightened girl, she reached the gristmill hill; and from this vantage point, she could see the swirling, frothy water of the river hungrily clutching at the pilings supporting the wooden structure that now looked frail indeed. As they approached the bridge, Blanche could see that the water had already risen some four or five inches above the planks. She pulled Topsy up to survey the situation. What should she do? Was the bridge safe, or would it give way when she was part of the way across, letting her fall into that dark, raging river? After a moment's indecision, Blanche urged Topsy forward.

"C'mon, Topsy. The longer we wait, the worse it gets."

The horse hesitated, put a tentative foot forward into the cold water, then stopped.

Blanche slapped the lines. "Please, Topsy, oh, please, get me across."

The old horse edged forward, slowly feeling with each foot as she put it forward. Twice she fell to her knees, whinnied in terror, got back up, and steadily moved ahead. Blanche closed her eyes. That was worse. She was in the middle now and could see the torrential waters.

"Please, God, help us across."

Blanche was crying in earnest now. Topsy, as if sensing they were nearly across, speeded up, and as soon as her feet struck land, she surged forward to a fast trot with no urging from Blanche. When Blanche reached home, she laid her cheek against Topsy's neck and cried.

Millie and Miney never knew how frightened their daughter had been. She told them why she was sent home, but made light of the situation. It was over and done with, so no need to alarm her mother was Blanche's reasoning. One thing she knew for certain, if she lived to be a hundred, she'd never ever forget old Topsy.

Ralph had been playing in the barn. It was just before the haying season, and the mows were nearly empty. However, there was still a sizable pile of timothy on the barn floor. Rate had been up in the mow, walking beams, swinging on hay ropes and generally enjoying himself. When he decided to leave, instead of descending the ladder as he normally would have done, he looked at the enticing pile of hay and, without hesitation, jumped from the mow. He gave a yell of pain as his right foot struck something. He looked aghast.

Oh, my God, how had that happened? The rusty tine of an old broken-handled pitchfork was stuck between the big toe and the next and protruded at least a quarter of an inch at the back of the foot near the heel. Jeepers, but it hurt! He sat and looked with dismay at the grotesque picture his foot made. Well, he'd best get busy and pull the thing out. He grabbed the broken handle and gave it a tug. It never even budged. Of course, it was rather awkward to get at, and he couldn't get much leverage. After a few more tugs, he knew he wasn't making any progress. Sweat beaded his forehead partly from the pain and partly from the anxiety. He had to do something. He tried to stand, but that didn't work at all since it hurt more to put pressure on the foot. He couldn't hop because the handle hung down in the way. Well, he had to get to the house somehow. He hitched himself backward on his buttocks, dragging the fork and foot carefully along; thus, he went out the barn door and across the barnyard to the house. He remembered to keep looking behind him since he didn't relish the idea of sliding through a fresh cowflop or of putting his hands in one either. His progress was slow and painful. When he reached the windmill, he began to holler.

"Ma! Ma! I'm hurt! Ma, do you hear me? Help me, Ma."

"Ralph Setterington, whatever is the matter now?"

"I'm hurt, Ma. Come see."

"Oh, my land! Oh, Ralph! However did you do this? Goodness, what shall I do? Hold still now. I guess I've got to pull this thing out. It will probably hurt."

"Hurts now, so I guess it can't be worse."

Miney grasped the handle firmly, and although her face looked a little white, she began slowly and steadily to pull the tine from Rate's foot. She gave an audible gasp when it finally came free. She made no effort to stem the flow of blood.

"Good. It's bleeding. That always seems to cleanse a wound, and there is less likely to be infection or blood poisoning. I'll have to get some salt pork and something to wrap it up with. Goodness, Ralph, what were you doing?"

"I jumped out of the haymow onto a pile of hay on the barn floor. This old fork was buried under the hay, so's I couldn't see it."

"Somehow, you just attract trouble. I'm afraid that foot is going to be mighty sore for a few days. I do hope it heals all right," she said with a worried frown. "I'll be right back with some salt pork and some bandages, so you sit right here until I get back. See, it has almost stopped bleeding."

When she returned, she had a basin of hot water with her lye soap to scrub the foot, salt pork to place over the punctures, and strips of an old sheet for a bandage.

"Land's sakes, Ralph, this is going to be an awkward thing to bind up. We've got to hold the salt pork over those holes. Here, you help hold this piece in place while I get a bandage around it."

When finished, if not a professional job, it was at least a serviceable one, although somewhat cumbersome. Ralph testily put some weight on the foot and discovered that it felt much better when he didn't try to step on it. Miney helped him into the house, gave him instructions to keep off his foot as much as possible, and returned to her work in the kitchen.

She decided she didn't understand boys at all. Ralph was forever doing something dangerous. She supposed she should consider herself fortunate that thus far he had sustained no broken bones. Good thing she generally had a supply of salt pork on hand to use on his wounds. Seems like all summer long he had a piece of salt pork tied to one foot or the other. Lucky thing the salt pork drew out any poison, so no infection set in, and the punctures had always healed nicely. If he'd wear shoes, it wouldn't happen, but he could hardly wait for the first dandelion in the spring, which proclaimed it was time for small boys to doff their shoes and go barefoot until fall. He hated to put on shoes to go to church—said they made his feet burn. Millie never seemed to worry about the lad but always reiterated that boys will be boys and found all of Ralph's antics on the humorous side.

What a blessing to have had Blanche. Girls certainly were different. It seemed that Blanche could keep busy for hours doing fancy work, practicing her piano lessons—although her progress was very slow—reading, or helping with the housework. Ralph was a horse of another color. He had more energy to wear off than a young colt—always on the move, hating to sit quietly for even a short spell.

Perhaps when he got further in school, things would improve. He did love to look at books if they had any pictures in them and simple reading; sometimes, he'd even ask her what a word was, then he'd try to remember it for the next time. She was sure Millie would keep adding to his chores as he got older. Something had to be done with all that ambition he had, and if it wasn't channeled into something constructive, she just didn't know what would happen to him. Millie laughed at her fears, when he bothered to listen to her continuous complaints and observations, and merely said the boy would turn out all right.

She had to admit Ralph had been doing a good job raising the lambs. He hadn't even complained during the rest of the school year when he'd had to get up early enough to feed them before setting off for school. All seven had lived, and if Ralph put in an appearance, all seven rushed to him expecting a bottle. Now, they were fed only twice a day since there was plenty of pasture. Millie said they looked as good as the other lambs who'd been more fortunate and hadn't been disowned by their mothers. Fact was, he sounded pleased that Ralph had accepted his responsibility so readily, although he never mentioned this to Ralph.

Goodness, that brought up another problem. Mina just knew Ralph wouldn't be able to get around that well, and someone else would have to feed those lambs. Well, Millie or Jim Keenan, who'd been working for them this summer, could just see to it. After all, it was hardly work for a girl, and she knew that she wasn't about to take on the chore. It was enough that she saw to warming the milk and filling the bottles.

Wonder where Millie had found all those whiskey bottles anyhow. She supposed he had stopped by one of the saloons as they'd more than likely have a good enough supply. She didn't like to think of Millie going in one of those establishments even if it was to get empty bottles to feed the poor lambs. The neck of a whiskey bottle just fitted the nipples that the drugstore carried, and they held the right amount of milk for one feeding when the lambs were older.

Miney knew for certain John went in saloons now and again. Hadn't been too long ago that she'd overheard Cash and Millie talking about John, but she hadn't heard enough to get the whole gist of things, so she'd asked Millie later. It seemed that a couple of men had started to fight while John had been in the saloon. Well, John had just grabbed each one by the scruff of the neck and actually picked them up so's their feet hardly touched the floor and had thrown them out the swinging doors onto the boardwalk with the admonition that they stay away until they sobered up. Hadn't made any difference that both of them had swung away trying to hit John, he had just hung on tight and walked right along like they were a couple of small boys. Of course, John stood six foot four and a half in his stocking feet, and not many men were that tall or as hefty as John since he usually tipped the scales at 280.

Miney had then asked Millie, who had told him about the incident. He'd given her this peculiar look, then admitted somewhat abashedly that he'd seen it with his own eyes. Well, that had not only surprised her, but it had also provoked her, and she had spoken her piece. Millie had hastened to explain that he had only gone in there to see his brother about some business and had left shortly after the incident. He had reminded her that Pa wouldn't like the idea of him frequenting a saloon, and not being like John, he didn't want to antagonize his father.

Mina had been more than a little upset over this admission because she felt her husband cared more about what his folks thought than what she thought. She would've liked to have told him so but, for once, bit her tongue, realizing there was no way she could change the ingrained feelings Millie had for his parents. It was a strange kind of love, built out of respect with a healthy dose of fear thrown in. Millie just never wanted to cross his father in any way. She supposed that he and John would have been better off if they could have been mixed up a little, thereby giving Millie a little more independence and letting John have a little more respect. She supposed Millie worked as hard as he did to be successful simply to please his father, looking for the words of praise, which never came.

Rate's foot remained sore for a few days even though it was healing with no sign of infection. Mina still kept it wrapped, but he hobbled around quite well and had taken over his chore of the lambs once more. Blanche still hauled his kindling for him and had been grumbling about it rather loudly the past two days. Rate thought it rather humorous and felt Blanche was getting her just due since she was gone so much enjoying herself. He really supposed he could get around well enough to do the work, but he'd hardly be the one to suggest it.

He simply aggravated Blanche all the more by sitting where he could watch her do his work. If she tried to ignore his presence, he was sure to make a big issue out of playing with Bruno, where she could hardly miss the barking dog or the loud words of praise for something well done. If not this, he merely sat on the porch and gazed idly toward the barn, whistling tunelessly when his sister came with a wagon of wood to unload. Blanche knew as well as he did that Ralph was doing this to get her goat, so she resolved not to let him know by her outward appearance that it bothered one whit. However, she promised herself that she would get even one day.

Chapter 15

B lanche had been asleep for some time, long enough for the first deep sleep to be finished. She stirred slightly in her bed. Something seemed to disturb her slumber. There it was again. Some thing or someone was on the porch below the north window. Whoever it was, was moving stealthily. Her throat constricted in fear. No use to look out the window. The porch roof would shield whoever was there. She was debating what to do when she heard a muffled voice.

"Miney! Miney! It's Ed. Lena needs you."

Blanche heaved a sigh of relief. She hadn't realized just how tense her muscles had been until she began to relax. She stayed very still, almost holding her breath, trying very hard to hear the muted conversation.

She knew it was Ed Clark, only she didn't quite understand just why Lena, his wife, needed her mother in the middle of the night. She wondered if Ma was going to get dressed and go with him. Try as she might, she could hear no further conversation. Stealthily, she slipped out of bed and hovered by the open door leading onto the east porch roof. There was enough moonlight, so she could easily see the road. Sure enough, there stood Ed's buggy with his old driving mare tied to a tree. Next, she saw Ed and Mina emerge from the shadows of the porch, get into the buggy, and leave. Blanche was completely baffled. She looked in to see if Ralph had heard anything, but he was sound asleep, so no use to rouse him.

There were many things lately that puzzled Blanche a great deal. A few months ago when her monthlies had started, she had been greatly upset and had asked Ma why this was happening, wanting some kind of reassurance from her mother that she was simply a nor-mal girl. Ma had acted rather embarrassed, and the only explanation she had given was that it was something a woman had to contend with every month. Blanche had not been satisfied with this meager bit of information, although any further attempts to discuss it had met with failure. Miney had merely indicated that when Blanche was older, she would understand, but until then, this scant bit of information would have to suffice.

Just like Blanche had been noticing that whenever any children or young girls came into the Ladies Missionary Society meetings, all talk stopped immediately. She, Fern, and Hazel had stood outside the door one day trying to hear what was being said, only the blamed door had been too thick, or the women had been talking too softly, because all they could get was the steady hum of voices. However, when they had burst in rather unceremoniously, all conversation halted, and some of the women looked ill at ease. Blanche had questioned her mother about this.

"Ma, what do women talk about at Ladies Missionary Society?"

"Oh, recipes, sewing, kids' ailments."

"Then, if that is all, why does everyone stop talking when we girls come in? Ralph says it was like that one day when he came by to ask you something. Just what is being said that we can't hear?" she demanded.

"Why—why, nothing," replied a flustered Miney. "It wasn't intentional, I'm sure. We just wanted to give you girls a chance to say what you'd come to say."

Blanche had realized her mother was putting her off, not giving the real reason. The girls had figured out that it must have something to do with being wives and mothers. That was another thing—no one seemed to know where babies came from. Everyone knew that a woman had to get married first, but none of the girls knew why. Blanche would have liked to have questioned her mother about this, only she realized Miney would not discuss such a topic.

Blanche finally drifted back to sleep although it was somewhat troubled and beset by weird dreams.

"Blanche! Time to get up."

That was Pa's voice. She wondered sleepily why he, instead of her mother, was calling her.

"Yes, Pa," came the drowsy answer.

She dressed quickly and came down the stairs. She noted that Rate was ahead of her, having had his share of chores to do before breakfast.

"Where's Ma?" asked Blanche, looking around.

"She's at Clark' s. Think you can rustle us up some vittles? I've got the fire going."

"I suppose so, Pa. But why isn't Ma here?"

"Because she isn't."

Blanche knew better than to press the matter further when Pa took that tone of voice. She went to the kitchen to begin breakfast. Pa had followed her.

"Here, Blanche, I'll slice the side pork."

"Thank you, Pa. I'll get the bread cut. Do you want eggs too?"

She had already put the coffeepot on to boil.

"Reckon I do. Man can't work on an empty stomach, you know."

All the while Blanche was getting breakfast, her mind was in a turmoil. Her actions were mechanical as she removed the cheesecloth from the table, set the plates in place, put on the jelly and butter, in between turning the strips of fat side pork in the pan. When the meat was done, she removed it to a plate that she promptly put in the warming oven above the stove top; she fried the eggs in the deep grease from the meat. Millie noted the meat with satisfaction—fat meat was his favorite, and the side pork had only a thin vein of lean.

Why hadn't Ma come home? Rate managed to ask Blanche if she knew why Ma had gone to Clark's, and she just shook her head.

Breakfast was over before Mina returned home. She looked plumb tuckered out, and her funny hip was sticking out, so she walked haltingly and with pain.

"Ma, where have you been?" demanded Blanche.

"Up to Clark's. Didn't your pa tell you that?"

"Why did you have to go there?"

Blanche's voice was petulant.

"Lena needed me."

"What for? Is she sick?"

"Not exactly."

Mina carefully lowered herself into a chair. My, but it had been a demanding and tiring night. She'd have liked to go to bed, only there was work to be done.

"If she isn't sick, why did Ed come get you?" persisted Blanche.

"When you're older, you'll understand," said Miney.

"Blanche, quit pestering your mother. Can't you see that she's tuckered out?" put in Millie.

Blanche shut her mouth in a tight line. She'd not ask another question, but she'd not do any more work than what she absolutely had to for the rest of the day. Much she cared if Ma's hip hurt. If that's the way they wanted to treat her, like some small child—well, let them. She had intended to do the sweeping after she finished dishes, only now she wasn't so sure. She supposed if Ma asked her, she would, but otherwise, she would just conveniently forget. Her stubborn English heritage once more took over.

A few days later, Blanche learned that the Clarks had a new baby boy, born the night of June 16, whom they named Milford after her own father. Somehow, Blanche tied together the two facts—her mother's absence and the new baby. Now, why couldn't her mother have given her just a simple explanation instead of being so secretive? Blanche felt guilty that she had used her mother so badly, but there were times when Ma just left her feeling frustrated because there were things she didn't understand, and where else was she to get the answers if not from her own mother?

Ralph had been getting around quite well for several days; in fact, his foot was almost back to normal. At the dinner table, Millie spoke to his son.

"Rate, there's a patch of bull thistles in the cornfield that need hoeing. That would be a good job for you this afternoon."

"Can I have Curly and Burl come help me?"

"I think not."

"But, Pa, I've helped them with their chores afore this, so it'd be only fair if they came to help me. Besides, we could get the job done lots quicker," he added hopefully.

"Rate, I know boys. One boy is fine, two boys are half a boy, and three boys are no boy at all."

Rate opened his mouth to ask his father what he meant, but the look on his father's face told him the question was settled. Blanche kicked him under the table and gave him a sweet little grin, which really meant she was laughing at him. His mother seemed lost in thought and had paid no attention to the verbal exchange between father and son. It was not the last time Ralph was to hear his father express these sentiments, and while not fully understood at first, in time, he came to agree that Pa's idea was not completely far-fetched.

Bruno was Rate's only companion that afternoon, and Ralph was more than a little miffed at the dog because Bruno had wanted to follow Millie instead of him. He concluded that dogs were not always the loyal friend they were supposed to be. Actually, he knew that Bruno preferred Pa to himself, and yet, Pa never paid him that much mind, so why the dog liked him best was hard to figger out. 'Course, he must admit that when he and Pa got to scuffling, which happened rather often, Bruno always took his part and was likely to give Pa a little nip. Sometimes, when Bruno nipped a little too hard, Rate thought it made Pa more than a trifle mad, but Pa never said much, and Bruno was pretty darn clever about dodging any blow directed at him.

Thinking of wrestling with his father brought a smile to Ralph's lips. He wondered if there would ever be a time when he'd be able to best Pa. As it was now, no matter how much by surprise he took Millie, Ralph was always the one to come out on the short end. Still, it was fun to try. There were times when Pa sure was fun. Guess he was lucky to have such a good father even if it did include hoeing thistles from a cornfield with no help from his friends.

"Blanche, where's Pa and Ma going?"

"Weren't you listening? Don't be such a dunce."

"I heard them say Nigra Falls, but what's that?"

"It's Ni-ag-ara Falls, and it is a big waterfall by Canada. They are also going to the exposition."

"Is that all? What they going there for?"

"Why would anyone go anyplace? To see something. Brothers. I wonder if they are all as dumb as you. Ma and Pa are just taking a trip for enjoyment. The exposition is like a big fair, I guess. I think

Niagara Falls isn't too far from where Pa was born. You do know that Pa was born in Canada and that Grandfather and our great-grandfather came here when Pa was two years old."

"I guess I know that. Leastways I've heard Grandfather talk about his home in Canada afore now, but I don't really know if it's far or not."

"Well, it's a lot farther than we've ever been from home."

"What are they doing with us?"

"Aunt Lorin said we could stay with her and Uncle Norman. I don't really like Aunt Lorin all that much. She's sort of odd if you ask me. I suppose I can put up with her for a few days."

Ralph pondered the situation. He had never been away from both parents before. Of course, he had spent a day or an afternoon with Grandmother, Aunt Lorin, or Grandma Smith all by himself. He was glad they were to stay with Aunt Lorin since he liked her, and she liked him. He guessed Pa wouldn't want to be gone very long 'cause he'd heard Pa say something about this was the only time they'd have before it was time to start putting up hay, and time would be short.

Mina and Millie, along with Clayton Sherman and his wife, left on Thursday from the depot in Elsie. Rate was sad to see his parents leave, but Ma had actually hugged and kissed him goodbye, and Pa had given him a bear hug and whispered that he'd bring back something special.

The days with Aunt Lorin passed pleasantly and quickly. Rate enjoyed the coddling from Aunt Lorin. She took him to the store twice and gave him a whole nickel each time to buy any kind of candy he wanted. Ma was never this generous. True, he'd had a difficult time deciding just what he wanted, but it sure had been fun. Aunt Lorin made awful good cookies too, and she wasn't near as fussy about how many he ate as Ma was.

When Millie and Mina returned, they picked up the children from Lorin's and hastened on home. Millie was anxious to get back to work. He was not a man to enjoy being idle for many days, so he was more than ready to get back in harness.

Ralph feared to bring up what was foremost on his mind: what had Pa brought him, or had he forgotten?

When Miney unpacked the valises, she brought out a paperweight and a beaded pincushion. Now, the paperweight was of plain, heavy glass with a browntone picture of the falls under the domed top. However, the pincushion was made of several kinds and sizes of brilliantly colored beads over a beautiful blue-gray satin. The beaded words read "From Niagara Falls." Rate didn't realize it was a pincushion, a girl's gift, so he thought it was beautiful. He was sure this must be the something special Pa had promised. Then, he realized Ma was speaking.

"Blanche, this pincushion is for you, and Ralph, yours is the paperweight."

"Oh, Ma, it's—it's—why, it's just gorgeous."

With that, Blanche threw her arms around her mother and kissed her in an unaccustomed display of affection.

"Thank you, Ma. I just love it."

"Ralph, you haven't said a thing," observed Miney.

"Thank you, Ma. It's nice."

"Don't you like the paperweight, Ralph?"

"Sure, Ma, it's fine. I like it."

If his voice faltered a little at the tiny white lie, Miney never noticed. She had already turned back to her unpacking.

Ralph was to learn that this was only the beginning; he would always come out second best, Blanche would always come first in everything. A bitter pill for one so young to swallow, yet neither Miney nor Millie would ever have admitted to anyone, much less themselves, that this partiality ever existed in any form. Perhaps they couldn't see the forest for the trees and, therefore, never realized they were being so very prejudicial. It was a very disillusioned and saddened small boy who went to bed that night. What had happened to Pa's promise for something special? He really couldn't see anything so special about the paperweight they had given him; still, they had brought something, so he guessed he should be pleased.

"Blanche, I'm a man short today, so you get to drive the team on the hay rope."

"Millie, do you think she can?"

"She's done it once or twice before. You just never knew about it."

"Well! It's not a woman's work, you know."

"Miney, just keep still. Blanche, I want you out to the barn when we come up with the first wagon."

"All right, Pa. But if I'm to drive that team, you are not to load the forks too heavy. If you do, I'll quit."

Ralph stared. Pa was letting Blanche get away with sassing him. Bet Pa would never let him talk like that.

"What do you mean?"

"Just what I said. Sometimes, you push those forks in so deep, the team can hardly pull them up. I'll not make them work so hard. You just never consider those poor horses. Now, promise me, Pa."

"All right, Blanche. We'll load light so the team won't be over-worked." Millie chuckled. Golly, but when she was like that, she sure did put him in mind of Ma. The tilt of her head, the way her eyes flashed, and the set of her mouth. He supposed he shouldn't let her talk to him in that tone of voice, and if it wasn't that she even sounded like Ma, he supposed he wouldn't have tolerated it.

The hay was forked onto a wagon in the fields, then brought to the barn. Here an inverted U-shaped hayfork, which was over three feet high with a spread of thirty inches or more, was lowered by means of a heavy rope from the car on a track fastened to the center of the barn roof; the other end of the rope passed through a pulley at the north side of the barn door and was fastened to the eveners where a team of horses was hitched. Each side of the fork had a finger that slid up out of the way as the fork was shoved into the hay on the wagon, then the finger was pushed out by a lever at the top of the fork and locked into place. If the hay was long and piled well on the wagon, when the horses were driven away from the barn, the fork rose with a large bunch of hay attached. When it rose high enough to clear the beams into the haymow, the team was halted; the car locked the fork in place automatically, and it was drawn over into the mow by another smaller rope and pulley series. A trip rope hanging from the lever locking the fingers was jerked, retracting the fingers and dumping the load of hay.

All this was if everything worked satisfactorily. Sometimes, when the hay was short, it did not cling together well enough, and some of it fell from the fork back onto the wagon. Once in a while, the trip rope got tangled up and couldn't be found, or if found, it failed to trip the forks. Sometimes, if a farmer didn't keep close watch of the ropes being used, a rope broke. All work had to stop until the two pieces of rope were once more spliced together.

All had been going well, and Blanche had been satisfied with the way Millie was loading the forks—until the last, small load.

Millie set the forks, and Blanche dutifully drove the team until Millie hollered "Whoa!" That load of hay was dumped in the mow, and the forks returned to be drawn down to the wagon rack to be set once again.

This time, Blanche had driven the team only about half the usual distance when she heard Millie holler.

"Blanche! Stop the horses!"

"Whoa! Whoa, there."

The team stopped as she pulled back on the lines.

"What's wrong, Pa?"

Blanche turned to look back to the barn and saw that not only was there hay clinging to the forks, but Millie had shoved them down so hard the pointed legs had stuck in the wagon rack, and that was going up along with the hay.

"Pa! Just look what you've done."

Blanche dropped the lines and ran to the barn.

"I thought I told you not to load heavy so's old Mage and Jen wouldn't have to work so hard. Now, look what you've gone and done. That rack is heavier than the hay. I'm done, Pa. I'm not going to drive no more. I told you I wouldn't if you didn't have some consideration for the team. I meant just what I said. Besides, it isn't a woman's work."

With a toss of her head, Blanche flounced off to the house. Millie gave Jim a sheepish grin.

"Sure riled her good, didn't I? Gets more like Ma everyday. Guess if this wasn't the last load, I'd have to change her mind for her. As it is, no harm's done. One thing about Blanche, when she makes up her mind to something, she's powerful hard to dissuade. Pity the poor man she's to marry."

"Your mother found one to match her. Leastways, I never felt your father couldn't hold his own. Maybe Blanche will do as well," said Jim.

"Could be. Guess we'd better get this mess straightened out afore the team gets tired of standing. Rate, you grab those lines and just hold 'em steady so they won't start walking off."

"All right, Pa. Can I finish drivin' 'em when you're ready?"

"We'll see."

Boy, Blanche sure had talked up to Pa. Bet if he ever tried it, Pa would trounce him to within an inch of his life. Wonder why Pa always seemed to let Blanche do as she pleased. Fact was, he always seemed to think it comical the way he chuckled. Maybe it was because she reminded him of his mother, and everyone knew that Pa had never spoken up to his mother in all his years. Must be that was the reason.

Blanche never liked to be told she resembled Grandmother Setterington. Guess she was just too stubborn to admit the resemblance. Blanche had told him once that in no way did she ever want to be anything like Grandmother. Still, Pa was always saying blood will tell, so he supposed she just couldn't help herself.

Miney had thought Blanche seemed rather quiet at dinner. She was the one who usually had something to say, and if Millie was to do much talking during a meal, it would be in response to some query from his daughter. However, today's meal had been a quiet one, and even doing the dishes afterward had been an unusually quiet occasion. Mina tried to draw Blanche into conversation, but her efforts were to no avail. Blanche remained quiet and morose, much unlike her usual self.

Work finished, she went upstairs to her room with no word of explanation. Millie left for town, taking Ralph with him, so Miney was left to herself as she sat on the porch to do some of the seemingly endless mending. July 26, her birthday. She doubted if the children even thought of it, and she knew Millie would never remember anything so trivial. Well, it didn't matter much. So she was a year older. Didn't make her feel any different.

She finished putting the hem in a dress for Blanche. The girl had grown taller so fast that the skirt had been too short. Why, it had been more than midway to her knees, showing over two inches of calf above the shoes. Well, now it was done. She supposed she should have made Blanche do her own sewing since she was getting to be such a young lady. However, she could most certainly finish the chore much more quickly than her daughter.

Dress in hand, Miney stepped to the stairway, opened the door, and called, "Blanche. Ma's got your dress finished. Come take care of it."

"Yes, Ma," came the rather muffled reply.

When Blanche reached the bottom of the steps and extended her hand for the dress, she kept her eyes downcast. Miney looked at her critically.

"Blanche, have you been crying?"

"Not…not much."

"Come here. Let me look at you. Why, child, your pretty eyes are all red. What is the matter? Aren't you feeling well?"

Miney took her daughter's chin in her hand and tilted Blanche's head back so she could see the girl's tearstained face, clearly noting the reddened, swollen eyes.

"Yes, Ma. I feel all right. I'm not sick."

"Then, why have you been crying? If you tell me, perhaps I can help. Don't you want to tell Ma?"

"Oh, Ma. It's just—it's just that I know what today is."

"Well, what is it?" came the baffled question.

"It's your birthday," she wailed.

"I've known that all day, but I don't see why that should make you cry."

"But, Ma, you're thirty-five today," blurted out Blanche. And with that, she burst into tears anew.

Miney began to laugh. "Child, child, child. Whatever makes you cry because I'm thirty-five?"

"But, Ma, it's so old, and I don't want to lose you."

Miney took the sobbing girl into her arms, dress and all.

"Sweetheart, Ma's not going to leave you. Thirty-five may sound old to you, but Ma isn't exactly ancient, you know. Don't you remember that Grandma was seventy-six, and that is more than twice my age. Blanche, is that what has been ailing you all day?"

"I guess so. Ma, I love you so much, and I just thought that you were getting so old, and however would I get along without you?"

"You silly little goose." Miney laughed. "Ma loves you too, and I'm not as over the hill as you think." Miney kissed her daughter noisily. "There. Give Ma a smile. You are so pretty when you smile. Go wash your eyes with cold water. The redness spoils their looks, and you do have such beautiful eyes. In fact, to Ma, you are a mighty charming and pretty young girl. 'Course anyone who's as old as I am certainly isn't much of a judge." Miney laughed.

"Ma, you're just teasing. Here, I'll take care of my dress. Thank you for fixing it. I guess I'll have to start doing these things for myself. Grandmother says I must learn to be independent," she announced as she went back up the stairs.

Fine thing for Lavina to tell a young girl when if Mother Setterington had her way, everyone would be dependent on her. Why, she hadn't thought Miney knew enough to buy Blanche's clothes when the girl had started school. Mina had made Blanche's dresses that first year, and Lavina had looked haughtily down her nose and asked if that was what she intended Blanche to wear to school. Miney had said that she thought Blanche would be dressed as well as the other girls; then, Lavina reiterated that she doubted if the Wooley girls or the Albaughs or any of the Bates children wore homemade dresses except for every day—or perhaps when they hired a competent seamstress to do something special. This had hurt Miney's feelings deeply, and she had felt quite taken down because she had put forth a lot of effort on those dresses.

Lorin, who often supplemented Norm's income and as a young woman had even earned her living as a dressmaker, had helped her with the more fancy of the three. Well, Mother Setterington had informed her that since she had already gone to the time and effort she, Lavina, supposed it would have to suffice for this year. "However, next year I will take her to Owosso to Christian's and buy her something which *I* find more suitable. Please keep that in mind," she had said in her most dictatorial manner.

Mina had wished the floor would open up and let her drop right out of Mother Setterington's sight and life. Of course, it hadn't happened, but true to her word, the next year, Mother had taken Blanche on the train to Owosso and bought Blanche not three, but four dresses and had presented them with the bill. Miney supposed she should have been grateful that Mother had paid the train fare and that Mother had only bought material for the new petticoats and pantaloons, not ready-made ones. However, Miney had been put out at the expense—she could have made the dresses for half the price, but Millie had made no objection and had shelled out the money without batting an eyelash. Miney had expected at least some kind of remark, but no, Millie still jumped whenever his mother snapped her fingers.

Last year, Blanche had raised her objections by asking why Grandmother always had to take her shopping because she would rather go with Ma. Miney was at loss as to what to say, so she had told Blanche to ask her father. Millie merely retorted, "Because that's what your grandmother wants." Even Blanche hadn't said more, knowing that her father would tolerate no criticism of his mother by his daughter. Blanche had told her mother that she wouldn't mind so much if only her grandmother would let her choose at least one dress herself. As it was, Lavina had her try on several and then told the saleslady which ones they would take, without even asking for Blanche's opinion. Blanche wanted to rebel, but she knew it would do no good. If Pa and Ma couldn't stand up to Lavina Setterington, how could she? Still, there might come a day.

Ruby had been visiting her mother and father for a few days. She and Lavina drove out to the farm one evening to visit Millie and his family. While there, it was decided that Blanche and Ralph would go home with her for the next week. Both children seemed enthused over the prospects of a trip to Big Rapids.

Perhaps Ralph was a little reluctant although he said nothing. He thought his aunt Ruby had changed a great deal since she was married. While they lived in St. Johns, she seemed much the same.

'Course Uncle Mac had only been a rather lowly paid bookkeeper for Masons. Now that he had a position in the bank in Big Rapids, Aunt Ruby put on airs. She had a seamstress come in to make her dresses. Grandmother probably paid for them, he thought maliciously. Anyway, she felt she had to dress the part as the wife of a bank employee who was certain to go up in the world.

Rate thought she rather looked down her nose at Ma and Pa thinking she and Uncle Mac were better than simple farm folk. Oh, well, she treated him pretty good and really never favored Blanche like the others did. Anyway, it would be a nice trip.

Rate hadn't figured on getting bored because he had no one to play with. A boy could only do so much to entertain himself during the day. 'Course, one day wasn't so bad as they had gone down to the Muskegon River and had taken a picnic lunch. Aunt Ruby was a good cook—no disputing that. She always let him have two pieces of pie, when Ma sometimes said one was enough. Anyway, they'd had fun. Uncle Mac had even played catch with him.

Another day turned out to be exciting. Aunt Ruby called to him where he was playing in the backyard.

"Ralph, the lawn needs watering. Do you think you can manage to water it? Here, hold the hose at an angle so it sprays like falling rain. That's it. Now, do along the sides and the front too."

"All right, Aunt Ruby. I'll do a good job, you'll see."

"I'm sure you will."

Ruby went back into the house to do her morning work. Blanche was doing the dusting, so there wasn't much to do. It was going to be a hot one, and so far, no breeze to help. The curtains hung limp at the open windows.

"Aunt Ruby! Aunt Ruby, come quick," cried Blanche from the parlor.

Ruby hastened to where her niece stood staring at the double windows. Water was coming in, thoroughly soaking the curtains, wetting the couch and the rug. Apparently, Blanche was so surprised, she did not realize the cause.

"Rate! Rate!" screamed Ruby. "You turn that hose away from the house this instant. Rate! Do you hear?"

"Yes, Aunt Ruby. I hear you. What's wrong?"

"You were spraying water into the house. That's what was wrong."

"Gosh, I didn't mean to. I was watering the bushes," he explained.

"But those bushes are in front of the windows, and the windows are open. Oh, Rate, my curtains will have to be washed, and it is going to take the rug a while to dry."

"I'm sorry, honest, I am."

"I know," sighed Ruby. "Go on and finish your job, but stick to watering the grass, not bushes."

"Boys!" came from Blanche. "Aunt Ruby, he just always gets into trouble. I'll get the mop and soak up what water I can."

"Thank you, Blanche. I'll get the curtains down and get them washed."

Washing curtains, while not difficult, was a time-consuming job. They had to be lightly starched and put on curtain stretchers until they dried. Next, they were sprinkled, rolled in a towel until slightly damp, and then ironed, being careful not to stretch them out of shape. It was not a job Ruby liked. But like it or not, it had to be done. She had always rather suspicioned that Mina and Mother exaggerated the stories of the mischief Ralph got into, only now she wasn't so sure. Still, the lad had meant no harm, and he was such a good-looking child. In fact, she felt that both of Millie's children were exceptionally good-looking. She would consider herself lucky if she and Oliver were ever blessed with children, to have them as nice-looking.

*****

"Rate, go down the road and fetch Jen from where I tied her in the fencerow this morning."

"All right, Pa."

"Don't dawdle. Supper is near ready."

"Yes, Pa."

Boy, when Pa wanted something done, he expected it done right now. What made him think it would take so long anyhow? 'Course, she was tied clear down to the line fence, but that wasn't so far.

Ralph hurried along to the black mare who stood contentedly by the roadside fence. Apparently, she had had a good feast since the grass was nibbled short as far as the rope would let her move.

"Jen, just you hold still while I get on your back. No need for me to walk back when I can ride you."

He maneuvered the horse next to the rail fence and slid over onto her back. He grabbed a handful of mane and kicked her ribs with his bare heels.

"C'mon, Jen. Let's go."

The mare ambled off at a slow walk, but the nearer she got to the barn, the faster she went, and Ralph was intent on the task of staying on her broad back. Just as she turned into the north driveway, *whomp!* Something struck his forehead, and off he slid. Wow! His head hurt something awful. He put his hand to his forehead, drew it away, looked at it tentatively, half expecting it to be covered with blood. It wasn't. Dumb horse. She'd turned too close to the oak tree, and he'd been caught by a lowhanging limb. His head throbbed.

Better put the fool mare into the barn. At least she hadn't run off, just stood patiently waiting in front of the barn door for someone to put her in the barn.

Ralph hurried to finish his job and get to the house so he wouldn't be late for supper. Neither Miney nor Millie tolerated tardiness at mealtime. He hastily washed and had slid into his chair before his mother looked at him.

"Whatever happened to you? Why, Ralph, your forehead is scratched and—here, let me look at it—you've got a bump as large as an egg. Millie, just look at this."

"I'm lookin', Miney. Well, Rate, want to explain?"

"Gosh, Pa, I hit my head on that low limb on the oak tree. Jen was comin' faster than I wanted, so I was workin' at stayin' on, and she cut too close to the tree. See if I ever ride a horse again."

"If you could ride well, you'd have had your horse under control and wouldn't have let her turn so short towards the tree," observed Blanche.

Ralph wrinkled up his nose at his sister.

"Like to see you do any better," he muttered.

"That's enough," said Millie, then added, "How's the head feel?"

"Sore. And it aches."

"My land, Ralph, must you always get hurt?"

"Honest, Ma, I didn't do it on purpose."

"I should think not. I just wish you would learn to be more careful. After you eat, a cold cloth on your forehead might make your head feel better."

"Miney, quit fussin'. The lad's no sissy and can take a little bump. Can't you, Rate?"

Lot Pa knew. It wasn't his head that hurt. At least Ma had showed some concern, but then, mothers were like that, he guessed.

A few days later, Millie came into the kitchen from the windmill door, then continued into the dining room. He looked somber.

Miney looked up from her crocheting.

"Millie, whatever is the matter?"

"Didn't you notice any of the fracas up at Clayt's?" he countered.

"Now that you mention it, I did notice three or four buggies in the yard. What was going on?"

"Young Ed just died."

"Ed Sherman, Clayt's nephew?"

"That's right, Miney. He's only about thirteen or fourteen."

"For land's sake, what happened?"

"Seems he was giving Burl a ride on the handlebars of his bicycle. They were down the Ridge a piece when a rig came along, and the boys had to get out of the way. Well, they brushed into some bushes, and Burl got his heel caught in the spokes, jerked the handlebars out of Ed's hand, and tipped them over. Ed got that handlebar right in the pit of the stomach when they fell. He just lay there doubled up in pain. Burl's heel was bleedin' pretty good, but he started for Clayt's yellin' his head off. The man in the rig stopped, Clayt came runnin' out, and they both got back to where Ed lay. The two of them picked

Ed up and carried him into the house. First they called Ed's folks, then they called the doctor. Guess his ma got there just before he died. Anyway, the doctor no more'n got there when he up and died."

"How awful."

"I happened along about then. Wondered why all the rigs so stopped to see what was wrong. Felt sorry for Burl. He said it was all his fault because he was the one who made them tip over. The kid had quite a cut on his heel, so the doctor took a couple of stitches. Guy tried to tell Burl it was just an accident, but the boy just cries and says he should have kept his feet away from the spokes."

"Poor child. Those boys have always been close, more so than some cousins."

"I know. Guess it was just meant to be. 'Course it was a dumb thing to give the boy a ride on the handlebars, but kids often do that. I'd better get my team put away. Where's Rate? He should be told."

"I don't know, but he's likely not far."

"You want to do the tellin'?"

"Suppose I can. If you find him, send him in. He'll feel pretty badly—him being so close to the Sherman boys."

Millie nodded his head in agreement.

Miney was the one who explained to Ralph what had happened. He hadn't said much, there wasn't much one could say. Rate wondered why one so young had to die. Poor Burl. It was sort of his fault, but then, if the rig hadn't come along—if, if, if. God sure had strange ways of running the world, and Rate guessed he would never understand why certain things happened, they just did.

Usually, Blanche began looking forward to school starting along about the middle of August. This year was different. The nearer the time came, the more she dreaded it; the reason was that this year she would be entering the seventh grade. This meant she would no longer be in one of the downstairs classrooms but would have to go to the second floor. It also meant she would have Miss Finch. What a horrible thought. For the past two years, she had heard many stories about how strict Miss Finch was and how she ruled the classroom with an iron hand. Why, it was said she even used a razor strap on the students for just any little infraction of the rules, which everyone knew were so outlandish it was just impossible not to break one once in a while. The thought of being in such an environment terrified Blanche.

The day of doom grew steadily closer. Blanche even considered faking some sort of illness just to put off the awful day a little while longer. Then, she thought of some of her mother's homemade remedies and changed her mind.

If Miney thought her daughter was less than exuberant about the beginning of the school term, she said nothing. She realized it would do no good to question her daughter because if Blanche did not want to share her thoughts, no amount of coaxing would entice her to divulge what she was thinking.

Miney need not have been concerned. Blanche came home from school on Friday night chattering like a magpie. It was Miss Finch this and Miss Finch that, and how she was looking forward to the school year.

"I thought Miss Finch was so strict no one liked her."

"Oh, no, Ma. She's just the nicest teacher. She says the funniest things without cracking a smile, but her eyes always laugh. Fern and I always ask if we can do things for her like erase boards and such."

Miney laughed. "See all that worrying you did for naught."

"I guess so. But she's not one bit like what we'd heard. 'Course, no one did anything wrong yet. I guess probably she wouldn't tolerate anyone fooling around. She expects work done on time. She is such an interesting person. I never liked history all that much, but she sure makes it fun to learn."

Blanche had made the observation that many a student was to make: Kate Finch was a demanding teacher, but an interesting one, and one who managed to reach each student who passed through her classroom—a truly dedicated teacher, devoted to the only children she was ever to have, for she never married.

Wheat had been a good money crop the past two years—almost as good as hay. While Millie was busy dragging a field for the crop of winter wheat he would soon sow, Miney waited for Ralph to come home from school so they could drive to town. The main reason was to get Blanche from her grandmother's, but if Mina went to town, she could always think of something she needed from the store.

Rate often wondered just why his mother always had to have him go along when she still considered him enough of a child that she had to drive instead of him. Mothers could be so blamed hard to figger out at times; now, Pa often let him drive knowing that a boy almost eight could handle a horse right well. Pa even let him drive by himself although he knew Ma often berated his father for this. 'Course, Pa was kind of careful which horse he gave him to drive since some of Pa's horses weren't exactly trustworthy. Anyway, Mina was driving Old Mikey today, and they pulled up to the hitching rail in front of Van Deusen's General Store.

Mina took her time about getting down from the buggy while Rate scrambled down in a hurry and tethered the horse securely—not that Old Mikey needed tying, he'd have stood there till doom's day, lessen someone came along and picked up the lines. Ralph waited, but just as Miney stepped down onto the boardwalk—the refuse from the multitude of horses over the years had resulted in the street being some six inches higher than the boardwalk—a young man accosted Miney, making unintelligible sounds, his arms waving and his fingers moving excitedly.

"Dummy" Harris was deaf and dumb. Rate knew his given name was Edgar, only everyone just called him Dummy. It was not the first time Ralph had seen his mother use her hands and fingers to "talk" to Dummy. Rate often marveled that they could carry on a conversation this way. Of course, since Mina was one of the few people other than his own family who could talk to him, and since she always treated him kindly, Dummy almost worshiped her. Rate could sense there was something urgent in what was being said.

The sign language flew, then Miney gasped, "Oh, no! Ralph, Edgar says that someone has shot President McKinley. Oh my goodness."

"How does he know?"

"He was down to the depot, and it came over the telegraph not long ago. Edgar can read, you know, and he saw the message. We'd best hurry with our purchases and get back home to tell your father."

"Is he dead?"

"Your father? Oh, you mean the president. No. Leastways not yet. Edgar said they didn't know much about it except he's been shot. I knew the president was to be at the Pan-American Exposition at Buffalo. Some man just up and shot him. Had the gun bandaged up in his hand like he had something wrong with his hand. Why would anyone want to kill the president of the United States?"

Rate pondered the question. Why would anyone want to kill anybody whether they was president or not? Grown folks were hard to understand, that was for certain. Ralph hoped they would sentence the man to death. Didn't the Bible say an eye for an eye?

Dummy Harris had been right in his information. On Friday, September 6, 1901, Leon Czolgosz, an anarchist, had shot President William McKinley; the president was still alive, and the wound was not thought to be critical. He had been taken to a hospital in Buffalo, and the doctors were rather optimistic. Then, his condition abruptly worsened. Vice President Roosevelt was on standby while a whole nation waited for the news each day. Special services of prayer for his recovery were held at churches all over this vast country; the Elsie Baptist Church was among them.

On September 14, the president succumbed to gangrene, and the nation set about to mourn a president. On the afternoon of the same day, Theodore Roosevelt took the oath of office; no nation can remain without a leader at the helm even though they lament the passing of a competent man.

Millie was optimistic. Hadn't McKinley chosen Roosevelt for his running mate? Well, then, the man must think along the same lines. Millie was not concerned with a foreign policy, he wanted only a good domestic trade with farmers earning a fair price for their various crops. Millie did not care for newfangled notions in the way of automobiles, nor could he envision farming being done by anything other than good draft horses and a reliable man.

Milford had always been a skeptic about something new; the old, if it worked well, would suffice. Machinery to save time was only for men who were lazy, and he was not to be counted in their number. Thus, while he felt saddened that a man had lost his life in so brutal a fashion, he felt no qualms about the twenty-sixth president doing a comparable job.

The schoolyard buzzed with talk of the assassination. The older boys made their boasts as to how they would have handled the situation. The younger ones, Ralph included, were awed by the event. Since to them, President McKinley had been only a man whom they had seen in pictures, they felt no personal loss or tragedy. So a president had died—the country still had a president, and life continued in the same manner as before. The guilty man should be punished because he had broken one of God's Commandments, nothing more, nothing less; to the very young, it was all exceedingly simple.

All summer the Detroit Bridge and Iron Works had been working on a new metal bridge across the Maple River by the gristmill. The old wooden structure had been deemed unsafe, especially after the near disaster of last spring's record high water. The new bridge was directly to the east of the wooden structure; men and horses were still hauling and leveling gravel since only the approaches were unfinished. Ralph had already walked across the new bridge. It was much higher above the water than the old one, and the sides were open. Rate had kept pretty much to the center since it was sort of scary being in the open with the water so far below; he kept expecting the bridge to wiggle, but it didn't. The planking on the old one really rattled when any vehicle passed over it; he was sure this one was going to be virtually soundless.

When the bridge was finally completed, the old landmark was torn down with only the pilings still standing like sentinels in the water, mute testimony that the bridge had once existed. At each end of the new bridge was a prominently displayed sign: Ten Dollars fine for riding or driving faster than a walk.

Chapter 16

Ralph and Don (Curly) Sherman were discussing a grievance at noon hour.

"Rate, it ain't fair that the older boys get to get out of school to bring the water."

"Maybe so. Only I don't think we could carry a full pail all that way."

Stafford School did not have a well. There was a flowing well on the east side of the road by the bridge across from where the Naegle family lived, and the older boys took turns carrying a pail at a time from there. It usually took two pails to last the day, one for the morning and one for the afternoon. The pail set on a stand just inside the door at the back of the schoolroom, and the children drank from a single dipper.

"Maybe by ourself we couldn't," Don agreed. "How about if she let us go together? We could either take turns or we could carry the pail between us."

"Suppose we could at that."

"Whyn't you ask?"

"Not me. It was your idea."

"Aw, Rate, you know she's more likely to say yes if you ask."

"That's not so."

"She likes you better'n she does me."

"Naw, she doesn't. She just got mad the other day 'cause you were fighting."

"That's what I mean. She ain't mad at you."

"What about how she hollered when I stuck both of Alice's pigtails in my inkwell?" asked Rate with a mischievous grin.

"I'd forgotten that. Maybe I should ask."

"I'll go with you, but you do the talking."

Ralph and Don went back into the one-room schoolhouse and approached Miss Peabody's desk situated off to the southwest side of the front of the room. They paused in front of her desk not knowing if they should interrupt her since she was correcting some arithmetic papers.

Looking up, she asked, "Do you boys want something?"

"Yes, Miss Peabody. Me and Rate—uh, Ralph, here, we want to know if we can get the water for this afternoon."

"Oh, Don, do you think you can carry it so far? You know it is quite a ways."

"Yessum. That's why both of us want to go."

"You know neither of you is very big. I'm just not sure you could manage. A pail of water can get pretty heavy."

"We know, ma'am, but we can do it. Honest. Just you give us a try. We're stronger than we look, ain't we, Rate?"

"I sometimes carry water for chickens and such at home," volunteered Rate. "Can we try? Please?"

"All right. You'll have to leave now so you will be back in time for your afternoon reading class."

"Oh, boy. Let's go. C'mon, Rate."

Rate carefully set the dipper aside while Don grabbed the pail. They set off with a vim down the schoolyard hill and into the road.

"Race you there," shouted Curly as he took off running.

Rate ran to catch him. Panting a little, he said, "There's no use to hurry. Reading class don't start when the bell rings, so we've got plenty of time."

"Guess you're right," admitted Don.

They slowed their steps, and Rate took his turn carrying the pail.

Upon reaching the bridge, they crossed the board planks and went down the path leading to where the cold, clear water flowed from the side of the riverbank, cascading down to the river. They soon learned a pail full of water was not an easy thing to handle as they scrambled back up the incline. Both boys together managed to get it back on the road where they set it down and rested.

"How we gonna do it?"

"You take it first since it was your idea. Then, I'll carry it a ways," said Ralph.

Don picked up the pail, holding his left arm out for balance. The pail banged against his legs, sloshing out some of the water.

"You're spilling it," observed Rate.

"I know. Like to see you do any better."

"Guess probably I could at that."

"Here. You take it then."

Ralph took the pail, but after a few steps, he banged it against his leg and sloshed water on his pants.

"You sloshed it too," pointed out Curly.

Rate set the pail down.

"Guess we'd better try carrying it together. Maybe that will work better."

Don took one side and Rate the other. Both lifted together on the bail, but the pail seemed to bang around worse than ever.

"This ain't no better, Rate. What we gonna do?"

"It was your idea. You figger it out."

Rate sat down on the roadside and looked at his friend. Don, who was usually so self-assured, looked completely baffled.

"I've got it," cried Rate. "We weren't in step. Let's try it again. We'll both start off with our right foot and then see."

They took up their positions, and sure enough, keeping in step helped. Slowly and surely, they made their way back to the school-house. If the pail wasn't quite as full as usual, no one said anything. Miss Peabody smiled to herself when the boys slid into their seats. She had watched their progress out of the window and knew they had nearly bitten off more than they could chew. She was almost certain neither of them would ask for that task again, and she was right, they never did.

*****

Miney had driven to town by herself to get groceries since Millie needed to get some feed ground for the hogs.

There seemed to be an unusual amount of activity at the mill when Millie and Rate drove up. Several men were standing in a group, talking excitedly about something. Millie threw off his bags onto the loading platform and then joined the group to see what was going on.

Mr. Cooley, the owner, was in the center.

"Just don't know why such a thing had to happen."

"What's going on?" asked Millie.

"We've just had us a drowning," said Cooley.

"A drowning? Who?"

"Little Harry Newington, Amza's boy."

"How in tarnation did something like that happen?"

"Seems he and his brother had been down there in the basement. The older boy wanted to come ask his pa something, so he cautioned the little fellow to stay away from where the boards cover the flume. When he went back down, he couldn't find Harry, so he gave a yell, and we all came runnin'. One of the boards looked askew, so we took up the others and used a rake to search. Sure enough, at the other end, against the grating, was his body. You know, it didn't take much of a hole for a five-year-old lad to slip through. That water in the flume isn't all that deep, but it is so swift, the tyke didn't have no chance at'all."

"Just never know how long a person has, do you? Kids always have to try just what they've been told not to do," said Millie.

"The brother took it pretty hard. Think he was afeared Amza was going to blame him. Right then, Amza was too broken up to put blame on anyone. 'Sides, it ain't like the boy did it on purpose."

"What in hell were they down there for?" asked someone.

"Don't rightly know. No one seen 'em go."

Rate had been standing to one side and had heard the conversation. My gosh, first Ed and now some little boy—both dead because of an accident. He had always known the water flowed fast through the mill to turn the two huge waterwheels set horizontally under the building. In fact, Pa had cautioned him to stay away from the bank that led to the millrace because when the doors were open, the water flowed through with enough force that Pa had explained a person would have been sucked under and held against the grating, which kept out debris, even if that person could swim. Rate had been given to understand that the millrace deserved a lot of respect. Made him wonder why Mr. Newington hadn't impressed this on his boys. Perhaps he had tried, but perhaps he was not as severe in his punishment as Pa, so his boys felt they didn't have to mind. Maybe Pa was so blamed strict for his own good.

*****

Millie decided it was high time the lambs were sold. He and Jim Keenan drove them onto the barn floor, and from there, they loaded them onto the wagon, which was equipped with a high rack so even the most agile or frightened lamb could not jump over it. They had already made one trip to St. Johns, where the largest stockyards were located, and were now about to leave with the second load.

Millie stepped into the dining room and spied Ralph sitting cross-legged on the floor, playing with a small cast-iron fire engine, pulled by coal-black horses, which was one of his favorite toys.

"Rate, Jim and I are leaving with another load of lambs. We've got yours this time. How much will you take for him?"

Rate pondered the question, then piped up, "I'll take a dollar for him."

"Boy, you've made yourself a sale."

Millie reached into his pocket, took out a silver dollar, and rolled it across the floor to his son. Without another word, he turned and left.

A whole dollar! He had almost been afraid to ask Pa for that much money, but Pa hadn't even tried to Jew him down—just forked over the dollar, a nice shiny one too. Boy, a dollar to do with just as he pleased. He had sure earned it feeding those lambs for all those weeks. Not that he had minded most of the time, but there had been a few days when he would have liked to play hockey and forgot about bottles for seven lambs.

Rate's feeling of euphoria continued until the day when Millie received the check in payment for the lambs. Ralph noticed the satisfied look on his father's face and heard him tell Miney, "We got a good price for the lambs. Best we've had for quite a spell."

Rate asked his father how much they had received, and Millie told him the amount of the check. Rate still did not have the information he was fishing for; he wanted to know how much each lamb brought. Well, he knew how many lambs they had; however, he hadn't learned that much about ciphering. When Ma wasn't busy, he would ask her, being certain she would figure it out for him.

Miney finished the dinner dishes, removed her apron, and sat down with some crocheting; Millie and Jim had gone back outside to return to the work they had interrupted for the noon meal.

Rate took this opportunity to ask Miney the all-important question. He told her how many lambs they had sold, what Pa got for them, and then asked the question.

"Ma, how much money was that for each lamb?"

"Well, Ralph, I'd have to figure it out. Now, let's see. Unless I made a mistake, it was just a few cents over three dollars apiece."

"Three dollars! Are you sure?" Mentally, she ran over the figures again and said, "Yes, that's right. Three dollars and about twenty cents, I didn't figure it exactly."

Three dollars a head, and he'd sold his lamb to Pa for one measly dollar. Pa had made two dollars on his lamb. Ralph knew there would be no use complaining to his father that it was unfair because Millie had asked him what he wanted for the lamb, and he had set his own price. Bet he'd never sell anything again without knowing the fair market value. A dollar had seemed like a good price, only compared to three, it was merely a drop in the bucket.

*****

As so often happened, Vere Brown had sure riled Miss Peabody this morning. Vere, who was a grade behind Rate, often seemed to vex his teacher. For one thing, Vere did not take his schoolwork seriously, so he seldom had his assignments done at class recitation time. This morning had been worse than usual.

Vere had not had his work done for his arithmetic class, then he had been disruptive at his seat; Miss Peabody had stood him in the corner, so close his nose was almost touching the wall, but he kept turning around, when she wasn't looking, causing the kids to laugh because he was making faces. Finally, in desperation, she had jerked him out of the corner and shoved him underneath her desk. The teacher's desk was crudely built of heavy boards with drawers on each side and a kneehole in the middle. It was situated so there was no way Vere could peek out at any classmates.

Just before dinner, Miss Peabody gave Vere permission to return to his seat.

He grinned a little sheepishly and amazingly went right to work.

It was noon, time for dinner. Books were put away, dinner pails brought from a shelf in the respective cloakrooms, each student bowed his head while the teacher said grace, and then the hungry children looked to see what their mother had packed for the day. Rate always had meat or egg sandwiches although a lot of students had only jelly—slightly soaked into the bread—for sandwiches.

"Land's sakes," exclaimed Miss Peabody.

The talking stopped, and each student looked her way wondering what was amiss. She held up an empty dinner pail. No one even snickered, but all eyes turned to Vere, who sat in his seat as unconcerned as could be, wolfing down a jelly sandwich.

"Vere Brown," came the stern voice. "Come here."

Smiling somewhat abashedly, Vere slid out of his seat and slowly approached the teacher's desk. Thereupon, he hung his head and looked at the scuffed toes of his shoes, not knowing if he dare grin or not.

"Vere, what happened to my dinner?"

The boy shifted from one foot to another and mumbled a reply.

"Speak up. I couldn't understand you."

"I-I...aw...Miss Peabody, I et it."

"Didn't you know that was wrong?"

"Reckon so, but I din't have no breakfast, an' I wuz hongry. I'm sorry. Is ya gonna lick me?"

"Vere, Vere. I don't honestly know what I'm going to do with you. You go back and finish your own dinner."

"Already did. Only had one sannich," he explained.

Goodness, a growing boy needed more than that to eat; little wonder that he had not been able to resist the temptation of her dinner. Well, she supposed she'd have to keep him after school and make him wash the blackboards or perhaps bring in kindling. It was cold enough to have a small fire most of the day now, so each night, wood had to be brought from the woodshed and piled by the stove for use the next day. She couldn't ignore the fact that the boy had taken something that did not belong to him, even if she did understand the reason.

*****

Miney was upset. She had just this day received some disturbing news in a letter from her sister Ettie. Miney had read and reread the middle portion.

> I just learned that I am in the family way. Miney, whatever am I to do? Why, I'm almost forty years old, and I just know I'll die having this baby. Look how old Glen and Free are. I haven't been one bit well, and I've told George how terrible I feel. I know he just thinks I'm being silly—says there's no need for me to worry, plenty of women my age have babies. Men are just heartless and unfeeling. I was always so sick before the boys were born, and I just know this is going to be worse. Don't suppose it would be quite so bad if I wanted another child, but I don't. Never actually wanted the boys, only once they were here, I loved them. George simply does not understand how I feel. Guess if he'd had his way, we'd have had a dozen. At least some of the time he realizes that my health is delicate at best. I just told him

that this is all his fault, and when I'm dead and
gone, he can just realize who it was who put me
in my grave.

There was more, but Miney gave that a cursory glance and
reread the middle again. Her heart went out to Ettie. Good heavens,
imagine being forced to have a baby at forty. Miney had always been
fond of George and thought he had been very understanding of some
of Ettie's eccentricities; now, she felt angry with him. Goodness, how
old did a man have to be before he no longer needed to satisfy his
desires? She agreed with Ettie—it was all George's fault. If a man
didn't always force his attentions on a woman, but she guessed that
was asking for too much. She would write to Ettie tonight and see
what she could do to put her sister in a better frame of mind. If Ettie
was determined that having a child would kill her—it likely would.
Miney decided to do what she could to improve her sister's outlook
although it was going to be extremely difficult since Miney shared
Ettie's beliefs as well as apprehensions.

That evening, after the children had gone to bed, she told Millie
about Ettie's letter.

"Forty isn't all that old. If Ettie would only forget about her
health, get interested in something for a change, she'd feel better."

"How do you know she would? You've never been forced to
have a baby."

"Don't think she was forced either. Still, there's many a slip
twixt the cup and the lip."

"It is all George's fault. Wonder if he will feel like a murderer
when Ettie dies."

"You sound as though her death is inevitable. She isn't dead yet,
so don't cross your bridges afore you get to them"

"I just know she has a woman's intuition. Men can't understand
these things. I know Ettie has a premonition, and I'll warrant it is
right."

"Humph," grunted Millie.

As far as he was concerned, Ettie was a little willy-nilly and a
chronic complainer. She had complained so much about Doc that

he'd given up medicine and become a lawyer. Millie felt that Ettie would be glad to die just to prove to the world that what she said was right. He bet poor Doc's life would be nothing but pure, unadulterated hell until that baby was born.

He was reminded of how Miney had treated him when she was carrying Ralph, always telling him it was his fault. If he knew Ettie, she'd be ten times worse than Miney ever was. Sometimes, he wondered if all women resented the intimate relations between a husband and wife.

Ma had never complained about having children—only about losing them after they got here. She had finally convinced Pa it was likely his sinful ways, and that was probably the biggest reason Pa had got religion. Hadn't made any difference, Millie thought, because even though Pa had been going to church ever Sunday in atonement, they had lost little Emma anyway. He guessed women just weren't happy if they didn't have a man to blame for something.

*****

It was Sunday morning, and while Ralph had been up to do his chores, he had gone to change his clothes for church.

"Ralph," called Mina at the stairway door leading upstairs to the children's rooms. "Ralph, you be sure and bring your dirty clothes down for the wash tomorrow. And don't forget to change your suit of underwear."

"But, Ma, I changed it last week."

"You didn't either. It was your father's suit I had in the wash last week. Didn't you put on your clean one this morning?"

"No. Shall I change now? I'm almost dressed," he added plaintively.

"Hurry and change. I'll not have you going to church dirty."

It never occurred to Miney that there would be a time when folks would change their winter underwear any more often than every other week. Those heavy, woolen flannel, long-legged underwear suits were dreadful to wash and dry, so she had Millie and Ralph change on alternate weeks. Woman's suits were not quite as bulky, so hers and Blanche's were not nearly the trouble. Some womenfolk said they only washed their menfolk's suits once a month, but Miney figured they would be rather smelly in that length of time. Two weeks' wear, and then a good scrubbing was much better. Of course, Ralph, like any growing boy, had to be reminded, or he would never think to change his clothes less'n maybe they got so's they would stand alone.

Rate hastily doffed his outer pants to strip off his dirty underwear, first having the clean suit ready to don as quickly as possible. Sure was cold upstairs although winter hadn't yet set in fiercely enough for him to dress downstairs by the fire. When he was just a child, he had always grabbed his clothes and hightailed it down the stairs to the welcome warmth of the dining room stove. Now that he was bigger, he stuck it out except in the very coldest weather of December and January. He was sure this had not been his week to change, but from past experience, he knew it was useless to argue with his mother.

He finished dressing, put on his long black woolen socks, and stuck his feet into icy-cold shoes. Oh, well, he would warm his feet on the fender of the stove when he got downstairs.

He picked up his underwear and wrinkled up his nose as he smelled it. The pungent odor of turpentine and goose grease assailed his nostrils. Guess he had worn it longer than he supposed since it was a week ago yesterday that Ma had started doctoring him for a cold on his chest. She had made a concoction of goose grease laced with turpentine to rub on his chest. She had also given him some of the catnip tea that she steeped every fall for just such emergencies. He liked the heavy onion syrup she had made from boiling onions in a small amount of water, then sweetening it with sugar until it made a heavy syrup much thicker than the maple syrup they used on pancakes. He had even carried a small bottle to school in case he got a fit of coughing there.

Come to think of it, half the kids in school smelled of turpentine since this was the time-honored remedy of most parents. At least he had never had to take chicken manure like Pa. With a mother like Grandmother Setterington, there would have been no talking her out of it either.

Thinking of his grandmother brought another thing to mind. He had heard his grandfather and Pa talking one day, and Grandfather had said something about moving to another town. Now, that really would make a change in their lives not to have Grandmother and Grandfather around. Bet Ma would like it a heap better without her bossy mother-in-law looking down her nose at everything Ma did and always telling Ma how she should do things. Pa just never seemed to mind. Guess he'd grown so used to being bossed by his parents as a little shaver, it had just been a habit to let them continue to boss him around. Ma would have liked to rebel, for it sure went against her grain to knuckle under all the time.

If they left Elsie, he wondered what Blanche would do. Blanche was perfectly capable of driving back and forth to school, only sometimes Ma sure did want her pampered. Sometimes, he wasn't sure Blanche liked staying with her grandparents since she often was headstrong, and she never quite gave in to her grandmother's whims—only on the surface while the inner girl seethed.

Mina was darning a pair of Ralph's socks while Blanche sat at the table putting the hem in the housedress they had just finished making for her.

"Ma, why don't Grandmother and Grandfather like Aunt Grace?"

"Lawsy, Blanche, who says they dislike her?"

"Well, for one thing, the girls at school talk. Then Grandmother is always finding fault with Aunt Grace. 'I'll never understand what Johnny saw in her. Grace just always overdresses. She just never knows how to dress suitably. If only she would attend church. Blood will tell,' she imitated. "Grandmother always talks like that. What does she mean 'blood will tell'?"

"I presume she means that Grace is adopted, so she really isn't a Cobb. Of course, no one knows who her natural parents were."

"Uncle John hasn't accomplished much, if you ask me, so why does she act like Aunt Grace is so much worse?"

"Well, her son just has to be better than someone else. I guess your grandmother thinks he married beneath him. Still, I'm of a mind that John was no bargain. Leastwise he has never been a steady worker like your father. Then, too, Grace sometimes argues with your grandmother, and you know for a fact Mother Setterington cannot tolerate anyone disagreeing with her."

"That's true enough. If I voice an opinion, it is always wrong according to her. You know how Grandmother is always asking what we want for Christmas. Well, you should have seen the list Uncle John gave her. She grumbled to Grandfather something awful, but she's already started buying the things he wanted. Guess it was practical since most of it was warm clothes for the kids. If she gets it all, Aunt Grace and Uncle John won't have to buy the kids any winter clothes. Of course, I suppose if we gave her a list, she'd buy what we want too."

"I presume she would, but that makes Christmas so commercial somehow. The giving of gifts is all right, only we must not forget that we celebrate Christmas because that was when Christ was born. That is the important thing. I don't think there have to be a lot of gifts, or expensive ones either, and they should come as a surprise to the one who receives them."

"I think so too. Only it just made me wonder why Grandmother is so generous when she always finds so much fault."

"Blanche, your grandmother has always been a mystery to me. I think she thrives on finding fault with others. You'll notice Ruby never comes in for her share though. Mother never says one word against Mac, and he hasn't always been the best provider. Of course, Mother always paid for a hired girl so Ruby wouldn't have to do the heavy work."

"Seems as though Grandmother wants to run everyone's life. I'll never let her run mine, you can count on that."

Mina glanced up at her daughter and noticed the set line to her mouth. The girl was right, thought Mina. I think maybe Mother has met her match here. Blanche is too much like Mother to be intimidated by her. Don't know as I like her being quite so strong-willed and spunky, but I do want her to lead her own life without interference from her grandmother. I expect there will be more than one clash of wills before Blanche is grown.

Christmas that year was especially nice. Rate got the usual amount of clothes—each year like clockwork, he had a pair of double knit gloves from Aunt Lorin—a book or two, but the present that left him wide-eyed and almost tongue-tied was the beautiful air rifle and huge box of BBs from Grandmother and Grandfather. He had been rather enviously eyeing Blanche's *The Adventures of a Brownie*, which had come from Aunt Ruby since the title certainly sounded enticing to Ralph; however, in all fairness, he had to admit he could not read that well yet. This inability had in no way kept him from wishing. Then had come the gun. My oh my, what a beautiful sight it was. Maybe Grandmother and Grandfather did like him as much as they did Blanche; well, anyway, they had given him a really nice present.

Ralph was soon to learn that his mother did not approve of the gun for a present—said he was still too young. He'd heard her and Pa discussing the matter. Well, maybe discussing wasn't quite the word since Ma had been doing all the talking, and Pa was just keeping still like usual.

"Millie, Ralph is too young to have a gun even if it isn't a real one. It still shoots those little pellets, and I don't think it is a safe thing for him to have. It's just like your mother to give him something like that without asking our opinion. Supposing he gets hurt or shoots one of the neighbor children?"

"Now, Miney, first of all, the lad's got sense. He's going to be careful, and those popguns aren't much anyway. Personally, I thought it a mighty fine gift. I'll be sure he knows how to use it safely, so I don't want to hear any more about it."

Miney knew from the tone as much as the words that it would be futile to argue further. "I just hope you're right," she muttered, half to herself.

Ralph was always one for getting into trouble, and giving him an air gun was just asking for some disaster to happen. She had told him that he could not use the gun when any of his friends were over. At least that would take care of the risk of having him accidentally shoot someone. True, a BB gun couldn't kill a person, but it could most assuredly put out an eye.

Perhaps Millie was right. Perhaps she was overprotective of Ralph and didn't want him to live the life of a boy. If only he had been a girl—no use pursuing that line of thought because she couldn't change the situation. Still, she knew more about what to do with girls, and a lively normal boy like her son was rather bewildering at times.

If only he wasn't always getting into mischief or trouble of some sort. But she guessed Millie liked him that way. Leastways, there were many things he encouraged; just like them always scuffling, and that always set Bruno barking until finally he'd join in the fracas to take Ralph's part. Sometimes, she thought it was a wonder that some furniture hadn't been broken during one of the wrestling sessions. Ralph always got the worst of it, but that still didn't stop him from starting it. Guess he was always in hopes that with the element of surprise on his side, he would be able to best his father sometime.

Raising children did take a lot of doing especially when one was a boy. Ma had been lucky to have all girls, and yet she recalled that her mother had often said she would have liked a son. Guess maybe Ma had wished she had known Pa's boys when they were small. Maybe that was so there would have been some family ties because after their father died, they hadn't seen fit to pay hardly any attention to their stepmother. 'Course, to be truthful, they hadn't seen much of Pa after they had married and had moved away.

Jim had been the restless one, always on the move, always looking for a better place. He had made those trips to Oregon by wagon train in the hopes of becoming rich, only each time he came back, he had been broke. Pa had always said Jim was a good worker for a year or two, and then his itchy foot began to bother, and off he would go. None of Pa's boys had been the homebody Pa was.

Miney missed her parents. Pa had been an interesting storyteller, and Ma had always been easy to talk to. If she complained to Ma about Ralph's antics, Ma always had some words of wisdom to make her feel better. 'Course, Ma had always thought a lot of Ralph. Perhaps it was because he was the youngest grandchild. She had plenty of grandsons: Lorin's Georgie, Mary's Frank, and Ettie's Glen and Free. Anyway, Ma had never shown partiality between Ralph and Blanche. Miney knew that she herself often favored Blanche, and try as she might, she couldn't help loving Blanche the most. Not that she didn't love Ralph—he was such a good-looking lad and usually very good-natured—it was just that he did manage to try her patience. Well, she would just have to keep asking the good Lord to help her out, for He knew she certainly couldn't do this job of raising children alone.

Ralph and Bruno were out in the yard romping together. A few days ago, Millie had brought Rate a dog harness, and Ralph had been trying to teach Bruno to haul the sled. At first, the dog had objected to all those straps of leather and had tried to bite and tug to get them off. Ralph had patiently worked with the young dog who now tolerated the harness. However, Rate had not tried to hitch him up as yet. At least Bruno would follow Rate anywhere without getting upset with all that leather hanging on his body. Ralph had made up his mind that today was to be the big day. Much to his surprise, the dog did not object. He simply pulled the sled wherever Rate called him.

That night, after supper, Ralph spoke to his mother.

"Ma, do you need some apples brought home from Clark's?"

This year, Millie had decided it was too much work to pit apples, so they had stored some of the crop in the Clarks' basement. Millie had been bringing them home a crate at a time.

"Why, yes, I could use some more. Millie, are there any apples left at Ed's?"

"Three or four crates, if I recollect right."

"Why are you so anxious to get apples? Last time, when you had to get some on your sled, you did nothing but complain."

Miney eyed her son suspiciously.

"I just thought I'd offer."

"You didn't answer my question."

"All right. It's 'cause I've taught Bruno to pull the sled. I figured I'd have him help me."

"So that's it. In other words, you won't have to do the work, Bruno will."

"Something like that," he admitted, giving her a smile.

"Land's sakes, do you think that dog is strong enough to pull that much weight?"

"He can pull me all right."

"I suppose you can try it," said Miney.

The next night after school, Ralph hitched his dog to the sled and made the trip to the Clarks' on the Ridge. Ed helped him bring up a crate of apples from the basement to place on the sled. At first, strain as he might, Bruno could not get the sled to move. Ralph got behind it and gave a shove. There it went! However, since the drive was slightly uphill, Ralph continued to push until they were in the road and headed for home. Bruno pulled with a will, seemingly enjoying his job. Ralph's murmurs of "Good boy, Bruno." "Attaboy." "You can do it." only served to urge the dog to a steady, rapid walk. This certainly was better than having to pull the sled himself, thought Ralph. Good ole Bruno. He sure was a good dog and a mighty smart one too.

Millie had come home through the mire that only slightly resembled a road. The rig and horses were both caked with half-dried clumps of mud. He was glad he had braided the horses' tails so they had not dragged in the slime. As it was, he knew he'd have to soak and wash Major's feet. Major was half Clydesdale, and that profuse amount of hair growing around each hoof had to be cleaned and soaked free of the icy mud particles if his feet were to be kept in good condition. It would have been much easier if the hair could have been trimmed off, only Millie knew that if this was done, a Clydesdale usually got scabies. Why those little parasites felt they had to pick on the poor Clydesdale, Millie never knew, but he and others had learned the hard way that the good Lord had given the horse all that hair for a reason.

Millie had a bit of news for Miney. The ice had gone out of the river and had jammed up against the new bridge in such a wild assortment of chunks, there had been some concern for the bridge itself. Men had even contemplated using dynamite to break up the mountain of ice lodged against the lower part of the bridge. However, there were those against this idea, and while they were arguing the pros and cons of the advisability of blasting the ice, nature had taken care of the situation. Now, they were arguing as to whether the bridge had been built too close to the water. There were those in favor of going to the expense of raising the bridge two feet, and there were those opposed. Millie felt that raising it would be a bunch of nonsense. It had withstood this ice jam, and like as not, there wouldn't be another one for years. The old wooden bridge had been nearer the water, and the ice had never destroyed it. No use borrowing trouble, and Millie felt trying to raise a bridge of that size was certainly asking for trouble.

It was true. Grandmother and Grandfather were moving the first of April. Rate wasn't just sure why as yet, and he didn't rightly care because he thought it was funny that Blanche no longer would have a place to stay. Ma had asked Blanche if she wanted to stay with Aunt Lorin, but Blanche didn't seem to cotton to the idea. She had said that it was a shame Aunt Mary and Uncle Jap had moved 'cause she would sure liked to have stayed with Aunt Mary, who was the grandest person and was her most favorite aunt.

A number of years ago, Mary and Jasper Sickles had moved north from Elsie into timber country where Jap had started a sawmill. Now, there was a little community there, and it was called Sickles after the original settler. They had moved from there to Chicago. Ralph remembered visiting them once, and it had been fun. Of course, they didn't have anyone for him to play with since Frank was lots older. Lelah was Blanche's age, so that was one more reason Blanche liked being with them. 'Course Aunt Mary reminded both of them of Grandma—at least more so than anyone else.

The weeks passed quickly, and Lavina and Horatio moved to South Lyon, where Horatio started a private bank. He had $16,000 in cash of his own money, and while it was perhaps not a spectacular amount, it was sufficient capital for the times. He still had numerous land holdings throughout Clinton, Gratiot, and Shiawassee counties, so if the occasion demanded, he could have raised at least twice that amount. However, he was getting a good return for his money invested, so he would let the situation remain as it was for the time being.

Ralph learned that Uncle Mac and Aunt Ruby had moved from Big Rapids to be with Grandfather in South Lyon. Since Uncle Mac was a bookkeeper, he presumed this was the reason Grandfather had given Uncle Mac the job.

However, he had heard his parents talking, and Pa had said, "Pa just took Mac into the business so Ma could have Ruby near her. Well, if Mac is ever to amount to a picayune, it will have to be because he rode there on Pa's coattails."

Rate wasn't quite sure what his father meant. Ma had said something about Ruby being so spoiled, and the way everyone doted on her now that Lois had been born was a sight for sore eyes. Personally, Ralph didn't think much of Lois. 'Course she was so tiny she couldn't even sit up by herself yet. Maybe if she'd been a boy, he would have been more interested.

After much haggling and discussing, it was agreed that Blanche could finish out the school year by driving back and forth to Elsie. Millie still had that dependable old mare, Topsy, or Old Mikey, and Blanche could stable either one in Grandfather's barn since he had not yet sold his house.

Miney had mixed emotions about it. She most assuredly wanted her daughter home with her, only she didn't take a notion to Blanche's having to drive. She was still more upset when Millie decided that since Blanche had to drive to Elsie five days a week, she might as well take their milk to the cheese factory there. He had been taking it himself each day to Knight's cheese factory over west, only there were rumors they were going to close, so now he figured this would save him the trouble, and it might not be a bad idea to get started somewhere else. While Blanche might not have been too thrilled with this idea, she also knew better than to voice any sort of dissension.

A few days before she was to start driving, Ed Clark came over to talk with her. Ed owned the farm west on the Ridge Road just past Sherman's woods, so part of his land bordered the back of Millie's eighty.

Ed had a proposition to make for Blanche.

"Blanche, since you'll be haulin' milk to the cheese factory fer yore pa, how 'ud you like to pick up a can fer me?"

"Well, I don't know—"

"I'll pay you say fifty cents a week. How 'ud thet be? Won't take much extree work, and you kin have some spendin' money. Be it agreed?"

"All right. I'll do it," answered Blanche.

The chance to earn money was a great incentive. Trouble was, she didn't know that Ed would never pay her a single, solitary cent, and her folks wouldn't let her ask him for what he owed, saying he was a good neighbor in other ways.

Blanche hated hauling milk. The cheese factory was on the east side of town, over a block off the main street, and had an odor all its own. Sometimes, she had to wait in line because there were several farmers ahead of her, and it nearly made her late for school.

There was a place where the milk was dumped, then she had to drive on a little farther and collect the hot whey, which came out of a canvas tube. Old Sam Packingham was the one who pumped the wooden handle to force the whey up into the tube, which he also controlled. The factory had tried once to let the farmers pump their own whey, but this had not worked out well at all. It seemed that some folks who only sold a very small amount of milk—and therefore had contributed an equally small amount of whey to the total amount—helped themselves overgenerously; thus, they ran out of whey before everyone had collected his allotment. This was why Sam tried to portion it out so everyone got some. It didn't always work out this way, and on occasion, they had pumped out the entire day's allotment before the last patrons came to collect.

Sam had lost a leg in the Civil War. He stumped around on his peg leg and, to Blanche, always seemed in a grouchy mood. More often than not, he missed with the first or last bits of whey, so it ran all over the floor of the springboard wagon. My, it did stink, and the flies sure did swarm.

Both Millie and Ed had pigs, and they wanted the whey to feed to them; thus, there was no way Blanche could be excused from getting their allotment of whey.

Blanche had to hurry back to Grandfather's house, put the horse in the stable, and then dash the two blocks to school. Of course, she still cut through by Grandma Smith's house, which did make it some shorter. Anyway, she always felt hot and messy when she arrived. Town girls never had to work like this—they maybe made their own bed or did the breakfast dishes, which wasn't very time-consuming. Guess maybe underneath she felt that this really was man's work; however, Pa wasn't one to argue with, especially when it concerned work.

Then, at night, after the whey was fed to the hogs, she or Ma or both worked at scrubbing out the stale, stinking whey, which clung tenaciously to the sides of the milk can. Then, the can had to be scalded with boiling hot water so it wouldn't turn tomorrow's milk sour. These thirty-gallon cans were large and cumbersome and difficult for the two women to handle. When full of milk, it took a good man like Millie to toss one easily onto the wagon.

At least old Topsy was an easy horse to drive and nothing seemed to frighten her; she just plodded along at her set gait. Even if Blanche was to touch her lightly with the whip, it only speeded her up for a few steps, and then she dropped right back to her regular gait, which was no more than a fast walk.

Half the time, before she could come home, Blanche had to stop at the general store to buy something for Ma. Actually, she felt her mother rather liked having her drive to school so she could get something from town every day. Much of it could have been bought when Ma shopped on Saturday, but for some reason, Ma always was forgetting something. Either that or Ma preferred to spend her grocery money a few cents at a time. Ma sure did like to pinch a penny. Bet when she grew up, she would be better than her mother at planning her shopping trips.

CHAPTER 17

April is traditionally the season of warm spring rains to awake the dormant vegetation, the time of rebirth. This year was no exception. The expression "April showers bring May flowers" had certainly held true this year because the mayflowers had already carpeted the woodlots with their delicate, pale pink because the last few days had been unseasonably warm. The woodlots were also full of puddles and marshy spots, and even the roadsides were much wetter than usual. The Ridge, because of its sandy composition, was normally well dried off by this time of year; however, such was not the case this year.

Blanche hated the wet spring even if it was a warm one. Some days she drove the wagon, but after being thoroughly wetted in a shower on the way to school, she had used the buggy even if it was more difficult to fit the milk cans on the back. She often wondered why the rain usually came in the afternoon when she was going home since most of the time, any wind also came from the southwest, driving the rain into the buggy, thoroughly soaking her. Now, in the morning, the wind would have been to her back, and she'd have had the protection of the buggy and side curtains.

Today was no exception. Blanche managed to get Old Mikey hitched to the buggy before the first splatters of rain began. There were large pelting drops, which came violently at first, lessened, then came violently again, and then quit altogether. Just maybe she could get home before the storm really broke. Huge black clouds were swirling in from the southwest, and Blanche watched them anxiously as she urged Old Mikey to a fast trot. At least his speed was greater than Topsy's.

She crossed the river and turned north by the cemetery before the rain commenced again. This time, the drops were small and wind-driven, and with each step that Old Mikey took, it seemed the storm increased in intensity. When Blanche turned west once more, the rain blew in sheets as the clouds dumped their cargo, the road became obliterated, and Blanche was immediately drenched.

She began to cry, her tears mingling with the rainwater running down her face. It was difficult to keep her eyes open; she wanted only to close them against the driving rain.

"Oh, Mikey, Mikey. What are we to do? I can't see the road, and I'm near soaked to the skin."

The old black horse, wise in so many ways, felt the lines slacken. In a moment, he had turned the buggy around in the road; he hung his head and hunched his rump to the lashing rain.

Blanche sighed with relief as now the top and sides of the buggy were bearing the brunt of the storm. No longer was the rain stinging her face; her clothes might be sodden and stuck to her in their wetness, but she was more comfortable.

"Good Old Mikey. You know more than I do. This is much better," she murmured.

When the storm had pretty much abated, Mikey lifted his head, glanced back at Blanche, nickered softly, then turned back to head for home where they found Millie anxiously awaiting his daughter whom he sent directly to the house to get out of her wet clothes while he took care of the horse.

Blanche let it be known that Old Mikey had had more good sense than she had. She ended by saying, "But, Pa, I remembered what you always said about not stopping under a tree. There were a couple of big ones, and they are all leaved out, but I minded what you said."

"Good for you, Blanche. Lightning does strike a tree now and again, so they just aren't safe."

"It was an awful temptation all the same. Old Mikey sure was a blessing. Guess I did learn something today."

Miney was busy rearranging Blanche's dress and coat where they hung near the stove to dry. She was worried for fear Blanche would take a cold, but her fears were unfounded; being strong and healthy, Blanche suffered no ill effects from her drenching.

The latter part of March, Clayt Sherman had moved off the farm. Swarthout, the tenant who had moved there the following week, had several children. It hadn't taken Rate long to become friends with Rollie, who was in his grade at school. Frankie was lots older, so he didn't always want Rollie and Rate tagging him around. There were some girls, but Ralph figured girls were only made to tease, and there were times when Rollie's sisters felt like skinning both boys alive if they could only have caught them. If Rollie had been somewhat of a tease before, he only became worse with Ralph around to help him think of ideas.

It had been one of those days when whatever Rate could think of to do didn't exactly appeal to him. It was still wet from April rains, and the day was more than a bit on the cold side, with a hint of still more rain in the angry black clouds swirling overhead, so playing baseball didn't suit his fancy either. He had thrown a few stones with his sling-shot, but quickly became bored. Bruno followed his master faithfully, obviously puzzled by his random wanderings. They went into the toolshed where Ralph poked around in the litter of odds and ends.

"Jeepers, Bruno. Look what I found. This stuff in this old jar is gunpowder sure as shootin'. Pa don't need it no more. He don't hunt much, and he's been buyin' his shells at Downey's. Bet we'd get a bang out of this just like a big firecracker. C'mon, Bruno. Let's go see."

Bruno sat on his haunches, tilting his head from side to side, ears perked forward, watching Rate's every move. Now, he bounded after the boy, not understanding, but ready to follow wherever the boy might lead. He watched as the boy carried out back of the granary the two-quart jar that was nearly full of black gunpowder. Rate plunked the can on the ground, rummaged around to find a length of board that he laid on the ground; next he poured the gunpowder in a small thin line from one end of the board to the other where he dumped the excess into a small pile.

"Now, Bruno, you stay back over here whilst I light this."

The dog obediently sat where Rate pointed. The lad fished around in his pockets and came up with two matches. He struck a match and held it to the dribbled-out fuse. It burned a few inches, then went out as the powder became too thin to carry it further. Ralph sighed in disgust, lighted the second match, and held it to the heavier line, which was much nearer the pile. *Whoosh!* Before he had more than dropped the match, the whole pile went up in one big puff of fire and smoke. Rate grabbed his face with his hands. Golly, but he had never expected results like this. He guessed he was all right. He didn't seem to be burned. Bruno whined and carried on until Rate absently patted his head.

"It's all right, Bruno. Don't guess I'm hurt any, but it seems like I can smell singed hair. Guess I'll go take a look-see."

While the acrid smell of burned gunpowder clung to the air, there was also the unmistakable odor of scorched hair. Rate entered the house rather cautiously having no desire to meet his mother until he had assessed his own damage.

"Ralph?" came the query. "That you? What do you want?"

"Nothin', Ma. I just got tired of being outside."

He headed for the stairway, but his mother came from the kitchen before he had more than put his hand on the doorknob.

"Ralph, are you hiding something?"

"No, Ma. I was just goin' upstairs."

"With those dirty shoes? Not much you aren't. Come back here and clean them off on the porch. When will you ever learn?"

Heaving a resigned sigh, Rate turned around.

"Goodness! Whatever have you been into now? Your face is blackened, and, and—why, you have no eyebrows, and even your hair is singed. Ralph Setterington, whatever have you been doing?" she demanded, her tone unmistakably stern.

"Nothin' much."

"Do you call getting your eyebrows singed off nothing? Your hair is singed where it sticks out from under your stocking cap. Did it scorch the cap?"

"Naw. Golly, Ma, I didn't do it on purpose. I just found this can of old gunpowder, and I took it out and set fire to it. I thought it would explode like a firecracker, but it jest burnt, and I didn't even have no time to get away it went so fast. Honest, I didn't intend to get singed."

"I suppose not," she conceded. "Lucky you were that it wasn't worse. Clean your shoes, and then wash your face and hands. I'll have your father speak to you tonight."

"Yessum."

Land's sakes, would she ever live to see that boy grown to manhood—that is if he didn't kill himself before that time. If it wasn't one thing, it was another. She'd long ago lost track of how many nails he'd stepped on during the summer months when he went barefoot, how many skinned fingers, knees, and oh, just about everything. My, he would certainly look a sight to take to church tomorrow, only there wasn't much she could do about it.

True to her word, Miney related the incident to Millie when he came in to supper. In his usual manner, Millie listened to his wife, yet said not a word, his face completely expressionless.

Blanche hissed at Ralph, "You're in for it now. Pa looks sort of mad."

"Does not. He's just thinkin'."

"Bet you get walloped."

"Bet I don't," Ralph said much more bravely than he felt.

"Boy, is what your ma says true?"

Rate swallowed hard. "That's right, Pa. That gunpowder went up faster'n you could say *scat*."

"Come here." Rate moved toward his father. "Stand here where I can see you. You don't appear hurt none, but I guess you don't have much of any eyebrows or eyelashes left." He touched Rate's hair. "Looks like you got rid of a little here too."

Rate watched his father warily. Pa was so blamed hard to figure out. He couldn't tell whether his father was angry or not.

"Did you learn anything?"

"Sure did. I learned that gunpowder burns awful fast, and it ain't nothin' to be foolin' around with."

"See that you don't forget that."

With that statement, Ralph knew he was dismissed. He flashed Blanche a triumphant look as he moved away. Later that evening, he spoke smugly, "Told you so."

"You're just lucky. You deserved a lickin'. Ma thinks so too. Bet she wishes she'd a done it herself 'stead of leavin' it up to Pa. Why can't you ever stay out of trouble? Boys!"

Rate laughed at his sister. He liked her well enough, and she was a lot of fun to tease. She got awful mad at him sometimes, but sometimes she was nice to him; and if she bought candy, she often saved a stick for him. If one had to have a sister, he guessed he would rather have her than any other girl he knew.

"Miney," called Millie from the wagon seat, "come look."

"What is it, Millie? Goodness, what have you got there?"

"Maple trees." And true enough, the wagon box was piled high with saplings.

"Whatever are you going to do with them?"

"Plant them. What else?"

"I know. But where?"

"I don't know for certain. Some in the yard and some along the road. Wouldn't some nice maples look good along the road?"

"I...well, I guess so. Guess I'd never given it much thought."

"Jim and I will get them planted soon's we eat dinner."

Later on, there were four new maples in the front of the house, maples between the south and north driveway, maples along the road north of the driveway, and maples along the road south of the front yard.

Rate had watched with interest. Upon completion, Millie had explained to his son that if these new trees were to live, they must be watered every day unless it rained. That was to be Ralph's job. He could use Major on the stoneboat and fill a thirty-gallon milk can with water and give each tree a good pailful of water. At the telling, it hadn't sounded so bad, but in actual practice, Rate found it was not the most desirable of jobs. The worst job was filling the blamed milk can in the first place. Seemed like it was going to be a long summer.

*****

Ralph, Burl, and Don were finished with their work. Instead of rereading their reading assignment as they should have done, they started whispering. Don and Rate shared a double desk while Burl sat across the aisle; their desks were located near the back of the room on the north side in the first row by the stove. The small children sat here since it was warmer in the winter; the larger boys sat on the south side near the windows, which was more than a little chilly on a cold, windy winter's day, no matter if the stove was kept red hot.

However, the back of the room was not exactly the ideal place for a pair like Don and Rate. Upon someone's suggestion, they began to play Simon says: thumbs up or thumbs down. As the game progressed, they began to laugh when someone was caught moving his thumbs when "Simon" hadn't preceded the order. Finally, they became noisy enough to gain the attention of the teacher. Mrs. Ingersoll gave them a withering look and caustically asked, "And just what are you three boys celebrating?"

"The Fourth of July," piped up Don with an impish look.

It seemed Don was always one to have a ready answer that on more than one occasion was to get him into trouble. He also looked like he enjoyed misbehaving, the devil danced in his eyes. Rate was the one with the wide-eyed innocent expression.

The students laughed. Mrs. Ingersoll didn't even crack a smile. She stalked to where the boys sat, yanked Burl out of his seat, and shook him until he was afraid his head was going to fly off. With no uncertain admonitions, she sat him back in his desk and grabbed Don. After shaking him severely, and at the same time berating him for his actions, she shoved him back down. It was Rate's turn.

Now, Rate had watched the process thus far with quite some trepidation. He had often provoked a teacher, but he had never had one get violent with him before. He wasn't about to be shook like a dirty dust mop. As she grabbed him, he clutched the desk with both hands. She grabbed his arm, then his shirt, and his heart sank as all four buttons went popping off. She pried the first hand loose, and as she began to work on the other, he held on tenaciously with the first hand again. Finally, she could see that this was getting her exactly nowhere, and she could hear the twittering of laughter as the other students watched with interest. Suddenly, she stopped.

"Frankie, go fetch me a willow switch from the patch across the road."

"Yes, ma'am," said Frankie Swarthout as he left his seat and headed out the door.

"All of you have work to do, and this is no concern of yours, so get busy."

All eyes returned to their books. Ralph was the only one who eyed the teacher. Cripes! If she gave him a licking, that meant he'd get one from Pa. The schoolmarm didn't frighten him, but he certainly didn't relish the thought of Pa trouncing him. He still remembered the last time Pa had licked him. Golly, here came Frankie. Well, he conceded, he supposed he had sort of brought it on himself.

Frankie gave Mrs. Ingersoll the switch and hastily sat down.

"Ralph, will you stand up and take your switching?"

Rate eyed her and shook his head. She raised the willow whip, aimed at his shoulders, and struck! Ralph ducked. The switch hit the desktop—and broke into several pieces. Frankie had done as he was bidden, but he had also cut the switch very carefully about every six inches in a circular motion so that only a small amount of wood held the switch together; thus, at the first whack, the willow had broken into pieces. Frankie had brought two switches. Mrs. Ingersoll picked up the second one, slowly bent it, whereupon it broke in the same fashion as the first. Without a word, she walked to the stove, opened the door, and tossed the pieces into the firepot, stood a moment as they caught fire, then closed the door with a bang.

If Ralph dawdled on his way home from school, it was with calculated intent. Golly, but Mrs. Ingersoll had been mad. Her face had turned a mottled red first and then more like a dull purple, and she had looked at him with venom in her eyes. Talk about if looks could kill—he'd be dead by now sure as shootin'. Then, she had drawn herself up very straight, to her full five foot six, and had marched stoically back to the front of the room, stood by her desk a moment, glared at the students as if inviting anyone to give hint of a smile or giggle, then calmly called the next class for recitation. A wave of relief had flooded the whole room.

Trouble was, no one knew if the matter was settled or not. Rate hadn't dared look around; he had ignored Don and Burl and got busy with his reading assignment. As usual, reading soon transported him from the world he lived in, and he had entered the pages of the book—if not physically, at least spiritually. For the entire length of the story, he had heard no more of the noise of the classroom. When dismissal time came, he slipped from his seat as quietly and unobtrusively as possible, grabbed his lunch pail, coat, and hat, crossed the schoolyard, and headed down the road at a rather rapid pace. However, the nearer he got to home, the slower his steps became.

Gripes. He'd have to tell his parents what had happened; otherwise, he'd have no explanation for the missing buttons from his shirt. Good thing there hadn't been any more, or they'd have been gone too. As it was, the shirt only opened halfway down the front, and that only gapped a little, showing a smidgen of his spring underwear underneath.

As he neared the driveway, he noticed a rig standing in the yard and recognized it. Worse luck! It belonged to his grandparents. How come they were back from South Lyon? As if it wasn't bad enough to have to explain to his parents, he was going to have his grandmother looking at him like the leader of the inquisition. Good heavens, this was some day!

He came quietly into the kitchen, put his dinner pail on the kitchen cabinet, and hung his coat by the door. Well, might as well get it over with. He squared his shoulders, pulled his shirt front together, and stepped into the dining room.

"Hello, Grandfather. Hello, Grandmother."

"Hello, Ralph," they replied.

"Goodness, Ralph, whatever happened to you? Have you been fighting again?"

"No, Ma, I haven't been fighting."

"Then, why are the buttons missing from your shirt?"

"Oh, that."

"Yes, that. Now, what have you been up to?"

Lavina eyed the boy sternly. Both Millie and Horatio watched the boy expectantly, no smile on their lips, but the crinkles around their eyes were deep, and the eyes shone.

Ralph scuffled his feet, looked down at the floor, heaved a sigh, and related his story, giving an accurate and concise account of what had happened. When he reached the part where the teacher had left him to return to the front of the schoolroom, his father interrupted.

"You mean she never actually whipped you?"

"No, Pa. I ducked, and she hit the desk 'stead of me. It made her madder'n a wet hen 'cause she knew what Frankie had done. She just let me alone. No, sir, she never walloped me at all."

"Lucky for you, boy. You do mind what I told you when you first begun school?"

"Yes, Pa. If I got a lickin' at school, I'd get another when I got home."

Millie nodded his assent.

Lavina and Miney did not seem to find the situation humorous; while neither of the men smiled, their features remained stern, the crinkles by the brown eyes were there, and the eyes showed merriment. Obviously, they viewed this infraction with a different viewpoint than their wives. Of course, it wasn't a man's job to replace the torn-off buttons either.

"There are times when the lad puts me in mind of when Millie and John were boys. Their clothes were always torn, buttons always missing, they attracted dirt like sugar does flies, and were always fighting with someone over something. Rate often found it comical," she accused.

"Now, Vine, did I ever uphold their antics even though they were just being normal boys? And many's the time they got a whipping over some mischief or for slacking off on their work."

"Well, I'd like for my grandson to be less trouble. I'd not wish all that on any woman."

Mina couldn't believe her ears. Her mother-in-law was actually thinking kind thoughts of Miney. Wonders would never cease. 'Course she knew Millie and John had been a handful to raise. Most of their mischief, Millie often said, was just good, clean fun, and they never hurt anyone. Guess Father had taken a dim view of some things because it was common knowledge that he had used the buggy whip on more than one occasion.

Millie had told more than once about getting a whipping, and how he would try to work himself closer to his father so he'd get struck with the part of the whip that was thicker because it didn't sting as much. His father would say, "Stand out there, boy, and take your licking." For sure, Father Setterington had been a stern father. Miney was glad Millie had never been that harsh with Ralph even if the boy did seem to be forever getting into trouble.

Rate watched his grandmother in wonderment as she talked. So Pa and Uncle John had torn their clothes too. The way Ma talked sometimes, he had thought he was the only boy who ever got dirty or had accidents with his clothes. Gosh, he wondered what kind of mischief Pa had got into. Sometimes, Pa liked to tell stories about when he was young, so Rate made up his mind to ask Pa about it. Maybe Pa had been just an ordinary boy after all.

It was a lovely, Saturday afternoon, warm and sunny, with the slightest of breezes gently rippling the leaves on the trees. It was the kind of day that gave a young lad itchy feet, the wanderlust, the desire to roam the meadows in search of a woodchuck hole; wander along the river and maybe observe a kingfisher sitting on a limb that stretched out over the water, patiently waiting for some unwary fish to swim by and then *whoosh!* down into the water it would plummet and up it would come with a fish in its beak. Yessir, there were just any amount of things Rate would have liked to be doing, but here he sat politely listening to the grown-ups' conversation while his thoughts wandered. The only consolation was that Blanche didn't look as if she was enjoying herself either.

Aunt Ruby, Uncle Mac, Grandmother and Grandfather, and, of course, Lois were visiting; Rate got pretty fed up with hearing Grandmother tell of the "darling" way Lois did this and that. She looked like any little girl to him, and she couldn't even walk alone, although Grandmother had been quick to show off how the child would take several steps to get to her grandmother, but would simply refuse to attempt walking to anyone else, even her own mother. Lavina fairly burst with pride.

Ralph wondered how it made Blanche feel not to be the apple of Grandmother's eye anymore. 'Course Grandmother didn't treat him any differently. Although there were numerous occasions when he remembered her being particularly kind, for the most part, she had pretty much ignored his existence. It was kinda funny seeing Blanche look so bored and Grandmother so wrapped up in Lois she had scarcely replied to something Blanche had told her.

Millie spoke of the two foals, a colt and a filly, born the first of the month. As usual, he wanted his father to look them over and give his opinion of the two youngsters. It was decided that the entire group would go along—all except Lois and Ralph.

"Here, Ralph, we'll only be gone a few minutes, and you can just watch Lois for us."

With that admonition, Ruby plunked Lois on Ralph's lap.

"But, Aunt Ruby, what if she cries?"

"Walk around with her, and she'll be quiet until we get back."

As the group trooped out of the house, Rate looked at Lois with misgivings. The child returned his stare, then broke into gurgles of delight as she grabbed his nose; next she latched onto the lock of hair that had fallen onto his forehead. Babies! Golly, they were a nuisance. He hoisted her into his arms and walked over by the door. Lois poked an exploratory finger into his ear, pounded on his cheek with a pudgy hand, and kicked and squirmed.

After a short period, Ralph figured the group had been gone long enough. He watched as they stood by the fence watching the mares and their foals. What on earth was taking so long? Bet if Lois started crying, they'd be back in a hurry. Ralph sat her on the floor hoping she'd cry; she just gurgled and crawled over to pull herself up to a chair. Guess that didn't work. He picked her up once again. Then, a secretive grin appeared. Lois started to wail loud and long. Rate had pinched her.

"Ralph," called Aunt Ruby, "what is wrong?"

"Don't know. She just started crying." He pinched her again. "See, I'm walking her, and she still cries."

Ruby hurried to the house followed by Lavina. Lois calmed as soon as Ruby took her; two big tears rolled down her fair cheeks as she looked accusingly at Ralph. Rate gave her his most innocent look. Sure was a good thing she couldn't talk, Rate thought as Ruby cuddled her child.

Blanche came close and hissed, "Bet you did something on purpose. Bet you pinched her just 'cause you didn't like taking care of her. Aren't you ashamed?"

"Did no such thing," came the reply. "Can't help it if she doesn't like me, can I?"

Blanche shook her head and moved off. Sure was odd that Lois had cried when she was such a good-natured baby. That Ralph, she knew he'd done something even if he never would admit it.

*****

Rate had been listening to students in the seventh and eighth grade as they recited some poetry for reading class. Mrs. Ingersoll had been more than a little upset when a few of the students were not able to recite the stanza without considerable help. She scolded and impressed upon them they would have to recite again tomorrow, and she expected a great improvement. The selection was canto 6, stanza 1 from *The Lay of the Last Minstrel* by Sir Walter Scott; perhaps a little difficult, but it contained such a good message.

At recess time, Ralph edged up to the teacher's desk.

"Mrs. Ingersoll."

"Yes, Ralph. What is it?"

"You know that poem the older ones is learning. I can say it."

"You can what?"

"I can repeat all of it."

The teacher viewed him with skepticism.

"Ralph, do you mean you can recite the entire stanza?"

"Ever bit."

"How did you learn it?"

"I listened while the others was sayin' it. Want me to show you?"

"Land's sakes. That's a lot for a third grader, but if you're sure you can do it, how would you like to recite it to everyone after recess? That ought to put some of the older ones to shame."

Ralph grinned. "I'd like it fine."

Recess time over, the students back in their seats, but instead of calling the usual class, Mrs. Ingersoll spoke to all the students.

"Some of you have been complaining about your piece to memorize. Well, we have someone who had memorized the selection because he wanted to. Ralph, will you say it now?"

Ralph flashed a smile, slid out of his seat, and walked to the front of the classroom. There, he recited clearly and with much more expression than the teacher had thought possible:

> Breathes there the man, with soul so dead,
> Who never to himself hath said,
> This is my own, my native land!
> Whose heart hath ne'er within him burn'd
> As home his footsteps he hath turn'd,
> From wandering on a foreign strand?
> If such there breathe, go, mark him well;
> For him no minstrel raptures swell;
> High though his titles, proud his name,
> Boundless his wealth as wish can claim,—
> Despite those titles, power, and pelf,
> The wretch, concentred all in self,
> Living, shall forfeit fair renown,
> And, doubly dying, shall go down
> To the vile dust, from whence he sprung,
> Unwept, unhonour'd, and unsung.

*****

Ralph knew that sometime this summer the mail would be delivered to a mailbox in front of their house instead of being left up on the corner. Couldn't happen any too soon to suit him. During the summer months, when the weather was good, Blanche often got the mail. Some days, they both watched to see if the mailman, Will Letts, stopped at the corner, and then they sometimes raced to see who could get there first. Blanche always liked to go on the day the *Toledo Blade*, a weekly newspaper, was delivered since she was becoming interested in world affairs. He rather liked having her get the mail and only raced her to tease. Still, if it was rainy, Blanche could never take a turn then, and since Pa had told him it was his job, there was no question as to who traipsed through the rain to the corner and back.

Then, another thing. Blanche was forever getting him into trouble. Pa blamed him for everything whether it was something he did or not. Like day before yesterday. Blanche had been the one to go get the mail. Well, when Pa came home from town, he had found a letter on the road that she had dropped. It had never occurred to Millie to ask who had gone for the mail that day, he simply assumed it had been Ralph and had berated him for being so careless. What had really angered Ralph was that he was almost certain Blanche had heard the whole thing, yet she had not come forward to admit her guilt. Perhaps he was being unfair to his sister. The way Pa always took Blanche's part in every way, he bet Pa wouldn't have believed her anyway. Rate had known there was no use trying to defend himself because Pa wouldn't have believed him, and then he would have been in trouble for lying. Wonder just why Pa always thought everything was his fault?

Sometimes, when the windmill didn't run, water for the live-stock had to be pumped by hand. Rate would do his turn, but Blanche often conveniently forgot her turn; then, Pa always yelled at Ralph to get out there and finish the job. Sometimes, lately, Pa was even worse than Ma. At least Ma yelled at Blanche on occasion; and when they were younger, he had seen Blanche get her legs switched for being sassy. Seems the older he got, the more Pa favored Blanche. He just wished he could figure out why.

Miney had just received a disturbing letter from Ettie. In fact, she sat with the letter in her hand and cried bitter tears. She washed her face and eyes with cold water, but the eyes were still red and the lids swollen. She was in control of herself now, so she reread the letter.

"My dearest sister," it began. "By the time you receive this, I might very well be dead. The child is due any day now, and, Miney, I am so huge, I know I'll never be able to have this baby. George tries to be cheerful, but even he is worried although he tries desperately not to show it. I can hardly get around, and it is difficult for me to get out of a rocker without help.

"I want you to know that you have been a good sister. Sometimes, I wish we had not lived so far apart and could have seen more of each other. Our children never really knew one another.

"I hope the baby dies with me. It would be a hard world for a baby to grow up without a mother, although George would no doubt marry again if there was a child. If not, he assures me he will live alone—says he wants no other woman.

"I must write to Mary and Lorin as well. God bless you, Miney, and know that I have cared."

It was signed, "Your loving sister, Ettie."

The letter was dated June 12, 1902.

Five days later, Miney received a telegram:

> Ettie and baby died this morning.
> Funeral Wednesday. Wire if coming. George.

Mina could not keep back the flood of tears. Ettie was her own sister, and while somewhat different in many ways, they had got on well as children. Perhaps it was the way Ettie had died that bothered Miney the most. She felt resentment toward her brother-in-law. Ettie was just too old to have been in the family way, and the blame for that was certainly to be laid at George's doorstep. She was glad her mother had not lived to see this day. 'Course, Ma had been forty-one when Miney was born, so Ma might have looked at the situation differently. From what little her mother had ever said about childbearing, Miney assumed her mother had had little, if any, trouble bearing children. She guessed some women were just luckier than others. Miney recalled with displeasure the intense pain she had borne while giving birth to Blanche, and it had been nearly as bad for Ralph. She fervently hoped she would not get in the family way again. What a horrible thought! She'd just view her feelings to Millie and impress upon him that she did not want to be in Ettie's shoes.

Goodness, there was always something for a woman to worry about. Mina had felt she was getting beyond the childbearing years, but Ettie was a dire reminder this was not so. A woman's lot certainly was a sorry one much of the time. Perhaps if she asked God not to have any more children, He would heed her prayers. It wouldn't hurt to ask, and she would start this very night.

Miney and Lorin were to take the train to Traverse City. Just before she left, Miney decided to check her money for train fare, which she had tied up in a handkerchief. She had already done this several times. The handkerchief was tucked in the bodice of her gown; only this time, there was no handkerchief and no money. Miney began a frantic search of the house. She enlisted Millie's help, and even the children began a rather haphazard search.

"Millie," she cried, "whatever will I do if I can't find it? I don't have enough money left for another ticket."

"Don't fret. It has to be here somewheres. I've got a little change, so I think we can scrape up enough for your ticket. Wouldn't give you any extree though. If Pa was here, we could get it from him."

"I'd sooner not go than borrow money from him," muttered Miney.

Millie chose to overlook that remark. He knew Miney often resented his relationship with his parents; she just never acknowledged that both Ma and Pa could be mighty generous people. Miney just never seemed to understand.

"Miney, you're running around like a chicken with its head cut off. Now, start by retracing your steps. Just what did you do after you put the money in the handkerchief?"

Miney stopped and thought.

"Well, I sat in front of the dresser and combed and braided my hair."

They looked under the dresser. Nothing.

"I went into the kitchen to see if the meat on the stove had enough water on it."

They even looked under the stove—to no avail.

"Oh, yes, I went out to get a pail of water."

A glance out the door showed nothing. However, the hired man went on out the door. There were wide planks covering the space between the house and the well curb. Charlie, playing a hunch, started moving the planks and saw the bit of white cloth standing out against the moist dark earth. Sure enough, it was the missing handkerchief with money intact.

"Now, Miney, are you ready to go? The sooner you get your ticket bought, the better. Think we should let Lorin carry your money and ticket for you?" Millie laughed.

"Don't be funny," snapped Miney.

"Well, you haven't been doing so good keeping track of it."

"Never mind. I'm ready to go."

Miney was slightly miffed. She had voiced her thoughts to Millie regarding her sister's death, and although he had said very little, she knew he did not share her sentiments. He had even had the audacity to ask her if she wasn't always the one who said we don't necessarily understand why the Lord does things the way He does. Of course, she had to admit this was so. Then, he had asked what made her think this was not the Lord's doing. She had no answer. When presented in this fashion, to say it was not the Lord's work made it seem as if her faith was not strong.

Miney truly did believe the Bible, and it was only her personal loss that had given her moments of doubt. She knew in her heart God had His reasons, even if she could not understand. Perhaps someday she would be enlightened.

*****

Blanche sat at the piano in the parlor dutifully practicing her lesson. Mina had pestered Millie to buy them a piano instead of the organ they had had when they were first married just so Blanche could be given lessons. Why, Mina had been playing the organ when the most difficult part had been to pump it because her legs were hardly long enough to reach. She had taken readily to music and had hoped her aptitude would be passed on to her daughter. However, Miney was beginning to have her doubts. She had been giving Blanche lessons for some time now, yet Blanche's progress seemed to be incredibly slow. Miney had other students who had started after Blanche and were much further in their book than Blanche. Goodness, that was a sour chord!

"Blanche! Blanche, you made a mistake. Can't you hear that it doesn't sound right?"

"I know, Ma, I just didn't feel like correcting it."

"If I've told you once, I've told you a dozen times, it only makes it worse if you don't take time to correct your mistakes. Now, start that last piece over."

"Oh, Ma, do I have to? I've already practiced over twenty minutes, and I'm not nearly through with all that you gave me for a lesson."

"It won't hurt to go over the half hour."

Mina came into the parlor wiping her hands on her apron.

"Now, try it again. Take it a little slower, and I'm sure you can play it right," cajoled Miney.

Blanche started the piece once again. A few measures later, her finger hit a wrong note.

"Blanche, you forgot you have two flats in the signature, not just one. Goodness, child, I just don't believe you keep your mind on your practicing."

"I try, Ma. I just don't know why my fingers always hit the wrong keys."

With that admission, she burst into tears. Miney gathered her daughter into her arms to comfort her.

"Now, now, it isn't worth tears. If we move into town, I'm going to speak to Mabel Wooley. Perhaps you would do better if you had someone else for a teacher. How would you like that?"

"I don't know. I just don't think I was meant to play the piano."

"Nonsense. Why, when I was your age, I played piano for church services for both the Methodist and the Baptist Church. They had their services at different hours, so it was an easy matter to play for the Methodist service then go across the street for the Baptist service. Once in a while, if the minister took too long for his sermon, I'd nearly be late." She chuckled. "If I could do it, so can you."

"Ma, it just isn't in me. But I'll try just to please you."

"That's my girl. One of these days you'll find that all of a sudden, it will come much easier. Just you wait and see."

The next afternoon, Mina called up the stairsteps, "Blanche, come down here. Pa just brought a package for you from the post office."

"What is it, Ma?"

"That's for you to find out. It's from your uncle George in Traverse City."

There it was, a package addressed to her in her uncle George's beautiful writing with his name as the sender. She eyed the package in awe. She'd never had anything sent to her through the mail before except cards or letters, and not many of them.

"Aren't you going to open it?" asked Miney.

"Yes, of course. Oh dear, my fingers are all thumbs," Blanche exclaimed as she tore at the wrappings. She managed to get them off, revealing a box, which gave her further difficulty.

"Ma, you do it. I can't seem to get the top off."

"Here, child. If you weren't so anxious, it would help."

In the box nestled in a bed of cotton was a lady's gold watch.

"Isn't it lovely? Look, Ma, it has a long chain to wear around my neck. It is just beautiful."

"It's Ettie's watch. George gave it to her before they were married."

"You mean this belonged to Aunt Ettie?"

"Here, there's a letter too," put in Millie. "Maybe Doc explains it in there."

Blanche read the letter. Before her death, Ettie Smith Curtis had expressed the wish that Blanche, her favorite niece, be given her watch since it had great sentimental value. She asked that Miney keep the watch for Blanche until she was fifteen, at which age Ettie felt the girl would be capable of appreciating so valuable a gift. George was only too happy to honor his wife's last request.

Aunt Ettie had passed away in June; however, Blanche had never cared much for her aunt, so she had not really grieved her passing. She had once heard someone describe Ettie as a "spineless creature." Blanche felt the words were apt and had forever after thought of Ettie in that way.

She remembered the time before she started school when she, Ma, and Ralph had gone to Traverse City to visit them. Uncle George had been a doctor then except Aunt Ettie had complained and complained, first about him being gone so much—especially at night when she was scared to death to stay alone—then about the long hours he worked, so he had been studying law on the side. Blanche guessed Aunt Ettie had complained less since Uncle George had opened a law office and kept regular hours; although she still complained about her health, which everyone felt was mostly in her head.

Blanche had liked Uncle Doc. George W. Curtis, better known as Doc to his old friends, was a promising attorney in Traverse City, and she had always been a little proud to let other playmates know that she had an uncle who was a lawyer. Now, it made her feel just a little bit ashamed of herself that while she had thought so little of Aunt Ettie, her aunt had sent her a prized possession. It made Blanche feel rather humble for a moment. Then, the terms of the gift registered in her mind.

"But, Ma, does that mean I can't wear it until I'm fifteen? That's…that's two whole years from now."

"That's what George's letter says. I'm afraid we must respect the wishes of the deceased. We'll just put it away until you're older."

That beautiful gold watch in that beautiful case. It looked alike on both sides until you pressed the release to open the front. Aunt Ettie would be just the one to think she wasn't old enough to take care of something of value. Now, Aunt Mary would have been different. Bet Uncle Doc hadn't had anything to say about it either. He'd probably been too upset over knowing Aunt Ettie was dying to give it much thought, especially since Ma somehow believed it was Uncle Doc's fault his wife had died. Well, two years was better than ten. She looked at the watch once more, returned it to the box, gave the box to her mother, and didn't mention it again. Of course, she wrote to Uncle Doc to thank him, but it was as if the watch had never existed. However, she and her uncle would keep up a correspondence until his death.

Don and Burl Sherman came over to spend the afternoon with Ralph. They had been back to the creek for a while, played catch for a while, and had ended up in the barn dangling from the hay ropes and walking the beams.

Later, no one was sure whose idea it was to hitch up the two yearling calves that were tied on the barn floor. The boys worked with a will using bits of a leather driving harness and rope to fashion harnesses of sorts. Finally, all was in readiness, and they opened the big barn doors to let the calves out. Don was driving.

Burl had taken one calf by the head while Rate had the other. They managed to get them outside with no problem. Then, all hell broke loose. Both calves began to kick and jump, one tried to turn around to face Don while the other bounded straight ahead. Neither Burl nor Ralph could get close enough to grab their heads as the two calves pulled and jerked Don along every way for Sunday. It seemed that the more the boys tried to calm them down, the more they kicked, and the more entangled they became in the hastily completed harness.

"Rate, whyn't you get ahold o' their heads?" yelled Don.

"Ha! Like to see you manage. Why are you lettin' 'em drag you?"

"I've got my feet braced. Burl, can't you help?"

"What am I supposed to do? I'm not gonna get kicked ifn I can help it."

"Well, somebody do something. I'm not gonna be able to hold 'em much longer."

"Hang on, Curly. I think they're getting tired," said Ralph as he grabbed the halter of one.

It was true, the initial fervor was dwindling as the calves' sides heaved, attesting to their exertion. Then, came the summons.

"Rate! Come here," commanded Millie from near the woodshed.

"We've gone and done it now," Rate confided to his companions. "I didn't know Pa was around. He sure sounded mad."

"We're goin' home," said Don. "He never yelled for us to come with you. Hope you don't get a lickin'."

"Me too."

Ralph managed to get the calves back into the barn while Don and Burl skedaddled cross-lots for home.

"You want me, Pa?"

"Called you, didn't I?"

"Yessir."

"Guess you know what you got coming."

"Reckon so," mumbled Ralph.

"Speak up, boy. What have you got coming?"

"A lickin', I 'spect. But, Pa—"

"No excuses. Rate, you should have known better. Since you didn't, I'll give you something so's you won't be likely to forget. Wouldn't want you to get into the same mischief twice."

With that, Millie proceeded to use a barrel stave to give Ralph his third and final whipping. As to whether he deserved others as time went by, there might have been a difference of opinion. In all probability, his mother could have cited numerous occasions when she felt a licking was warranted. However, this final whipping was not one he was to forget very readily.

Blanche was doing the dusting as usual. Miney normally did the sweeping, so that left the dusting up to Blanche. She used the turkey wing to dust the intricately carved legs of the marble-top table; she used the dustcloth on the top. Next, she moved into the spare bedroom. Here, she ran her cloth along the exposed part of the dresser. They only took the dresser scarfs off on Fridays when they did the weekly cleaning. The daily dusting was more of a hit-or-miss job. Blanche paused before a picture that had two long peacock feathers crossed above the frame. They were so pretty, the colors varied and beautiful.

She turned and went out to the kitchen where her mother was just taking up a dustpan of dirt.

"Ma, where'd you get those peacock feather you're so choice about?"

"Mrs. Stafford gave those to me several years ago."

"Did the Staffords have peacocks?"

"They did. Said they were better than a watchdog to let you know if someone strange was around. I used to watch for them when we drove by, always hoping to catch one with its tail spread. They are so beautiful with the sun glinting on the various colors. Once in a while, they'd be sitting on the peak of the barn."

"Did they raise them?"

"Sometimes. Guess they aren't all that easy to raise. Anyway, I was talking to Mrs. Stafford one day, telling her how much I admired her birds, and she up and gave me those two feathers. I suppose the colors will fade in time, but they are certainly gorgeous now."

"They are that. Wish we had some peacocks."

"Blanche, your father would think I had lost my senses if I was to suggest such a thing." Miney laughed.

"Why?"

"Well, he's not one to keep something that doesn't earn its keep. 'Course I guess way back in history, royalty used to eat peacocks, but I'm sure I could never kill one to eat."

Blanche digested this as she went back to finish her dusting. Yes, she guessed Ma was right. Pa just wasn't one to go in for something frivolous, and she was sure he'd feel peacocks were definitely frivolous.

It was Saturday, and the family was just finishing breakfast when Millie turned to his young son.

"Rate, I've got a job for you this morning."

"What is it, Pa?"

"Heard in town yesterday that old man Cobb has a heifer calf for sale. You can go over there this morning, and if you can get it for a reasonable price, buy it."

"What's a reasonable price?"

"As little as he's willing to take."

Ralph knew better than to question his father further. Big lot of help that answer had been. Well, Pa would have to give him some money, so he guessed he'd just try and buy the calf for less than what Pa gave him.

When Ralph came to leave, Millie gave his son ten dollars with the admonition that he not spend any more than he had to.

Rate kept going over and over in his mind what he would say to Mr. Cobb. Nothing seemed to sound just right. He wanted to do a good job so his father would be proud of him. He knew for certain if he gave more than Pa figured the calf was worth, Pa would be quick enough to tell him about it.

When he arrived at the Cobb farm east of Elsie, Arthur recognized him right off. They tethered the horse and went to the barn to look at the calf.

"How much you askin', Mr. Cobb?"

"Wal now, I did reckon she'd be wuth maybe ten dollars, but since you're Millie's son, I guess I could take as little as eight."

"I dunno, Mr. Cobb. She seems kinda scrawny to me. I doubt she's worth more'n five," Rate said with much more bravado than he felt.

"Rate, you just look her over good. See how deep the body is. She'll make a fine cow. How about seven?"

"Mr. Cobb, I still think she's a mite small. She may make a good-looking cow, but she sure looks to be on the small side. No, sir, Mr. Cobb, I don't figger she's worth no more than six," Rate said with a determined note in his voice.

The boy watched the older man, almost holding his breath, waiting for the older man's answer. Mr. Cobb took off his hat, scratched his head, looked at the calf as if this was indeed a monumental decision.

"Don't think she's wuth seven, huh? Got the cash, was I to take six?"

"Oh, yessir, right here in my pocket."

"You drive a hard bargain, mind you, and I'm not saying she ain't wuth the seven, but I don't want to monkey with feedin' her, so I guess you've bought yourself a calf."

Whew! Rate heaved a sigh of relief as he dug into his trouser pocket for the six dollars. Boy, that was four less than Pa had given him, so Pa sure oughta be pleased.

However, when Ralph got the calf home, Millie looked it over critically and only nodded when Ralph explained that Mr. Cobb had come down to six dollars.

"Wouldn't take five?"

"No, Pa, I didn't think he was even gonna let her go for six. Not at first anyway."

Millie made no further comment as he tied the calf on the barn floor. He told Ralph to bed her down and moved off to finish his chores.

Ralph tried hard not to show his disappointment. He had wanted so badly to get a word of praise from his father. For some unknown reason, Millie always found it impossible to praise Ralph for anything.

Later that night, Millie related the event to Miney.

"By golly, Miney, the lad's got horse sense. I'd have given eight for that calf, but he got it for six. He's a right sharp one when it comes to knowin' his livestock. He'll do all right for himself, he will."

Millie never realized how much good it would have done a small boy to have heard these words of praise.

Rain dripped from the eaves; the leaves of the cottonwood hung mournfully low, clasping droplets that became glowing crystals in the sun. Ralph gazed idly out the window absently rubbing Bruno's ears. The dog sensed his master's preoccupation, so he whined and moved a little closer with his head resting on Rate's knee. Rate was so completely lost in thought he scarcely noticed the dog. Jeepers, he'd heard Ma and Pa talking. They might move to town for the winter since Blanche didn't have a place to stay anymore.

Girls were one heck of a lot of bother. Blanche couldn't drive to town all year, yet Pa could make the trip to the farm twice a day, and Rate knew there would be plenty of times he'd have to accompany his father. That wasn't the worst part. It meant he'd have to go to town to school too, and that meant not having Curly and Rollie to play with.

Rate was right. Millie and Mina decided that it would be too much to expect Blanche to drive to school each day when the weather got bad. Since they would be moving the first of November, they decided there was no sense in letting Ralph start in at Stafford. He could just go to Elsie with Blanche.

Little did either Miney or Millie realize the resentment this would cause. Ralph disliked the idea of leaving his friends. On top of that, he resented the fact that everyone, including Blanche, accepted the fact that Rate assume all responsibility for caring for the horse. They still had milk to take to the creamery although they only took their own. Blanche had been perfectly capable of handling the work last spring; Rate wondered why all of a sudden it became too difficult for her to do.

Blanche usually got off down town while he continued on to the creamery by himself. When it was time to go home, she managed to talk to a girlfriend or two until Rate had the horse hitched up to the wagon or buggy, whichever they were driving for the day. Wouldn't do any good to say something to Pa or Ma because they would just tell him it wasn't a woman's work. Things sure did seem unfair at times.

Rate missed seeing Curly although he quickly made new friends. Bud Grell, who was older, even let Rate learn to ride his bike at recess time. Naw, he liked his new friends all right, only he did wish he could see more of Curly. Perhaps he missed the mischief they had gotten into together. Curly always had a big mouth, and it did get him into trouble, but Ralph had usually thought it funny even if it involved him and he had had to share the punishment.

Mostly, he resented that their whole world must revolve around Blanche. He didn't realize that Blanche never asked for all this adulation, and that at times, she found it somewhat stifling. He just knew that more and more it became apparent his parents loved Blanche and seemingly only tolerated him. Yet, he and Pa did get along. They teased one another, and Pa never really got mad at him. Still, the older they got, the more Millie favored his daughter. Sure was hard to figger out.

Pa often was quite vociferous in his opinion that his parents made fools of themselves catering to Ruby. It always seemed that Pa resented the fact that Ruby was the favorite, yet it was sure enough easy to see Blanche was Pa's favorite. Just didn't seem fair. If Pa could criticize his own parents for their behavior toward a daughter, then why was he doing the exact same thing? The Setterington men were somehow all very similar.

Rate had already driven to where the milk had been unloaded. The big arms had come out, taken the milk can, stopped for the scales, and then dumped it into a huge vat. Now, he pulled ahead and around the corner of the building to pick up the whey. Just ahead of him were the Garrett twins, Mabel and Muriel. They looked back and waved, so he rather nonchalantly waved back. The thought flitted across his mind that these two girls weren't as old as Blanche, and they didn't seem to mind hauling milk. In fact, they had a ready smile for everyone. He didn't know them well enough yet to tell them apart because they were identical twins.

When he finally pulled up to the pump for his portion of whey, Sam Packingham stumped over, and being in a particularly affable mood, he was in no hurry to get on with his job of pumping the hot whey into the milk can.

"Wal now, Rate, I seen you makin' sheep's eyes at those two purty gals. Ain'tcha a little young fur gal friends?"

"I only waved 'cause they did. Haven't known 'em long," he explained.

"Sure. I seen 'em tryin' to catch your attention. Didn't see you ignorin' 'em any. 'Course they's mighty nice gals. Don't do no harm to start lookin' early."

"I'm not looking," came the patient elucidation. "I had to be polite, didn't I?"

"'Course you did, boy. I seen you wuz jest bein' perlite." He winked suggestively at Ralph while he turned to the pump, held the canvas tube over the milk can, and methodically worked the old wooden pump.

Now, what was wrong with returning the girls' waves? Sam was just makin' a mountain out of a molehill. Besides, he was sure the girls were at least two grades ahead of him. Why would Sam think he'd be interested in girls anyhow? Sam was a funny old coot; the way he stumped around on his peg leg always made it seem as if he was in a terrible rush. Blanche always thought him grumpy, but he didn't seem that way to Ralph.

Each day for several days, the Garrett girls were just a rig or two ahead of Ralph at the cheese factory. Just like clockwork, Sam took time to comment about Ralph and his girlfriends.

"Rate, ain't no one never told you they's a law again havin' two wimmen? Bein's that's so, which one are ya gonna take, Mabel or Muriel? 'Course, not many could tell the diffrunce anyhow." He laughed.

Ralph stared straight ahead at his horse's ears. He'd simply not give that old man the satisfaction of knowing all these jibes bothered him. He'd just ignore him, that's what he'd do.

He was soon to learn that a man like Sam was hard to ignore. He was like a hound on a hot scent; he knew he was bothering the lad, so he continued the attack.

"Why, Rate, you mean you can't make up yore mind? Want me to give you a hint on how to choose?"

"Would you hurry up and give me my whey? You're going to make me late for school."

"Couldn't have that, now could we?"

Sam laughed and soon finished his job. Rate was glad to get away from there. He was sure some of the other farmers could hear what Sam had to say. How embarrassing.

The next morning, Ralph was in no mood to hear any more of Sam's words of wisdom. Drat it all, he was tired of being teased about girls. An idea came to mind. Just this once, he'd go home without any whey; he'd tell Pa that he'd been kinda far back in line, and they ran out of whey before they got to him. He knew it wasn't right to lie, but just this once he felt it might be justified. After all, he'd taken all the guff he was going to from that old man.

Although Rate was somewhat apprehensive when he told his father the little white lie, it worked, and Millie just nodded his head in acknowledgment and said nothing. This was not the last time Ralph was to come home without stopping to get any whey. If Millie ever surmised that his son was not being completely honest, he never let it be known.

Ralph did not know how to cope with being teased about girls. In the first place, he hadn't thought of liking girls because they were girls—he just liked them because he could always think of something to do to vex them. Had Sam chosen to pick on Ralph about anything else, he would have found a quick mind, with a parry and riposte for any attack. The old Civil War veteran took much delight in watching the youth squirm, and he enjoyed it even more when a deepening red blush crept over the lad's face.

Come November, before snow flew, the family moved into Grandma Smith's house. Millie drove back and forth to the farm to do chores. After school, Ralph was expected to go with his father, and often on Saturdays, they spent most of the day at the farm. Now, Ralph saw less of Curly than before. Still, it was rather nice not to have chores to do mornings before he went to school. Well, at least not many. He had to go across the street to the barn and take care of the two driving horses, but that didn't take long. Guess living in town wasn't all bad.

However, Ralph did look forward to spring since he knew they would once again move back to the farm. During the summer, he would have Curly and Rollie for companions. No matter how well he got on with his new friends, no one could quite replace Curly Sherman; theirs was indeed a lasting friendship.

CHAPTER 18

Blanche was upstairs in her room. Ma had gone to visit Aunt Lorin, and Ralph was heaven knew where, so just she and Pa were home. Because Pa was seldom one for carrying on much of a conversation, she had taken the book she was reading to her room.

She heard the front door open and close and thought perhaps her mother had returned early. A few moments later, she laid her book aside to go downstairs to talk with Miney. As she reached the back stairway, she heard voices raised in anger coming from the sitting room. She recognized her father's tones immediately, and then she realized the other voice belonged to her uncle John.

She sneaked down the stairs to listen to what was being said. Eavesdropping was not something she should be doing, but she wondered why the brothers seemed so angry, why the raised voices; something had greatly agitated them both.

"I tell you, Millie, that damned old man hates my guts. He's never been a father to me, and you know it. He can rot in hell for all I care."

"Now, John, simmer down a bit. What's Pa done now?"

"I needed a loan, so I went to Pa. Where else should a man turn but to his father, especially when his old man's well-off? He just looked at me as though I was a piece of vermin and began lecturing me on what he calls my irresponsible ways."

"What in particular was he referring to?"

"How in hell should I know? Said he'd lent me enough money over the years to start out ten sons, and I'd managed to squander and mismanage ever red cent. Said I hadn't begun to repay the other loans. That ain't true, Millie."

John glared at his brother, daring him to disagree.

Blanche edged closer, wanting a better view, but not wanting to be discovered. She found her heart was pounding. Never had she seen Uncle John look so angry or Pa so distraught.

"John, be honest with yourself for once. You know you've traded more pieces of land than a dog's got fleas. Somehow, your trading never gains you one thin dime. You can't do a half-assed job of farming and make a go of it. Pa just wants you to put in six days of work each week like—"

"Like you, Milt? Go ahead and say it. You've always done just as the old man says. He says 'jump,' and you say 'how far?' How can you forget all those hidings with a horse whip? I suppose you'll tell me they were for our own good."

"In Pa's way, he thought they were. He was teaching us to accept our responsibilities in life. You asked for what you got. If you hadn't always slacked off on your share of the chores, Pa would never have got so mad. Own up to being on the lazy side, John."

John glared at his brother. He would've liked to have slammed his fist in Millie's face like when they were boys, but he thought better of it.

Sullenly, he muttered, "Still didn't give the old reprobate no right to whip me so. I always got it worse than you, an' you know it. Why in hell does he do everything for Mac and Ruby? Everyone knows Mac's not worth a hill of beans. Still, everything has to be done for Ruby. She's always been Ma's favorite. Ruby is perfect in their eyes. They get along with you because they can push you around. Me? I'm shit under their feet."

Millie tried in vain to reason with his brother. Just when he thought he had calmed John down, the man erupted all over again.

John's voice shook with emotion as he looked at his brother and said, "Milt, I could take that old man by the hair of the head, take a razor, and slit his throat from ear to ear with not an ounce of remorse." He shook his clenched fist as though holding his father's head and made a movement with his right hand as if drawing an imaginary razor across his father's throat.

Millie stared at his brother in disbelief. No words came for a moment; there was utter stillness in the room.

"By God, John, you have gone too far. I'll hear no more from you about Pa. Just get out of my house, and stay out until you've got some sense in your head. After all Pa's done for you, you could repay him like that? Ma's done her damnedest for you and Grace and the kids. Seems like you ought to be grateful for the help you've had. Think it over. When you can talk rationally, I'll talk to you. Not before." Millie had not raised his voice, but the tone was ominous.

John said nothing; he simply stomped out of the house. Millie leaned forward, his head in his hands, his mind in a turmoil. His own brother wanted their father dead. He couldn't think. He couldn't understand. Pa had been strict, but Pa had taught them honesty, responsibility, integrity, an honest day's work brought an honest day's pay.

How could John's warped mind speak of killing their father? Everyone knew John Setterington had a horrible temper, although it took a lot to rile him. Millie took comfort in believing John would simmer down and be sorry for his words. Still, it made him see John in a different light. It opened a breach that never completely healed.

Blanche wanted to comfort her father, but she didn't know how. Besides, she didn't want him to know she had overheard the conversation. She found she was trembling. Never would she feel any love for her uncle John. He had killed her love just as he wanted to kill her grandfather. Quietly, she slipped back upstairs to her room. Over and over she heard Uncle John's strident tones, and she shuddered.

Two nights later, Milford was gone for the evening, and Rate was spending the night with Don Sherman. Blanche and Mina were alone. Miney had her rocking chair drawn up close to the Rayo lamp on the table so the light would be good enough to do the crocheting she had started a few days ago. She was doing some wide lace for a pair of pillowcases to give as a Christmas present. She hadn't decided just who she was going to give them to, perhaps Ruby—although Ruby could be so uppity she might not think them good enough.

Blanche sat at the table engrossed in a book. In truth, her thoughts were elsewhere, and it had been several minutes since she had turned a page.

Finally, she spoke to her mother.

"Ma, did you know Uncle John came to see Pa when you were at Aunt Lorin's the other night?"

"Millie did mention it, although he never said what John wanted."

"I'm not sure what he wanted either, but he was awful mad about something. They didn't know I was in the house."

"Do you know what they were talking about?"

Blanche explained in detail what she had heard.

"Land's sakes. Oh, Blanche, I'm sorry you had to hear that."

"Me too. Honest, Ma, it just makes my stomach hurt. After all, Grandfather is Uncle John's father. How can he hate him so?"

"I don't know. I have never understood John with his shiftless ways. Well, that explains what was wrong with your father that night. I thought he acted strange. He said something about John being here, but he'd have been better off not to have come. When I questioned him about what he meant, he said something to the effect that his brother wasn't good for much and that he was the most unappreciative person he'd ever known. That was all I could get out of him. Goodness, Blanche, no wonder he was upset. To think that John could think such a thing, much less put it into words. God will certainly punish him for this."

"Ma, if Uncle John comes here again, do I have to be nice to him?"

"Yes, Blanche, you do. He is your uncle, and we are not to judge. God will do that. Oh my, I doubt if he will be back for some time. Your father will not forget easily, so I think he will avoid his brother whenever possible. Sometimes, down in his heart, I'm not sure your father always agrees with his father, but he has always had a great deal of respect for the man. Of course, Father Setterington has certainly been an astute businessman," she said grudgingly, "although I have always felt he was more than a little heartless."

Blanche digested this. She realized that sometimes Grandfather could be unreasonable in his demands and that he was terribly stubborn. 'Course, she felt Uncle John was equally stubborn. However, not to feel remorse if Grandfather died was unthinkable. Blanche loved and respected her grandfather. Besides, it was Grandmother who usually aroused her ire by her constant fault-finding. Grandfather never had a lot to say, but he was always pleasant to be around.

Blanche never forgot what she had heard John say, and she never found it in her heart to completely forgive him. She wasn't sure her father ever forgave him either.

*****

Christmas this year was a more exciting time since they had been invited to spend the day at South Lyon with Grandmother and Grandfather. Rate was glad of the diversion. He could remember the time he, Georgie, and Ma had gone by train to Traverse City to see Aunt Ettie and Uncle George, and the time when he and Blanche had gone to visit Aunt Ruby and Uncle Mac at Big Rapids; he could even remember going to Aunt Mary's in Chicago, and he had always enjoyed the train ride. True, going to South Lyon wasn't going to take very long, but even a short ride was better than none.

Besides, Christmas was the one time of year he enjoyed going to his grandmother's. She always fussed a lot more than Ma did. There was always plenty of oranges and bananas and fancy little candies that Grandmother so proudly made and all kinds of nuts to crack. For dessert, they always had what Grandmother called plum pudding, a steamed pudding with lots of raisins, although it tasted just like Ma's suet pudding. Anyway, Grandmother said hers was an old English recipe that came from Horatio's side of the family. Whether it was rightly named "suet" or "plum" pudding didn't matter much to Ralph since it was one of his very favorite desserts.

Grandmother served generous portions of the dark hot pudding with sweetened milk to pour over it. Just thinking of it made his mouth water, and he could almost taste it.

Since Grandfather was the town's only banker, he no longer wore full chin whiskers. Rate heard him say that the neatly trimmed Van Dyke was more in keeping with his new station in life. Personally, Ralph liked the transfiguration; he felt it gave his grandfather the distinguished look of an aristocrat. Horatio was tall, wiry, and by now his beard and the thinning hair was a steel gray, yet the eyes were as bold and black as they had ever been. Perhaps the lines at the corners of the eyes were more deeply set, the forehead was certainly higher, but Horatio carried his years well. The broad shoulders were still square, and there was no stoop; he stood as erect as a young man. Rate often watched his grandfather with a sort of inner pride.

Ralph had never really known his grandfather's brothers. He knew Uncle Albert and Uncle George had visited, but he scarcely remembered them. He only knew they had seemed large, much like Willie and John, who were Uncle Albert's boys. He did remember that the youngest brother, Uncle Vest, had come to see them. However, he just knew that his grandfather was the best-looking of the boys in the family. He had never seen any of Grandfather's sisters, although he assumed them to be large women. Blanche had always been tall for her age and broad-shouldered for a girl, and Ralph had heard Grandfather compare Blanche with his sisters. He guessed Setteringtons were just special 'cause no one ever talked much about Grandmother's side of the family. Aunt Nan and Uncle Lem Bingham had once lived just west of the village limits on the north side of the road, and Aunt Nan was Grandmother's sister. He hadn't been all that old when Lem had sold the place to Grandfather. Rate remembered that was where he had seen his first and only barn raising.

Aunt Nan had died of cancer a few years ago. He remembered Uncle Lem as being a rather odd sort of person. He'd heard Pa say that was because Uncle Lem was a morphine addict. When Rate had questioned his father, Millie had told him that Lem Bingham had been hurt very seriously in an accident and had been given morphine for several weeks to make the pain bearable. The doctors had not realized that such prolonged use of the drug created a dependence on it, and the body developed a craving for the drug. They had been able to lessen the dosage, but Lem had never quite been able to forgo the withdrawal pain, so he had continued his use of the drug. Pa had told Ralph that before the accident, Lem had been a much different personality. Ralph had digested this bit of information resolving that if he ever got hurt, he'd tolerate the pain rather than be given drugs upon which he would become dependent for the rest of his life.

He knew a Lizzie Loynes called Grandmother *Aunt Vine*, so he supposed she was Grandmother's niece. He had asked Blanche about it one day, and Blanche had said that she sort of remembered Aunt Bet Loynes, who she guessed was Grandmother's sister. Blanche had told him that Grandmother never talked much about her family. Perhaps they weren't as prosperous as the Setteringtons, or perhaps Lavina just didn't get on well with them, neither Blanche nor Rate ever knew for certain.

Grandfather met them at the station with the cutter. As usual, he drove a highstepping, spirited team. Blanche and Miney clambered into the back seat and were snuggled under a beautiful horsehide robe, their hands shoved deeply into their muffs. Ralph asked to ride in front with the menfolk, who scoffed at such necessities to keep them warm. Even though the weather was in the lower teens, men had to be tough enough not to need coddling. When they moved away from the depot, Rate wished he could drive the team, but he was afraid to ask even though Grandfather looked in a particularly jovial mood, smiling and chatting with his son as though their arrival was indeed special.

If anyone wondered why John and Grace, with their five children, were not present for Christmas dinner, no one made mention of the fact. Grandmother was almost pleasant and found no fault with anyone, which Ralph felt must have set some sort of record. She played a great deal with Lois, so it was easy to see that there was now someone in her life who mattered more than Blanche. Well, perhaps it was only because Lois was still a baby, and Lavina did love babies— especially baby girls.

It was late March when Milford and his family moved back to the farm. Now that Ralph and Blanche once again had to drive back and forth to school, Rate decided that living in town had had its compensations after all.

First, there were the raw, cold, blustery winds of March. Since it had come in like a lamb, it was sure going out like a lion. The roads were a complete sea of mud. Ralph felt sorry for the poor horse picking his way through that cold, sloppy mess. It took a lot more time to clean a horse after they had been driven and splattered so with mud. All that caked dirt had to be cleaned off each evening, only to be equally as bad after a few yards on the road the next day.

Next came the April showers. Showers! Some of them were downright cloudbursts. Seemed like half the time, he and Blanche came home looking like something the cat dragged in—wet, mud-splattered, and not in the best of humor. 'Course, sometimes it was worth getting wet just to hear Blanche bellyache about her clothes getting sodden even though she had a blanket to cover her lap and legs. Sometimes, their coats had to be sponged off where another rig had splashed them, and then, Miney carefully tended them by the stove to have them dry by the next morning. Thinking of his mother, he guessed this kind of weather only added to her work too. Blanche tried to help, but Ma always said Blanche didn't do a good enough job. At least Blanche must have felt sorry for Ma too since she did the chicken chores to help Ma out a bit.

Rate guessed he'd be glad when school was done with for the summer. Besides, he'd heard talk that Elsie was going to build a new school this summer and that it was likely to have a basement and two stories. Sure would be different from the crowded wooden structure that served all eleven grades. The new building was to be built of brick and located just east of the present building. He supposed they'd start on it right after classes finished. Bet it was going to cost a tremendous amount of money.

The spring planting season was over. The winter wheat had survived the harsh winter weather well; the small field of oats looked good, and the corn was just beginning to peek through the ground, so the checkrows could be picked out here and there. Pa hadn't always checkrowed his corn, but he said this field would do better if it could be cultivated both ways to keep down the weeds. Rate knew it would mean less hoeing by him and the hired man, so he was all in favor of it. You see, when rows were checked, the hills of corn were the same distance apart from north to south as they were from east to west. Many farmers planted corn this way and used one horse on a single row cultivator to keep the weeds under control and to preserve the moisture for the corn.

*****

It was Monday morning, and at the breakfast table, Millie spoke to his young son.

"Rate, just got word that the sheepshearers will be here on Wednesday, so we'd best get the sheep washed today. I don't want you running off. I've got a few things to tend to, so I'll be ready about nine thirty or ten. Make sure you are within callin' distance."

"Yes, Pa."

This was the first year Pa had asked him to be around to help wash the sheep. Rate had known it was a job that needed doing since wool brought a better price if it wasn't so heavy with oil. He had asked Millie about this, and Millie told him he guessed the buyers would rather give a better price for clean wool and have the weight be all wool than to give less and have part of the weight be the sheep's natural body oil that had permeated the thick wool. Anyway, it made sense. Last year, he'd asked to go along, only Pa had told him he wasn't big enough. Rate hadn't figured to ask this year, so he was surprised and delighted with this new task delegated to him.

It was almost ten when Millie, Jim Keenan, and Ralph opened the gates to let the flock of seventy-five ewes out of the yard surrounding the sheep barn. One old ewe with a bell hanging on her collar, bellwether as they referred to her, was in the lead. Rate stood in the road to keep her from going south, and since she turned north, the rest of the flock automatically fell in behind. Sheep are notorious for following the leader; this was all well and good if the leader could be kept going in the right direction. The dust from the late June dryness rose in clouds as the sheep scurried on their way, darting here and there to nibble the lush, tender grass along the roadside.

Jim circled out into the fields to get by the flock because at the first corner north, the flock needed to turn east.

Rate chased a few stragglers out of the Garretts' front yard. When Ezz saw them coming, he had helped keep them from coming in around his buildings like any good neighbor would. Neighbors were always ready to lend a helping hand. Farmwork had to be a shared industry since it required so many hours of backbreaking hand labor. Some things were nigh impossible for a man to do by himself, and it wasn't every missus who was strong enough to be of assistance; besides, most farm men felt that fieldwork was not for women anyway. If she tended house and children, did the washin' and cookin' and bakin', tended garden and chickens, not to mention the sewing and patching, she had plenty of work of her own.

They made the turn east, and Jim kept the ewes from wandering into the Moores' or the Tabors'. By now, the old ewe settled down and acted as though she knew where she was going. Rate dashed to get ahead by the school to make sure she didn't turn south although he needn't have worried. She went north of her own accord, across the bridge spanning Maple River, and then turned east once more.

Not too much farther, there was a trail leading back to the river where a holding pen had been built across the river. They drove the sheep into the shallow water.

"Well, boy, get in there and start washing."

"Pants and all?"

Since it was summer, he wore no shoes, so no problem there.

"How else? Water's not very deep. Most likely won't come much over your knees."

Rate hardly relished the idea of wet pants even though they only came to his knees, so he quickly rolled his pant legs as high as they would go.

The water, for all it was a warm June day, was still rather chilly. Rate watched his father and Jim wading amongst the sheep—they hadn't even bothered to roll up their pant legs—so he did likewise. They kneaded the wool on the sheep's back, pulling it up this way and that so it became saturated with water. Then, they moved on to the next.

Rate was busy at work and hadn't noticed that his father had come up behind him. The next thing he knew, he was bumped from behind, and down he went into the water, completely soaking his pants and the front half of his shirt.

"Oooops. Didn't know you was that close to me, boy. Guess you needn't have taken the time to roll up those pant legs. They look a little wet now."

"Pa, you did that on purpose," accused Ralph.

"Did what, Rate? Couldn't help it if I didn't know you was behind me, now could I?" Millie's chuckle rankled just a trifle.

"You could look around once in a while," suggested Rate.

"No harm's done, boy. You'll dry out by afternoon." Millie laughed.

Ralph knew his father had bumped him intentionally. Well, one of these days he'd get even.

When they were ready to leave, the bellwether took the lead once again, and the others obediently followed. They would be no trouble since all of them realized they were headed for home.

Rate, uncomfortable in his wet clothes, walked silently beside his father. Millie seemed to sense the lad was put out with him, so he became voluble.

"Several years ago, Rate, there was a man killed right where we were today. Seems he had a pretty good-sized ram in with his flock. He was squatted down, and for some reason, that ram lowered his head and charged. Before the man could get out of the way, the buck butted him right over the heart. Killed the man. Just like that. 'Course, don't think there's anything any harder than the head of a buck sheep. Just don't never pay not to keep an eye on them since no animal can always be trusted. It's usually the mild ones that do the damage 'cause farmers are notorious for not being cautious, get to havin' too much confidence in a well-mannered animal, and then bang! the animal goes wild, and the unwary farmer pays. Keep that in mind, boy, don't never put too much faith in a male animal, they can be awful treacherous."

Rate digested that bit of information. In later years, he was to say that never did he come by where the holding pens had once crossed the river without thinking of the unwary man who had lost his life there.

Wednesday, two men came to shear sheep. Ed Clark and Jim Keenan kept busy catching sheep to be sheared, one man did the shearing, while the second man kept a pair of sheep shears freshly sharpened. Millie was kept busy tying the wool in bundles.

A sheep bent on keeping its wool is not the easiest animal to handle. A body knew just how to grab the ewe, set her down between his legs, and commence. Around the ears and legs, it took some careful trimming. However, with shears razor-sharp, there was no need to open and close them along the belly, sides, and back; he could just keep them in an open position and slide the shears quickly down, neatly cutting a swath of wool close to the body. On occasion, he cut a little too close, usually around the head, and would nick a sheep. The red blood showed a sharp contrast to the glaring white coat of the newly sheared sheep. The bleats chorused a cacophony of sound as the frightened sheep cried out their despair. However, as soon as they were released to join their newly shorn companions, they became once more at ease and didn't seem to mind that they had just lost their heavy winter coat. How white they looked! Rate always felt that they looked completely naked until the snow-white wool began to get darkened with oil and dirt once again.

A couple of days after the sheep had been sheared, Millie loaded the bundles of wool on the wagon to take in to H. J. Hankins to sell. There was over 250 pounds of wool, and he was paid nineteen cents a pound, thus getting almost fifty dollars. Millie felt this was a fairly good price and was well pleased with the amount, figuring he'd had a good return for the work involved.

Fact was, things were going pretty darned good this year. Prices had held steadier than normal. The first of June, he had sold Hankins over sixteen tons of hay at a price of $6.75 a ton. Since he hadn't been feeding so many hogs over the winter, he'd had a goodly quantity of corn left over, so he'd sold some at fifty-five cents a bushel, and he'd had extra oats, which he'd sold for forty-two and a half cents a bushel.

He still had some of both commodities left just in case he didn't get a crop this year. However, the corn was off to a good start, and the oats looked good. Still, Millie always said a bird in the hand was worth two in the bush—he knew just how quickly adverse weather conditions could ruin the prospects of a good harvest. He had long ago learned that the old saying of "don't count your chickens before they're hatched" sure applied to a good-looking crop in the field. Frost before corn was ripe, heavy rain at harvest, which knocked the wheat and oats flat or perhaps sprouted them while they stood in the shock—these were always an ever-present threat to the farmer.

Millie had just always accepted whatever came as being something he couldn't control, and since he couldn't control it, there was no sense to worry about it. If things went wrong this year, likely next year would be better. Besides, Miney worried enough for the both of them—that was one reason he figured she was always so close with money; she was always afraid there wouldn't be any more coming, so she pinched her pennies and stretched a dollar until it hollered. He laughed as he thought of it. 'Course Miney was a right fine wife, and he liked her just the way she was.

Miney came flouncing into the house, banging the screen door.

Millie looked up expectantly from the paper he was reading, an amused expression on his face.

"And who's always yellin' at Rate 'bout slammin' doors?"

"I just don't care. That George Schenck makes me furious."

"What's he done now?"

"Remember last week when I told you he saw me coming out of the house to mail a letter, and even though I hollered and waved at him to stop, he just drove right off? Now, this time is even worse."

"What's worse?"

"See this?" She waved a piece of paper in the air. "Well, it's a note he left along with the letter he never took. You see, I didn't have any stamps, so I put my letter in the mailbox along with two pennies to cover the cost of a stamp. Well, sir, just listen to what he wrote. 'Lick your own stamps!' Now, doesn't that beat all? He left the letter, took my money, and left a stamp." She showed the letter and stamp. "Just you wait until I see that man. I'll give him a piece of my mind."

Millie started to laugh.

"I don't see why you think it's so funny. I did want this letter to go out today. Isn't it part of his job?"

"Don't think it says anywhere whether he has to lick stamps for his patrons or not."

"Always knew when we were in school together that he was lazy and irresponsible. How'd he ever get to be a mail carrier anyway?"

"Now, Miney, don't make such a big thing of it. Just learn to buy more than one stamp at a time, and then you won't be likely to have that problem."

Miney moved off to the kitchen muttering to herself.

Ralph had listened to the verbal exchange. Frankly, he thought the note was comical. Somehow, Ma was always late going anyplace, and even though she knew Mr. Schenck was always here so regular you could set your clock by him, she always waited until the last minute to go to the mailbox. She just hated to buy more than one stamp at a time, so she was always running out. Mr. Schenck had tolerated this a few times. Must be he'd just plain got tired of Ma putting the money in the box. Bet from now on, Ma would stamp her own letters even if it did rankle a mite. Of course, if she did meet Mr. Schenck up town, she'd give him a tongue-lashing even if it wouldn't do any good. From what everyone said, Mr. Schenck could be an ornery cuss. Ma just needed to have a better sense of humor at times. Now, Pa had seen the funny side of it too. 'Course the note almost sounded like something Pa would say, so that was probably why it tickled him.

When Millie had purchased his farm from his father, there had been two tracts of eighty acres of land, so it had extended as far north as the next road. However, after a short period of time, he felt this was an excessive burden of debt, so he had sold the north eighty to his brother John. Now, being the trader he was, John had no sooner acquired the property when he traded it back to Horatio in exchange for a farm north of Elsie. This had left Millie with the south eighty and Horatio once again in possession of the north eighty.

A portion of the north eighty had been cleared of timber, the stumps burned out, and the fields had been plowed a few years before these transactions. Horatio had approached his son about the advisability of continuing to farm the fields rather than let them lay idle. Whether Horatio actually hinted that if Millie worked the place on shares, it would someday be his is rather doubtful. However, Millie assumed that this was the agreement. Of course, nothing was put in writing, and at this time, neither Horatio nor Millie realized this was to be the genesis of a quarrel.

Millie was glad of the extra land for crops since most of his own land back of the ditch had only been used for pasture, and stumps still dotted the terrain. Often on a Sunday afternoon, Rate would accompany his father to these back fields while Milford set fire to a stump or two. The sheep kept the vegetation nibbled so short all around the stumps, there was little danger of the fire spreading.

Sometimes a stump would smolder underground a day or two with small wisps of smoke rising intermittently above the blackened hole, a silent indicator that the fire was still feeding on the roots of the once forest giant.

This year, like last, the field across from the Garretts had been a hayfield. Several days of rain the first part of July delayed the final putting up of the hay from this particular field, which was the last one Millie had. Then, came two days that were beautifully bright and sunny and hot, ideal haying weather. The hay had been cut, raked, and was now standing in the haycocks, waiting for someone to load and haul it.

Millie, Jim, Merval, and Ralph were getting ready to do that very thing.

A few days ago, Millie had traded off Mage to Cash Waldron for a younger mare. Rate hadn't been sorry to see Mage go since the boy had never forgiven the horse for standing on his foot. Besides, Mage hadn't learned from the episode, and the only thing that kept there from being a recurrence was that Ralph had learned to be extremely careful when in the stall alongside Mage. He paid particular attention to how close he got to the horse's feet and was prepared to move his own in a hurry. Anyway, the new mare hadn't been hitched up with any of Millie's horses since the acquisition. Millie decided the hay wagon was a good time to try her out, so they harnessed her in with Cap.

All went well. Rate drove the team while Merval and Jim pitched the hay from the cocks onto the wagon and Millie made the load. When Millie decided they had put on a good enough load, Jim took the lines to take the team into the road and home.

There was a slight incline to go up before they reached the road. When spoken to, Cap stepped into the collar to pull, but Dolly hung back; when Cap stepped back, she surged forward. Poor Cap didn't know what to do. He tried again, and as soon as his tugs tightened, Dolly stepped back. She began to prance, she tried to turn sideways, she even tried to rear. Jim, who was uncommonly good with a team, could do nothing with her.

There was a small sapling growing in the fenceline a few yards off, so Millie stepped over to this and cut it off with his jackknife. He took the lines from Jim and told the others to stand back; he stood off to one side, the lines firmly grasped in one large hand, the sapling in the other.

Millie spoke, his voice deep and powerful, "Get up there."

Dolly didn't even make an effort.

Millie raised the sapling and struck her rump a resounding blow; she neighed and pranced, but didn't attempt to pull. Again a blow fell with much the same results. Poor Cap danced and pranced and didn't know for certain what was expected of him.

By now, Millie was fast losing his patience. He began to rain blows methodically and with vigor while a string of profanity came forth, the likes of which Rate had never heard. To be sure, he sometimes heard Millie swear, but nothing that held a candle to this. He fairly stared at his father. What if Ma had heard? His mother was not one to condone taking the Lord's name in vain, and yet here was Pa spewing out blasphemous words with gusto.

Millie stopped as suddenly as he had begun. He tossed the sapling aside; it looked a little worse for wear, no leaves, and the bark hung in shreds. His voice took on a new tone as he spoke soothingly to the team. Cap quieted, but every muscle along Dolly's ribs and flank quivered with anticipation, and her eyes rolled white in fright.

"Cap. Dolly. Get up there," spoke Millie firmly.

There was no hesitation this time. Both horses surged forward as a team should, and the wagon creaked into the road.

"Whoa!"

The team stopped. Sweat was running off Dolly as she awaited the next command.

"Jim, you get back up there and see if she don't drive all right now," ordered Millie.

There was no further confrontation. Dolly did not balk again that day; her decorum was perfect in every way.

Several days later, Jim was once again driving Dolly when she refused the command to go. Millie didn't even bother to pick up the lines. He merely shouted from some distance away, "Dolly, you sonofabitch, get up there." Dolly obediently did as she was told.

Rate figured he had learned at least one thing. He hadn't liked seeing Dolly beaten, and Pa had sure dressed her out good, but he did understand that horses had to be taught to mind if they were to be of service. A horse that balked every now and then was not much use to a farmer. He hoped he would never have to take such drastic measures because he didn't like hurting an animal. 'Course, he remembered that Pa hadn't struck any too lightly when giving him a whipping, so he guessed a horse, being so much bigger, could tolerate a lot more.

*****

"Millie, I'd like a few extra dollars to buy some material for aprons, and I do need a couple of new housedresses. I thought since you just sold some hay and grain, now would be a good time to get what I need."

Milford's face took on an uncommunicative expression.

"Perhaps you'd best wait until I sell those yearlings."

"Why on earth do I have to wait? You said it would be a month or more before you sold them."

"I'm a little short of cash right now," he hedged.

"Short of cash? You can't be. There haven't been that many expenses, and I know you've been getting a good price for what you've sold. Don't you want me to have the money?"

"It's not that, Miney."

"Well then, what is it? I don't usually ask for much."

He knew by the tone of her voice that her feelings had been hurt, and he hadn't intended to do that.

"I know you don't ask for much. I never complain, do I?"

"No, but you've never refused me before."

Millie heaved a sigh.

"I honestly don't have the cash because I bought a flock of a hundred sheep from Pa."

"Sheep? Why do we need more sheep, and how'd your father get a flock anyhow?"

"He had loaned a man some money and taken a mortgage on the flock. Well, the man couldn't pay, and Pa had to foreclose. Anyway, they aren't far from here, so he gave me first chance to buy them."

"For a good price, I'll bet."

"Pa only asked $210 for the whole lot. That's what the note was for. He didn't even make any to cover his trouble."

"$210! Good heavens, Millie, since when are sheep worth that much? I thought you just sold one for $1.50."

"I did, but she was an ewe that hadn't got bred, so I sold her cheap. No, Miney, I'm sure they are worth that much."

"You'd think they were just because that is the price your father set on them. I honestly don't understand you even a little bit. You think your father knows all there is to know, and, Milford, I don't always trust your father when it comes to business. I still remember how he took Pa on trading horses."

"Let's not dredge that up. Pa's always been fair with me. He just thought I'd stand to make a tidy sum on these sheep."

"I know, and you're still willing to let your father do your thinking for you," she said bitterly.

"Now, Miney, that's not fair. As soon as I get some extree cash, I'll see that you have whatever you need."

From the tone of his voice, Miney knew the matter was settled. Sometimes he did try her patience. She had thought when Father and Mother Setterington moved to South Lyon, Millie would be free to be his own man, but she had been wrong. Millie was still like a puppet on a string where his father was concerned. Of course, in all fairness, she had to admit that there were times when Father had helped Millie to invest money and, in a short time, make a sizable amount on his investment.

She was certain it had been on his father's advice that Millie and Mr. Curtis had bought a couple of houses in Elsie—one for taxes and one was estate property. They had fixed the houses up a bit, new paint and paper, and made a few minor repairs. They'd sold the one house for a tidy profit and had been renting the other one, which made a steady income, although when it was divided in half, it wasn't very much. Of course, just the fact that they could count on that rent money each month made it worthwhile.

She honestly doubted if Millie would have had the courage to attempt something like that without his father standing behind him, prodding him along. Father Setterington had just the right amount of gambling spirit to make him dare to speculate. Millie wanted to invest only in a sure thing. Perhaps some of this was her influence because she simply hated putting money out when they might not get it back. Still, Father did seem to get his back, and he usually got a generous profit. Why, she'd heard that as far back as in the 1880s, he had charged 10 percent interest. She didn't even dare guess what he charged now. No getting around it, Father knew how to make money. 'Course, he never let his emotions enter into a business deal. No, sir, there were times when he was coldly calculating, and a person would have thought he had ice in his veins.

She supposed she'd just have to wait for her material. It did rankle a bit because Millie never discussed anything with her—just went ahead and did as he pleased, or rather what his father pleased. Well, she'd just keep close track, and as soon as he sold something, she'd be sure she got her money, and just maybe she'd buy some material for a good dress even though she had thought she'd make do until fall.

The summer was passing quickly. Haying season was finished, and it was time to harvest wheat. Next, the oats would be turning, and then there would be only a short time left of summer vacation. Rate and Curly were enjoying being together again. They often went over to Maple River back of the Pages' and fished. Sometimes, they had good luck, sometimes not. If Rate was lucky, Ma could have fish for a whole meal. If not, she always cooked what he caught just for him. Yup, in ways like that, Ma was awful good to him, and she never complained about doin' it neither.

When the boys were back to the river, they often saw blacksnakes slither into the water only a few feet away from where they walked along the bank. Some of these snakes were six feet long and almost as large around as Ralph's wrist. The boys had no fear of them since the snakes made every effort to get away from them as quickly as possible. In fact, they liked to watch the snakes swim effortlessly in the water.

Mostly, they fished from the trunk of a tree that had become uprooted and had fallen into the water. This made a good place to sit, and there was no need for long poles. Besides, neither of them had a proper store-bought fishing pole, they had simply cut themselves a hefty willow from along the roadside, trimmed off the leaves and small branches, and tied a piece of string to the end. A washer served as a sinker, a used cork from a bottle as a bobber, and sometimes a bent pin had to suffice as a hook. Both boys wore straw hats pushed back on their heads; while Rate had a white, unblemished complexion, the bridge of Don's nose and his cheeks were peppered with freckles, giving him an impish look. For boys who sometimes found it difficult to remain quiet for very long while in school, they could sit on that old tree trunk for hours, seldom talking because they didn't want to scare the fish. Their legs and feet were deeply tanned from sitting so long in the sun. Their arms were tanned as far as the rolled-up shirtsleeves allowed. They seldom argued, although neither was above playing a prank on the other now and then, and they often wrestled for the fun of it.

They became inseparable, seeming to want to cram a whole lifetime of living into these few brief summer months. Miney had even let the two of them sleep in the haymow one night when Don had slept over with Rate. It was at the end of haying season, and both boys had looked so enthusiastic about the idea, she hadn't had the heart to refuse. Newly mowed hay had a pleasant odor, so perhaps she could understand their desire just a little. Besides, she knew if Millie had got wind of the request, he would have overridden any negative decision of hers. In some things, Millie was quick to side in with Ralph—unless it in some way affected Blanche.

Blanche was watching out the south window, her eyes following a man leading a cow along the road toward their place. As he drew nearer, she recognized him as Monroe Swarthout from up on the corner. Out of idle curiosity, she moved to yet another window so she could watch the man's progress. The man turned into their driveway and, after some problem at the gate, took the cow into the barnyard.

Blanche wondered what was going on. This was not the first time this had happened. A week or so ago, it had been Roy Brown, a few days ago, John Fizzell, and now Mr. Swarthout.

Then, she remembered that one afternoon she had been the only one home when Mr. Brown had come by. He had seemed rather embarrassed when he found out her father wasn't at home. He'd dug a work-dirty hand into his overalls and come out with a folded piece of money; he'd smoothed it out and given her the dollar saying he owed it to her father. When she had asked what it was for, he'd only become more embarrassed and had even got red around the ears. He'd hung his head and said, "For a service last week an' the week afore thet. He'll know." Then, before she could say anything more, he'd taken off like a burnt boot, and she'd been left there holding the money.

When she'd given her father the money, he'd just nodded and said it was to settle an account.

Blanche hated being treated like a child. So today, feeling in a particularly spunky mood, she descended on her unwary mother in the kitchen.

"Ma, why's Mr. Swarthout bringing a cow here?"

Miney looked around at her daughter, the expression on her face showing how completely taken aback she was by the suddenness of the question.

"Why, why," she stammered, "I didn't know he had."

"I just watched him come through the gate. Mr. Brown and Mr. Fizzell have brought cows too. What's going on? They always take them back home, so I know Pa's not buying their cows."

"They…well, they bring them to visit our cows."

"What for? Seems like a dumb idea to me."

"Well, that's what they do. They come for a visit," she stated emphatically, then added in a more modified voice, "When you're older, you'll understand better."

"Understand what? If you don't explain anything, there's nothing for me to understand. Well, if you won't tell me, I'll just ask Pa when he comes in for dinner."

With that declaration, Blanche made a hurried exit.

Goodness, Blanche obviously meant what she said. Miney had no idea what kind of an answer Millie would give the girl. It was such a delicate situation. If only Blanche hadn't been quite so observant.

True to her word, Blanche put the question to her father. He gave her a long expressionless look, then said, "They bring them here to be serviced."

The tone of the answer told Blanche she was not to ask any more questions. Now, she was more perplexed than ever.

That night, after she and Ralph had gone upstairs to bed, she sneaked into his room and sat on the edge of his bed. Rate looked at her wonderingly. It wasn't often his sister did this, only if something was bothering her.

"Ralph, do you know why the neighbors bring those cows here?"

"Sorta," he said hesitantly.

"Tell me," she demanded.

"They take 'em in where Pa keeps the bull. Pa hasn't never let me go along, but I peeked through a crack once, and I could hear them talking. Whatever they do had to be done if the cow is to have a calf."

"Oh."

Blanche had known that cows had calves, mares had foals, sows had pigs, because there were some things that farm children just grew up with and accepted as the normal course of events. However, no one ever quite got around to telling them why the animals gave birth; this was something to be ignored—the fact that a female had to have mated with a male.

"Ralph, do you suppose that is why we keep a ram with the sheep?" she asked wonderingly.

"Guess I'd never given it much mind. Could likely be. Everyone I know who keeps sheep keeps a ram, or they sometimes lease one for a short time."

"Thanks, Ralph. Now, go to sleep."

Blanche returned to her bedroom more puzzled than ever. There were so many questions she would like to ask, but Ma just never was one to explain anything. Sometimes, she felt Ma hated to admit there were male and female anything.

Not all farmers kept a bull on their farm, especially if they only kept three or four milch cows. Millie had let it be known that he had a good-looking Holstein, and those who brought a cow to be serviced paid fifty cents. It had turned out to be quite profitable. Millie also found that he could command a much better price for a bred heifer than one that was open, so the bull was surely paying his way and then some.

Once again, come the latter part of October, the Setteringtons moved back into Grandma Smith's house. It wasn't all that bad. In fact, Ralph was glad to see some of his friends again. Guess maybe he had the best of two worlds—the farm in the summer when it was really the most pleasant place to be, and town in the winter when the weather was bad.

Yes, the summers were really pleasant. Rate enjoyed doing any fieldwork, which involved driving a horse. Now, the hoeing was something he could do without, but it could have been worse. He liked working with the animals. Sometimes, it took a heap o' doin' to outsmart them.

Winter work wasn't anything to enjoy. The ice froze in the tank, and a hole had to be chopped so the livestock could get a drink. Then, when the water had to be pumped by hand, he stood there half frozen, methodically moving the pump handle up and down while his nose lost its feeling and his fingers felt numb. He also remembered the time he had stuck his tongue on the pump handle and had been completely surprised to learn that it stuck there. When he pulled it away, he left a small patch of skin on the iron handle. At dinner, when he hadn't eaten very much because of his sore tongue, Millie chuckled like it was something extraordinarily comical. Then, he explained, "Rate, I'd bet my bottom dollar that in town, every kid at some time or other sticks his tongue on a hitching post, and every farm lad tries a pump handle—all with the same result. Guess you won't never do it again, will you?"

Rate had been emphatic in stating he had learned his lesson. Pa's words had made him feel better even if Pa had laughed since he realized now that he wasn't the only dummy in the world. The next generation of boys was to learn on ice skate keys—they were such a handy size to pop in the mouth with the same results.

Since the horses stood in the stable all the time, there was a lot of manure to fork out daily; they had to be bedded down extra good to try to keep their stable blankets as clean as possible. In fact, it took a lot of time to pull straw from the stack behind the barn and carry it into the stable. He'd get a really big forkful, with the straw hanging together well, then just before he got into the stable, it would have loosened enough, so half of it fell off. Sometimes, it was enough to make him swear even though he knew Ma didn't approve of swearing.

True, he still had horses to care for in town, but usually there were only two instead of six or eight. Usually at night, a group would go sledding or skating. Sometimes, the older ones went on class sleigh rides. Well, a couple more years, and he'd be old enough for that.

'Course, it really didn't matter whether he liked the present arrangement or not, Blanche was the only one who counted. In all fairness, he did realize that during the heaviest part of the winter, it would not have been all that pleasant for Blanche to drive to school, yet other girls did it. Of course, they weren't the only daughter of Milford and Mina Setterington. Wonder why the only son never seemed to matter?

Rate was well pleased with the new school building. It was a huge, two-storied, red brick building with cut stones set in at the corners for design. The gray slate roof sloped sharply upward, making the edifice look taller than it actually was. The front of the school faced east where the arched, stone-decorated entrance shielded the double doors leading upstairs to the classrooms. The new building had been built in front of the old two-storied wooden structure that had since been sold and moved away.

Even the belfry held a brand-new bell, the old one being considered too small for the growing community. The building looked naked standing there with no bushes to make it appear part of the landscape; it was stark, and bare, and its newness made it stand out like a sore thumb. 'Course, once a person got inside, all this was forgotten, and if the outside had an austere look, like it didn't yet belong, the rooms were pleasant, and the teachers gloried in the new space and improved facilities.

Since Ralph was now in the fifth grade, his classroom was on the main floor. However, he had gone upstairs where the high school students had their classes and had even been on an excursion to the basement just to look things over. He noted the classrooms were light, airy, and spacious after the cramped quarters of the old building.

Blanche had long ago decided she liked town best. She was not one to care for the smells often emanating from a farm. She could do without the smell of freshly spread manure in a field, the stink of the hogpens, the stuffiness of the chicken coop when she went to gather eggs. The flies were not nearly as bad in town, and she certainly didn't miss carting milk to Doyle's cheese factory and smelling the stink from that, not to mention the smell of the whey they took home for the pigs.

Besides, she had friends in town, and they always had something to do. They often met at each other's house and sometimes did their homework together. Often, on the farm, she was lonely, lacking someone her own age to talk to. She had never been close to the Swarthout girls or Selina Clark, who were her nearest neighbors. Farm girls had a different outlook on life and accepted not having money much of the time. Blanche had seen too much of the comforts money could buy to be content living a meager existence on a farm like some folks did.

Miney felt it was easier living in town. She didn't have chickens to take care of, and she no longer had the milk can to wash since Millie took care of that. She could send Ralph to the store every day instead of having to wait until Saturday to buy groceries. She had to admit that on the days when she sent him to the store before school, at dinnertime, and after school, he sometimes seemed a little resentful. Well, she tried not to make him go before school, but there were times when it was a dire necessity. She knew exactly how much each item cost and carefully doled out the money. Often Ralph was sent for exactly one pound of beefsteak, cut thin, and since it was twelve cents a pound, twelve cents was all Miney gave him. She expected the butcher to be that accurate with his cutting.

Besides, Miney had grown up in town, and she liked having neighbors next door. Lorin lived just down the street, and while there was a great difference in their ages, she and her half sister did get on well. Lorin did a lot of knitting, so she often brought her knitting and spent the afternoon with Miney. Miney always had something she was crocheting, or sometimes in the winter, she worked on braiding a rug. For this, she used heavy wool material from old coats or trousers, cutting the material in narrow strips, then deftly turning under the raw edges as she put the three strands into a braid. The extra warmth of the material on her lap was a welcome feature when the winter winds howled and the curtains moved lazily back and forth because nothing fit snugly, and the cold air sneaked through each and every crack.

At the back of the house was a large attached woodshed, so one didn't have to go outdoors to bring in kindling. At the farm, Ralph had had to keep kindling piled by the door, but it was often snow-covered and somewhat damp to put in the stove. This was much better.

Then, too, she was within walking distance of church. Miney always dreaded getting a horse around in the winter. The horse had to be blanketed when they stopped, and it was such a nuisance getting the blanket on and off. She was always just a little afraid of tipping the cutter over when they had to go through uneven drifts, and sometimes there were drifts as high as the horse's belly. Of course, the menfolk often did some shoveling in these spots, and the thills of the cutter were off-set so the horse could travel in the tracks of a team rather than having to break new snow. Still, when all was added up, the convenience of being in town was greater than the pleasures of the farm. Perhaps one of the greatest plus factors was that Miney realized it made life easier and more pleasant for her daughter.

Millie knew without a doubt that both Blanche and Miney liked living in town. Although it made more work for him having to drive to the farm twice each day, he really didn't mind all that much. However, he had been giving considerable thought to the farming situation. He liked the work well enough and had been making a comfortable living, but he knew he would never acquire the wealth his father had. Perhaps he could do better if he owned a business. Pa had been lucky to have had his father help him get started. Millie didn't like bookwork all that much, and being in the banking business held no fascination for him, but there must be something he could do. He had a little money saved, so perhaps he should keep watch for someone wanting to sell his business. Millie felt there were several things he could adequately handle. A general store couldn't be all that difficult, a livery stable, or perhaps a butcher shop. Well, it was food for thought. He wondered if Pa would think some sort of business was a step in the right direction.

Whether Milford decided he liked living in town better, or whether he felt it kept his womenfolk happier, or if he simply wanted to emulate his father, that next summer, he decided that come fall, they would move to town for good. He had found someone to rent the farm on shares, and he had the offer to sell farm implements for Roy Pierce's dad. Besides, he could still trade horses and supplement his income there. He intended to keep his flock of sheep on the south forty and would bring them back to the eighty for the winter months and lambing time. He had meticulously worked this out with the renter and had had papers drawn up so each knew what to expect; there was the division of the wheat Millie had planted in the fall to be harvested by the renter. The renter was also to take responsibility for doing Millie's roadwork.

Each year the farmers took turns grading, hauling gravel, or perhaps improving a ditch alongside the road; an elected roadmaster was the one who assigned the duties for a given area, and this now became the duty of the renter.

In the fall of 1904, the Setteringtons moved bag and baggage into Elsie. Before, they had never moved any of their own furniture, they simply had used Grandma Smith's. Now, they moved some of Grandma's to the attic, sold some, and added the rest to their own— that which was kept included four chairs with cane bottoms, which had been made by Miney's grandfather Barnes and a rocking chair that Miney's mother had brought from New York State. Miney had been quite upset on moving day when the glass on the secretary had been cracked. Well, she guessed she was lucky it hadn't been completely broke out; she could live with it only being cracked near the bottom of the door.

Ralph couldn't dispel a feeling of sadness as he settled down to permanent town life. He had liked the farm, he liked the animals, he even liked what little bit of fieldwork he was allowed to do. Chores weren't all that bad either—they were just like anything else, they had their bad moments when the weather wasn't good.

He enjoyed hearing the whip-poor-wills call, and often the silence of the night was broken by the cry of a screech owl. Some people hated hearing them because folks said a screech owl foreboded death. Ma said this wasn't rightly so, and he believed her. Besides, how could one of those cute little bundle of feathers have anything to do with people dying? Just like some folks were scared when a dog howled at a full moon—said the dog did this because they smelled death in the air. Rate didn't believe this either. Folks always had to come up with an explanation for everything, and some of the explanations were pretty far-fetched.

Often a barn owl or two lived in one of the outbuildings, and Rate liked to watch the sleepy-eyed bird sitting oblivious to anything going on during the day. Then, too, in town, one seldom saw the hawks sailing in the sky. He knew that chicken hawks sometimes helped themselves to a meal of baby chicks, and he'd seen his father grab his shotgun and shoot more than one of these predators as they hovered, ready to plummet down on an unwary chick. After one such occurrence, the chicks went into a frenzy every time a shadow passed overhead. Anyway, there were other kinds of hawks who ate only rodents, and he loved to see them sailing the wind currents, their wings outspread and motionless, a true spectacle of beauty.

In town, there sure weren't going to be the woodchucks, not to mention seeing the muskrats along the river or ditch or swampy areas. Living in town all year long was sure going to be a lot different.

He wondered just what he would find to do to occupy himself come summer when school was out. During the winter, there was ice-skating or sledding right after school, then hurry home to get chores done before it was time to eat; there was no going out again after supper, but there were lessons to be done and books to be read, so he didn't have all that much free time. They even had a library at school now. It didn't have many books as yet, but he had brought a few home. He always looked forward to getting books for Christmas; besides, if a book was really good, he didn't mind reading it two or three times.

Oh, well, summer was a long ways off, no use giving it too much thought now.

ABOUT THE AUTHOR

Donna Gene Stankey grew up on a small farm in the rural area of Elsie, Michigan. The youngest of three children, she was never babied. She loved the challenges everyday farm life brought during the 1930s. She was from a large family with many aunts, uncles, and cousins to visit with. She went to a small country school through the fifth grade. Donna Gene excelled in school and was promoted to the third grade after only a few weeks in second grade. Her parents decided to send her to the public school in Elsie for sixth grade where there would be more students and opportunities to challenge her. She graduated co-salutatorian at the age of sixteen. From there she attended a business school in Lansing. She worked as a secretary during WWII. Her job was eliminated after the war, so it was back to school at Michigan State College. There she met Roman and dropped out of school to get married. They moved to Roman's family farm outside of Wayland, Michigan. While being a housewife and mother of eight, Donna Gene decided to once again go to school. Western Michigan University was where she got her BS degree with a major in group science and a minor in English. This was where she began to write from the encouragement of her professors.

This book was published by co-author Ramona Hammel, Donna Gene's daughter.

CPSIA information can be obtained
at www.ICGtesting.com
Printed in the USA
LVHW012248081020
668387LV00001B/62